BLINDFOLD

Lyndon Stacey is an animal portrait artist by trade and has a love of Western-style horse riding. She lives on the outskirts of the New Forest and is currently writing her third book, *Deadfall*.

Praise for Lyndon Stacey's previous novel, *Cut Throat*:

'The closest to taking Dick Francis' crown . . . terrific, pacy stuff', *The Bookseller*

'Splendidly exciting . . . moves at a cracking pace . . . A sparkling debut' *Publishing News*

'Entertaining . . . fast paced . . . absorbing, enlivened by witty dialogue and vivid descriptions of the show-jumping circuit' *Publishers Weekly*

'Great characters both human and equine . . . Offers the reader plenty of surprises' *Horse Magazine*

'Clears its fences neatly . . . wonderful' *Kirkus Reviews*

'Lively, absorbing . . . the reader has a very good time' Gerald Kaufman, *The Scotsman*

D0826462

By the same author

Cut Throat

LYNDON STACEY

BLINDFOLD

arrow books

Published by Arrow Books in 2004

1 3 5 7 9 10 8 6 4 2

Copyright © Lyndon Stacey 2003

The right of Lyndon Stacey to be identified as the author of this
work has been asserted by her in accordance with the Copyright,
Designs and Patents Act, 1988

This book is sold subject to the condition that it shall not, by way
of trade or otherwise, be lent, resold, hired out, or otherwise
circulated without the publisher's prior consent in any form of
binding or cover other than that in which it is published and
without a similar condition including this condition being
imposed on the subsequent purchaser

First published in the United Kingdom by Hutchinson in 2003

Arrow Books
The Random House Group Limited
20 Vauxhall Bridge Road, London SW1V 2SA

Random House Australia (Pty) Limited
20 Alfred Street, Milsons Point, Sydney,
New South Wales 2061, Australia

Random House New Zealand Limited
18 Poland Road, Glenfield
Auckland 10, New Zealand

Random House (Pty) Limited
Endulini, 5a Jubilee Road, Parktown 2193, South Africa

The Random House Group Limited Reg. No. 954009

www.randomhouse.co.uk

A CIP catalogue record for this book is available from the
British Library

Papers used by Random House are natural, recyclable products
made from wood grown in sustainable forests. The
manufacturing processes conform to the environmental
regulations of the country of origin

Typeset by SX Composing DTP, Rayleigh, Essex
Printed and bound in the United Kingdom by
Bookmarque Ltd, Croydon, Surrey

ISBN 0 09 942944 6

For Pam Stembridge, who has a really special way with animals; and to the memory of Charlie, my equine companion of twenty years, who taught me all about Alphas.

Acknowledgements

My thanks go to Tessa Clarke, MBA, NPSD, of West Kington Stud Stallion Centre; to Firefighter Tony Smith and Leading Firefighter Den Barrow; and once again to PC Mark Randle, and Martin Peaty, MRCVS.

1

The light bulb had blown.

With a resigned sigh Gideon stepped into the darkness of his hallway and turned to close the front door against the cold night wind.

There were two men waiting unseen, one outside and one in. Neither of them took the trouble to introduce himself.

As Gideon reached for the handle, the first man kicked the front door viciously from the outside, smashing it into his face and shoulder and sending him stumbling back into the waiting arms of the second. The arms wrapped around him without hesitation, enclosing his own in a hug of rib-cracking enthusiasm.

Pausing only long enough to regain some sort of footing, Gideon threw his head back hard, feeling it make contact with a satisfying crunch. There was a muffled curse and the owner of the arms fell away, freeing his captive as he clutched at his face in agony.

Gideon had little time to appreciate his freedom, for as he staggered upright he was first blinded by blazing torchlight, and then floored by an unseen fist which took him just below the ribs with all the force of a kick from an offended mule.

He found himself face down on the cold stone floor, his nose pressed to the uneven flags and one arm twisted up behind his back. There didn't seem to be anything he could usefully do about it, so he preserved what was left of his dignity and did nothing.

Something cold clicked on to his right wrist and the other one was pulled to join it.

Handcuffs! What the hell?

A hand pressed down none too gently on the back of his neck, forcing his face into even closer contact with the stone, and somewhere above his head a voice said conversationally, 'Be a good boy and lie still, and nobody will hurt you.'

A bit late for that, Gideon thought. He already felt steamrollered, and the left side of his face, which had taken the major part of the impact from the door, had begun to throb. He heard footsteps moving away and took the opportunity to roll on to his side to try and ease his painful breathing.

'You just try it!' a voice warned thickly from behind him. 'An' I'll put your lights out for good!'

Gideon had no intention of trying it, whatever *it* was. His head felt unpleasantly muzzy and he had a strong suspicion that for the time being he was probably best off horizontal.

A light clicked on across the hall in his sitting room.

'Leave him alone,' the first voice said from the doorway. 'Why don't you do something useful, like putting that bulb back in?' It was a strangely soft voice with strong undertones of some northern city, probably Liverpool. The other voice sounded similar but much rougher.

'He broke my fucking nose!' number two protested thickly, distinctly aggrieved.

'Well, I've felt like doin' it myself, more than once, so he's saved me the trouble,' the first voice remarked, further off now.

Gideon felt that had the circumstances been different, he could have liked this man.

In the shaft of light from the sitting-room doorway, he could see the heavy pair of work boots worn by assailant number two as they crossed and re-crossed his vision, three or four feet away. After a moment, the hall light came on once more.

He could hear the other man moving about in the next room and wondered what he was doing. If the object of the exercise were robbery, then they would find they had picked the wrong house. Gideon had little of value to this sort of thief: no television or video, no computer system or microwave, and very little cash about the place. His hi-fi was good but hardly state-of-the-art. Admittedly some of the furniture was antique – Gideon liked old, mellowed things – but its condition was unlikely to arouse much joy in the heart of a collector. Apart from his credit cards and the keys to the Norton, both of which were in his pockets, the only really valuable things in the house were the paintings, but none of them was particularly well known and his two visitors didn't strike him as connoisseurs.

The boots paused in their perambulations and came towards Gideon, abruptly banishing any thoughts of paintings to make room for more urgent considerations. A meaty fist descended and, hauling him to a sitting position, proceeded to drag him across the flagstones to the wall, where he leaned back gratefully and waited for the other walls and the ceiling to start behaving as walls and ceilings should.

Broken Nose hadn't finished with him. He crouched down to Gideon's level and, still holding him by the front of his leather biker jacket, pointed at his own heavy-featured, blood-streaked face, saying in a low but nonetheless menacing voice, 'I'll make you sorry you did this!'

Gideon was saved by the return of the other man, who was clearly in charge.

'Leave him alone! The Guv'nor wants him in one piece.' He pushed his injured colleague out of the way and bent down to hold a tumbler to Gideon's lips with a hand enclosed in a thin, black leather glove. 'Drink this.'

Gideon smelt brandy – his best Courvoisier – and obliged with no argument. The burning liquid did wonders.

'Thanks,' he said, and immediately felt stupid. It was, after all, his own Cognac.

His jacket was grasped once more and he was pulled to his feet, where he was surprised to find himself standing face to face with his captor. Surprised, because he himself stood six foot four and was accustomed to looking down at most people. This man was as tall or taller. He wore a black woolly hat over very short fair hair, and a cotton bandanna pulled up over his nose, bandit-style, so that all Gideon could see was a pair of uncompromising, ice blue eyes. Presumably the other man had also worn his neckerchief in the same way but it had since been removed and used to mop his face. Both wore black jeans and black leather jackets over dark roll-necks.

The tall one patted Gideon down in the manner of one who had done it before and slickly removed his mobile phone, wallet and keys from an inside pocket.

'You won't be needing those,' he said, tossing them on to a chair. 'Now, turn round.'

Gideon wasn't in a position to argue. He turned. From behind, a thick, soft pad was placed over his eyes and bound tightly in place with another piece of material. Darkness was absolute. Firm hands took hold of his shoulders and pushed him in the direction of the front door.

'Right, let's get moving. We waited half an hour for you, pal, and the Guv'nor doesn't like to be kept waiting.'

'What the hell's going on?' Gideon protested. 'Where are you taking me?'

'The Guv'nor said to bring you, I don't ask why, I just do it.'

'I don't understand. Who is this Guv'nor?'

'Yeah, right. I'm really going to tell you.'

Gideon stumbled over his front doorstep and stopped. 'Are you sure you've got the right man?' he persisted, mystified. Less than an hour before he had been celebrating the completion of a commissioned racehorse portrait with some delighted clients. The situation was unreal.

'You *are* Gideon Blake and this *is* the Gatehouse to Graylings Priory?'

There seemed little point in denying it, since one look in his wallet would give the game away. Gideon nodded.

'Then we've got the right man. Now shut up and keep walking.'

Gideon did as he was told. There was nothing else he could do. Shouting for help would have been a fruitless exercise with his nearest neighbours the best part of half a mile away.

Moments later, he was shoved unceremoniously into the back of a van. A van which, on reflection, Gideon remembered seeing as he'd ridden past on his motorbike. Such things were notable in a country lane as quiet as this one. Broken Nose climbed in beside him, muttering darkly, the doors were slammed shut and with the tall man at the wheel, they moved off.

The bed of the van, on to which Gideon had

been pushed, was completely devoid of any form of upholstery, leaving him lying on the bare metal ribs of the bodyshell. The pervading smell was of oil, and from the hollow sound of it, the vehicle was more or less empty.

With a sustained effort, Gideon managed to inch his way into an upright position by pushing his shoulders against the side of the vehicle and wriggling. Suddenly, just as he relaxed, the van turned and accelerated, throwing him against his companion, who swore and pushed him flat again.

'Cut it out!' the tall man said over his shoulder.

Gideon wriggled his way up once more and by bracing himself firmly with his feet, managed to stay there for the rest of the journey, which he judged was about twenty minutes. About halfway he began to shiver, due partly to the cold of the February night and partly to shock, but in the noisy darkness of the van his travelling companion didn't appear to notice, for which he was grateful.

Fear was pushing at the edges of his consciousness, but his overriding emotion at the moment was complete bewilderment. He was still half-convinced that it was all a case of mistaken identity. He was certainly not an obvious target for kidnapping, his family being no more than comfortably off, and he wasn't aware that he owed anybody any money. He was thirty-four, single, and a self-employed artist with a sideline in animal psychology, although sometimes it seemed to be the other way round. As far as he knew he had never stepped on anyone's toes.

What the hell were they playing at?

The van slowed, turned sharply and proceeded to bump violently over an extremely uneven surface for a few yards before coming to a halt. The engine rattled into silence and Gideon heard the tall man get out, then the back was opened and Broken Nose scrambled out, pulling Gideon after him. He landed awkwardly and would have fallen, had it not been for the hand grasping the collar of his jacket. His head was throbbing in earnest now and it took him a moment or two to regain his balance.

Footsteps could be heard approaching over the frosty ground and a new voice said, 'You certainly took your time. What happened?' The tone was terse and held no discernible accent.

'He was out,' the tall one replied. 'We had to wait half an hour.'

'Well, bring him in. We've been here too long as it is.'

They all began to move forward, Gideon stumbling between the two from the van.

'Did he give you any trouble?'

'A little,' the tall man admitted. 'He's a big bloke.' Then, with a chuckle, 'He bent Curly's nose for him.'

On the other side of Gideon, Curly swore viciously.

A door creaked open. It sounded like an outside door, Gideon thought, to a shed or a barn, not a house. They stepped inside. He was right. Under his feet the ground was soft like trodden earth.

He was propelled forward a few feet and then stopped by a hand dragging on his leather jacket. The third man, who he assumed from his manner was the Guv'nor, spoke from his left side.

'We've got a little job for you to do, Mr Blake. If you co-operate you'll be out of here in no time and none the worse for it.'

He didn't say what would happen if Gideon didn't co-operate but somehow he didn't feel the need to enquire.

'You're an animal tamer, right? A – what do they call it – a horse whisperer?'

Gideon cringed inwardly. He hated the term, with its mystical connotations.

'I'm a behaviourist,' he amended, 'of sorts.'

'Well, whatever,' the Guv'nor said impatiently. 'But you sort out horses.'

'Sometimes.'

'Well, we need you to catch one. It's farting around in there and we can't get near it. Bloody mad it is! Kicked one of us already.'

Oh, cheers! Gideon thought. Aloud he asked, 'What's upset it?'

'I don't know!' the other man said testily. 'It's just like that. Maybe it's stressed. Maybe it's had a bad hair day. Just get on with it!'

'Well, I'll need something to catch it with and you'll have to undo my hands,' he observed practically.

'It's already got a bridle on. A headcollar or whatever you call it.'

'So how did it get loose?'

'What *is* this?' the man hissed, losing patience. 'Twenty fucking questions? You don't need to know what happened. Your job is to catch it. Right?'

Gideon took a steadying breath. The force of this man's personality made Curly's threats seem like those of a child.

'Okay,' he said, as calmly as he could. 'And my hands?'

'I can't let you free but you can have them in front,' the Guv'nor conceded.

'And the blindfold?' Gideon asked as one handcuff was undone and swiftly reapplied in front of him.

'No. That stays.'

'What's to stop me pulling it off myself?' he asked reasonably.

The Guv'nor leaned close. 'Nothing except the knowledge that if you do we won't be able to let you leave here.'

Gideon took his point.

'Useless to mention you're making my job almost impossible?' he suggested.

'Useless,' the other man agreed. 'Think of it as a challenge. Now get on with it!'

'And if I can't do it?'

'I don't think that's an option, do you?' he said softly.

Gideon was turned through ninety degrees and once again pushed forward.

'It'd be a help if I knew the horse's name,' he ventured hopefully.

'Tough.'

He took a deep, steadying breath and applied his mind to the problem. 'Okay, so how big is the area? How big is the horse? And where is it in relation to me at the moment?'

'About thirty feet by fifty. The horse is in the far corner, diagonally right from you. It's . . . I don't know, about average size. What does it bloody matter?'

From the rear another voice volunteered the opinion that the horse was about seventeen hands. Gideon assimilated the information, wondering at the same time just how many more people were standing silently around. It was almost eerie.

Anyway, one thing was clear. Whoever the Guv'nor was, he wasn't a horseman. Seventeen hands wasn't really average. Difficult to say what was. It just wasn't the sort of thing a horseman would say.

Trying to put his audience out of his mind, Gideon began to walk slowly in the direction of the animal, hoping that his way was unimpeded by obstacles. It was going to be difficult enough to gain the horse's confidence; doing a nosedive under its muzzle would seriously damage his chances of success.

The blindfold was a major hindrance. So much depended on body language with animals. Tiny changes of posture, movements of a horse's ears and eyes and the swishing of its tail, all gave away important information about the state of its mind. Normally, Gideon intuitively reacted to that

11

information with his own body language; dominant posture when it was required, at other times submissive. Without it, it felt uncomfortably like a game of Russian roulette. He was frighteningly vulnerable.

This is crazy, he thought, I can't do it. And at the same time he knew he had no choice but to try.

Somewhere ahead and to the right of him, he heard the horse begin to shift restlessly, its feet thudding softly on the loose dirt underfoot. Gideon paused, reaching out with his mind to the animal. What came back was a powerful mix of emotions; anxiety and distrust, certainly, and fear, but laced through with an unmistakable vein of aggression, fairly unusual in a horse.

Gideon turned his head. 'He's a stallion?' he asked softly.

'Yeah. Get on with it.'

'Oh, shit!' he muttered under his breath. Concentrating hard, he reached out once more to the horse, trying to project an aura of calm and reassurance.

He could sense the stallion watching him.

Anxiety.

Indecision.

It wasn't sure whether to stand its ground or run. Fight or flight. Given the option, horses almost invariably choose the latter. Nature has equipped them with the means to escape and they make good use of it. Stallions, however, are often the exception. Fired with the instinct to protect their herd, they meet aggression with aggression, challenge with physical attack.

Gideon turned slightly sideways. He had no wish to appear challenging.

The horse was still.

Tense.

Watching him.

He would have given anything to be able to see it. Was it standing facing him, head high, defiant? Or had it lowered its head, considering the situation? The electricity in the air between them suggested the former.

Still trying to radiate reassurance, Gideon stepped closer, head slightly bowed, shoulders still angled away.

He'd moved too close, too soon.

With a flurry of hooves the stallion rushed him, its teeth closing with a painful snap on his shoulder before it backed away.

It hadn't gone far though. No more than a couple of paces. Gideon could feel the huffing of its breath on his face. He steeled himself to remain motionless, trying not to think of the damage those steel-sprung jaws could do; what havoc the immensely powerful legs could wreak on a soft, unprotected human body. Important not to think. He must be steady. Horses are strongly telepathic.

The stallion was unsure now. He could sense its bewilderment. It didn't know how to respond to somebody who neither fled nor tried to dominate. At least it hadn't run. If it started to race around he wouldn't have a chance, handicapped as he was. The signs were encouraging.

Gideon relaxed. He tried to project serenity, picturing the horse in his mind, lowering its head and coming to him quietly. He was offering a refuge.

If the animal hadn't already been thoroughly unsettled by earlier, more direct attempts to catch it, the procedure wouldn't have worked, but after what seemed like a lifetime, he heard the stallion give a deep gusty sigh and smiled to himself. The horse was as good as his now. He took a step sideways, away from the animal, keeping his movements soft and slow.

The horse stepped warily closer, dropping its nose and blowing softly on Gideon's hands. The rope trailing from its headcollar flopped against his leg. He let the horse snuffle his hands, not allowing himself to think that it might suffer another flash of temper and take a couple of fingers off.

It didn't.

Much calmer now, it let Gideon rub its muzzle gently with his fingers and slowly, oh, so slowly, take hold of the rope. Hoping nobody would be stupid enough to call out, he turned away from the captive horse and took two or three experimental steps. There was a momentary resistance on the rope and then he heard the muffled hoofbeats of the stallion as it gave in and followed.

Strange, but when it came to it, most tame horses were glad to be caught again. Breaking free was instinctive but after the first wild exultation had ebbed they seemed almost relieved to have order restored.

Gideon told the horse quietly that it was a good boy.

Somewhere ahead and to his right, a low voice said 'Well done!' and he made his way towards it, slowing when the horse's hesitation told him he must be nearing the waiting group.

'He's very head-shy but I think he'll be all right now if you all stay calm and don't crowd him,' Gideon said, quietly. Then, almost surprising himself, 'He's in pain. Is he injured?'

'Shut up.' The Guv'nor again.

'Okay,' Gideon said, with a slight shrug. 'Well, who wants him?'

Somebody came quietly forward to take the rope from his grasp. He felt the horse's head go up a notch or two as control was transferred but it offered no further resistance as it was led past him and away.

Gideon heaved a deep sigh of release, aware for the first time that his shoulder was painfully bruised, and wishing he had his hands free to rub it. He was also aware that he only had the thickness of his padded leather motorcycle jacket to thank for the injury not being many times worse.

'Right.' The Guv'nor was speaking, back in charge. 'Fetch the other one and let's get it over with and get out of here! It's all taking far too bloody long!'

His task completed, Gideon stood still. Presumably someone would come for him before long. His knees felt shaky and he would have liked to have sat down but he could scarcely just collapse

15

where he was. Ahead of him he heard a door open and then the low whickering of a mare and the answering excitement of the stallion.

Why hadn't they used the mare to catch the stallion? he wondered wearily. Surely somebody could have caught hold of the rope while he was about his business, if that was what they'd intended him for anyway. Any horseman would have thought of it, surely? And if there wasn't a horseman amongst them, what the hell were they doing in possession of a stallion?

Feeling overlooked, he began to step cautiously forward.

'You! Blake! Stand still.'

Gideon obediently stood.

'You. Take him outside.'

Somebody grasped his arm and within moments he was out in the frosty night air again. His arm was released and the door shut behind him. Only the sighing of the bitingly cold wind disturbed the silence. Gideon stood where he'd been left.

Was everyone with the horses? he mused after a while. Was anybody actually watching him now or was he standing like a sucker with nobody near? He lifted his hands and rubbed experimentally at his cheekbone, just brushing the edge of the blindfold.

'It would be a shame if I thought you were trying to get that blindfold off, when all you had was an itch.'

Soft Liverpudlian accent. Curly's tall companion.

'That *would* be a shame,' Gideon agreed.

Nothing was said for a few moments then

Gideon broke the silence. 'Do this sort of thing often, do you?'

'Makes a change from the pubs and clubs,' his companion replied evenly.

'Been down south long?'

'Long enough to know my way around.'

'Yeah?' Gideon affected mild surprise. 'So, where would you say the nearest town would be to here?'

A low chuckle greeted this admittedly feeble attempt to draw him out.

'Listen, pal. I may have been born at night, but it wasn't *last* night. Now just shut up and wait.'

Gideon did as he was told.

He couldn't be sure how long he stood there in the bitter wind with his silent companion. Long before there was any sign of an end to his wait, he had begun to shiver violently and was in danger of losing all feeling in his hands and feet, but eventually the barn door creaked open and a horse was led past within a few feet of him. Shortly after, another followed and he heard the unmistakable hollow sound of hooves on wood, as they were loaded into a horsebox or boxes.

Footsteps approached, crunching on the frosty ground.

Gideon's heart began to thump uncomfortably. He hoped that his being blindfolded meant he was going to be freed as promised, but he was realist enough not to be sure of it.

The footsteps stopped in front of him.

'You know what to do,' the Guv'nor said quietly

to Gideon's escort. 'Just give us all some breathing space and make sure no one sees you. And you,' he said, leaning close to Gideon. 'You'd do best just to think of this as a bad dream – one you were lucky enough to wake up from. Remember, we know where you live but you know nothing about us. Best let it stay that way. Understand?'

Gideon felt he probably did. At any rate, he wasn't about to argue.

There followed a journey which was essentially the same as the first, except – presumably – in the opposite direction. Gideon was seated next to the rear doors of the van, with Curly close beside him having an amusing time opening the door a crack occasionally and threatening to push him out. His tall friend had taken the precaution of cuffing Gideon's hands behind him again before they had set out, and with the road noise and the rushing of the wind, he felt desperately exposed in the open doorway.

After a while, Curly's companion caught sight of the baiting in his rear-view mirror and put a stop to it.

Gideon sent him a silent blessing.

Presently, after bumping for a hundred yards or so along an unmade track, the vehicle swung round in a semi-circle and stopped, engine still running.

'You've not far to walk,' the voice from the front informed him, 'but I'm afraid we can't take you any closer. We don't want you calling the boys in blue, do we?'

Gideon didn't see that an answer was called for,

18

and he couldn't think of a polite one anyway.

'I've been admiring your boots,' the soft voice went on. 'I should think they'd fit me just fine, we're much of a size. Curly, would you do the honours?'

For a moment Gideon considered baling out voluntarily for the sake of keeping his boots but the idea died a death. He wouldn't exactly be able to sprint away, blindfolded and with his hands behind his back. He began to have second thoughts about the blessing so recently bestowed.

'I hope they pinch, you sonofabitch!' he muttered uncharitably.

'So, he does have feelings,' the tall one observed as Curly got to work.

Gideon simmered with helpless frustration. The boots were favourites of his, bought in America for a small fortune some six months before and now just nicely worn in. It wasn't only this, however, that depressed him, but the prospect of a hike of indefinite length over frosty, stony ground, with feet clad only in socks. It was ironic that half an hour ago he had been far from sure that he would be freed at all and now he was quibbling over the theft of his boots. It was a bit like being picked up at sea and then moaning because your rescuers weren't going your way, but the thought didn't appease him.

'Well, we'll be off, then,' the tall one said. 'It was a pleasure doing business with you.'

'Oh, the pleasure was all mine,' Gideon assured him sarcastically. Then, as Curly put a hand on his arm prior to pushing him out, 'What about the handcuffs?'

'Oh, you can keep them. We've got some more.'

Gideon's protest was cut short as Curly gave him an unnecessarily hard shove that pitched him helplessly out of the back of the van. He landed heavily on his shoulder and the side of his head on what felt like hard-packed gravel.

The van moved off promptly, as if they were afraid that he would somehow climb back in, but as Gideon rolled on to his back and sat up, he heard it stop again, a little way off. He felt a moment's sharp panic. Was Curly coming back to fulfil his earlier promise, after all?

'The key's in your back pocket, pal,' the soft voice called. 'Have a nice walk.'

Listening to the van pull away and breathing a choking lungful of exhaust fumes, Gideon nevertheless sent up a prayer of thanks to the stars.

His first impulse upon regaining his feet was to feel in his pocket for the key, but even as his fingers located it he realised he had little hope of using it successfully with his hands still behind his back, and stiff with cold into the bargain. It was more than likely that he'd drop it and, judging by the size of it, once dropped – in the dark and on an uneven gravel surface – it would stay dropped. Much better, if he could manage it, to get his hands in front of him, remove the blindfold and do the job properly. Carefully he palmed the key and closed his fist around it.

Bending forward, Gideon then attempted to

slide his joined wrists down over his hips and buttocks, feeling the muscles in his back and chest strain with the effort. The pull of the metal bracelets on his wrists was intensely uncomfortable but he persevered and, with a groan of relief, made it.

His hands were now behind his knees. He knew he'd been able to step through his hands as a teenager but he was somewhat bulkier these days. After a pause to breathe he emptied his lungs, balanced on one socked foot and dragged the other through from front to back, his shoulders taking the strain this time. A sharper pain in his right shoulder bore witness to the damage the horse's teeth had done. The second foot was slightly easier and he stood up straight, feeling justifiably pleased with himself.

The irony was that if he'd been wearing his boots, with their inch or so of heel, he doubted very much if he would have succeeded in stepping through, and he would have found it exceedingly difficult, if not impossible, to have taken them off with his hands secured behind him. They weren't always easy at the best of times.

Lifting his joined hands, Gideon removed the blindfold, wincing as it pulled clear of his left eye where blood had run from the gash on his brow and done a painfully efficient job of sticking the material to his skin.

Blinking, he looked about him.

It was a fairly clear night with a moon that was a little more than half-full. Against the starry sky he could make out the shapes of trees surrounding him and see where the gravel track stretched away towards the road. There wasn't enough light to be of much help in undoing his handcuffs but twisting one hand to touch the other bracelet, he could feel the small hole that presumably accommodated the key. This done, it was a relatively simple task to release himself.

Feeling much happier, Gideon snapped each cuff shut once more and stowed them in his jacket pocket. The key he returned to the back pocket of his jeans, wondering as he did so just when the tall man had put it there.

A growing numbness in his feet reminded him that he had far more urgent concerns. The temperature was well below freezing and the ground frozen hard. He had at least a hundred yards to cover before he reached the road and no idea how much further after that. He thought he might possibly be in the lane that led to the old gravel pits just outside the village of Tarrant Grayling and, if so, his gatehouse home was going to be some three-quarters of a mile away. The spectre of frostbite reared its ugly head.

Peering at the lighted dial of his watch he discovered it was almost three in the morning; hardly the best time to try and hitch a lift on what was never a busy road.

With a heavy sigh, Gideon began his trek, trying to console himself with the fact that he had at least been left with his jacket, but in reality swearing bloody revenge every time his unprotected feet located a sharp stone.

The walk was a very long one.

2

The sun was up and shining through the gothic arches of his bedroom windows when Gideon eventually surfaced the next morning. He lay motionless for several minutes, enjoying the warmth and hoping that sleep might reclaim him, but the hope was shattered by the trilling of the telephone on the floor beside his bed. With a groan he put out a hand and located the handset.

'Yes?'

'Gideon? It's Pippa. Are you running late or had you forgotten?'

Gideon's brain felt woolly. 'If you give me a clue what we're talking about, I'll tell you whether I've forgotten or not,' he offered helpfully. Pippa Barrington-Carr and her brother Giles lived half a mile away at Graylings Priory, and were not only his landlords but also very good friends.

'Riding? This morning? Ten o'clock? You were

going to try out the mare,' she prompted with a pardonable touch of asperity.

'Ah,' Gideon responded, vaguely recalling an arrangement made two days before; a lifetime ago. 'Is it ten already?'

'Quarter to eleven,' Pippa informed him, not in the least taken in.

'I'm sorry,' Gideon said, genuinely so. He was properly awake now and sat up, swinging his legs over the side of the bed. His feet, as they made contact with the floor, forcibly reminded him of every single stone and thorn he'd trodden on during his interminable journey home. The thought of pushing them into his boots . . .

Boots.

Damn!

'Look, Pippa, I had a spot of bother on the way home last night and I'm not really with it this morning. Can I catch you later? I'm sorry about the ride.'

'Are you okay?' She sounded concerned. 'You didn't come off your bike, did you?'

'No, nothing like that. Look, I'll be over later. Tell you then. Will Giles be around?'

'As far as I know,' she said. 'Come for lunch, why not? See you about one?'

Gideon agreed and hung up, fighting the urge to lie back down again. A full bladder helped win the battle and, wincing with every step, he made his way to the bathroom.

When, some moments later, he turned his attention reluctantly to the mirror over the

24

washbasin, he grimaced. On a normal morning the reflection in the glass showed Gideon a face with strong, regular features; pleasant enough, if not quite film-star material. Now his sun-bleached thatch of long dark-blond hair framed a disaster area.

The edge of the door had left him with an inch-long vertical cut rising from his left eyebrow, surrounded by a spectacular purple bruise. With a cut and swelling below his eye too, he looked like a failed title-fight contender. Blood had run and crusted blackly. With a handful of moistened cotton wool, he set to work.

Half an hour later, bathed and shaved and feeling slightly more human, Gideon made himself toast and scrambled eggs, which he ate leaning against the Aga for warmth.

Considered in the light of day, the events of the previous night still failed to make a lot of sense. He had eventually reached home just before four in the morning to find that, thankfully, the front door was open. He was mildly surprised that Curly hadn't taken the opportunity to make his life even more difficult, but quite possibly in this age of almost universal Yale locks, he'd taken it for granted that the door would lock itself. The heavy, old-fashioned key lay inside, on the floor near the wall, where it had fallen when Gideon had been attacked.

The stout, oaken door seemed to have survived its rough treatment with no ill-effects and Gideon had closed it behind him and turned the key with something between a sigh of relief and a groan of exhaustion. On the hall table he'd found the tumbler containing the remains of the Cognac the tall man had offered him, and had swallowed it gratefully before giving the house a cursory check and heading for his bed.

Now, making coffee after his late breakfast, it was hard to believe what had happened. It was almost as though, for two or three hours last night, he'd swapped lives with someone else. It just wasn't the sort of thing that happened to your average, fairly law-abiding person. His bruised face and shoulder, tender ribs and throbbing feet, though, said different. For the first time in his stay at the Gatehouse, Gideon wished he had some painkillers in the house.

Collapsing into the one comfortable chair in the kitchen, he displaced his Abyssinian cat, who glared at him accusingly.

'I'm sorry, Elsa. But my need is much greater than yours,' he told her.

She refused to be mollified and after licking her beautiful lion-coloured coat, as if to indicate that human contact had dirtied it, sauntered gracefully out of the room.

Gideon shrugged. 'Suit yourself.'

He liked the company of the cat; she was quiet and undemanding. No trouble when he was painting and a balm at times when he'd had a difficult day with someone's stressed-out horse or delinquent dog. She suited him.

Shortly before one o'clock, Gideon rode the

Norton, helmetless, up the gravel driveway that led from the Gatehouse to the Priory itself. He felt faintly silly as he turned under the stone archway into the stableyard after a journey of only two or three minutes, but it couldn't be helped. His normal preferred modes of transport for the short distance, namely his push bike or his own two feet, required rather too much pressure on his bruised soles for comfort.

Graylings Priory was a sixteenth-century manor house that nestled in the Dorset countryside on the edge of the Cranborne Chase, near Tarrant Grayling. It took its name from a much earlier building that had presumably fallen foul of Henry VIII's reformatory zeal. Giles Barrington-Carr, an old schoolfriend of Gideon's, had inherited it soon after his thirtieth birthday four years ago, when his parents were killed in a car crash.

Gideon had seen little of Giles since leaving university some ten years before, until a chance meeting at Salisbury races six months ago had thrown them together again. Gideon had been there discussing a possible future portrait commission with an owner, and on hearing that he was temporarily between lodgings, Giles had offered him the Gatehouse for as long as he needed.

Now, as Gideon stepped off the bike and propped it on its stand, a young woman came out of one of the old, ivy-clad stables, leading a horse. Pippa Barrington-Carr, younger sister of Giles, was tall, well-built, and possessed a pair of fine hazel eyes and a short mop of unruly curls that had originally been light brown but which changed hue with startling frequency as the whim took her. Today they were auburn.

'Hi, Pips.'

'Hi, yourself,' she responded, squinting against the winter sunlight as she crossed the yard towards him. 'I hope I didn't get you out of bed this morning.'

'No,' Gideon disclaimed airily. Then more truthfully, 'Well, yes, actually. But I didn't get in it until past four this morning, so I think I'm excused.'

'Why, for heavensakes?' Pippa exclaimed. 'What happened?'

'Tell you over lunch. Is that the mare you wanted me to try?'

'Yes.' Pippa stood her up for Gideon to look at. 'She'd just suit you, wouldn't you, Cassie?'

'She's not a Cassie!' Gideon protested, regarding the mare's ample proportions. 'Cassie's a slim young thing with flowing hair. *She's* built like a Russian female shot-putter. More of an Olga than a Cassie!'

'Oh, don't listen to him,' Pippa told the horse. 'He's just a male chauvinist pig. Big can be beautiful too.'

'Oh, I agree. Some of those shot-putters are real stunners.'

Pippa tossed her curls. 'It's too late now, the damage is done. Come on, Cassie, let's find you some grass.' She led the mare out through the arch, saying over her shoulder that she would only be a minute.

With an infinitely practical mind, a good head for business and a degree in catering, Pippa could easily have been a high flyer in the world of society parties and wedding receptions but chose instead to follow her heart, buying, training and selling potential three-day-eventers for a living.

Gideon sat back against the Norton to await her return, looking up at the golden stone walls and mullioned windows of the house. The sun glinted on the tiny diamonds of the leaded lights, and way up on the roof two fantail doves were basking in its rays. The Priory wore time like an old coat; creased and a little shabby, but with an air of comfort and serenity. Gideon loved it.

In a very short time Pippa was back, walking with an energetic mannish stride, the lead rope swinging from one strong brown hand. As always she reminded Gideon sharply of her brother. Three years separated them but they could easily have been twins.

'Right, let's go get some lunch,' she said, draping the rope over the nearest open half-door and turning back to Gideon.

'My God! What have you done to your face?'

'I walked into a door,' he said with partial truth.

Pippa wasn't amused. 'Don't be silly. Was this something to do with last night?'

'Let's go in,' he suggested. 'I'll tell you both together.'

'But it doesn't make sense!' Giles protested for the fourth or fifth time. They had eaten lunch and were sitting round the scrubbed oak table in the Priory's huge kitchen, drinking coffee. 'Why would anybody steal a stallion in the middle of the night and use it to cover just *one* mare? It's such a risk. I mean, stallion fees aren't *that* huge, are they?'

Pippa shook her head. 'Not unless you're talking about a Derby winner or something. But thoroughbreds have to be registered. What's the point of breeding a potential top-class racehorse if you can't race it?'

'They stole Shergar.'

'That was political,' Pippa pointed out. 'I don't think they ever intended to use him.'

'I suppose they couldn't forge its papers?' Giles suggested, a frown on his good-natured face.

Pippa shook her head emphatically.

'Not a chance. Thoroughbred breeding is a multi-million-pound business. The official stud-book is kept at Weatherbys and they monitor everything. Foals are blood-tested to prove paternity. A stallion can't even break wind without them knowing about it. It's a watertight system. It *has* to be.'

Gideon nodded. 'She's right. But I'm like you, I can't think what on earth they were up to. I mean, they went to a hell of a lot of trouble, didn't they?'

'They certainly did,' Giles agreed, glancing at Gideon's bruised countenance. 'They must have heard how much you charge!'

'Very funny.' Gideon pushed back his chair and stretched his long legs out, feeling drowsy. The old black range was pumping out heat and, well fed, his lack of sleep was catching up with him. Black-beamed, with warm ochre walls and an assortment of rugs on the uneven flagstones, the old kitchen was one of the cosiest places he knew. Herbs hung in fragrant bunches from the ceiling, and onions on the back of the door. Opposite the table, three ancient armchairs and a large dog bed completed the furnishings.

'How did they get in, do you know?' Giles' voice brought Gideon back from the brink of nodding off.

'No. No sign of damage. I don't know if you can pick those old locks. Or perhaps they got through the studio window; that catch is very loose. Whatever, I shouldn't think it was the first time they'd done it. The tall one in particular was very slick.'

'So where did they let you go, in the end?'

'Down that track to the gravel pits,' Gideon told him. '*Sans* boots.'

'Oh, for heavensakes!' Pippa said. 'What did the police say?' She scanned his face. 'You didn't call them, did you?'

'Well, no,' Gideon admitted, sheepishly. 'To tell the truth, I didn't even think of it last night. All I wanted was my bed.'

'Don't blame you,' Giles said.

'And this morning it all seemed – well – rather daft. I mean, I'm still here, aren't I? More or less in one piece. What are the police going to do about it?'

'I still think you should report it,' Pippa said. 'It's assault, after all.'

31

'Maybe I will.' He decided against telling them that he had been warned in no uncertain manner to forget the whole affair.

A door opened to admit a dumpy, bustling person with short grey hair and glasses. Formerly Giles' and Pippa's nanny, now their capable housekeeper, Mrs Morecambe was a treasure, and if her rosy cheeks owed more to the occasional drop of spirits than simple blooming health, it was never spoken of.

She came now from the laundry room, which had originally been the scullery, with her sleeves rolled up and an apron over her navy blue tunic dress, and immediately busied herself collecting empty plates and mugs and offering more coffee, which was declined.

She gathered the last of the crockery and turned towards the sink, saying as she did so that one of the terriers had brought a rat into the boot room and if anybody thought she was going to remove it they had better think again.

Giles' brace of terriers, Yip and Yap, were the bane of the household. If they weren't under somebody's feet it was invariably because they were up to no good elsewhere, and they seemed to delight in baiting Mrs Morecambe.

Pippa, whose own black Labrador, Fanny, was presently laid up with two-week-old pups, was strongly of the opinion that Yip and Yap should have been taken firmly in hand long ago. She regularly applied to Gideon, asking – tongue in cheek – if he couldn't have 'a word' with them.

However, Giles regarded their antics rather in the manner of an indulgent uncle, saying that they were terriers; one didn't train terriers.

In due course, the three of them wandered out to the stableyard evicting both terriers and rat, en route, and Giles soon returned to the subject of Gideon's abduction.

'Pippa's right, you know. You really ought to go to the police. I mean they could have killed you. The *horse* could have killed you, for that matter!'

'I don't think they even considered that,' Gideon said. 'They seemed to think that all they had to do was get me there and the horse was as good as caught. I mean, I wasn't even told it was a stallion to start with. It was as though they didn't think it was important.'

'Gideon Blake, witchdoctor and animal tamer *extraordinaire*!' Pippa teased him. 'Your reputation precedes you.'

'I wonder if anyone's reported a stallion missing,' Gideon said, ignoring her. 'Perhaps I will contact the police, after all.'

'But surely the stallion could have come from anywhere? It may not have been local.'

Gideon shook his head. 'If it *was* stolen – and that's the only reason I can think of for all the deadly secrecy and the strong-arm tactics – then they wouldn't want it on their hands for very long, especially a half-wild creature like that one. No, they were in pretty much of a hurry. Why else would they take the risk of abducting me? I mean, given time the stallion would have calmed down of its own accord and they could've caught it with a bucketful of food.'

'You said the boss chap kept saying they'd been there too long, as well,' Giles pointed out. 'So you can bet they didn't own the place. It must've been an empty barn or something. Maybe up for sale.'

Pippa shivered. 'If that horse *had* attacked you, I bet they'd just have left you there. You might not've been found for weeks.'

'Thanks for that,' Gideon retorted. He'd skipped some of the details concerning the capture of the horse, for his own comfort, but it would be a long time before the deep bruising in his shoulder would let him forget.

'Well, I just think you should tell the police and let them deal with it. It's their job, after all.'

'I wonder why they wouldn't let you take the blindfold off after you got there,' Giles pondered. 'I mean, it's not likely you'd recognise the inside of a barn, is it?'

They had reached the yard and were sitting variously on the stone mounting block and the hitching rail, enjoying the last of the sun.

'Maybe they thought he'd recognise one of the people. Or the horse,' Pippa suggested, drawn into the mystery again despite herself.

Gideon shook his head. 'I'm pretty sure I didn't know the horse,' he stated. 'I don't think it's one I've worked with.'

Pippa squinted at him against the sunlight. 'How can you be sure with a blindfold on?'

34

'I don't know,' Gideon said. 'I can't explain it. It's just a feeling.'

'The people, then.'

Gideon shrugged. 'Who knows? I've certainly never met Curly and his pal before.' He paused reflectively. 'I wouldn't mind meeting them again though, in the right circumstances.'

'If you go looking, give me a call,' Giles said, a martial light in his eye.

Pippa groaned, rolling her eyes heavenwards. 'Oh, God, give me strength! This isn't a game, you know. These people are criminals. Leave it to the police.'

'Okay, Pips,' Gideon said fondly, sliding off the hitching rail. 'Well, I'd better be on my way if I'm going to tell my sad tale to Her Majesty's Finest.'

'And get that cut stitched,' Pippa advised as they walked towards his motorbike. 'Have you had an anti-tet?'

'Yes, Mother,' Gideon said gravely. 'And I've washed behind my ears, too.'

'Well, you men, you need looking after! You're like overgrown school kids.'

'Ouch, she's got a sharp tongue, that one! You want to get her married off before she turns into a harridan or else you'll be stuck with her,' he warned Giles.

The gathering broke up in a welter of insults and Gideon was still chuckling as he rode home.

The following day, with no urgent business to pursue, no appointments, and no particular desire to paint for painting's sake, Gideon found himself on the Norton, bound approximately north and west.

It wasn't really a conscious decision. He'd felt like taking the bike out, having a vague notion that he might buy some replacement boots, and somewhere along the line the idea of discovering the whereabouts of the infamous barn had suggested itself.

Recalling the direction and the first few turnings the van had taken, he knew roughly which way to start out, and an estimate of speed and the duration of the journey combined to give him an idea of the probable radius. It was worth a try, he thought.

When he'd called the local police in Blandford the previous evening, they had asked Gideon to go in to the station to give a statement and reluctantly he'd obliged.

Once there, it had been several minutes before he could convince the duty officer that his complaint had nothing to do with a brawl between two motorcycle gangs which had apparently shattered the peace in Blandford the night before. He supposed it was understandable, especially with his battered face, but no less annoying for all that. So many people took one look at his longish blond hair, jeans and motorbike gear, and labelled him Trouble. He'd even been refused service in pubs before now. He knew he'd cause less consternation if he had his hair cut but something inside him rebelled at the idea of giving in to the pressure of unfair pigeonholing.

The officers to whom he had eventually related his experiences were polite but a little sceptical, and Gideon was left with the feeling that they suspected him of knowing more than he was saying.

He wished he did.

His grievance duly recorded, he was told that somebody would be out to inspect the scene of the kidnap within the next day or two, depending on when they could be spared. There was apparently a shortage of manpower due to policing a band of protesters at a bypass construction site.

He had called in at the local surgery to have the cut over his eye seen to and ridden home wondering if anything would actually be done about his report or whether he would be filed away in some dark corner and forgotten about.

Now though, with Giles' suggestion in mind, he decided to begin his search by checking estate agents' offices in the towns which fell close to the radial line he had drawn on his map of Wessex. The three most likely seemed to be Shaftesbury, Sherborne and Chilminster, and for no particular reason other than that he liked Chilminster, he headed there first.

The town was host to a veritable rash of estate agents, each of which seemed to have several dysfunctional farms on its books, due partly, he was told, to the collapse of the market for British beef. One or two of these were duplicated and not all were completely untenanted. Gideon narrowed his search down to five, and just three he considered remote enough to be possible candidates.

In the last estate agent's it occurred to him to ask whether they'd had any other people asking for the same specifications that he had. He was told politely that there was a good deal of interest in all of their agricultural properties – which Gideon doubted, given the reason for their sale in the first place – but that naturally they could not divulge any details about prospective clients.

'Naturally,' he agreed, and departed the office with a handful of paperwork on the three short-listed farms. He had gone less than twenty paces when he heard the tap-tapping of rapidly approaching stilettos and a breathless voice just behind him said 'Hey, Mister!'

He turned. A small, titian-haired female stood beside him, the top of her carefully tousled head barely reaching his shoulder. He vaguely recalled seeing her at a corner desk in the estate agent's he had just left.

'I heard you asking about the farms and if anyone else wanted to know about them,' she announced, looking up at him with more than a hint of flirtatious admiration in her eyes. 'There was a man, last week. Mr Wilkins was with him for ages. He said he had ready money and was in a hurry to buy. Mr Wilkins was all over him like a rash! You could see the pound signs in his eyes, the silly bugger! That bloke wasn't any more interested in buying than you are. Any idiot could see that!'

'How could you tell, Miss . . . er . . . ?'

'Debbie.'

'Debbie. What made you think that?'

'Women's intuition,' she said archly, then as Gideon showed his scepticism, 'Nah, just kiddin' you. I was brought up on a farm – you wouldn't think it, would you?'

Gideon shook his head obligingly, showing the requisite surprise.

'Well, I was, and this bloke asked all the wrong questions. I mean, he didn't ask anything about acreage, milk quotas or crop yields to start with. All he really wanted to know was how close the nearest houses were and whether it had a barn and out-buildings. I ask you, it was obvious what he wanted it for, wasn't it?'

'Was it?' Genuine surprise this time.

'Yeah. Where've you been hiding? He wanted to put on a rave, didn't he?' Debbie nodded know-ingly. 'You know: music, drink, drugs, the works. I told the boss that's what he was up to and he just told me to mind my own business. Treats me like shit, he does!'

Gideon made a sympathetic face. 'Can you remember what this man looked like, Debbie? It'd be a great help.'

She put her head on one side. 'Are you a cop?' she asked curiously.

'Not exactly.'

'A private investigator!' she said eagerly.

Gideon began to see that a white lie or two might be in his best interests.

'Sort of. But I'd rather you didn't tell any-one . . .'

An emphatic shake of the head. 'On my honour,' she promised.

Gideon was uncharitably glad he didn't have to rely on that.

'What happened to your face? Did someone beat you up to warn you off?' Debbie asked, her eyes shining with bloodthirsty relish.

'No. I walked into a door,' he said dampeningly. 'Now, what can you tell me?'

Debbie thought it would be a good idea if they went somewhere quiet to talk, in the best detective tradition, and Gideon found himself buying her lunch in one of the town's smarter pubs. She made the most of the opportunity, displaying a hearty appetite and expensive tastes.

Afterwards, having failed to entrap him into taking her out that night, Debbie returned to the tyrannical Mr Wilkins, leaving Gideon to a bitter-shandy and his thoughts.

Debbie's memory of the other interested party had in the event been rather vague, and much of that recalled only under fairly extensive prompting from Gideon. The result was a description that could really have been applied to any number of people at present in the pub.

The man had apparently been of medium height and fairly stocky build. She had said at first that he was quite old, but when pressed said maybe about forty, which in view of his own age, Gideon found rather sobering. He had had dark, greying hair, no particular accent that she could remember, and had been wearing jeans, a waxed jacket and a flat cap. Standard country issue.

Gideon gazed contemplatively at the subsiding froth on his shandy. The description might be of some use if he had any idea where to start looking for the man. It was not, of course, certain that the person looking for a remote farm with a large barn was the same one who'd ordered Gideon's kidnap, but it was a sizeable coincidence, if not.

Back on the Norton, some ten minutes later, Gideon found himself debating the wisdom of taking his fledgling detective work any further.

On a purely emotional level he was furious that he should have been manipulated entirely against his will by a bunch of complete strangers and then told to forget it ever happened. Common sense, on the other hand, dictated firmly that he should swallow his wounded pride, be glad he had come out of it relatively unscathed, and let well enough alone.

In the end he convinced himself that just taking a look at the three farms was unlikely to land him in any further trouble. The bad guys were almost certainly long gone, and the most he would find would be evidence of their passing, in the shape of a few hoofprints and maybe a tyre-track or two if the frozen ground had yielded any.

In the event, there were no tyre-tracks. At the second farm he tried, he found the door to the barn at the end of the yard had been forced and the trodden earth floor inside bore evidence of recent disturbance.

41

It was strange, seeing the interior of the barn for real. Unconsciously he had built up an impression of what it was like, and what instantly struck him was the size of the place. Even though he'd been told its approximate dimensions, he'd imagined the barn so much bigger. The area the stallion had been running in was bounded on three sides by wooden walls sitting on a metre or so of brickwork, and on the other by the rails of three, square livestock pens.

Gideon wandered into the centre of the open area and crouched to inspect the hoofprints.

The imprints were fairly small for a seventeen-hand horse, indicating that it was probably a well-bred animal, but they had no other distinguishing features except for the absence of shoes. A young horse, perhaps, not yet broken to ride?

Here and there he could make out his own boot prints. He could see where he had stood and allowed the horse to come to him. Custer's last stand, he thought wryly. And it could so easily have been just that.

In spite of the very real fear though, the episode had given him a kind of buzz. He found himself able to relate to most horses on one level or another, mainly by way of mutual interpretation of body language, but just occasionally he came across one that was exceptional. He had described it to Pippa once as like tuning in a radio. Sometimes, no matter how you turn the dial, no matter which way the aerial is pointing, reception is poor, a series of crackles and half-heard words that you have to guess at. Then, another time, feeling your way through the frequencies, you hit it right and the signal comes through sharp and crystal clear. It was rare in Gideon's experience but this was such a horse, and the memory stirred excitement in his veins.

He wondered if the blindfold had played any part in clearing a path to the animal's consciousness. Perhaps, like blinkers on a racehorse, it had ruled out distractions and allowed him to concentrate his mind fully on the stallion.

He realised he was still crouching, making patterns in the dirt with his finger, and straightened up to turn his attention to the railed pens.

One of these bore evidence of recent occupancy in the shape of more hoofprints and two or three scattered and trampled piles of dung. Frowning, Gideon bent once more to inspect the prints. These presumably belonged to the mare that the Guv'nor and his pals had brought along to receive the services of the stallion. Her hooves too were unshod – not unusual in a broodmare that isn't being ridden at all – but what *was* surprising was the size. They were far bigger than the stallion's and much rounder.

As it was unlikely that the mare was going to be very much taller than seventeen hands, which is near the top of the scale for horses, size-wise, it looked as though she was a good deal heavier than he was; less well-bred, more of a weight-carrier. She certainly wasn't a thoroughbred.

But why steal a stallion, and probably a valuable

one at that, and then breed it to a mare of a completely different sort?

Gideon took a final look round the barn, finding nothing but an empty cigarette packet of a common brand, which was unlikely to prove useful. With a sense of having reached a dead end, he let himself back out of the heavy wooden doors.

The rest of the outbuildings held no surprises and the house, which was locked, looked as though it hadn't been lived in for years. It seemed as though Mr Wilkins' many clients had not been tempted by this particular farm.

The blurb had described it as an attractive period property in need of some refurbishment, with a good range of outbuildings that offered development potential for a variety of uses.

You're so right, Mr Wilkins! Gideon thought as he kicked the Norton back to life.

3

The next day had little to recommend it. Gideon woke to cloudy skies that drizzled icy-cold rain and had his breakfast disturbed by the long arm of the law knocking on his front door.

The two policemen stayed for the best part of two hours, asking questions, peering at the front door, noting the layout of the hall and getting Gideon to show them just where each of the players in the drama had been throughout. They inspected the lane outside the Gatehouse for suspect tyre-marks, then asked him to relate his movements during the day preceding his abduction. They enquired again if he didn't think he might have known one or both of his attackers, and wanted to know precisely where and how he'd been released.

On this last point there was much shaking of heads. If he'd reported the incident immediately, he was told, an inspection of the release site would quite possibly have yielded much of interest, but as things stood, with all the traffic that regularly used the lane to the quarry, any evidence would probably have been destroyed.

Gideon produced the handcuffs and watched with amusement as they were carefully removed from his palm on the end of a pen, deposited in a polythene bag and labelled.

'They wore gloves,' he pointed out. He had already told them once.

'Can't be too careful, sir,' he was informed.

Gideon was tired of it all after the first twenty minutes and heartily regretted having notified them at all.

They had come, as he had requested, in plain clothes and an unmarked car, just in case the Guv'nor or one of his thugs were watching the place, but Gideon didn't seriously believe they were. He supposed he would soon find out if they had been though, for the thorough way the two officers quartered the ground outside signalled their business as clearly as if they had come with blue lights flashing and sirens wailing.

When eventually they left him in peace, he couldn't see that anything whatsoever had been gained from their visit. In fact, quite the opposite. After supplying numerous cups of coffee, he had run out of milk.

The policemen, it seemed, had departed still under the impression that Gideon knew more than he was letting on, and their manner clearly indicated that although they would naturally do their best, they wouldn't be able to make much progress until he came clean.

He'd intended to spend the day adding to a small collection of pictures he was assembling for an exhibition, but his session with the police left him feeling unsettled and he abandoned the idea.

It didn't seem worth putting his wet weather gear on and getting the bike out just for the sake of going to the village for a bottle of milk, and ten minutes later he found himself trudging instead in the other direction, along the lane towards the Priory.

Both Giles and his sister were out when Gideon reached the house but three of the stables were empty so he sat on the stool in the tack room to wait and, sure enough, Pippa soon returned, clattering into the stableyard riding one horse and leading two more.

'Oh, good,' she called as she saw him. 'Another pair of hands. Can you take Sebastian for me? He will keep making horrible faces at Griffin – who's terrified of him – and if he does it just as I'm getting off, I shall probably end up in an undignified heap!'

Gideon obligingly took the lead rein and removed the bay gelding from the vicinity of the beefy-looking chestnut that Pippa was waiting to dismount.

'Why take them together if they have such a personality clash?' he enquired curiously.

'Well, I *wouldn't* have done if I'd *known*,' Pippa said with a trace of indignation, 'but they're both

47

perfect gentlemen normally. You just can't tell.'
Then, slanting a teasing look at Gideon, 'Well,
perhaps *you* could. I'll have to employ you as my
consultant equine psychologist. You can interview
them all and find out their personal likes and
dislikes before I take them on.'

Gideon treated this idea with the contempt it
deserved. He was well aware that Pippa understood, more than most, the limits that there
necessarily were to communicating with horses.
Words, for a start, didn't come into it.

'Have you come to ride Cassie?' she enquired
over her shoulder as she tied one of her charges to
the hitching rail.

'Well, not precisely,' Gideon admitted, 'but if
she needs exercise . . .'

'I was going to lead her out from Skylark but it
would do her more good to be ridden.'

'Okay then. Glad to be of service.' Gideon
bowed.

'What did you come for, really?' Pippa asked, an
hour and a half later, after they had come back
from their ride, and settled all the horses with feeds
and nets of hay. 'Only, Giles will be out 'til quite
late, I should think. He's gone to Surrey to see a
man about some ostriches.' She grimaced. 'It's his
latest money-spinning idea. I'm just keeping everything crossed that they peck him or something, and
put him off. I mean, *ostriches*, for heavensakes! You
can imagine what the horses would think of them!
They'd go ballistic!'

'I thought you liked birds,' Gideon said provocatively. They'd forsaken the yard for the warmth of the Priory kitchen, and Pippa was heating up soup and French bread.

She cast him a withering glance over her shoulder. 'There are birds and birds,' she stated heavily. 'But *ostriches?* I mean, one minute he's concerned about everything being in keeping with the character of the place and then he's thinking of importing birds from Africa or wherever they come from!'

'Yeah, Africa,' Gideon agreed. 'Still, it could be worse. It could be crocodiles or something.'

'Don't you dare suggest it!' Pippa warned, swinging round and brandishing the bread knife.

Gideon held up his hands, laughing.

'So what *did* you come for? You still haven't said.'

'Well, actually, I've run out of milk.'

'So what's wrong with the Post Office? Have they run out too?'

'Er, no,' Gideon admitted. 'But they've never yet offered me lunch, and I didn't like to ask them if I could borrow their car tomorrow.'

He ducked as the last two hard-crusted inches of the French stick whistled past his ear.

Afternoon, the following day, found Gideon in possession of the borrowed wheels and on the road to Dorchester. The vehicle was Giles' four-wheel-drive Mercedes, which compared to the Norton for comfort rather as an armchair would to a milking stool.

Gideon had had cars of his own over the years but when the most recent of these had finally coughed its last just four months ago, he'd taken to borrowing from Giles and Pippa on the odd occasion when a motorbike just wouldn't do, and the habit had stuck. Today was just such an occasion. He was to do the preparatory work for a portrait commission and the combined bulk of his camera, sketchpad and portfolio was more than the Norton's topbox could accommodate.

This afternoon he was headed for a small village just beyond Dorchester, and a heavy-horse stud called Winterbourne Shires. The stud was owned and run by one Tom Collins, in whose family heavy horses had plodded since time immemorial.

Gideon had known the Collinses, Tom and his wife Mary, for several years now. They had met when one of Tom's horses had been severely traumatised following a road accident, and a mutual acquaintance had recommended Gideon.

The horse, not a shire but a top-class show-jumper who had competed at the Olympics and on several successful national teams, had sustained horrific injuries when the horsebox he was travelling in had been involved in a motorway pile-up, one foggy autumn morning. The vet called to the scene had been inclined to put the horse down there and then, but the Collinses worshipped the horse and were not prepared to give up without a fight.

They pointed out to the vet that besides being a stallion with an ongoing career at stud, Popsox was the current darling of Britain's horsy public and there would be a national outcry if any effort was seen to have been spared. The vet saw the force of this argument. He had no wish to be cast as the villain of the piece; labelled forever as the man who shot the nation's favourite.

After extensive surgery by their own vet, and two months of dedicated nursing by the Collins family, the horse had made a fair recovery, although he would never again be completely sound, which spelled the end of his competitive career.

What had worried his owners, however, was his mental state. The once bright and energetic horse seemed to have lost all zest for life. He stood at the back of his stable with his head low and ears back, not even coming forward when somebody came to his door. He was reluctant to leave the security of his box to exercise, and loud noises made him break out in a sweat.

Sedation could obviously not be considered as a long-term solution and the vet had said there was nothing more he could do, as there were no longer any physical symptoms for him to treat. He could offer no assurances as to whether Sox would ever regain his confidence.

Gideon first saw him four months after the accident, at which point there had been no improvement in his mental condition at all and Tom Collins was at his wits' end. Gideon found the case fascinating. The horse was totally withdrawn and for the first few days he could make little progress. There was no spark, except when something alarmed him and then he exhibited fear bordering on panic.

After studying the horse closely, Gideon decided that in common with all herding or pack animals, what the horse needed was leadership. Ignore the fact that, as a stallion, this horse had hitherto assumed that role himself; the accident had robbed Sox of all his confidence and he needed the security of a strong personality to follow. The tendency so far had been to shield and reassure him in his distress. A natural enough instinct, but Gideon sensed that this had in fact only reinforced his anxiety. He felt sure that the way forward was through discipline and bonding. Sox needed, above all, to rediscover his place in the world.

Gideon had spent the best part of a month at the stud, working daily with the stallion, and by the end of it the horse had started his journey back to normality. It might be many months before he would stop jumping at sudden noises – maybe he never would – but he was coming up to his half-door and looking out, and although he wasn't yet fit enough for stud work, he was once again taking an interest in the mares.

That had been three years ago and Gideon had visited two or three times since, gaining great satisfaction from seeing the stallion gradually growing in stature until he was once more the vital, shining star he had been in the prime of his career.

It had given him great delight too to see the

visiting mares, one or two of whom already had Sox's sons or daughters at foot, coming to be mated again last year. The showy stallion had not been forgotten by his fans, and there was no shortage of people who wanted to breed a potential Olympic mount for themselves.

It was especially nice, Gideon thought, as he swung the Mercedes through the arched gateway on this cloudy February day, that Sox so often passed on his own distinctive colouring to his offspring. His coat was a bright coppery chestnut and he sported a broad white blaze on his face and four brilliant white, knee-length socks; hence the name. Only time would tell whether any of the youngsters would also inherit the phenomenal jumping ability that had made their sire famous.

Mary Collins came hurrying out of the house almost before the vehicle had come to a halt. Short and well-rounded, with a sort of faded prettiness, she held out both hands as Gideon got out of the Mercedes, and kissed him fondly on the cheek.

'Gideon. How lovely to see you again! My goodness, whatever have you done to your face?'

'Hello, Mary. The old story. Walked into an open door. It looks worse than it is.'

Concern furrowed her brow for a moment and then she recalled her reason for contacting him. 'Listen, I'm sorry to call you at such short notice, did you mind dreadfully? The thing is, it's our wedding anniversary next month and I couldn't think what on earth to get Tom. Then suddenly I remembered your paintings and I thought that'd be just the thing. You know how proud he is of Sovereign.'

'He's a lovely horse,' Gideon said as she finally paused for breath. Sovereign was Tom Collins' top prize-winning shire stallion. 'And, no, of course I didn't mind.'

'That's sweet of you. Now will you have a cup of coffee first or do you want to get on? Tom's away looking at some youngstock up Bristol way. I don't expect he'll be back before dark, so I'm on my own here except for Gerald.'

'Gerald? I don't know Gerald, do I? Where's Roly? With Tom?' Roly French was the Collinses' stud groom, and Gideon had come to know him pretty well when he'd stayed at the stud to work with Sox.

'No.' Mary sounded surprised. 'Of course, you wouldn't know, would you? Roly left us last year, very suddenly. I was away at the time visiting my sister, and when I got back he was gone.'

'Gone where?' Gideon asked, puzzled. They turned and started to walk towards the house.

'Well, that's what's so odd about it; he didn't say exactly. Down to the coast somewhere, to be closer to Connie's mother, so Tom said, but he didn't seem to want to talk about it at the time. In fact, I accused him of falling out with Roly, which didn't go down too well, I can tell you! I was just so surprised.'

'But haven't you heard from them since? Surely Connie's written?' She was Roly's wife, and Gideon had often eaten with the Frenches in the old farm cottage at the top of the south drive.

'Once. She said they were staying in a boarding house while they looked for somewhere else. There was no address and I haven't heard from her since.'

'I can hardly believe it,' Gideon said, shaking his head. 'Roly lived for this place, and that stallion was the apple of his eye. I would have sworn he'd have left his wife sooner than leave Sox. And it doesn't make sense either, does it? I mean, to leave suddenly after – what was it – fifteen years?'

'Nearly twenty-five,' Mary said.

'To leave his job and a tied cottage after twenty-five years, and in such a hurry that he doesn't even stop to find somewhere else to live first . . . It's crazy! They *must* have fallen out.'

'That's what I thought,' Mary said, unhappily. 'But Tom swore it was none of his doing, so what could I say? Anyway, now we've got Gerald. He lives in the village. Tom's decided to do up Roly's old cottage for summer letting, to bring in a bit of extra cash. He's just started work on it last week.' They stopped in front of the house. 'Coffee?'

Gideon opted to see Sovereign first, while the light was still reasonable. He needed to take a good selection of photographs and do a couple of sketches, so that when he came to work on the portrait in his studio he could be sure he wouldn't miss any detail, however small.

As it transpired, it was a good thing he did see the horse first, for while they were sitting in the big farmhouse kitchen, drinking coffee and eating

55

Mary's home-made scones, Tom Collins made an unexpectedly early return.

They heard his Range Rover swish to a halt in the gravel yard and the door slam as he got out and came towards the house. Mary sat and stared at Gideon with an almost comical expression of dismay.

'It's all right, Mary. I'll take care of it,' he said quietly.

The door opened. Below average height, stocky and in his mid-forties, Tom Collins looked the archetypal farmer, dressed as he was in baggy corduroy trousers, tweed jacket and cap. He stopped short with a look of consternation.

'Gideon!'

'Well, don't sound so pleased to see me.'

'No, of course not. I mean, I am, it's just that . . . Well, it's so unexpected.' He appeared to gather his wits. 'If you'd let me know you were coming, I'd have arranged to be in.'

'Yes, I'm sorry,' Gideon said. 'But I didn't really know myself. I was coming out this way anyway, to visit my sister, and I thought since I was so near, I'd drop in and see you both. And the "Golden Boy", of course.'

Out of the corner of his eye he saw Mary relax. He'd really had no idea, when he first started painting portraits, how many lies he was going to have to tell in the interests of keeping his clients' commissions a secret from their partners. It was almost like being a spy at times. Coded messages over the phone; arranging times to ring when the spouse, parent or child would not be in; even once, in a desperate case for a friend, creeping around outbuildings while the family were at dinner, to take photographs of a horse in its stable.

'Have you seen the lad?'

'No, not yet. I'm afraid we've been chatting over coffee.'

'Oh, yes?' Collins slanted an uncharacteristically sour look at his wife. 'Been telling you all her little problems, has she?'

Mary flushed darkly and Gideon glanced from her to Tom in shocked surprise. He'd never heard Tom talk of his wife in that way before. They had always been so close. Certainly, Tom was brusque by nature, but not deliberately unkind.

Gideon masked his bewilderment for Mary's sake. 'We were talking about your plans for Sovereign, as a matter of fact. Should be a good season ahead.'

'Shouldn't it just?' Tom agreed, so warmly that Gideon could almost have believed he'd imagined the previous remark.

There was Mary, though, gathering up the plates and mugs with a bleak expression that said that the unpleasantness had been all too real. And, Gideon thought, not completely unexpected. She had looked deeply unhappy when her husband spoke but not surprised. It had the appearance of a problem with far deeper roots than just a marital tiff, and he was greatly saddened by it.

*

When Gideon finally took his leave of the Collinses after having duly admired not only Popsox but also Sovereign again, he decided he might as well live up to the story he'd told Tom and pay a call on his sister.

The telephone at Naomi's flat in Dorchester was answered by her flatmate who told Gideon that Naomi was out and not expected back until quite late.

'I know where she is, though,' the girl added helpfully. 'She's gone to see Tim at the Sanctuary. You could get her on her mobile. I'm sure she'd love to see you.'

Gideon thanked her and rang off, wondering who 'Tim at the Sanctuary' was. One way to find out.

Naomi answered her mobile after half a dozen rings. 'Jack? Is that you?'

'No, Sis, it's not. Sorry to disappoint you.'

'Gideon! Gosh, is it my birthday or something?'

'I thought you'd stopped having birthdays,' he countered. 'You said you were stopping at twenty-nine.'

'So I did. Well, in that case, to what do I owe the honour?'

'I was in the area and I thought I'd come and see you.'

'Oh, that'd be nice.'

'Yes, well, it might, if I knew where you were,' he said dryly. 'Your flatmate said you were at a sanctuary or something. Don't tell me you've gone all religious on me?'

Naomi laughed. 'No. Listen, I'll give you directions. It's rather out in the sticks. Where are you coming from?'

Directions duly given and followed, Gideon found himself, some fifteen minutes later, rolling to a halt in front of a gate bearing the legend *Hermitage Farm Wildlife Sanctuary*. Two or three miles off the main road, down a lane that cut through farmland and passed only two other properties, the Sanctuary was, as his sister had said, fairly remote. The gate stood open and beyond it a grassy gravel lane wound away invitingly between two huge hawthorn hedges that were in sore need of being cut and laid.

The lane led to a farmyard with a multitude of rambling Victorian buildings in various stages of renovation. To Gideon's left, as he drove up, a line of six old brick stables faced a number of newer, wooden structures, forming a corridor which led to what looked like an aviary. Standing back a little from the yard was a farmhouse partly encased in scaffolding. In front of it was a paved area on which stood a mobile home and beside this, directly ahead of him, was a range of whitewashed out-buildings, one of which boasted two steps up to a newly painted door and a sign that read *Reception and Surgery*. To the right of this again stood a large black barn and a field gate.

Gideon parked the Mercedes beside a Volvo estate and a bright yellow sportscar that was presumably his sister's. She'd always liked bright colours.

Going up the steps, he let himself into a room with cream-painted walls, a beamed ceiling, three chairs and a table with a bell on it. He rang the bell.

Almost immediately an inner door opened and his sister Naomi leaned round it. 'Hi, Big Bruv! You found us then?' She came forward and hugged him warmly. 'It's lovely to see you.'

Tall and lithe, with dark-lashed blue eyes and a long, shaggy blonde mane of hair, Gideon's sister Naomi was a dancer, currently 'resting' while she recovered from a tendon operation. They had been very close as youngsters, with a father who was more often away than at home and an artistic mother who, although sweetness itself, seemed sometimes to be in a world of her own.

Now brother and sister were grown up, they saw each other no more than two or three times a year but continued to be close, staying in touch by phone and letter. Side by side, it was obvious to all who saw them that they were brother and sister, Naomi having the identical, if slightly more delicate, straight nose, wide mouth and firm chin that her brother had.

'So who's Jack?' Gideon said, returning the hug and mentally digesting the possible significance of her use of the word 'us'. Had Little Sis found herself a man, then? 'And, come to that, who's Tim?'

'Jack is my agent,' Naomi said, stepping back and looking up at her brother, 'and Tim you're about to meet. He's . . . well . . . he's a very good friend. Whatever have you done to your face?' she

60

asked, frowning suddenly and putting up a hand to gently touch the bruise on his forehead.

'I walked into an open door,' Gideon said again.

'Oh, yes? And who was behind it?' Naomi enquired with a depth of perception that was typical of her. He'd never been able to pull the wool over her eyes. She scanned her brother's carefully impassive face, her wide blue eyes troubled, then a look of resignation settled on her. 'Okay. So you're not going to tell me. Just do me a favour and be careful, all right?'

Gideon nodded obediently.

'Come on then, I'll introduce you to Tim.'

She whisked away with characteristic energy and Gideon followed her through to the room beyond, glad to have got off so lightly. He had no wish to burden his sister with the tale of his abduction. She would only worry.

The room in which he found himself was immediately recognisable as a surgery, with tiled floor, a table, cupboards, equipment trolleys and several multi-position overhead lights.

Naomi stepped to one side. 'Tim, this is my huge brother, Gideon. Gideon, Tim Reynolds who owns the Sanctuary.'

'Pleased to meet you.' A slim, wiry man came forward with a diffident smile and hand outstretched; bearded and bespectacled and totally unlike any boyfriend Naomi had ever introduced to her brother before, which admittedly wasn't many. Usually boyfriends came and went in his sister's life without ever lasting long enough to meet her family.

But boyfriend he undoubtedly was, for as Gideon shook his hand, Naomi linked her arm through his and said proudly, 'Tim's a wizard vet, Gideon. He can practically bring back the dead!'

Gideon's eyebrows shot up. 'This I must see.'

Tim laughed. 'I'm afraid your sister is rather easily impressed. The first time we met was when she brought me a rabbit she'd found lying at the side of the road. I admit it did look pretty far gone, but it was either just stunned or playing dead because no sooner had I touched it than the bloody thing leapt up and started haring round the room. No one was more surprised than I was, I can tell you! But what about you?' he went on. 'Naomi tells me you're a horse whisperer or some such thing.'

'No. Nothing so fanciful,' Gideon said, shaking his head. 'I suppose you could call it animal psychology, but I've had no training. I guess I have an empathy with animals, that's all.'

'Oh, no! It's a lot more than that!' Naomi protested. 'Lord preserve me from false modesty. If I didn't sell myself better than you two I'd never be in work! He's practically telepathic,' she added, turning to Tim once more. 'I've seen him stop a charging Dobermann in its tracks without a word. It was amazing!'

'Body language,' Gideon said to the vet. 'It's ninety percent of the battle. People can believe what they want to believe but there's nothing supernatural about it.'

'But he does it with people too,' Naomi persisted. 'You can't lie to him, he always knows.'

'You're a hopeless liar anyway; you always go red,' Gideon said, keen to change the subject. He could see Tim looking faintly sceptical and had no wish to engage in a debate about his talent or lack of it.

Generally the vets he had dealt with had been open-minded, or at the very least took the view that he could do little harm by his methods. Some had been very interested and a few even called him in themselves when they suspected they were going to have trouble with an animal.

A minority, though, saw him as some kind of threat. A poor reflection perhaps on their own failure to solve a problem. Gideon just kept his head down and did whatever he could to help, whenever he was asked.

He spent what was left of the afternoon and all the evening at Hermitage Farm. Tim seemed disposed to be friendly in spite of what he might privately feel about Naomi's claims for her brother, and showed Gideon round the Sanctuary with justifiable pride.

He had only been in operation about three months and said he wasn't making any effort to advertise the Sanctuary's existence until the conversion of the farm buildings had been completed. Even so, there were already over two dozen needy animals and birds in residence. At the moment he was living in a mobile home while the builders finished making the farmhouse habitable.

Gideon learned that Tim Reynolds had been a vet in a small animal practice for several years before a distant aunt had bequeathed him the farm and enough capital to turn a childhood dream into reality.

'Apparently my great-aunt moved out when the army moved in during the Second World War, and she never came back. Nobody knew where she was, although it's thought she might have gone abroad to escape the bombing. Anyway, the place has been empty ever since. She died five years ago leaving no will and her executors finally tracked me down last summer as her closest living relation.' Tim shook his head in wonderment. 'I didn't even know she existed! I still have to pinch myself occasionally to make sure I'm not dreaming. And to top it all, along comes a glamorous assistant to help out and give moral support.'

Naomi laughed. 'Don't try to pretend you didn't plan it. I know damn' well you paid that rabbit to lure me in. Just before we let him go I bribed him with a lettuce leaf and he confessed all!'

'I'm found out!' Tim exclaimed tragically. 'You can never trust a bunny.'

Gideon joined in the laughter, deciding that, atypical or not, his sister's latest conquest was by far her best choice yet.

When he finally left the Sanctuary it was past eleven o'clock and sleet had begun to fall, whipped into a stinging misery by a keening wind. The weather made driving difficult and it was nearly midnight before he got back to Blandford. As he approached the turning to Tarrant Grayling he passed a Mini parked untidily on the verge, and a couple of hundred yards further on his headlights picked out the outline of a woman walking with her head down, hunched against the sleet.

Not wanting to startle her, Gideon slowed up and drove a little way beyond her before stopping and lowering the passenger window. In the mirror he saw the woman hesitate and then come on, keeping well out to the side of the vehicle. Level with the open window she stopped, peering in.

Gideon turned the interior light on so she could at least see that there was only one of him.

'Can I help?' he asked.

'No, thank you,' the woman said, but she made no move to walk on.

Gideon could see a pale face in which huge dark eyes showed as hollows. She was fairly young, he judged, and more than a little frightened.

'Do you want me to call anyone? A recovery vehicle or the AA?'

'The battery's flat on my mobile,' she said, her lip quivering with the cold or anxiety, or both. 'I was trying to find a telephone.'

'Well, it's a longish hike to the village,' Gideon said. 'You can borrow mine.'

The girl looked back at him with a troubled frown. 'I'm sorry?'

Gideon picked the phone up off the passenger seat and offered it, wondering if she was foreign or merely half-witted.

'Oh, thank you.' Her brow cleared and she took

the phone but didn't seem inclined to make use of it.

'Who do you want to ring?' Gideon said, striving to keep his growing exasperation from his voice. 'Don't you know the number?'

'I'm sorry,' she said. 'You must think me very stupid but I don't know who to ring. I only passed my test last year and I've never broken down before.'

'Well, where were you going then?'

'I was going to try and get a room in the village. In a pub or something. I can manage by myself. Thank you anyway.'

The girl sounded slightly defensive and very close to tears. Gideon decided it was time he took charge.

'You won't find anywhere much open in the village at this time of night. If you like I could take a look at your car for you,' he offered. 'Or if you're not happy about that I could ring the police and let them know where you are.'

The girl pulled a small and totally inadequate handkerchief out of the pocket of a coat that looked as though it had long since ceased to repel the sleety rain, and blew her nose. A soggy strand of dark hair fell across her face and she pushed it back behind her ear. She looked at Gideon and shivered, her teeth chattering audibly, but didn't answer.

'Would you like me to call the police?' he repeated, holding out his hand for the phone. 'You certainly can't stand there all night, and I wouldn't mind getting home.'

'I'm sorry,' the girl said helplessly. 'I don't know what to do . . .'

Gideon leaned across and opened the door. 'Come on, get in. Let's go and look at your car and see if we can't get it started.'

The girl took hold of the door handle and hesitated.

Gideon understood her reluctance. He reached into the glove compartment and took out a can of de-icing spray. 'Here. If I make a wrong move you can spray that in my face,' he said lightly. He rummaged once again and withdrew a large spanner. 'And then, while I'm helpless, you can hit me with this!'

The girl smiled shyly, relaxed a little and slid gratefully into the passenger seat. She put the spanner back but hedged her bets by holding on to the spray. Gideon affected not to notice. He put the Mercedes in gear and swung it into a three-point-turn across the road.

'So, what exactly happened with the car?' he asked as they headed back towards the Mini. 'By the way, I'm Gideon. Gideon Blake.'

'My name's Rachel Shelley,' the girl answered, her teeth chattering again. 'I don't really know. It was making an odd noise on the corners and then all of a sudden there was a bang and the back seemed to drop down. Now it won't move at all.'

'Oh, dear! That doesn't sound too healthy. At a guess I'd say one of your UJs has gone. If so, it'll need towing and then it'll be a garage job.'

A cursory inspection of the car proved Gideon

right. He went round to the passenger window of the four-wheel-drive. 'I can tow it back to my place if you like, to get it off the road overnight,' he suggested. 'And then we'll have to decide what to do with you.'

Now she had taken the first step towards trusting him, Rachel seemed happy to leave everything in Gideon's hands. She nodded from the depths of a blanket that he'd found for her in the back of the Merc. Giles seemed to have everything that one would need for an Arctic expedition in there.

'Thank you,' Rachel murmured. 'I'm sorry to be such a nuisance.'

Gideon repositioned the Merc, attached a tow rope to the back of the Mini and pulled it up to lift the rear wheels clear of the road, then climbed back into the driver's seat, thoroughly cold and wet himself. He smiled at Rachel, who responded in kind, and began the steady journey home, noticing as he did so that she had abandoned the protection of the spray can.

4

The sun was just clearing the hedge at the bottom of his garden and beginning to melt the ice that had formed on the kitchen window, when Gideon lifted the cat from her customary position on the top of the Aga and replaced her with a pan of porridge. Elsa complained sleepily and he soothed her, draping her over his shoulder as he stirred the milky oatmeal.

The frost-rimed garden looked magical in the watery sunlight, and Gideon was possessed of a momentary urge to fetch his camera and take a photograph to reproduce later in watercolours. The angle of the sun was wrong though, and the thought of venturing out into the cold effectively quelled the impulse.

There was a movement in the doorway and the cat dropped lightly to the floor. He looked across to see Rachel standing there, warmly clad in grey slacks and a soft white jumper that reached halfway to her knees. She blinked at him, as though not fully comprehending the situation, and then smiled shyly.

'I must have fallen asleep.'

Gideon smiled in return. 'You did. Twice. Once in here, over coffee, and again when you went upstairs to change out of your wet clothes.'

'I'm sorry. I took your bed, didn't I?'

'No problem,' he lied, restraining an urge to flex his stiff neck. The sofa was at least ten inches too short to be a comfortable alternative. 'Would you like some porridge? It'll be ready in a moment.'

'Thank you.' Rachel moved hesitantly towards the table. Elsa rubbed around her ankles and she put a hand down to stroke the cat, absent-mindedly.

'Well, I'd put some shoes on if I were you. You'll freeze on this stone floor without anything on your feet.'

Rachel had a way of watching him with dark-eyed intensity while he spoke, as if worried about what he might say. Now she smiled, relaxing visibly as she nodded and disappeared, presumably in search of some suitable footwear.

She was a remarkably attractive girl when she wasn't looking like a lost kitten, Gideon thought, returning his attention to the Aga.

By the time she returned the porridge was ready and divided into two steaming bowlfuls on the table.

Gideon was finding spoons.

'There's brown sugar, white sugar, golden syrup and/or cream,' he announced, hearing her take her place at the table. 'Which would you like?'

Rachel didn't answer and Gideon turned to find her stroking Elsa and looking away from him, out of the window.

'Rachel?' he said quietly.

She gave no sign of hearing him so he waved his hand slightly and the movement caught her eye.

'I'm sorry,' she said, seeing him poised with the sugar and cream. 'I was miles away. Did you say something?'

'I was asking what you'd like on your porridge, but it doesn't matter, I'll put them all on the table and you can help yourself,' he said, suiting his actions to the words. Then, as he sat down, 'Why didn't you tell me you were deaf?'

'I'm sorry,' she said again, colour rising in her cheeks. 'I'm not completely deaf. I have some hearing in my right ear and I suppose I hope people won't notice.'

Gideon helped himself to brown sugar and cream.

'But why? It's nothing to be ashamed of.'

Rachel shifted uncomfortably. 'I know. It's just
. . . I don't know, I suppose I don't want to be pitied.' She tucked a section of her thick, dark hair behind one ear and reached for the syrup, her eyes flickering up to meet his and away again as if afraid that she would find him laughing.

'You haven't always been deaf, have you?' he said.

'No, I had an accident three years ago. I fell over and hit my head, and when I woke up in hospital I couldn't hear anything at all. After a few days I got some hearing back in my right ear but not the left. The doctors say it could still improve but it hasn't yet.'

'Is that how you got the scar?' Gideon asked gently. A curving, slightly puckered, white line showed noticeably across her cheekbone against the olive of her skin.

'Yes.' She unhooked the hair from behind her ear and let it fall forward, her hand stroking the blemish almost subconsciously as she did so. 'People don't usually mention it,' she said then.

'I'm sorry,' Gideon said mildly. 'I didn't mean to be rude.'

There was silence for a few moments as they both occupied themselves with their porridge, then Rachel said, 'I don't mind really. I mean, you always know people will see it sooner or later, and sometimes they try so hard not to say anything that you feel like screaming at them, "Yes, I know I have a scar, but it's no big deal!" I think you're the first person to actually come straight out and ask me about it.'

'Me and my big mouth,' he said with a rueful grin. 'Still, I'm not exactly unblemished myself.'

'I wondered about that,' Rachel said shyly.

'I'm not surprised you were reluctant to accept a lift. The truth is, I was on the wrong side of a door that somebody opened in a hurry.'

'Ouch!' Rachel said, wincing. 'I bet that hurt!'

She scraped her bowl, pushed it away and asked if he knew of a garage that she might telephone to see about her car.

Gideon rang the garage he occasionally used, in Blandford, and they said they were busy but would send a truck out for the Mini sometime that afternoon.

'I'm sorry if you were in a hurry,' he said, putting the phone down. 'We could try somewhere else but I know they'll do a good job for a reasonable price. I wouldn't know who else to recommend. I can ring round if you like, or alternatively I can give you a lift to wherever you need to go and you can pick the car up when it's ready. I expect it'll be a couple of days.'

'I'm not precisely in a hurry,' Rachel told him. 'The room I was after will probably have gone by now. The landlady told me in no uncertain terms that if I didn't take it up by yesterday she would rent it to someone else. She said she had someone waiting.'

'I expect that was just a ploy. We could ring her and find out if you like?'

'Well,' Rachel said without much enthusiasm, 'I guess it might be worth a try . . .'

'But you're not keen?'

'I didn't like her very much but it was the only place I could find other than a B and B, and that's outside my budget.'

'Why are you moving? Not that it's any of my business.'

'No, that's all right. I move around quite a lot.

I'm an interior designer – just qualified – and I go where my work is. I can't afford to turn anything down. I was living in a rented flat while I studied and haven't decided where to base myself yet.'

'Don't you have any family?'

'No. Not really,' she said, looking down at her hands.

Gideon read the signals and backed off. 'So, where do you need to be?'

'My next job's in Bournemouth but the people are on holiday for another week or so. I'm treading water at the moment until they get back.'

Gideon got up and began to clear the table. 'Well, there's a spare room upstairs you're welcome to until you can arrange something else,' he offered. 'It's quite habitable once it's warm but I couldn't face it last night. In fact, if you're here for a few days, you can work your design skills on it. It could do with smartening up!'

Rachel laughed, unsure whether to take him seriously. 'Are you sure you don't mind? You've been so kind already.'

'No problem. As I said, you're welcome.'

'Well, er . . .'

'There's a lock on the door,' he informed her.

She turned pink again. 'Well, thank you. If you're sure . . .'

Later in the morning Gideon took the Mercedes back to the Priory, taking Rachel with him and leaving the Mini with its keys under the wheel-arch in case the garage tow-truck turned up early.

Both Pippa and her brother were in, and when Rachel showed her delight at the old house, she was given a guided tour of the building.

As he followed Rachel into the sitting room, Giles raised his eyebrows at Gideon who lowered his and shook his head. Giles looked sceptical for an instant before turning to resume his narrative.

'She's a pretty girl,' Pippa said in a low voice to Gideon as they trailed the others through the house. 'If you don't act quickly, you'll lose her to Giles.'

'She's not mine to lose,' he responded. 'I only met her last night. Her car had broken down and she needed a place to stay.'

'Ever the Good Samaritan,' Pippa teased.

'Well, I couldn't just leave her there.'

'I'm surprised she felt safe staying overnight with a strange man – I'm sure I wouldn't!'

'She's just an extremely good judge of character,' Gideon said, tongue in cheek. 'And I have this trustworthy, avuncular air about me.'

Pippa spluttered. '*Says who?*'

Gideon affected deep hurt.

An invitation to lunch was issued and accepted, after which Pippa took Rachel out to see the horses.

'Well!' Giles breathed as the two girls went out. 'If *I* ever stop to help anyone they always turn out to be a toothless granny or a lump of a girl with pigtails and braces on her teeth. Trust you to pick up a stunner.'

Gideon laughed. 'She didn't look so stunning

last night, I can assure you. She looked like a half-drowned kitten. And what's more, she fell asleep on my bed so I had to sleep on the couch. I don't think my neck will ever be the same.' He rubbed it, grimacing.

Giles laughed. 'A white knight with saddle sores,' he observed. 'It doesn't happen in the fairy stories.'

'So, how did it go with the ostriches yesterday?'

'Ah. Pippa told you about that, did she?'

'Mm. She's not too keen.'

'Well, I've gone off the idea myself, a little,' Giles admitted. 'They have this way of looking at you . . .'

'They can be very dangerous, I believe.'

Giles looked crestfallen. 'The guy I spoke to didn't say that. In fact, he said they were very easy to keep.'

'He wasn't trying to sell you some, by any chance?' Gideon asked, eyebrows raised.

'Okay. Point taken. It was just an idea.'

'If you want to do something, why don't you build Pippa a decent cross-country course to school the horses over,' Gideon suggested. 'You could even hold a one-day-event yourselves. You've got room.'

'Does she want one?' Giles asked doubtfully. 'She's never said.'

'She'd be tickled pink,' Gideon assured him. For all his lively mind and abundant generosity, Giles often missed what was right under his nose.

'Yeah, maybe. Anyway, what's the news on

your front? Confronted any more desperate criminals?'

'Not for a day or two,' Gideon said. 'No. No news. I should think that's probably the end of it.'

'Well, I call that downright poor-spirited!' Giles exclaimed. 'Where's your sense of adventure, man? Don't you want to know what it was all about?'

'Not enough to get beaten up for it. Or worse,' he added darkly. 'Besides, I wouldn't even know where to start looking.'

Giles wasn't about to give up. 'Well, what about the barn they took you to? Couldn't you look for that?'

'I did.' Gideon told him about his search.

'Ah, so you do have some red blood in your veins, after all.'

'Yes,' he agreed dryly. 'And I'd like it to stay there, if it's all the same to you.'

'I like your friends,' Rachel told Gideon as they walked back to the Gatehouse.

'So do I,' he responded flippantly.

She ignored him. 'Pippa has offered to take me riding if I stay long enough.'

'Well, I should take her up on it,' Gideon advised. 'If you *want* to, that is. The garage may very likely take several days, I should think. *Do* you ride?'

'I have done, but I'm not very good. I'd love to try again. Would you come too?' She watched his face for his response.

'I might. It depends when you go.'

Rachel looked pleased.

Gideon's resolve to spend the best part of the next day working on his much-neglected exhibition pieces, was tested first by the allure of the cold, bright, frosty morning and secondly by a telephone call from Naomi, shortly after breakfast.

Rachel, in spite of his slightly embarrassed protests, had taken him up on his joke about decorating the spare room, which she temporarily occupied, and had begun to plot its transformation. Gideon gave in, seeing in her a need to justify her presence, if not pay her way. And the room *was* sorely in need of attention, it had to be said. Giles would be pleased.

Gideon dutifully set out his easel and pastels, sat for a full twenty minutes staring at the paper with its half-completed painting and seeing nothing, and then got up and made a cup of coffee he didn't really want. Tramping upstairs with a cup for Rachel, he found himself telling her he was going out for a couple of hours.

Rachel assured him she'd be all right, and within ten minutes he was on the Norton, bound for the wildlife sanctuary and his sister.

Fleetingly it occurred to him that he might return to find Rachel gone and all his valuables with her, but the idea didn't seriously take root in his mind. Unless she had an accomplice with transport, she wouldn't get far with very much.

What if she'd been planted by Curly and Co.? he

wondered in an amused flight of fancy, and dismissed the thought just as easily. Rachel's big, expressive eyes were a mirror for her soul and in their troubled depths Gideon sensed traces of some unspoken fear, but they were the eyes of a frightened child, not a scheming criminal.

Riding along the Dorset lanes in the bright sunlight, he couldn't have said with certainty just what had prompted him to visit Naomi again so soon. It wasn't anything she'd said; more what she hadn't said. Although they had spoken for almost a quarter of an hour, she had rung off without ever really saying why she'd called.

It was possible, he supposed, that the lure of a ride on the bike on such a morning had influenced his decision to check on her but he didn't feel it was entirely that. Whatever the reason, he hadn't been in the mood for painting, and a visit to the Sanctuary was as good a way to spend the morning as any.

He was barely a hundred yards from the place when it happened.

Riding along the narrow lane, the Norton doing forty or so, Gideon was totally unprepared for the small figure that came hurtling out of a gateway to his left, almost under the wheels of the motorbike.

He swore and swerved violently, the Norton skidding on the loose stones at the side of the lane as he tried to brake. Mounting the grassy verge, the bike pitched and bucked like an unbroken horse and finally succumbed to the forces of gravity, throwing Gideon off sideways into the hedge.

He was not best pleased.

He extricated himself from the brambles and broken twiggery, supposing he should be thankful there hadn't been a ditch, to find himself under the scrutiny of a scruffy, tow-headed and apparently entirely unrepentant child.

'My brother says people shouldn't ride big bikes if they can't control them,' the child announced, looking from Gideon to where the Norton had come to rest, its engine still ticking over and back wheel spinning. 'He says half of them should never be allowed on the road.'

Gideon nearly choked. 'And what does he say about running out into the road without looking?' he asked irritably, taking his helmet off and removing a hawthorn twig from the collar of his leather jacket.

The lad stared up at him through narrowed, insolent eyes.

'My brother's bigger than you,' he said with the air of one who thought that answered everything.

'Well,' Gideon said, 'if *you* want to get any bigger, you'd better start looking where you're going. I only missed you by inches!'

'You were going too fast.'

'And so were you!' Gideon retorted, unwarily allowing himself to be drawn into the childish argument.

He reached down and switched the motorbike's engine off, pulling it upright with an effort. He was relieved to see that it seemed to have escaped serious damage. One bent mirror and quantities of grassy mud plastered in every conceivable nook and cranny appeared to be the extent of it. He removed the worst of the mud and straightened up to find that the lad was still watching him.

'It's not a bad bike,' the kid said judiciously in his curiously sing-song voice. He stood there in denim dungarees and a none-too-clean jumper, his blond, tousled head tilted slightly to one side and bright blue eyes regarding the Norton with reluctant admiration.

Gideon's sense of humour came sidling back.

'But your brother's bike is better,' he suggested, with the ghost of a smile.

'Well, it will be,' the urchin asserted, 'when he gets it going. He's gonna take me out on it.'

'So, where's your brother now?' Gideon asked, feeling that it was high time somebody else took responsibility for the brat. He looked back at the driveway from which the child had hurtled. 'Is that where you live?'

He was rewarded with a look of deep scorn. 'Me! Live there? *Get real!*'

'Well, where then?' Gideon asked with what he felt was commendable patience. 'And what were you doing in there, if you don't live there?'

'None of your business.'

'No, I guess not,' he agreed. 'But I expect whoever lives there would be interested to hear what you've got to say.'

The child regarded him sullenly for a long moment. 'I was looking for my dog,' he said finally.

'He saw a squirrel and ran off. I went after him but this man chased me.'

'What man?'

'The man that came out of the house. He 'ad a stick,' he added for good measure.

'What were you doing?' Gideon asked suspiciously.

'Nothin'. Just trying to catch Tyke. I didn't touch anythin'. Honest!'

If Gideon thought the child's denial was a little too vehement, he kept it to himself.

'Well, we'd better go and see if we can find this dog, then,' he said reluctantly. 'But if I find you've been lying to me, I'll hand you over to the man with the stick!'

The blue eyes widened and the curls shook. 'I haven'. Honest!'

Wondering what he'd let himself in for, Gideon wheeled the Norton back along the lane and into the curving driveway, where he propped it on its stand, screened from the road by the hedge. As they set off towards the house they exchanged names and he learned that the diminutive figure determinedly trying to match strides with him went by the name of Jez and purported to be twelve years old. This last he doubted, but he held his peace.

Jez had been in favour of approaching the building commando-style, under cover of the shrubbery, calling the dog as they went; a notion that Gideon dismissed in no uncertain manner. His involvement in the whole affair was uncomfortable enough as it was and wouldn't be helped in any way, shape or form by being discovered skulking in the undergrowth. Jez was visibly disappointed.

The house, when reached, proved to be sizeable. Not quite on the scale of Graylings Priory but not far short. An unlovely, grey block of a building, it sat squarely in a sea of mown lawns and dormant rhododendrons, with rows of shuttered windows like closed eyes, repelling unwelcome visitors. Above the double front doors a stone bore the carved inscription *Lyddon Grange*.

Gideon mounted the steps and rang the doorbell.

Nobody came.

'Let's go,' Jez suggested.

'No.' Gideon shook his head firmly. 'We came for the dog. We'll get the dog.' A suspicion occurred. 'There *is* a dog?' he said, fixing Jez with a warning eye.

The curls nodded vigorously. 'Of course there is!'

Gideon took time to glance around him. On a sweep of gravel to his right a number of vehicles were parked, among them a gleaming Jaguar, a powerful sports saloon and a blue van with *Barratt the Boiler Man* emblazoned on the side, along with a childish representation of a boiler gushing smoke, and a telephone number. Gideon leaned on the bell again.

On the third ring the door opened. The man behind it was of medium height and heavy build, with short-cropped hair, tattoos and an earring. He looked as though he might well be ex-Forces.

'Yes?' His tone was decidedly short on welcome.

'Sorry to bother you. We're looking for a dog that ran in here. It's a—' Gideon looked round helplessly for Jez and found him standing at the foot of the steps almost out of sight behind the wall.

'A sheepdog,' Jez supplied. 'A puppy.'

'A sheepdog puppy,' he confirmed, turning back to the door.

'Well, I haven't got it, have I? What does this look like? Battersea bloody Dogs' Home?'

'I wouldn't know,' Gideon responded mildly. 'I've never been there. All we want is your permission to look for the dog.'

The man's eyes narrowed. 'If it's a little black and white bugger, I kicked it into them bushes about ten minutes ago,' he said, pointing across the drive to a stand of rhododendron. 'It yelped a bit,' he added with satisfaction.

'If you've hurt him . . .' Jez cried from the foot of the steps, anger lending him courage.

'You'll what?' The man enquired, sneering. 'You gonna bite my ankles like that dog of yours did?'

'I'm beginning to like this dog,' Gideon murmured. 'Jez, go and call Tyke, will you?'

Jez obediently turned away, but couldn't resist muttering, 'You wait. My brother will sort you out.'

'Yeah?' The man said, looking belligerently at Gideon. 'Well?'

'I'm not his brother,' Gideon said, weary of the

whole business. Across the drive, Jez had disappeared into the bushes and presently came out cradling a small black and white bundle. He carried the pup over to Gideon who was just preparing to take their collective leave when he noticed that the child had tears in his eyes.

'Tyke's bleedin',' Jez said on a sob. '*He* must've kicked him in the mouth and now he's bleedin'.'

Gideon was normally slow to anger but cruelty to animals did the trick every time. He turned back to the man at the door. 'There was no need for that,' he said through clenched teeth.

The man merely grinned. 'So?'

'Hit him, Gideon!' Jez advised from the bottom of the steps.

Gideon could cheerfully have strangled the pair of them but certainly had no intention of starting a brawl over a point of principle with somebody so obviously devoid of them. Keeping a tight rein on his temper, he turned away, telling the bloodthirsty child that it was time to leave.

'My *brother* would've hit him!' Jez muttered.

'Yes, I expect he would,' Gideon agreed dryly.

The tattooed one hadn't finished with him, however. 'A big mouth but no guts to back it up!' he shouted scornfully after them.

Jez looked up at Gideon hopefully but was disappointed.

'Come on, just ignore him.'

A burst of laughter followed them but was cut short as a new voice made itself heard.

'What is the meaning of this confounded

racket?' it enquired testily in high-pitched tones. 'How in hell's name am I supposed to work with all that bloody noise going on?'

As Gideon turned, an elderly man appeared in the doorway, wiping his hands on a piece of paint-smeared cloth and glowering at each of the offenders in turn. Of less than medium height, he was nevertheless an arresting figure, his spare frame topped by a crown of snowy hair which waved untidily around a bald pate speckled with liver spots. His face was weathered and lined, and he had deep-set brown eyes, a nose that would have been the pride and joy of any storybook wizard, a moustache and Van Dyke beard. A pair of pince-nez perched near the end of the improbable nose and the upper part of his body was covered by a painter's smock. Gideon felt sure he had seen him somewhere before.

The acute, monkey-like eyes finished their survey of the unwanted visitors and returned to the man at his side.

'Who are these people? Why haven't you got rid of them?' he demanded. 'What the hell do I pay you for?'

'I told them to get out but they wouldn't go,' Tattoos complained sullenly.

The snowy head tipped forward again, and Gideon and Jez were subjected to a deep frown over the top of the man's pince-nez. Jez slid sideways to shelter from the glare behind Gideon.

'Well? What do they want?' the man addressed his doorman again.

Gideon had had enough of being discussed as if he wasn't there. He mounted the steps once more and advanced with hand outstretched.

'Gideon Blake,' he said by way of introduction. 'I'm sorry if we disturbed you but my young friend here lost his dog and we came to ask if it had been seen.'

The elderly man looked suspiciously at Gideon's hand, as if hand-shaking was a custom he was not familiar with, and then looked past him to where Jez stood clutching Tyke.

'You would appear to have found the animal,' he observed, returning his gaze to Gideon. 'Do you have any other business here to detain you?'

Gideon's eyes narrowed at this display of bad manners, and behind the old man, Tattoos smirked annoyingly.

'I appreciate your right to privacy,' he said quietly, 'and I can tolerate rudeness, but this man viciously kicked a puppy, and that I *won't* tolerate. I suggest you have a serious word with him or you'll have others to answer to besides me!'

He was the recipient of another simian frown. '*Gideon Blake,* you say? Not the Gideon Blake who paints horses?'

'Amongst other things, yes,' he agreed, amused by this change of subject. He'd placed the man now: Meredith Milne, an eccentric but highly successful artist; he'd seen a photograph of him in a Sunday supplement alongside a review of an exhibition of his paintings. He was held to be something of a recluse, seldom emerging from the privacy of his home and then travelling, whenever possible, in his own helicopter.

'I've seen some of your work. There's a lot to like about it,' the old man conceded. Then, as if coming to a decision, finally held out his hand. 'Meredith Milne,' he announced.

Gideon affected not to notice the hand. 'I know,' he said calmly. 'But my warning stands. Your man was out of line and the very least I expect is an apology to the kid.'

'Yes, yes. Whatever.' Milne was patently tired of the subject. 'Benson, Renson – whatever your name is – give the boy some pocket money and then get out of my sight. I've had enough of you. Where's Slade anyway?'

'In his flat. He's got somebody with him.' Renson's mood was not noticeably improving. He dug in his pocket and withdrew a note that he held out to Jez, muttering something under his breath. Then he went back into the house, favouring Gideon with a look of pure venom as he passed. Jez pocketed the note with alacrity, raising two fingers to Renson's departing back.

'Well, and that's that,' Milne said, dismissing the affair. 'Children and animals . . . always trouble. Always.'

If Gideon thought this generalisation a little unfair, he let it go. Arguing the toss with Milne would quite obviously be fruitless. The man was a quite brilliant artist, known the world over, and his work an obsession with him. People like that were often, in Gideon's experience, a little naive in matters not pertaining to their ruling passion. He prepared to take his leave, wondering as he did so just what he was going to do with Jez.

The problem was taken out of his hands. Footsteps scrunched on the gravel drive to the side of the house and a voice said in surprise, 'Jez, you little bugger! What've you been up to? I told you to stay in the van.'

Gideon stiffened. At the top of the steps and out of sight for the moment, he didn't need the evidence of his eyes to tell him who the newcomer was. Those soft, lilting tones were stamped into his memory for a lifetime. What crazy coincidence had thrown them together again so soon?

His mind raced as the steps crunched closer. How should he react? Should he show that he recognised his abductor of five nights ago? Would he be believed if he didn't?

Jez apparently had no reservations. 'Joey!' he cried. 'I lost Tyke and a man kicked him. He's bleeding, look!' He held the puppy out for inspection.

Gideon made a snap decision. As far as he could see, he had nothing to gain by showing that he recognised the man, and possibly much to lose, here at this remote spot, outnumbered and with only a child for a witness. And hardly an impartial witness at that. With an odd feeling that fate was playing games with him, Gideon turned towards the newcomer, schooling his features to give no sign of recognition.

Joey had had no such warning. 'He'll be okay,

Sis, he's a tough little bugger,' he said, looking the pup over and handing it back to the child. 'But if you'd done as you were told in the first place . . .' He broke off, eyes widening with shock as he caught sight of Gideon on the steps.

'He helped me. His name's Gideon and he helped me find Tyke,' Jez declared looking anxiously up at Joey. Then to Gideon, 'I told you my brother was bigger than you.'

Her brother? So this obviously wasn't Slade, who lived in the flat.

'So you did,' Gideon acknowledged, still mentally adjusting to the revelation that Jez was a girl.

'*Gideon?* That's a name you don't often hear,' Joey remarked casually, watching him.

'No, you don't,' he admitted blandly. 'Look, the guy next door is a vet. He's a friend of mine. How about I take Jez and the puppy round to get that cut looked at? It won't take a minute.'

Joey wasn't entirely happy with that. He opened his mouth to decline but Jez forestalled him.

'Oh, *please*, Joey. It's still bleedin'. He might bleed to death!'

'He'll be all right.'

'Well, it might need stitching,' Gideon prompted, enjoying his reluctance. It seemed Joey wasn't quite sure whether he'd been recognised or not, and was anxious that Gideon should have no opportunity to question Jez. Gideon held out his hand to the girl. 'Come on. I was going there anyway. Let's get Tyke sorted out, shall we?'

Jez went to him, looking back at Joey in mute entreaty. At this point, Milne, who had been temporarily forgotten, decided to take a hand.

'I don't personally care where any of you go, just so long as you go somewhere,' he observed impatiently. 'All I want is some peace and quiet, so clear off, the lot of you!' He made a shooing motion, much as one might to a stray dog or cat, and then turned back into the darkness of his hallway, pausing on the threshold to say to Gideon, 'You! You can come back one day and see my studio. I wouldn't mind talking to you, and you might learn something.'

With this gracious invitation he disappeared, slamming the door behind him.

'It seems we've been dismissed,' Gideon said into the silence that greeted this display of arrogance. 'Well, Jez, are you coming? Your brother can come too, if he wants,' he added, slanting a quizzical look at Joey.

Jez gave him another pleading look and Joey gave in.

'All right. But don't be long. I'll meet you outside in ten minutes. And don't go chattering on about things, okay?'

'I won't, Joey. I promise.'

Naomi answered the bell in reception, and if she was surprised to see Gideon, complete with a small scruffy child and an even smaller and scruffier dog, she gave no sign of it.

'Oh, poor little mite!' she exclaimed immediately,

holding out her arms towards the puppy. 'What happened?'

Jez regarded her warily and held Tyke even more tightly.

'This is Jez. Her puppy met with a slight accident,' Gideon explained briefly.

'Let's go through and find Tim, shall we? He's a vet,' Naomi said to the girl, who nodded and went obediently through the door she held open. Over her shoulder Naomi murmured, 'Another of your strays, Brother?'

'I'll explain later,' Gideon promised.

It was some three-quarters of an hour before Gideon finally restored Jez to her brother, and he was gratified to find Joey tapping his fingers impatiently, sitting on the bonnet of the blue van that was now parked at the end of the Sanctuary's driveway.

'It won't take a minute, eh, pal?' Joey remarked sourly as they approached. 'Did you lose your way or somethin'?'

'Tim showed me round and I saw all the animals,' Jez told her brother, her eyes alight with remembered joy.

Joey wasn't impressed. 'Yeah, well, I've got a business to run, so hop in quick and let's be going, shall we?'

With one last unloving look at Gideon, he got into the van himself and within moments they were gone.

'Don't mention it,' Gideon murmured, but he

was smiling faintly as he turned back to the farm. Jez had held true to her promise, telling him nothing other than her surname, Fletcher. But Joey wouldn't be human if he didn't have some doubts. Now it was *his* turn to wait and wonder.

'So, what brings you out here this time?' Naomi asked, licking chicken fat off her fingers as she rolled up the remains of her takeaway lunch in the paper in which it had arrived. Having eaten, the three of them were relaxing in the warmth of the Sanctuary's office. 'Two visits in one week. It must be a family record!'

'I don't know, really,' he admitted. 'It was just something about your phone call this morning . . . I got the impression something was wrong. Tell me to mind my own business if you like, but there it is.'

'You didn't tell me you'd phoned Gideon,' Tim said, looking at Naomi in surprise. 'You said the note didn't worry you. Why didn't you talk to *me*?'

She flushed unhappily. 'I wasn't *really* worried. I don't know why I called Gideon. I didn't tell him about it even then.'

Tim still looked a little hurt.

'I'm sorry,' Naomi said, putting her hand on his. 'I thought you'd got enough to worry about without me adding to it.'

'At the risk of seeming abominably nosy, just what was it that everybody was worried about and Sis rang up specifically not to tell me?' Gideon asked. 'Or is it still a deep dark secret?'

Tim shook his head. 'It's really no big deal,' he

said. 'Somebody with a sick sense of humour pinned a note to the surgery door in the night. By far the best thing to do is to treat it with the contempt it deserves and forget it.'

'What did it say? Can I see it?'

'I binned it,' Tim said dismissively.

'And I took it out again,' Naomi said, reaching behind her to open a drawer in a nearby desk. 'Well, if anything did happen, the police would be bound to ask to see it, wouldn't they?' she added defensively, passing a sheet of paper to Gideon.

'Nothing is going to happen,' Tim said, soothingly.

'You can't know that!' Naomi protested. 'It's not as if we haven't had our problems already.'

Gideon didn't miss the 'we' and the 'our'. It appeared their relationship had quite solid foundations. He turned his attention to the note. '*Dear Dr Doolittle,*' it read. '*You can't have a hospital without any patients. Why don't you go back to wherever you came from? You're not wanted here.*' It was unsigned but bore the postscript, '*Ever had rabbit stew? It's really very good.*'

He looked up. 'Have you any idea who sent it?'

Tim shrugged. 'Suspicions but no proof.'

'What does this last bit mean? About the rabbit stew?'

Tim shrugged again.

Naomi wasn't having that. 'You know perfectly well what it means!' she exclaimed in exasperation. 'Someone brought us a litter of baby rabbits two weeks ago, their dog had killed the parents or something. But anyway, three days ago I went to feed them in the morning and the cage was open. They'd all gone, of course, and I was mad at myself because I thought I hadn't shut the door properly. Now we know better!'

'Not for sure,' Tim protested.

'Well, how else could they have known about it, if it wasn't them?'

Tim didn't have an answer for that. He subsided into thoughtful silence.

'And other things have happened?' Gideon prompted.

'Several things,' Naomi said unhappily, looking at Tim.

He didn't speak.

'Tim's dog was poisoned. Rat poison, we discovered. At the time we thought it was an accident, that he'd picked something up at the farm down the road. He was always getting out – we haven't had time to do the fences yet – but he never went on the road, always across the fields, so we weren't too worried. It was awful,' she said, sadness in her eyes as she remembered. 'We found him in the barn. He'd just managed to make it home but he'd bled to death. Haemorrhaged. Now we're wondering if it wasn't those bastards next door!'

'*You* are,' Tim put in, somewhat half-heartedly.

'And you are! You know you are! You just won't admit it,' Naomi declared passionately.

'The people at the Grange?' Gideon asked, trying to sift the facts from the emotional detritus. 'Why?'

'Milne tried to buy Tim out soon after he got here, apparently. Don't ask me why he wants the place, he doesn't do anything with the land he has, as far as I can see. And they've got their solicitors working to try and dispute the boundaries. Everything they can do to make things difficult for Tim, they do. And still he tries to see the good in them.'

Tim looked uncomfortable. 'I admit, their solicitors *have* been a pain in the backside but the chap who came round that time was very obliging. It's not his fault, anyway. He doesn't own the place, he just works for the guy.'

Naomi was undeterred. 'I didn't trust him. He said all the right things but he didn't mean any of it. And it was after he came round that the trouble started.'

Gideon couldn't imagine any of the players in *his* recent drama being described as obliging, even on a good day. 'We're not talking about a guy called Renson, I take it?'

'No,' Tim said. 'This man's name was Slade. Dark, slightly Latin-looking chap, dressed all in black. Expensive-looking clothes, too. Said he was Milne's administrator, whatever that means.'

'He gave me the creeps,' Naomi put in, wrinkling her nose at the memory. 'He was so smooth. Like a dangerous snake, beautiful but deadly.'

'He *did* make an impression, didn't he, Sis?' Gideon was surprised. Accustomed to the rich, diverse mix of humanity that made up the acting fraternity, his sister was not given to snap decisions based on outward appearances. This Slade had obviously touched something much deeper.

'All right,' Tim said, acknowledging defeat. 'The thing is, given that I admit I didn't like the man myself, and given that he's quite possibly a lying, unscrupulous bastard, what can I do about it? I mean, I've no proof that he's done anything. He hasn't even been *unpleasant* to my face.'

'No, it's a problem,' Gideon agreed.

'There's a path that goes from the gate by the stables, across the field towards the Grange,' Naomi said. 'Somebody had obviously used it regularly before Tim came. There's a gate into Milne's property at the other end.'

'But nobody's used it since,' Tim pointed out. 'The gate's locked now. It was probably just a shortcut.'

'To where?' she asked incredulously, but he had no answer.

'You said several things had happened,' Gideon said, concentrating on known facts. 'Anything other than the dog and the solicitors?'

'Well,' Tim looked uncomfortable, 'somebody sent the RSPCA inspectors round, saying that we were ill-treating the animals. Then we had some of our fences cut, and we've had one or two notes.'

Naomi looked at him in consternation. 'You didn't tell me! I thought this was the first.'

'I didn't want to worry you. It was some time ago, just after you first came. To be honest, I didn't take much notice of them until Sam was – until Sam died.'

'Could you get a trained guard dog?' Gideon suggested. 'Or better still a flock of geese or guinea fowl? A friend of mine's got some and they make a hell of a racket when anyone comes round. I was thinking they'd be less easy to silence than a dog. I mean, if they've already poisoned one . . .'

'It's an idea,' Tim mused.

'I think it's a good idea,' Naomi said. 'You've got to do something. Maybe we could get a security camera too.'

There was silence for a moment as the three of them were busy with their thoughts. In one of the nearby sheds a squirrel chattered noisily and was answered by the raucous squawk of a bird. Some- where further off there was the sound of a helicopter starting up.

'Anyone want any more coffee?' Naomi asked, getting to her feet. 'We haven't got much milk, unless you like powdered.'

Tim said he would have half a cup and Gideon was in the act of declining when the drone of the helicopter swelled to a thudding, thundering roar, and the machine rose into view from behind the trees on the farm boundary. Almost brushing the topmost branches, it swooped across the open field and headed for the Sanctuary buildings where it hung in the sky like a giant white dragonfly, gazing down on them with its huge glass eyes.

'Christ!' Tim exclaimed, leaping to his feet. 'The animals!'

Gideon sprang up beside him. 'Quick!' he said to Naomi. 'My camera! Inside pocket of my jacket!'

The helicopter drifted even closer and the windows of the office were vibrating so violently that Gideon seriously wondered if they would stand the shock. With shaking hands and wide, frightened eyes, Naomi handed him the tiny compact camera that had been a Christmas present from Giles. In seconds he was out through reception and into the open air.

Here, in addition to the incredible racket, the downdraught was wreaking havoc. Everything not firmly secured was rolling or flying away, a young conifer hedge was bent almost double and the corrugated-iron roof to what Gideon knew was the toolshed rippled along its length like a sheet of paper in a breeze.

Steadying himself, he pointed the camera and held the shutter down, thankful that it was the foolproof, auto-everything model and not his best, professional-quality one.

The helicopter was sensationally low. God only knew what terror the animals and birds in the shelters below were suffering. The noise and buffeting were awful.

It seemed a lifetime that the machine hovered there but it could in reality only have been a matter of half a minute or so. Gideon could see two figures through the darkened glass of the cockpit and after a moment one of them spotted him. He shook the pilot's arm and pointed, and almost immediately the helicopter dipped slightly in Gideon's direction and began to move.

There was no real danger that it would hit him,

shielded as he was by surrounding buildings, but nevertheless he instinctively ducked into the shelter of a nearby wall, the motor drive on his camera still whirring inaudibly against the greater cacophony.

Seconds later the ordeal was over. The helicopter curved sharply away and droned off into the distance almost as quickly as it had come, leaving behind it a comparative silence that was broken only by the panic-stricken cries of the creatures in the cages below.

Gideon pushed himself away from the wall and looked at the camera in his hands. It had been a new film, now it had wound on right to the end. Twenty-four pictures of a helicopter hovering dangerously, illegally, low. Twenty-four pictures of a helicopter that must have identifying marks upon it.

Now they had some proof.

5

When Gideon left the Sanctuary later that afternoon he took the incriminating roll of film straight to Chilminster police station to lodge a complaint, and returned to the Gatehouse by way of Blandford where he picked up the developed photos of Sovereign.

He finally got home just after six, with a Chinese take-away tucked under his arm, and found Rachel curled up asleep on the couch, arms hugging her knees and long lashes dark against her creamy skin. The fire was a faintly glowing mound of embers and a book lay open on the floor where it had fallen.

Gideon smiled and put a hand out to gently shake her shoulder.

With an inarticulate cry Rachel sat up and lashed out at him, catching him a stinging blow across the face.

'Whoa, Rachel! Steady on! It's me,' he exclaimed, catching the swinging arm before it could do any more damage. 'I'm sorry. I didn't mean to startle you. Who did you think I was?'

For a moment she stared at him with wide, anxious eyes and then, remembering, she subsided, looking horrified at what she'd done.

'I'm *so* sorry!' she said in anguished tones. 'I must have been dreaming or something. Did I hurt you?'

Gideon let go of her wrist and rubbed his face. 'I daresay I'll recover,' he said with a quirky smile. 'It's probably only concussion.'

Rachel managed a faint smile in return.

'Really, I'm fine,' he asserted. 'It was my fault for making you jump. Anyway, let's forget it, shall we? Come on, I've got some Chinese. You *do* like Chinese, I hope?'

'I love it.' She relaxed a notch or two, got up and followed him into the kitchen. 'I'm sorry about the fire, it's almost out. Shall I stoke it up a bit?'

'I'll do it in a minute. Come and have this while it's hot.'

After they had eaten, Gideon settled down at his drawing board in the small front room that he used as a studio. Small it might be but the light was perfect – when there was any, of course. Now he worked under an angle-poise lamp, using the photographs and sketches of Sovereign to rough out an outline in charcoal for the portrait he was to do.

Progress was slow.

The time it took to do a complete portrait from rough sketch to finished, ready to frame product varied from subject to subject but averaged about two weeks. He rarely worked on it every day. It was more likely to be between five and eight periods of three or four hours – longer sessions producing counter-productive tension. A fortnight was normally enough, even accounting for off-days such as today, and in fact he found the self-discipline needed to sit down and get on with it came more easily under pressure.

Fundamentally, he never really thought of himself as an artist. It was a useful and occasionally lucrative gift, not a calling. He certainly didn't feel compelled to reach for his sketchpad every time he had a moment to spare, as some artists did. Finishing a really good portrait was very satisfying but the process of setting up and making a start required a mammoth effort almost every time and, with his mind on the day's events, this time was no exception.

Maybe making countless cups of coffee that one didn't really want, much less need, was a normal consequence of working from home, he mused twenty minutes later as he spooned instant powder into two mugs. At this rate Rachel would be a caffeine addict too by the time she left.

Now *there* was a person who could apply herself to her work wholeheartedly and to the exclusion of all else. He decided that his own inability must be a character defect, but the thought didn't bother him unduly.

Coffee distributed and back at his drawing board, Gideon picked up his charcoal pencil and bent over the paper. In the living room Rachel was sitting on the sofa in front of the fire, cup of coffee at her elbow, cat on lap, and colour charts and swatches of material all around her as she happily planned the next stage of the transformation of the spare room. She had a compact disc of classical music playing with the volume turned well up and Gideon had left the door ajar so he could hear it too. Another distraction, he supposed, but sometimes, when the creative juices weren't flowing, the silence could become deafening and he often had music playing when he worked.

Once again he found thoughts of the day intruding.

His session with the Chilminster police had been less than completely satisfactory. Apparently there had been another complaint about the low-flying helicopter from a motorist who had been driving past the Sanctuary at the time, though the police had not held out much hope of tracing the culprit until the advent of Gideon with his film.

He knew it was unlikely that the prints would be masterpieces. With a compact camera, taking snaps of a white helicopter against a pale blue sky with the winter sun slanting into the lens was about as far from the ideal as possible, but the constable to whom he'd initially spoken had seemed confident that the images could be enhanced.

The constable, a PC Logan, was listening with what appeared to be a great deal of interest as

Gideon related a summary of the troubles Tim had encountered at Hermitage Farm, when the scene changed abruptly. A passing sergeant paused to listen and almost before Gideon was aware of what was happening, he had dismissed Logan and taken his place.

This, much older, officer was far more inclined to treat the incident of the helicopter, which he admitted was extremely reckless, as quite separate from any other harassment which Mr Reynolds might have suffered: 'whether real or imagined', he had added unnecessarily. He thought it would be proved to be a gung-ho young pilot showing off to a friend, and although it should be punished, such behaviour should not be confused with anything of a more personal nature. He added that, in the unlikely event of the helicopter being Milne's, a quiet word would doubtless put things right.

Gideon left the station feeling decidedly put out. The officer, one Sergeant Greening, had taken charge of the roll of film, issuing Gideon with a receipt and an assurance that it would be returned to him in due course.

'We often find that pictures taken in the heat of the moment don't come up to much,' he warned dismissively. 'If the subject is moving they tend to be rather fuzzy and indistinct and there's often a degree of camera shake.'

'Well, I took twenty-four shots so I'm sure there's at least one decent one amongst them. But if your guys can't make anything of them, I know a chap who certainly can,' Gideon told him, his

105

patience wearing thin. He had begun to wish, in fact, that he had taken the film to the specialist first. Time had seemed of the essence but now he wasn't so sure. He found he'd had quite enough of being patronised.

He had reported his efforts to Tim and Naomi on his mobile before setting off for home, and Tim had thanked him for trying but sounded resigned to there being no real result. It seemed he'd had dealings with Sergeant Greening before. He also reported that one of his patients, an injured peregrine falcon, had suffered a heart attack and died shortly after Gideon had left.

All in all, he felt it had been an odd sort of day, and it had left him with a strangely restless feeling. So much seemed unsatisfactory. His second brush with Joey had revived his sense of grievance about the way he'd been used on the night of the abduction, and he was conscious of a strong protective instinct towards his sister regarding the troubles at Hermitage Farm.

He came out of his reverie to find half a cup of cold coffee on the table beside him, and on his drawing board an expensive piece of paper covered in sketches of helicopters and a rather good caricature of Sergeant Greening. With disgust he clicked the angle-poise off and decided to go to bed.

Friday was a good day for Gideon work-wise. With what he felt was commendable self-discipline, he had completed a detailed charcoal study of Tom

Collins' horse and started sketching in the background. So when, on Saturday morning, he received a call from a lady who was having trouble with her dog, he could abandon the picture with a completely clear conscience in order to respond to what he felt was a genuine and fairly desperate cry for help.

Rachel had gone out, Pippa having called to invite her up to the Priory for lunch and to see Fanny's puppies. She had also suggested that the three of them ride on Sunday if the weather was kind, a plan which Rachel seemed very keen on.

It was another cold, clear day, superb for biking, and after a fairly hassle-free run, Gideon slowed down to ride carefully through the pretty, golden-stone villages below Bath, following the extensive instructions he had taken down over the telephone. He finally propped the bike on its stand outside a beautiful, ages-old cottage that stood next door to an equally ancient mill.

It was real picture postcard stuff. Had it been May there would have been roses flowering over the door and probably ducks from the nearby stream waddling past the gate.

Gideon had to bow his head to get into the porch, and the lady who presently answered the jangly bell focused first on his jacket front and then in succession on the loosely tied neckerchief and his battered face.

'My goodness!' she said, taking in the sizeable figure that was almost totally blocking the light

107

from her doorway. Somewhere in the background a dog was barking furiously.

'Mrs Weatherfield?' Gideon enquired, hiding his amusement. 'I'm Gideon Blake.'

'Yes, I'm sorry,' the lady said, collecting her wits. 'I do beg your pardon. I don't quite know what I was expecting . . .'

'But I'm not it?' he supplied with a twinkle.

'Well, no,' Mrs Weatherfield admitted. 'But where are my manners? Please, do come in. And it's Jenny.' She stepped back to let him past; a slim, neat, fiftyish lady with salt-and-pepper hair, and a world of trouble in her eyes.

Inside, the cottage was exactly as the outside had suggested it would be; chintz, dark beams and whitewashed walls. The room they entered was dominated by an impressive inglenook fireplace and lit by three tiny leaded lights that were about waist-high to Gideon. Head bent to avoid the beams, he divested himself of his leather jacket, which was taken from him and placed, along with his helmet, on a dark oak chair in a corner.

'Please, have a seat. Can I get you something? Tea? Coffee? Something stronger?'

Gideon sat down. 'No, thank you. Later perhaps.'

Sitting on a big squashy settee to one side of the fireplace he was evidently more manageable, for the lady relaxed a degree or two as she settled in the chair opposite.

'Now,' he said gently. 'Tell me what's been going on.'

'Well, I'm not really sure,' Jenny began, and Gideon could see her eyes shining over-bright in the muted light of the cottage. 'As I told you on the phone, Willow's been acting so strangely these past few weeks . . . I can't understand it. She's always been so affectionate but lately, well, she doesn't seem to want me to touch her and she's even growled a couple of times.'

'She's not in pain or uncomfortable in some way? You've seen a vet?'

'He can't find anything wrong.' Jenny looked distressed.

'Can I see the dog?' Gideon asked, and as she nodded, getting to her feet, 'Alone, possibly?'

She paused, looking doubtful. 'Well, I suppose so. She's not very friendly with strangers . . .'

'Just for a few moments. It'll be all right, I promise.'

She gave him another long look, then nodded again. Nevertheless, after letting the dog in she watched it approach Gideon before she withdrew.

He had picked up a magazine from a side table. From the corner of his eye he saw the dog, a handsome German Shepherd bitch, come slinking into the room and pause, but gave no sign of noticing it. As with the horse, it was important not to challenge; not to appear to threaten. When unsure, German Shepherds often prefer to circle and approach from behind. His position on the sofa was robbing her of this option but by keeping his eyes averted he was taking the pressure off her.

109

The bitch advanced, sniffed at one of his hands and wagged her bushy tail a little uncertainly.

'There's a good girl,' Gideon said quietly, still not looking directly.

Her velvety ears pricked enquiringly.

'Lie down, then.'

The bitch hesitated. Across the room the door closed softly and she flicked an ear back. Uncommonly useful, German Shepherds' ears. They mirror the direction of their thoughts in the same way that horses' ears do.

Willow padded away and back again, coming closer this time. Gideon sensed that she wanted to make contact.

'Come and lie down,' he said, a little more firmly. With a sigh, she sank down at his feet and quietly he put a hand down and gently rubbed the side of her face, looking at her for the first time. Willow returned his regard; a sign of a strong character.

'Good girl,' he told her again.

When Jenny Weatherfield put her head round the door a few minutes later, Gideon was sitting back on the sofa with Willow at his knee, her chin resting trustfully on his leg.

'Oh!' she said, a little wistfully. 'She used to sit like that with me but she's stopped doing it since . . .'

'Your husband died?' Gideon hazarded.

'Yes, that's right.' Ready tears sprang to her eyes. 'Did Pippa tell you? I asked her not to. People always sympathise and it sets me off. It's too recent.'

'I haven't spoken to Pippa,' Gideon said. 'At least not about you.'

Jenny frowned. 'Then how . . . ?'

Gideon didn't really know. 'A guess, I suppose. I think it's the root of the trouble with Willow, anyway.'

'But she wasn't close to him. She's always been very much my dog. Wouldn't go to anyone else. Until now,' she added thoughtfully.

'But *you* were close to him,' Gideon said gently. 'Very close, weren't you? And it's hit you hard.'

Jenny sat down, her eyes fixed firmly on Willow who looked back but made no effort to go to her. She nodded wordlessly.

'This dog adores you,' Gideon told her. 'You're her whole world. And suddenly you've changed. You act differently. From being her rock, you've become unsure, unhappy and indecisive. She doesn't know what to make of you any more. She's worried and you see that, so you make a big fuss of her because you're relying on her to get you through the bad time. Hugging her, perhaps crying at the same time. Needing her.' He paused and Jenny nodded, tears again in her eyes.

'She's totally lost. She feels insecure, and because she's anxious she becomes defensive. When you behave out of character, she growls. You're hurt; she's even more at sea, and so the downward spiral begins.'

'Poor Willow!' Jenny exclaimed.

111

'Yes, "poor Willow", but that's not what she needs to hear,' Gideon said. 'What she really needs is the Jenny she used to know. She needs to know where she is again; needs some direction. You must be matter-of-fact with her. If she growls, remember that it's in response to your mood. Ignore her or brush it off lightly. You have to be strong for her. Put on a show and one day you'll find it isn't a show at all. You can help each other through this but sympathy isn't what either of you need right now, however much you deserve it.'

Jenny sat and looked at her dog, a mixture of doubt and hope showing on her gracefully ageing features. 'I understand what you're saying,' she said. 'But I don't know if I can do it.'

'I think you can, for her sake,' Gideon told her. 'But if I were you, I'd get out of this house for a bit. Go and stay with a friend. Place yourself in a situation where you've no choice but to put on a brave face. Each day it'll be a bit easier and if you're happier, Willow will be happier. Spirals work both ways, you know.'

He got to his feet and reached for his jacket. 'I'll ring next week and I don't want you to be here,' he said firmly.

Jenny achieved a watery smile and followed him across to the door.

'When you arrived I thought I'd made a big mistake,' she told him. 'To be completely honest, if it hadn't been for Pippa, I probably wouldn't even have let you in. She said not to be put off by appearances and she was right, you have a gift.'

She *did*, did she? Gideon thought, filing that bit of information away for future use. 'I understand animals, that's all,' he protested, mildly embarrassed.

'And people,' she added softly. 'Thank you, Gideon. I'll let you know how we get on.'

Willow had padded across to stand behind her, watching Gideon leave. Jenny put a hand down and the bitch backed off a pace or two.

'Silly old girl,' she said lightly, and Willow looked up and waved her tail.

'That's fine,' Gideon said. 'Don't crowd her and she'll come back to you.'

'I understand,' Jenny said, and he could see that she did. 'Thank you *so* much.'

Sunday's ride went well. Rachel was a bit nervous at first but soon picked up the threads of her past experience and looked quite at home on Cassie. She was very taken with the handsome black horse that Gideon was riding and asked Pippa about him.

'Blackbird? He's a menace,' she said flatly. 'He's the most devious horse I've ever had the misfortune to come across and he can be a sod to ride. You just can't trust him.'

Rachel considered the black horse for a long moment. He was walking beside her own mount with an expression of beatific innocence upon his good-looking face. Butter, quite plainly, would not even become soft.

Pippa followed the direction of her gaze.

'Oh, don't be misled by that look,' she advised. 'He's probably planning something dastardly behind that saintly mask. Besides, our friend the witchdoctor there always sends horses to sleep. I don't know what it is, but put him on any horse and no matter how unruly it's been, within minutes it's walking like a seaside donkey.'

'It's a trade secret,' Gideon informed Rachel conspiratorially. 'You have to belong to the SSHW.'

She frowned. 'What does that stand for?'

'Don't listen to him,' Pippa said, exasperated. 'He's having you on. He'll tell you it's the Secret Society of Horse Whisperers, but there's no such thing.'

Gideon pretended to be hurt. 'Well, if you'd heard of it, it wouldn't be very secret, would it?' he reasoned.

Pippa looked heavenwards.

Monday morning brought a call from the garage in Blandford to say that the Mini could be picked up that afternoon. Both Gideon and Rachel needed to shop so they decided to travel in on the Norton, with Rachel driving the Mini back.

Once in Blandford they agreed to go their separate ways, meeting up again at a teashop before picking up the car. Gideon needed some art supplies, to call in once again at the police station, and to do a major grocery shop, which he arranged for Rachel to pick up in the Mini. What she needed she didn't say and, as it was none of his business, Gideon didn't enquire.

He arrived at the appointed teashop ahead of her and ordered cappuccinos and cream cakes for them both. He was a firm believer in healthy eating but an equally firm advocate of the value of what he called soul food, his theory being that if something was *really* enjoyable, then the satisfaction derived from eating it cancelled out any harm it might do in terms of cholesterol or calories.

His session with the Blandford police had been singularly unsatisfactory. He'd called them on Friday morning to report his findings about Joey, which had been received, if not with warmth and gratitude, then at least with interest. Today, however, his reception could at best have been described as tepid.

There were, he was told, seven Joseph Fletchers in the Chilminster area; three of whom were pensioners, two of school age, one out of the country and the last five foot four, bespectacled and a hairdresser. Gideon had laughed at this, which hadn't improved the warmth of his welcome, but the idea of *his* Joey as a hairdresser, with hairpins in his mouth and a towel over his shoulder, was hilarious.

They had also drawn a blank with the van. It wasn't registered, as Gideon had dared to hope, to Joey's partner-in-crime Curly, but to a bona-fide heating engineer called Ray Barratt. Barratt was unhelpfully away on a fortnight's honeymoon at present, but had apparently been described by those who knew him as skinny, dark-haired and quietly spoken, none of which could have applied to Curly. Nobody seemed to know where his van was, except that it might have gone in for a refit.

The coffee and cakes arrived, and taking one cup, he stirred the froth into the liquid, hoping Rachel wouldn't be too long.

She wasn't. By the time Gideon's coffee had cooled to remotely drinkable she appeared, laden down with shiny bags and looking very pleased with herself. She slid into the seat opposite him, depositing her purchases upon the floor beside her where they promptly subsided and slid across the tiles.

'Here,' Gideon said, holding out his hand. 'Put them over this side between my chair and the wall.'

When the bags were safely stowed, Rachel heaved a sigh of pure pleasure. 'Oh, I *love* shopping!' she said. 'It just gives you such a high. It's great!'

Gideon made a face. 'Whereas I spend the whole time thinking of all the other things I could be doing. The quicker it's over and done with, the better I like it.'

'Isn't that just typically male?' Rachel exclaimed, shaking her head in exasperation. 'All I can say is, it's no wonder most single men have nothing edible in their larders and a wardrobe full of jeans and tee-shirts!'

'Ouch!' Gideon said, laughing. 'A cruel indictment against the male of the species.'

'But true, nonetheless,' Rachel pointed out.

Gideon had to acknowledge defeat. 'The defence has no further comment,' he said stiffly. 'But it wishes to go on record as saying that it regrets buying Miss Shelley that huge and extremely expensive cream cake.'

'Oh, a poor loser!' Rachel said giggling. 'I wouldn't have thought it of you.'

'I'm renowned for it,' he told her seriously, but she was getting used to his teasing and turned her attention instead to the eclair.

He thought how much she had come out of herself in the few days he'd known her, and supposed her deafness must make it difficult for her in her first dealings with strangers. It was a shame she allowed her fear of pity to rule her life, though. In reality it was more of a handicap than her deafness, making her appear offhand and unfriendly. Nothing could be further from the truth. When she got past that first hurdle she revealed a warm and generous nature. And for himself, he found her intense way of watching him as he spoke quite appealing.

Coffee and cakes consumed, he paid the bill and they gathered up their collective purchases and made their way out into the cold once more. Rachel was ahead of Gideon and just turning to say something, when suddenly her face froze into an expression of shock.

'What is it?' he asked, and when she didn't answer, he turned to follow the direction of her gaze. The pavement was relatively empty. Nobody was looking their way in particular. Nothing appeared out of the ordinary.

He turned back. Rachel was as white as a sheet, her eyes huge.

'What's the matter?'

She dragged her fascinated gaze away from the street. 'I thought I saw somebody,' she said in a small voice. 'It doesn't matter. Please, can we go now?'

'Who?'

'Please,' she repeated, starting to move. 'Let's just go home.'

She would say nothing more and so Gideon led the way to the garage to pick up her car, telling her about the groceries to be collected from the supermarket, as they went.

As the mechanic at the garage explained what they had done to the Mini and produced the bill, Rachel gave the distinct impression that her attention was somewhere else entirely. The repair bill was very reasonable, to Gideon's mind, but he felt they could have added another two or three noughts and Rachel would still have thanked them and handed her credit card over with the same slightly dazed expression.

Every few moments she looked over her shoulder to where the big double doors stood open to the yard and from thence to the street. Her apprehension was so contagious that Gideon found himself glancing that way too, though he'd no idea who he was looking for.

When she slid behind the wheel of the Mini

he reminded her about the groceries but as she drove away he still wasn't sure whether she had taken the information on board.

As Gideon thanked the mechanic once more and made his own way out on foot, he heard a voice in the yard calling out, 'Okay, mate. See yer later,' and rounded the big sliding doors just as a blue-overalled figure came the other way. They collided in the doorway and over the shorter man's head Gideon caught sight of another man in a boiler suit waving and disappearing round the corner into the street. Medium height, heavy build, very little hair and a big plaster across his nose.

Curly?

'Sorry, mate,' the mechanic muttered, moving to one side, but Gideon caught hold of his arm to detain him.

'That man,' he said. 'The one you were talking to. Does he live round here?'

'Nah, Chilminster. What's it to you, anyway?'

'Oh, I . . . er . . . owe him some money,' Gideon improvised hastily. 'But I've lost his address.'

The mechanic laughed shortly. 'If you owe Curly money, *he'll* find *you*, believe me.'

'Well, to be honest, it's Joey I wanted to see,' Gideon admitted, roughening his voice a degree or two, and adding, 'We used to be mates.' He thanked providence that he was wearing his jeans and leather biker's jacket.

The mechanic looked him up and down doubtfully a time or two but Gideon could see that his mentioning Joey had tipped the scales in his favour.

'If you're Joey's mate, how come you don't know where he lives?'

'Christ! What are you, his bloody minder? I used to know him in Liverpool, if you must know, but forget it, I'll find him myself.'

He turned and started to walk away.

'They've got a bodyshop. Big Ellie's, it's called, just off Church Road in Chilminster,' the mechanic called after him.

Gideon smiled to himself and, without turning, raised a hand in thanks.

Chilminster wasn't more than fourteen miles away, and in view of his earlier reception, Gideon decided to verify this latest information himself, before running to the police with it. Rachel should be safely on her way home by now, so he thought he might just as well go right away. Another argument for going immediately was that if Curly and the Blandford mechanic were mates then Gideon might well come up in conversation over a pint, and he had far rather that Joey and Co. were not warned of a possible visit.

Arriving in Chilminster some twenty minutes later, Gideon propped the Norton on its stand just outside the Post Office at the end of Church Road, went in and bought some stamps to justify its being there, and then went in search of Big Ellie's, helmet in hand.

The bodyshop was, as the mechanic had said, just off Church Road. It stood at the end of a short alley, behind a row of dilapidated red-brick houses that were due for demolition, according to a graffiti-covered sign.

Gideon edged cautiously along the alley, pausing at the point where it opened on to the forecourt of the garage. He didn't have to worry about being heard. On the other side of the high wall to his left, what sounded like a JCB was working industriously. He could have approached on the footplate of a steam engine and nobody in the building ahead would have been any the wiser.

There were a few cars parked on the forty feet or so of tarmac in front of the aircraft hangar-like structure but little other cover. The idea of marching openly up to the building and asking if Curly was there didn't appeal greatly to Gideon, but equally unattractive was the thought of being caught sneaking up for a closer look. His initial plan had been to watch from an unseen vantage point in the hope of seeing either Joey or Curly moving about the place. Unfortunately, the way the garage was situated, this wasn't going to be possible.

He could, of course, retreat to the end of the alley and wait to see who left at the end of the day, but the prospect of kicking his heels for what might be the best part of two hours didn't exactly fill him with joy either. And quite apart from the fact that it was bitterly cold and beginning to rain, it would also by that time be dark and almost impossible to make out faces.

Gideon was just considering the possibility of withdrawing and approaching the building from another side altogether, when the decision was taken out of his hands.

'Lost our motorbike, have we?' a rough voice hissed in his ear, and before he could respond, hands grasped his collar and the back of his jacket, pulling him away from the wall and then slamming him back into it with sickening force.

The impact drove every ounce of breath from Gideon's body and when the unseen hands released him he dropped to his knees, gasping and leaning against the rough brickwork for support. *Damn that JCB!* he thought sourly. A few feet away his helmet rolled in a slow arc and came to a halt against the wall.

Showing a marked lack of human kindness, his assailant followed up his initial assault with a kick which flattened Gideon against the wall once more, before turning him and hauling him roughly to his feet by the front of his jacket. A little air found its way painfully into his lungs.

'We knew you was coming, see,' the voice informed him triumphantly, and he didn't need the evidence of his eyes to tell him that it was Curly who had jumped him. 'I bin watching you all the way down the road.'

'Well, bully for you,' Gideon said a little thickly. The side of his head had connected, rather too firmly for comfort, with the brickwork and he was having trouble thinking straight. As before, flippancy cut in first, and as before, it wasn't appreciated. This time though, there was no Joey to keep a rein on Curly's temper.

'Still got the smart mouth on yer, haven't cha?' he snarled, his breath foul in Gideon's face. 'Well, I can shut that for yer!'

Gideon saw coming the backhanded blow that accompanied the words but could do little to avoid it. It rattled his teeth and made his ears ring but because of the restraining hand on his jacket, he stayed on his feet. He blinked a time or two to restore focus and returned Curly's gloating look with a more or less steady one of his own. He was rewarded by a glimmer of disappointment in the pale eyes.

'What now?' he asked, running his tongue over a split lip and chalking up a mental IOU to Curly's account. Breathing was becoming easier and with the return of strength came confidence. Behind the wall, and aeons too late, the racket from the machinery rattled away into silence. Voices sounded briefly then moved off. A coffee break perhaps, or maybe even packing up for the day.

'Well?' Gideon persisted.

'Shut up!' Curly seemed to sense that the advantage he'd gained through surprise was ebbing away. Gideon had the edge over him in both height and reach. He put his hand into the pocket of his boiler suit and withdrew a hefty spanner in an attempt to redress the balance.

Gideon smiled faintly. 'That should do it,' he observed approvingly. In fact, the presence of a weapon, especially so clumsy a one, made his task that much easier. He'd done a little karate at university and one of the first things he'd learned about self-defence was that if your assailant picks up a weapon you can be ninety-nine percent sure that he's intending to use it, and can then concentrate your defence in that one area. A man with open hands is a far trickier proposition, with the possibility of attack from hands, feet, or both.

The hand on his jacket front tightened convulsively. 'You're comin' with me. Joey wants to talk to you.'

'Well, tell him to make an appointment like everyone else,' Gideon said mildly. He was almost enjoying himself now, confident of his ability to handle Curly.

Footsteps sounded behind him.

'I'd say you've got a tiger by the tail there, Curly,' a soft voice remarked. 'I'd tread carefully, if I were you.'

Telltale relief showed momentarily on Curly's face but gave way to resentment as he realised Joey had observed his dilemma.

'I can manage,' he asserted, but in reality put up little resistance as Gideon disengaged his grasp with a twisting movement of his own arm.

'Sure you can, pal,' Joey said, not troubling to disguise the scorn in his voice.

Gideon turned to him. 'You wanted to see me?'

With the big man's arrival the odds had turned against him in a decisive way but if he no longer had the upper hand, he could at least retain the semblance of control.

'Not here,' Joey replied shortly, turning away towards the hangar-like building.

124

He seemed confident that Gideon would follow, as indeed, after picking up his helmet, he did. For one thing, he felt that having come so far looking for information without any luck, he was unlikely to get a better opportunity to shed some light on things; and for another, he probably had little choice.

They trailed across the tarmac past a number of parked cars to a small door in the side of the structure, Joey leading, Gideon following, mopping his lip with his neckerchief, and Curly bringing up the rear, grumbling under his breath.

The room they entered was square and spartan, with white-painted breeze-block walls, a coffee table of sorts and an assortment of chairs offering varying degrees of comfort. It appeared to be the workers' restroom-cum-canteen, with a cupboard in the corner, on top of which stood a microwave and a kettle, and half a dozen mugs on a tray.

In one of the least uncomfortable-looking chairs a boiler-suited youth reclined. He looked round, eyes widening as he caught sight of Gideon's battered features.

'Out,' Joey said with a jerk of his head. The lad didn't argue. As the door shut behind him, Joey turned to Gideon. 'Coffee?'

Surprised, he shook his head. 'No, thanks.'

Curly made a noise that was something between a snort and a cough, and was chock-full of stifled indignation.

Joey glanced at him with disfavour. 'You keep out of this. You tried the bull-in-the-china-shop approach and it gained you sod-all. I warned you it wouldn't work, so now we'll try it my way. Sit down and shut up.'

Curly retreated to the side of the room where he stood looking out of the window, visibly seething. His refusal to sit down presumably salved his wounded pride, Gideon thought, but it bothered Joey not at all. He was by far the more dangerous opponent.

The big man seemed in no hurry. He lit a cigarette and drew in a lungful of pollution with an air of enjoyment.

Gideon propped a hip against the back of one of the PVC-covered armchairs and waited. Under the jacket and the thick, white fisherman's jumper he wore, his heart was doing double-time but he was determined Joey shouldn't know it.

Joey began to pace the room, passing Gideon twice.

Gideon didn't so much as look at him.

On the third circuit he stopped and blew smoke into Gideon's face. Their eyes met.

'The thing is, pal,' Joey said finally, 'this whole business has nothing to do with us – with Curly and me. We were just extra muscle, hired on the night. Even if you tell the police about us, it won't get you anywhere. We'll deny everything. We'll say it was just a lads' night out that got out of hand. We can find witnesses that'll say we were all drinking. You and me had an argument and things got a bit rough. You took it the wrong way. The police won't be interested, you know. They've got better

126

things to do and not enough men to do them, as it is.'

Gideon watched him steadily. He knew Joey was right. Presented in that way it would just confirm what the police were already more than halfway to believing.

'And the horse?'

Joey shrugged, lifting his hands expressively. 'A horse, officer? What would I want with a horse? Cars are my thing, cars and bikes. Anything you can't mend with a spanner and I don't want to know.'

'All right, I take your point. So what's the deal? If I lay off the police, will you tell me what it was all about?' It was a forlorn hope but worth a try.

Joey laughed shortly. 'I think not, pal. No, this is the deal: you stay away from the police and I don't tell the Guv'nor you've been poking your nose in where it's not wanted. That way *we* don't get no grief and *you* get to keep your kneecaps. Right?'

Put like that, it was quite reasonable, Gideon thought, but one part of him just wouldn't let it go. As Joey started to turn away, taking his silence for assent, he said, 'Who flies the helicopter?'

'What helicopter?' He paused, frowning over his shoulder.

'At the Grange.'

'That's got nothing to do with this.'

'Is it Renson or Slade?'

Joey whirled back incredulously. 'You just don't get it, do you? They'll take you apart if they find you snooping. You mess with them and you'd better make sure your affairs are in order!' His ice blue eyes flashed not six inches from Gideon's own.

'Thank you,' he said quietly.

'For what?'

'Now I *know* they're up to something. Before, I wasn't sure.'

Joey looked at him long and hard, shaking his head slightly. 'Why do you care?' he asked finally.

Gideon hesitated. He'd been about to mention his sister but instinct held him back. Apparently Jez hadn't said anything so he wouldn't either. It was better if the relationship wasn't known.

He shrugged but before he could formulate an answer they were interrupted by the reopening of the door by which the mechanic had left. They all looked round and Joey backed off a step.

'So. What's going on here, boys?' The busty blonde who stood in the doorway wore a red boiler suit, pulled in above curvy hips with a white, elasticated belt, and managed to look both tough and sexy at the same time. She spoke in the same northern accent that the 'boys' did.

'Terry told me we had company, and he said he thought there might be trouble.' Her large, mascara'd blue eyes narrowed as she looked the visitor up and down, and Gideon was sure she hadn't missed Joey's hasty retreat. 'You been in an accident?'

'He fell off his bike, Ma,' Joey lied easily, and Gideon did a double take. *Ma?* Good Lord, she couldn't be his mother, surely? She wasn't much more than five foot four!

'He *fell*? Or he was pushed?' the blonde asked dryly, coming into the room and closing the door behind her. 'I don't suppose Curly had anything to do with it.'

Curly scowled from across the room and Joey retreated a step or two more. Neither of them answered.

As the silence lengthened, the woman shrugged her shoulders. 'All right. Whatever I may feel about what you get up to on your own time, it's obviously none of my business. But that being so, I'll thank you to keep it off my premises. Ellie Fletcher,' she announced, advancing upon her visitor and holding out a somewhat oily hand.

Gideon shook the hand, feeling a degree or two happier about his situation. He surveyed her with interest. Her age was difficult to gauge. At first sight she could be taken for mid-thirties but closer scrutiny revealed lines around the eyes and mouth, and knowing her for Joey's mother, Gideon guessed she must be nearer fifty.

'*Big* Ellie?' he enquired with amusement.

'The very same,' she confirmed, with a twinkle. 'And you are?'

'Gideon Blake.'

She glanced at the motorbike helmet still looped on his arm. 'I didn't hear a bike. Did you really fall off?'

'No.' Gideon saw no point in elaborating. From Joey's reaction it was obvious that Ellie knew little or nothing of their affairs.

'I see. You're on a vow of silence, too,' she

observed with a touch of exasperation. 'Well, as I said before, I won't have any trouble here. There's a Citroën out there waiting to be masked for spraying, so I suggest you two get back to work.' She waved a hand in their direction. 'Go on. Get out!'

Still scowling, Curly started for the door, followed with obvious reluctance by Joey who gave a warning shake of the head before he disappeared from view.

Gideon responded with a mocking half-smile.

'I'm not going to pry,' Ellie said as the door shut behind them, 'but I'll just say this. Be careful around Curly, he's got a nasty temper. He got that from his father. He was the biggest mistake I ever made and I've made a few, I can tell you!'

'So they *are* brothers?' Gideon probed, casually.

'Half-brothers,' Ellie confirmed. 'Joey's the eldest, he's a good boy. His father was killed racing motorbikes. Mike Dylan; you may have heard of him. But Curly . . . well, he's my son and I probably shouldn't say it, but he's a bad one. Always in trouble. Jealous of his brother, I think. Joey's the one with the looks and the brains, and Curly's never known whether to love or hate him for it.'

'And Jez?'

'What do you know about Jez?' she demanded suspiciously.

'Not a lot. I . . . er . . . helped her find her puppy the other day,' he said, ruthlessly editing the facts.

'Ah, that was you, was it? Thanks, and thank your friend the vet. Jez was made up over visiting

130

that place. She's a good kid really, you know. Just a bit wild at times. Her father works the oil rigs, so we don't see much of him.'

She looked harassed and Gideon felt sorry for her. For a woman with principles, as she seemed to be, hers must be the family from hell.

'Christ, I don't know why I'm telling you all this!' she said suddenly. 'What must you be thinking?'

Gideon was saved from the necessity of answering by the reappearance of Joey, doubtless uneasy about the direction the conversation might be taking.

'You're wanted in the workshop, Ma.'

'Can't you manage for five minutes without me?' she asked testily.

'Sure we can, but you said you wanted to see the paint mix before we loaded it.'

'Yeah, I know I did. I'll be through in a minute, love. I'll just see Gideon out.'

Joey shot him a look of intense dislike before going back to the workshop.

At the door, as Gideon took his leave, Ellie put her hand on his arm. 'I don't pretend to know what's going on, Gideon. But you seem like a nice bloke. Take my advice and stay away from Curly and his crowd. I've seen his work before, and believe me, you got off lightly this time!'

6

When Mary Collins telephoned Gideon three days later for a progress update, as arranged, he was able to report that he'd nearly finished the portrait of Sovereign. One day of bitterly cold winds and two of sleet had been a strong inducement to stay in and work. He did, however, suggest that to complete the picture it might be nice to have Tom himself depicted at the horse's head. Mary fell in happily with this idea, and invited Gideon over the next day to choose a suitable photograph from which to work.

The day was a slightly better one than of late, less windy but still dull and cold. A phone call to the Priory had failed to unearth any available transport and he had to resign himself to piling on the layers and taking the Norton. As he made his way to the shed that served as a garage for the bike, he cast a thoughtful look at Rachel's Mini but it really wasn't a viable option. The thought of driving the twenty or so miles to the stud with his knees up round his ears and his head bowed didn't attract him at all.

Rachel had spent the best part of the last three days in the spare room, emerging from time to time to change the compact disc, dispense coffee and admire Gideon's work.

Although she hadn't mentioned it recently, he supposed she would be moving on in a day or two when her new commission started in Bournemouth. He'd have to make his own coffee again then. For now, he was banned from the spare room, forbidden to look until she'd completed its transformation; a plan with which he fell in good-humouredly, only hoping that the result was something that Giles, as his landlord, would find acceptable.

Happy living alone, Gideon had nevertheless adjusted almost seamlessly to Rachel's undemanding presence. She wafted around the Gatehouse in a haze of mohair and silk, leaving a trace of light perfume on the air, and causing as little disturbance as did Elsa the cat. Elsa herself, usually disdainful of strangers, had also quickly accepted Rachel, apparently regarding her now as part of the fixtures and fittings and even going so far as to curl up on her lap in front of the fire once or twice.

Although she seemed a little on edge for a day or two, Rachel had never spoken of the incident in Blandford and beyond enquiring, upon his return, if she was all right, Gideon had not done so either. After all, it was her business and none of his.

For his own part, once he'd cleaned up, the results of his second brush with Curly were more uncomfortable than visible, and if Rachel noticed anything amiss she didn't comment on it.

Stripping off helmet, gloves and scarf in the yard outside the Collinses' rambling, stone farmhouse, Gideon noted with relief the absence of Tom's Range Rover. Mary didn't drive but there were one or two vehicles parked there, including a large, muddy car he didn't recognise, and he wondered if perhaps either Mary or the stud had visitors.

He found the back door unlocked and let himself in, softly calling out as he did so. Mary was seated at her kitchen table, surrounded by masses of photographs and newspaper cuttings, some neatly arranged in albums and scrapbooks, some loose. As Gideon shut the door behind him, she jumped visibly, apparently not having heard his call and coming back with a start from a world of memories.

'Gideon! You made me jump!'

He apologised, grinning, and went round the table to give her a hug.

'I'd almost forgotten you were coming,' she said pulling a handkerchief from a pocket in her cardigan and blowing her nose. 'Which is silly, because that's the reason I got all this lot out in the first place. Anyway, I'll make a pot of tea. The kettle's already boiled once and I expect you're frozen if you came on that bike of yours.' She twisted out of his embrace and went over to the old-fashioned range.

'I am a bit,' Gideon agreed, moving to stand beside her and warm his hands. Out of the window to his right he could see someone moving about by the stables. 'Visitors at the stud?' he asked, ducking his head to get a better look.

'No, that's Gerald.' Mary said, reaching up to a shelf for an old Coronation tin. 'Roly's replacement, remember? He and Anthony are down in the yard helping the vet.' She began to put an assortment of biscuits on to a willow-patterned plate.

'Trouble?'

'Oh, no. Just jabs and teeth. It's that time of year again. You should go down and see Anthony afterwards. He's changed a lot since you last saw him. He should really be in college today but as Tom's not here he stayed behind to help the vet.' She poured boiling water into the teapot and turned to clear a space on the table for the cups and saucers.

'Still determined to take over from his dad when the time comes?' Gideon asked with a smile. Anthony Collins, fourteen when he'd first met him, had even then been ready to dedicate his whole life to the stud and the horses.

'Oh, yes,' Mary said with pride. 'I don't think *that* will ever change.'

She put the plate of biscuits on the table and paused, putting her hand up to cover her mouth.

'What's the matter, Mary?' Gideon asked gently,

stepping towards her. 'You've been crying haven't you? Do you want to tell me about it or would you rather be alone?'

She sniffed, shook her head and pulled her handkerchief out of her pocket again. 'No, don't go. I shall be all right in a moment.'

'Is it Tom?' Gideon remembered the tension between them on his last visit.

Tears rushed to her eyes and she gulped. Gideon put his arms round her and the simple act of sympathy released the floodgates. Mary buried her face in his shoulder and wept convulsively.

A minute or two later, when the sobs had subsided into sniffs, she pulled away from him and dried her eyes.

'I'm sorry,' she said after a moment. 'It's just, I've been so miserable and I've no one to talk to. Anthony's too young, and anyway he's a boy.'

'Well, I can't change my sex,' Gideon observed. 'But I'm told I'm quite a good listener.'

Mary lowered her gaze, silent for a moment, then said, 'Oh, Gideon, he's changed so! I suppose it first started about three years ago, just after Annabel went off to university. I thought he was worried about the expense, or perhaps that she was leaving home – you know how close they were. And it's true, after a few weeks he seemed better. But about a year or so ago it started again and these last few weeks he's been like a bear with a sore head. I can't seem to do anything right. Whatever it is that's worrying him, he's taking it out on me.'

136

'How does he seem with the horses, and Anthony?'

'Oh, fine,' she said quickly. 'He's always got time for them, but I hardly ever see him now except for mealtimes. We . . . well, he's even taken to sleeping up at the yard sometimes.' Her voice shook and she dabbed her eyes with her handkerchief. 'He says it's to keep an eye on the mares when they're foaling. It's what Roly used to do.'

'But surely that's Gerald's job now?'

'You would have thought so, wouldn't you, but Tom wants to do it all himself. Seems obsessed with it, almost.'

'Sit down,' Gideon said, pushing her gently but firmly into a chair. 'I'll bring the teapot over and we'll have that cuppa. It must be brewed by now.'

Mary cleared a space amongst the memories for the tray, and Gideon put it down carefully.

There were dozens of photographs. Some in colour, some black and white, many faded and spotted with brown oxide; they all recorded the past triumphs of the Collinses' horses, some still living, others long gone. Here and there lay newspaper cuttings that had fallen out of scrapbooks. '*Local Breeder Takes On The Heavies and Wins!*' shouted one; '*Winterbourne's Shires Do The Business!*' declared another. There were many, too, that recalled the meteoric career of their show-jumping legend, Popsox.

'That's a good one of Tom,' Gideon said, pointing to a ten-by-eight colour print of the stud owner holding one of his horses. 'Can I take that one?'

'Yes, of course,' Mary nodded. 'That's the one I'd picked out too.'

'Tom isn't worried about money, is he?' Gideon asked, taking a seat. 'I mean, any more than usual?'

'No. Not that he's told me, and he's always been open about it in the past. I really don't understand. It's as though I've done something awful but he won't say what.'

'Well, I'm sure you haven't,' Gideon said soothingly. 'I guess one of these days you'll find out what it's all been about. I just hope, for your sake, it's sooner rather than later.'

'Thank you, Gideon. I'm sorry for having dumped it all on you like this, but I do feel better for having told you.'

'Gideon Blake, Agony Uncle at your service,' he announced grandly. 'No problem too big, no donation too small. Or have I got that the wrong way round?'

Mary smiled. 'Thanks,' she said again.

After tea and biscuits, Gideon left Mary tidying away the photographs and made his way out to the stables, where he eventually tracked Anthony and the vet down to one of the shires' boxes.

'Okay, let's give it a rest for a minute or two, shall we?' someone said as he reached the doorway, and he almost bumped into two men who were on their way out.

The younger of the two, who was fractionally ahead, looked up at him with instant recognition.

'Gideon!' he exclaimed. 'What are *you* doing here?'

'I needed a photo of your dad for the portrait. You know about that, Mary says.' Gideon shook Anthony's hand, thinking that if he hadn't come looking for the boy, he might not have recognised him. He'd grown a great deal more mature in the two years or so since Gideon had last seen him, not just physically but in his manner, too.

Now he turned and said over his shoulder, 'Sean, this is Gideon Blake, the chap who worked with Sox after the accident. Gideon, meet Sean Rosetti: vet, stallion man, and useless rugby player.'

Gideon offered his hand to the vet in turn but Rosetti grinned apologetically and held up hands covered in a mixture of horse saliva and chewed hay. 'Anthony's just sore at me because I dumped him on his arse at practice last night,' he said with a sideways look at the boy. He had a deep voice that held a hint of a foreign accent, possibly Italian, which was borne out by his dark, curly hair and a pair of eyes that were as near black as made no difference. He was unknown to Gideon. The vet he'd originally worked with at the stud had retired shortly afterwards.

'Why did he call you a stallion man? Or is that a private joke?' Gideon asked curiously.

'Yeah, kind of,' Rosetti said dismissively, but Anthony wasn't going to let it go at that.

'He did the AI for the shires once or twice. Artificial insemination, that is,' he explained.

'Anyway, Dad used to joke that the mares all started to get randy when they saw him coming, so we called him the stallion man.'

'This old girl doesn't look as though her mind's on sex at the moment,' Gideon said, looking beyond them to where the huge carthorse stood, eyeing them distrustfully from the back of the stable. The middle-aged man at her head he didn't recognise; presumably it was Gerald, Roly French's replacement.

'Yes. We're having a spot of bother with her,' Anthony said, frowning. 'She hates having her teeth done and she's so strong she can tow the lot of us round the box without any trouble at all. Sean reckons she's had a bad experience at some time but she's got this hooked tooth right at the back that's making her mouth sore. We can't leave it. Hey, I don't suppose you could give us a hand? You know, work some of your magic . . .'

Out of the corner of his eye, Gideon caught the flash of a frown, hastily disguised, with which Rosetti greeted this suggestion, and declined. He had no wish to step on anybody's professional toes.

'Oh, Sean doesn't give a stuff for all that professional courtesy clap-trap, do you, Sean?' Anthony declared airily.

'Not at all,' Rosetti said smoothly. 'I'd be glad of the help. We were going to try a twitch but if you can do it without . . .'

Gideon hesitated fractionally, but if the vet was lying now, then he was a past master at it. He wondered if his own reluctance to interfere where

140

he wasn't wanted was becoming an obsession. Perhaps he was imagining antagonism where it didn't exist.

'Okay,' he said finally. 'But I can't make any promises. A lot depends on whether she's genuinely frightened or just bloody-minded. If she's just buggering about for the sake of it, there's not a lot I can do. Except add my weight to yours,' he added, as an afterthought.

When he approached the mare, however, there was no question of his imagining the antagonism in the stud groom's face. Gerald looked like a bulldog chewing on a wasp. He almost threw the lead rope at Gideon, muttering something under his breath about quacks as he passed on his way to the door.

Gideon ignored him. Everyone was entitled to their own opinion, after all. He concentrated on the horse instead.

When he, Anthony and Rosetti finally shut the door on the mare some twenty minutes later, they all felt the satisfaction of a difficult job well done. With Gideon's help, they had managed to keep her calm enough for the vet to clip off the worst of the hook and rasp smooth the remainder, pausing occasionally when she showed signs of stress.

'We could have done with you earlier,' Rosetti said with feeling, as he rinsed his various rasps in a bucket of water and put them away. 'The mare in the end box clamped her teeth on the rasp and wouldn't let go. That's a new tactic on me! And old

Queenie just puts her head up so high that I can't reach. They're a cunning lot here.'

'You were right about Rosie, though,' Gideon said. 'She *was* frightened. I expect somebody jabbed her with the rasp sometime and she hasn't forgotten. The trouble with that is that the more they play up, the more likely it is they'll get hurt again, and so it goes on.'

'Give the old girl a sedative and have done with it,' Gerald muttered as he emptied away the water the vet had used. 'I don't hold with all this alternative mumbo-jumbo.'

Rosetti disagreed. 'Oh, no, I'd much rather do it without using drugs, if I can. For one thing, it's not always easy to judge the right amount to give, especially with these giants. I mean, too little and you might as well not have bothered; too much and you can have them falling over on you, and that's not funny!'

The groom mumbled something under his breath and stomped off, carrying an armful of headcollars, ropes and buckets.

'I don't know why Dad ever took him on,' Anthony said, watching him go. 'He's such a miserable old bastard and not a patch on Roly when it comes to the horses. I don't think Dad really likes him. He does a lot more of the work himself these days.'

'He must know his job, though, surely,' Gideon protested. 'Your dad would never have taken him on if he hadn't got the relevant experience.'

'Oh, yes, he knows his job all right, and he

knows all the textbook stuff, word for word almost, but he hasn't got the feel for the horses that Roly had. I mean, Roly could tell if something was wrong with one of the broodmares long before anyone else could see anything, even Dad.'

'You've been spoilt, having Roly,' Gideon agreed sadly. 'He was one in a million. You won't find many with that kind of horse sense.'

At the farmhouse, Mary, showing no traces of her earlier distress, was reheating some home-made pasties and it required very little persuasion to induce the two visitors to stay to a late lunch.

The group broke up some three-quarters of an hour later, with Rosetti saying that he was due at a nearby riding centre for routine vaccinations. During the course of the impromptu meal, he had told Gideon all about his newly built equine surgery, of which he was obviously very proud.

'You must come and see it sometime,' he suggested as they parted. 'It's not far from here. I'll give you the guided tour.'

'I'd love to,' Gideon told him truthfully, and left the stud feeling pleased with his new and renewed contacts. The only cloud to mar his enjoyment of the morning had been Mary's worries about Tom, and he really couldn't see what he could do about that.

As he was more than halfway there, Gideon decided to call on Naomi and Tim at the Sanctuary to see if there had been any further developments in their troubles. There was no answer at reception so he wandered across the yard and up the concrete walkway towards the aviaries with the old stables on his left and the newly erected wooden buildings on his right, still reeking of creosote.

He could see Tim and Naomi two-thirds of the way along, leaning over the half-door of one of the old stables that housed the larger inmates. His sister turned and waved in greeting as he approached, then put a warning finger to her lips. Obediently, Gideon stepped quietly up to the door and peered over.

Inside, kneeling in the thick golden straw, was Jez, wearing what looked like school uniform and completely absorbed in the task of bottle-feeding a fawn that was not much bigger than a large cat. A small area of the stable had been penned off with boards and infra-red lamps installed to keep the youngster warm. They watched in silence until, the bottle emptied, the fawn took a few tottery steps away from the tousle-headed child and sank, exhausted, into the straw. Jez looked up at them with a radiant smile and climbed carefully to her feet so as not to alarm the tiny creature.

'Did you see?' she demanded excitedly once they were well away from the stable. 'She drank it all! That's much better than yesterday, isn't it? D'you think she'll get better now?'

'We'll have to wait and see,' Tim said cautiously. 'She's still very small and young animals can quite suddenly take a turn for the worse, for no apparent reason. But, if she does survive, she'll have you to thank for it, that's for sure.'

Jez beamed, and at Tim's suggestion, ran off to take the bottle to the surgery for sterilisation.

'Another helper?' Gideon asked quizzically. 'You'll soon be able to put your feet up and watch an army of women and children scurrying round at your bidding.'

'Sounds good to me,' Tim agreed, and received an indignant punch from Naomi.

'That fawn's tiny, isn't it?' Gideon said. 'I don't know why but I assumed deer had their young in the summer.'

'Yes. Most deer do but this is a muntjac fawn and they breed all year round.'

'What happened to it?'

'The old story,' Tim said resignedly. 'Well-meaning people who find what they think is an abandoned fawn and pick it up. Some kids found this one, though God knows where; muntjacs are as rare as hens' teeth round these parts! It's a damned shame because the doe was almost certainly nearby and would have returned as soon as they'd gone. As it is, I doubt we'll be able to save it. Deer are so nervous, and muntjacs worse than most. We could do with Jez here more often. She's got a certain way with her. That fawn will take its bottle from her much better than from either of us.'

'Children's minds are usually uncluttered. Free to concentrate completely,' Gideon suggested. 'I think that's why animals trust them sometimes, when they won't trust an adult.'

'He's doing his psychology bit again, Tim.

You'd better watch it or he'll be sending you a bill!' Naomi warned, tongue in cheek. 'I've heard his fees are exorbitant.'

'Only if you're stinking rich or a pain in the backside,' Gideon retorted.

He spent a couple of hours at the Sanctuary, looking at the new arrivals and helping to catch a chicken which dodged past Naomi when she went in to feed it. He also stood watching in fascination as Tim performed a delicate operation to pin the leg of a rabbit that had not crossed a road quickly enough.

'So have you had any more trouble from your neighbours?' he asked as he handed surgical instruments to the vet on demand.

'No, it's all been quiet. Nothing since that business with the helicopter. Perhaps your visit to the police did the trick and they'll leave us alone now.'

'Ever the optimist,' Naomi remarked, busy at the sink. 'I don't think they're going to be put off that easily.'

Gideon was inclined to agree with her. He had no idea why Milne or Slade should want the Hermitage Farm land but far from withdrawing from the fray, he thought it more likely they had called a temporary halt to re-think their strategy.

From certain things that were said, he gathered that Naomi had taken the step of moving into the mobile home with Tim and it appeared that Jez had become a frequent visitor too, arriving on the doorstep mid-afternoon and staying until teatime.

When questioned she had told Tim and Naomi that she caught the school bus out of Chilminster and ran the rest of the way. Although Tim admitted to worrying about a twelve-year-old girl roaming around the countryside on her own, there seemed to be little they could do about it and her obvious delight in the place made it hard to turn her away.

It was almost completely dark when Gideon finally took his leave and Jez had still shown no sign that she was preparing to do the same.

'How are you getting home, Shorty?' Gideon asked, ruffling her curls.

'Oh, that's all sorted,' Jez muttered evasively, ducking out from under his hand.

'Then you won't mind telling me.'

'She always says her brother picks her up,' Naomi put in.

'Yeah, but she knows that won't work with me. Because I've met brother Joey, and I can't see him running to and fro with his kid sister every day, fond though he is of her.'

'He does sometimes.' Jez glared defiantly at him.

'And the other times?'

'I hitch a lift. I know loads of truckers. Curly used to be one.'

Gideon felt that being a friend of Curly was a damning reference for anyone, but he let it go. 'Well, you're not hitching tonight,' he said firmly. '*I'm* taking you home.'

Jez knew when she was beaten. 'All right, but just to the end of my road,' she haggled. 'Joey'd do his nut if he knew I'd been with you.'

'Well, we can't have that, can we?' Gideon remarked dryly, handing her his spare helmet. 'Here, put this on and do it up tight.'

By the time Gideon reached Tarrant Grayling, having detoured to Chilminster to drop Jez off, it was completely dark. About a quarter of a mile down the road from the Gatehouse, the Norton started to splutter and within a very short distance, the engine coughed and died.

Gideon cursed, remembering that he'd intended filling up with fuel on the way home. Going to Chilminster with the kid had put it out of his mind. With a sigh, he started to push the heavy bike along the road. Shortly after, to add insult to injury, the sullen skies fulfilled their promise and began to throw sleety rain earthwards. He was consequently not in the best of moods when, some minutes later, he steered the Norton off the road and over the cattle grid at the end of the Priory's drive.

No welcoming lights shone out from the Gatehouse, although Rachel's Mini was parked, as usual, in the gravel pull-in in front of the wicket gate. He propped the bike on its stand next to the car and took his helmet off, wondering if Rachel was visiting Pippa up at the main house. Normally, if he was out late, she would turn on the outside light so he didn't fall into the shrubbery on his way to the front door. With the tall trees on the other side of the Priory drive, it was very dark at the front of the house.

Normally? My God! She's only been here ten

days or so and already she's part of my routine! he thought.

Unwelcome thoughts of permanence were effectively banished the next moment by the discovery that he wasn't alone in his front garden.

Somebody had just come round the side of the house and was moving about between him and the building. Gideon froze, still close enough to the hedge to merge with it. Even as he watched, eyes straining in the gloom, the figure peered into one of the dark windows. Apparently seeing nothing, it then moved to the porch and hammered on the heavy front door in frustration.

'I know you're in there!' an unmistakably masculine voice shouted, loud against the gentle hissing of the sleet.

Aware of an uncomfortable prickling sensation at the back of his neck, Gideon glanced around him, but if any accomplices lurked in the shadows, they were keeping themselves well hidden. The man at the door hammered on it once again and then stepped back, looking up at the first-floor windows. Gideon felt it was time to intervene.

'Just what the hell do you think you're doing?' he demanded, stepping forward.

Surprisingly, instead of the guilty start he'd expected to provoke, the intruder merely turned his head slightly and said, 'Fuck off and mind your own business!'

'No, *you* fuck off!' Gideon retorted. 'I live here!'

The man turned round.

Squinting against the sleet that seemed to have

set in for the night, Gideon estimated that the man was a little less than six foot tall and fairly stockily built. As far as he could tell, it wasn't any of his recent acquaintances, but he couldn't swear to it in the dismal light.

'So you're the bastard!'

'Not as far as I know,' Gideon replied.

His companion wasn't in the mood for jokes. Taking a short step forward he swung his right fist at Gideon's chin with vicious intent.

Caught slightly unawares, Gideon side-stepped hastily, bringing his helmet up to block the punch and swinging his right foot backward to sweep his assailant neatly off his feet.

Moves that had become instinctive in his karate days had not deserted him, and it afforded him great satisfaction to see his would-be attacker flat on his back on the soggy grass, nursing what were, no doubt, very bruised knuckles, and turning the air blue.

The problem was, what to do with him now? Even if he'd felt it would do any good, Gideon couldn't really see himself interrogating his captive. And calling the police would no doubt entail his spending the rest of the evening at the police station giving statements and trying once more to convince sceptical officers that he honestly didn't know what was going on.

'I don't suppose you're going to tell me what you're doing here,' Gideon said with little optimism.

He wasn't. With more foul language the man

scrambled to his feet, backing off a pace or two in the process. Gideon's rather imposing bulk still stood between him and the gate, and he clearly wasn't sure what Gideon intended, because he looked around for other avenues of escape.

'Did Slade send you?' Gideon asked, although he really had no idea why Slade should have.

'Fuck off!' the man said, in his endearing way.

Gideon sighed. 'Oh, sod it!' he muttered wearily, stepping to one side. 'Go on, get out of here.'

To get to the gate the trespasser was obliged to come within a couple of feet of Gideon, close enough to reveal a stud through his eyebrow and a tattoo on his neck. He edged past with an almost palpable aura of mistrust, and Gideon had to stifle a mischievous urge to stamp a foot as he went by.

Once the gateway was reached, the man's confidence returned. He turned and pointed a warning finger at Gideon. 'You're going to wish you hadn't fucking messed with me!' he hissed. 'And you can tell that bitch I'll be back for her, and she'd better be ready.'

He disappeared into the darkness without waiting for a reply, which was just as well because Gideon wouldn't have known what to say. That the man had been looking for Rachel had simply not occurred to him. He waited a moment or two to make sure he really had gone before turning thankfully back towards the house. In that instant there came a crashing sound from the lane that had him cursing and retracing his steps. His visitor had vented his spleen on the Norton on his way out.

Having picked the bike up and stowed it safely in the shed-cum-garage, Gideon trudged back to the front door, turned the key in the lock and then proceeded to flatten himself against the woodwork as the door unexpectedly resisted his weight. Perplexed, he pushed again.

Nothing. It didn't shift.

Someone had bolted it from the inside.

Gideon thumped the door a couple of times with his fist, scanned the dusky garden for possible assailants, and then bent down and hailed Rachel through the vertical, brass letterbox.

'Gideon?'

The reply came immediately, followed by a scraping noise as the heavy bolts were drawn clear. He pushed the door open and went in, shutting it quickly behind him and reaching for the light switch with a strange sense of déjà vu.

Nobody kicked the door in from the outside, and the hall light came on, bright and comforting. With an inarticulate cry of relief, Rachel flung herself at him, clinging to his jacket and burying her face against his chest.

'Whoa there, Rachel! Steady on!' Gideon exclaimed, rocked back on his heels by this sudden assault. 'What's been going on?'

He was answered by a stream of disjointed words, rendered even less intelligible by being lost in the folds of his leather jacket. Gently he prised her away from him.

'Rachel, Rachel!' he said, breaking in gently but firmly. 'Hey, slow down! I can't hear a word. Let's go into the kitchen, have a cup of tea and you can start again. Okay?'

She looked up at him, her dark eyes tragic, and nodded. 'I'm sorry,' she said. 'It's just – he wouldn't go away and I thought you were never going to come! I was so frightened!'

'Well, I'm here now,' Gideon said soothingly. 'And whoever it was has gone. We'll sort it out, okay?'

She nodded again, trusting, like a child, but with his hands on her arms Gideon could feel her trembling.

'Good girl,' he said, and turning her round, steered her into the kitchen, switching on the lights as he went.

Minutes later, sitting in the chair by the Aga and cradling a cup of tea in her hands, Rachel seemed a lot calmer. In fact, she'd become quite subdued and appeared to be in no hurry to unburden herself.

'Rachel?'

Gideon turned a chair round and sat astride so that he was facing her over the back of it. He reached out a hand and touched her arm, causing her to look up briefly but she shied away from meeting his gaze and her eyes dropped again.

'That man – the one outside – did he do this?' Gideon asked on an impulse, brushing her scarred cheekbone with a gentle finger.

Her head came up sharply. 'How did you know?' she breathed. 'How could you possibly know?'

153

Gideon shook his head. 'I didn't. It was just a guess.' But he *had* known, ever since that first morning, that there was a lot more to Rachel's past than she was prepared to tell.

'I can't believe he's out,' she said, running a shaking hand through her hair. 'He's supposed to be locked away. I can't believe they let him out and didn't even tell me!'

'Who is he, Rachel?'

'Duke – Duncan Shelley. He's my husband . . . was my husband. They gave him five years. Everybody said it wasn't enough but he's still got three to go and he's out already! I just can't believe it!' Tears welled up and one overflowed, rolling slowly down her pale cheek. She looked at Gideon and her lip quivered. 'I thought I was safe for another three years . . .'

Gideon didn't know how to comfort her. Almost absent-mindedly he reached out and fielded the tear with a finger.

'I think the first thing we ought to do is find out if they really did let him go. I mean, I suppose it's just possible he's escaped, in which case somebody somewhere will be very glad to know we've seen him.'

He got to his feet and went out into the hall to telephone. After a moment, with an uneasy glance at the black, uncurtained windows of the kitchen, Rachel followed him.

'They don't know anything about it,' Gideon said, replacing the receiver after his persistence was finally rewarded by contact with a senior-ranking officer. 'The chap I got hold of said they'd look into it and get back to us. Sorry.'

Rachel nodded. She put her mug of tea up to her mouth and her teeth chattered audibly on the rim. Gideon took her firmly by the arm and led her into the sitting room where the woodburning stove stood black and cold.

'Come on, sit down here,' he said guiding her gently towards the sofa. 'I'll make up the fire and then you can tell me everything. No half-truths this time, okay?'

She nodded, sitting obediently, finishing her tea while he crumpled newspaper and arranged kindling in the hearth. When he'd finished and the fire was crackling cosily, he sat beside her on the worn leather of the chair and she told him her story.

She had met and fallen in love with Duncan Shelley, who was known as Duke, when he was serving at an army base near her home. She was barely eighteen and very impressionable, and when he'd been called up to serve in a war zone overseas, it had seemed vastly romantic to marry her soldier before he went. She had subsequently lived as an army wife for nearly five years and although she suffered long periods of loneliness while he was away, the joy of their reunions more than made up for it. Then Duke's regiment was disbanded, he came home for good, and it all fell apart.

Unable to settle to civilian life he found it difficult to hold down a job, and within a very short time, eaten up with bitterness and feelings of inadequacy, he turned to the bottle.

Rachel was at this time engaged on a design course at a local college and waitressing in the evenings to make ends meet. It wasn't easy but she hadn't minded, she said, could even have been happy if Duke had let her be.

He wouldn't. Accustomed to the macho image of himself that the army had helped foster, he couldn't adjust to the idea of Rachel playing the more useful role in their relationship. He began to come home violently drunk and once or twice he'd hit her.

Rachel's voice quivered as she related this part of her history.

'I know what you'll say,' she declared with a sniff and a pathetic touch of defiance. 'Everybody said it. I should have left him . . . but he needed me. How could I leave him just because things were bad? I still loved him then, and *he* loved *me* when he wasn't too drunk to think straight. I really thought things would work out; that he'd get a job and we'd pull through.' She sighed. 'I guess I was just kidding myself.'

Gideon slid an arm round her shoulders, pulling her towards him. Childlike, she curled her shoeless feet under her and snuggled against him for comfort. He had only meant it as a brotherly gesture of reassurance and that was obviously how she'd taken it, but as Gideon felt the warmth of her slim body and caught the scent of her familiar musky perfume, he was suddenly aware that she was all woman.

However, he was also aware that being needed

held a certain attraction of its own, and that quite possibly what she'd awakened in him was primarily a fierce protectiveness towards her. Whatever it was, no power on earth could have made him betray that he felt anything more than friendship. Her trust was too fragile for that.

'Wanting to see the best in someone is no crime, Rachel,' he assured her, speaking softly, close to her good ear. 'But go on. Obviously things got worse.'

'Yes. Some old army mates he used to drink with started teasing him about his . . . well, they kept asking him when he was going to start a family. We'd been trying. That was something else he was getting depressed about. The doctor said it was probably because he was so stressed, and said that the drinking wouldn't help, but Duke wouldn't hear of it. He went mad. He said it was my fault and accused me of taking the pill because I didn't want a baby to interrupt my study. It wasn't true!' she said, tilting her head so that she could see Gideon's face; desperate for him to believe her. 'I would have done anything by then to make him happier, but I couldn't get pregnant. It wasn't my fault. I had tests and I was clear. The doctor wanted to do tests on Duke but he wouldn't have it.'

She paused, looking down at her own tightly clasped hands, the knuckles showing white. 'He came home from the pub early one night in a terrible mood. They'd been teasing him again and he only had one thing on his mind. I didn't want to. It – well – it wasn't a good time for me, but he wouldn't listen. He dragged me into the lounge and then he – he raped me.'

Her voice faded and she began to tremble, and Gideon murmured comfort into the dark, shining hair.

'Was that how you got the scar?' he asked after a moment. 'Did he hit you?' Talking seemed the best way to exorcise her demons.

'I lost my temper,' Rachel said. 'I know I shouldn't have but he'd hurt me and I wanted to hurt him back. I told him it was his fault we couldn't have children, not mine. I told him that he'd never amount to anything if he didn't pull himself together and stop drinking. I said – I said if he hit me again I'd leave him. I know I shouldn't have said those things, but I was really mad.'

She paused again, staring straight ahead, then continued in a colourless voice, as if to disassociate herself was her only way of remembering safely. 'He broke a bottle – just as if it was a pub brawl or something – he broke a bottle and he said he'd make it so that no man would ever look at me again. He said I'd be glad to stay with him when he'd finished, because nobody else would want me around. And then he did this.' She fingered the scar almost absent-mindedly.

'I fought him. I really tried! I even tried to . . .' She stopped abruptly, her eyes flickering up to glance at Gideon and then, as quickly, away again. 'Well, I hit him with a candlestick but it just made him madder. I remember him coming at me and then everything went black. The doctors think he banged my head against the wall, maybe several times. He fractured my skull and when I woke up I couldn't hear a thing. I was *so* frightened. Eventually my right ear improved but my left one never has.'

Filled with compassion, Gideon put a finger under her chin and gently tilted her head up. 'You shouldn't feel guilty, you know,' he told her. 'You did everything you could to help him, but there isn't really anything you *can* do to help somebody who's determined to self-destruct. His life had gone off the rails and I guess you were the one area he felt he could still control, only you weren't playing the part right. You were building a life for yourself. He couldn't live with what he'd become and was just looking for someone to blame for his own weakness. There was nothing you could have done to stop it happening, Rachel. Don't torture yourself.'

Her eyes filled with tears. 'Perhaps if I'd been more patient . . .'

'No, Rachel. It wouldn't have made any difference. He was looking for a confrontation, and sooner or later he'd have found a way to goad you into retaliation. What we've got to do now is to make sure he can't take up where he left off. He obviously hasn't learned his lesson.'

'When they sentenced him he said he'd be back for me. I moved out of Kent as soon as he'd gone; I thought if I moved around he'd never find me. How *did* he find me?' she finished on a half-sob.

'I don't know, sweetheart,' Gideon said, the endearment slipping past his guard. She gave no sign that she'd noticed. 'But we'll sort it out, I promise.'

'He came about an hour before you did. He knocked on the door and I went to answer it, but then I caught sight of him peering in the lounge window so I pretended to be out. I thought he'd go away but he didn't . . .'

'Was it him you thought you saw the other day in Blandford?'

'Yes, but then I thought I must have been mistaken. You don't think it *was* him and he followed me home?'

'I don't know. It's possible, I suppose.'

'He kept knocking on the door and then he started prowling round the back. He tried all the doors and windows, and at one point he was shouting for me to come out. I just kept quiet. I don't think he was sure I was in here or he would have broken in. I didn't know what to do. I was just praying you wouldn't be too long.'

'I'm sorry,' Gideon said. 'I had to drop somebody off in Chilminster on my way home.'

'When you did come I didn't hear the bike,' she went on. 'I didn't know you were back until he stopped thumping on the doors. Did he – did he say anything?'

'Oh, one or two things,' Gideon said. 'Nothing repeatable. And then he took a swing at me.'

Rachel's eyes widened. 'Oh, Gideon, I'm sorry! He didn't hurt you?'

Gideon shook his head with a smile. 'O, ye of little faith! I dumped him on his backside.'

'Oh, I wish you hadn't done that!' she said, looking deeply unhappy. 'He won't forget. He never forgets.'

'Well, I won't forget either,' Gideon said with an attempt at lightness. 'He flattened my snowdrops.'

Rachel wasn't in the mood to appreciate his humour – such as it was – so he gave her shoulders a shake and suggested they get themselves something to eat.

An hour and an impromptu lasagne later, a telephone call from the police did nothing to set Rachel's mind at rest. It appeared that Duke Shelley had been paroled ten days before but had almost immediately gone missing and his probation officer was keen to know of his whereabouts.

'I expect they'll soon catch up with him,' Gideon said encouragingly, as he put the phone down. 'And if he gives you any more trouble, he'll end up back inside.'

'Is that what they said?' Rachel asked with hope in her eyes.

'Well, not in so many words,' he admitted, 'but he's not a completely free man. He'll have to watch his step.'

'How could they do that?' Rachel demanded. 'Just let him out and not warn me. Surely I had a right to know. I wasn't expecting it. He was supposed to be locked away for ages yet.'

'I don't suppose they knew where you were,' Gideon pointed out reasonably.

'Duke found me.'

There was that, of course. Gideon shrugged. 'I don't know, then. Perhaps they're not required to. You haven't given this address to anyone, have you? Your mother? Friends?'

Rachel shook her head. 'I haven't spoken to my mother in years. She never liked Duncan and we fell out when I married him. I haven't told anyone where I am.'

Gideon led the way back into the sitting room, where he busied himself in stoking the wood-burning stove up with more logs.

'Well, anyway. Now they know where he's likely to be, I'm sure they'll soon be on his tail. If he's got any sense he'll move on. We probably won't see him again.'

Rachel sat on the sofa, curling her feet under her, and offered no reply. She obviously wasn't convinced either.

It was about midnight and Gideon was just dropping off to sleep when a clatter from downstairs reawakened him. Silence followed and he settled down again, unwilling to leave his warm bed to investigate what was undoubtedly just the cat exploring the kitchen work surfaces. Moments later though, his bedroom door was pushed hesitantly open and somebody padded in.

'Gideon?'

'Yeah?'

Rachel stood halfway between him and the door, a slim figure in flower-print pyjamas.

'Did you hear that?'

'It was probably Elsa,' Gideon murmured sleepily.

'Yes, I suppose so.' Doubtfully. She didn't move.

Resigned, Gideon sat up and swung his legs over the side of the bed.

In the kitchen, Elsa blinked in the sudden light and turned her head away, the end of her tail twitching in annoyance. On the floor a saucepan lid provided the expected answer to the mystery. Gideon replaced it on the wooden draining board, yawned, told the cat to be more careful in future, and retraced his steps.

'I'm sorry,' Rachel said when he told her. 'It's just, well, I couldn't sleep and it sounded so loud, I thought . . .'

'It's all right, Rachel. I don't think he'll come back here, at least, not tonight. He's bound to realise we'd tell the police.'

'I suppose so . . .'

Gideon climbed back into his bed, which had cooled somewhat in the interval. Rachel showed no inclination to return to hers. She stood in the doorway, twisting a fold of her pyjama jacket between her hands in a characteristic gesture of worry.

'Oh, come here,' Gideon said eventually. 'If you're not going back to your bed, you'd better come and get in this one. And shut the door, for goodness' sake. You'll catch your death if you stand there much longer. There's a force-nine gale blowing through that doorway.'

Rachel approached the bed but still hesitated.

'It's all right. You're quite safe,' he said with a smile. 'I don't make a habit of seducing damsels in distress. Surely you know that by now?'

Gratefully, she slipped in beside him.

7

There was plenty of room in Gideon's king-sized double bed for two, quite separate, sleepers and he allowed Rachel her own space. It was she, in fact, who as she was finally succumbing to the effects of emotional exhaustion, turned over and snuggled close to him, her head resting on his upper arm and her body curled foetus-like at his side. Gideon resigned himself to a long and uncomfortable night.

He awakened in the early morning after dozing fitfully. It was still quite dark but a glance at the illuminated dial of his alarm clock told him that it was past six.

Rachel was sleeping deeply, the dreams that had caused her to cry out several times during the night seemingly over for the time being. She still lay across his arm and it took much gentle manoeuvring to extricate it without waking her.

Having done so, it was another five minutes or so before feeling returned with an uncomfortable attack of pins and needles. He dressed quickly and quietly in the cold of the morning, the fingers of that one hand still refusing to do their full share of the work, and trod softly downstairs.

He had revived the flagging Aga, and had porridge thickening in a pan on the top by the time Rachel put in an appearance. She padded in on slippered feet, wearing jeans and one of her hugest, hairiest jumpers, to be greeted with pleasure by Elsa, who rubbed, purring loudly, around her ankles.

'Oh, fickle feline,' Gideon said reproachfully. 'Only five minutes ago you swore you wouldn't look at another if I let you have the top of the milk. Now look at you!'

Rachel laughed, bending to stroke the beautiful, flecked coat.

Gideon tapped the saucepan sharply with the wooden spoon to get Rachel's attention. 'Porridge is ready. Sit yourself down.'

She hesitated, looking half-shyly at him through a cloud of dark hair.

'I'm sorry about last night, Gideon. You must think me very silly.'

'I don't.'

'Well, the thing is, I just wanted to thank you, for not – well, you know . . .'

He raised an eyebrow quizzically, then said, 'Do you want brown sugar or white?'

*

It was a lovely morning once again and Gideon was glad when Pippa called to invite Rachel out for a ride. Not only would it do her good to get out of the house, but also Gideon had a mind to visit Lyddon Grange again. He was prompted by a telephone call from Naomi who was tired and rather emotional after a sleepless night at the Sanctuary.

There had been, it appeared, one disturbance after another. It had started with the telephone ringing every couple of minutes and the caller hanging up the moment they had answered. Whoever it was had, unsurprisingly, withheld their number and Tim and Naomi had been forced to leave their receiver off the hook; something they disliked doing in case anyone tried to call about a sick or injured animal.

The disruptions had continued with a number of fires being set in the farm's outlying fields. When Tim had cautiously investigated, he discovered that piles of old car tyres had been ignited, probably with petrol, and they continued to burn throughout much of the night.

Things were relatively quiet then until just after two in the morning when the helicopter began circling overhead. At this point, Tim had telephoned the police, who promised to send a car out to investigate as soon as they had one free.

The helicopter had departed about two minutes before the police car drew up. The officers who accompanied the vehicle were very sympathetic but gave it as their considered opinion that the fires were set by kids having a bit of fun, and as the helicopter was no longer in evidence, were afraid that there was little they could do.

Naomi begged them to stay around for a while, sure that something else would occur, and they did for thirty silent and uneventful minutes. At this point, however, they received a call about a drunken brawl outside a nightclub and apologetically took their leave, saying that it now looked as though things had quietened down for the night.

Barely five minutes later, the first of several fireworks exploded above the Sanctuary.

'And you still think it was your next-door neighbours?' Gideon asked.

'Who else?'

'If only we knew why they want the place so much,' he said thoughtfully. 'I wonder if old Milne would give anything away.'

'Even supposing you could get to see him,' Naomi said, sounding tired and dispirited. 'From what I've heard, he's pretty much of a hermit. Maybe that's why he wants Hermitage Farm,' she added with a feeble attempt at humour.

'Ah, but I have an invitation.'

'You have?' Naomi was disbelieving. 'Why on earth would he invite *you*?'

'Because I am a fellow artist, my dear!' Gideon announced grandly.

'Yes, but hardly world-famous, you must admit,' she pointed out with sisterly frankness.

'Well, okay. I was surprised too. But apparently he's seen some of my work and he said there was

168

"a lot to like about it". So there. Official recognition.'

'I'm impressed,' she said, sounding anything but. 'But seriously, he's not likely to tell you anything, is he?'

'Not intentionally, maybe,' Gideon admitted. 'But it's worth a try, isn't it?'

Naomi agreed, warning him to be careful, and Gideon had hung up wondering what to do about Rachel while he was out. He could hardly leave her on her own, under the circumstances. Now that problem was solved, he was free to go visiting.

Meredith Milne, when Gideon was finally ushered into his presence, was more than a little taken aback, and to be honest, Gideon couldn't blame him. He must have felt rather like someone who, having issued a vague invitation to people met on holiday, suddenly finds the whole family on his doorstep less than a week later, suitcases in hand.

To Gideon's relief it had once more been Renson who answered the door. He'd a strong suspicion that from what he'd heard of the man, he wouldn't have found it so easy to bluff his way past Slade. As it was, he'd stepped in on Renson almost before the door was fully opened, saying that Milne was expecting him and that he'd be obliged if Renson would show him in.

At this point, finding his visitor already in the hall, Renson made his first mistake, that of shutting the front door behind him.

He protested that Milne hadn't mentioned

Gideon's visit, at which Gideon laughed and said he'd never met anyone as absent-minded as Meredith. He'd then turned towards the nearest door and asked, 'Is he in here?'

Thrown off balance again by Gideon's obvious intention to make himself free of the house, whatever his objections, Renson made his second mistake when he said, 'No, not in there. He's in his studio,' and waved a hand towards the stairs.

Gideon immediately set off in that direction, allowing himself a small, secret smile as Renson hurried to follow him, protesting all the while.

Thus Milne found himself the recipient of a completely unexpected – and just as completely unwanted – guest, and being a man of solitary habit, he took no trouble to hide his annoyance.

'What in thunder are you doing here?' he demanded, his snowy brows lowering like storm-clouds. He was wearing, as before, a much-stained painter's smock with a red and white kerchief knotted around his neck.

'I'm sorry, Mr Milne, I tried to stop him,' the hapless Renson began in his own defence, but Gideon cut in, ignoring him.

'You invited me,' he informed Milne in tones of mild astonishment. 'Have you forgotten?'

'That's what he told me,' Renson asserted eagerly.

Milne also ignored him. 'I *did*?' he asked Gideon, no longer totally sure of his ground.

'Of course you did. Just the other day. You told me – oh, I say,' he interrupted himself

170

providentially, 'isn't that the watercolour you exhibited at the Southampton Exhibition?' He transferred his whole attention to the massive harbour scene on the wall behind Milne.

The artist followed his gaze helplessly. 'Er . . . one of them, yes. In 'ninety-eight. You were there?'

'Not exhibiting,' Gideon replied with perfect truth. He had never been to the Southampton Exhibition in his life. Nautical art, while all right in small, select doses, was not really his cup of tea. Mentioning the exhibition had been a calculated gamble that had paid off. His foot was, metaphorically, in the door.

'Shall I call Slade?' Renson offered, vainly trying to win back a little favour.

'What? Are you still here?' Milne said testily, as if noticing him for the first time. 'Go on. Go away! Haven't you got anything else to do?'

Renson left.

Gideon looked around him at Milne's studio. It was impressive, to say the least. Everything that an artist's studio should be. It was a corner room that Gideon guessed had originally been a bedroom and light came into it by way of four large windows, two in each of the outside walls. Now it contained none of its original fittings beyond a huge vanity sink and mirror in one corner, and adjustable blinds had replaced the curtains. A range of work surfaces had been built in down one side, into which a stainless-steel sink and drainer unit had been plumbed. Under the work surfaces, wide shallow shelves held rolls of canvas, sheets of

171

paper and mounting card of every conceivable hue, and on top, trays contained hundreds of tubes, pots and cakes of paint, brushes, pencils and pens. Palettes and mixing trays lay on the draining board, and several liquid-holding receptacles were dotted about, along with bottles of turpentine, white spirit and linseed oil, and pots of varnish.

Paintings, sketches and photographs lined the upper parts of the walls, presumably to avoid the fading effects of direct sunlight, and countless dozens more lay in stacks against the inner walls. The man was prolific, if nothing else, one had to give him that.

Gideon wondered if he would feel more inspired to work if he had a studio like this one. With something that was akin to regret, he decided that it would probably make little difference. Art, whether good, bad or indifferent, had to be a calling and he just wasn't getting the shout. He had a feeling that with him it would always remain more of a whim than a compulsion.

Two or three works in progress stood about the room on easels and Gideon gestured towards the closest. 'May I?'

Milne nodded. 'Go ahead.'

The painting was in oils and depicted a Spanish fiesta. Horses, dark-haired girls in bright, flounced skirts, and proud young men in wide-brimmed hats and red sashes, all dappled by sunlight filtering through the branches of an avenue of trees. The style was Impressionist and the effect dynamic. Gideon could almost hear the flamenco guitars and the clopping of horses' hooves on the cobbles, and yet when he looked closely there was no detail at all, merely suggestion.

Milne was watching him for a reaction. 'I spent the summer in Andalucia last year,' he said.

'Is it finished?' Gideon asked; the eternal question with which most artists tortured themselves. Would that one more touch of the brush turn the thing into a masterpiece, or take it to irretrievable ruin?

'I'm not sure,' Milne mused, frowning slightly. 'What do you think?'

Gideon looked at it again. 'I'd say so. It's not a style I've ever been very successful with. I always try to do too much. It takes courage to stand back and leave it alone.'

'D'you like it?'

'It's beautiful,' Gideon said simply. He had come prepared to flatter for the sake of his mission but found he had no need to do so.

'It's well enough,' Milne said with a shrug. 'I shan't know until I come back to it whether it's finished or not. I cover them up for a couple of weeks and then look at them again with fresh eyes. Sometimes then you can see properly what has been staring you in the face for days.'

'You're so right,' Gideon said. 'Sometimes when I see pictures I've done for people in the past, it's as much as I can do not to say "let me have it back, I can see where I went wrong now".'

He wandered across to the next easel which held a portrait of a small child in a party dress, sitting

173

with her arm round a spaniel. It was beautifully crafted but a little sugary for Gideon's taste.

Milne came up to stand beside him. 'We all have to eat,' he stated without apology. 'This is the bread and butter that makes the jam possible.'

'Andalucia?'

'Yes. Andalucia. And this year, Normandy.'

'I envy you,' Gideon said honestly.

He looked at several more of the paintings, enjoying both them and the company of their creator a lot more than he had expected to.

After twenty minutes or so, Milne summoned the long-suffering Renson by means of what appeared to be the original household bell system, left over from its Georgian beginnings. When he arrived, he was immediately despatched to fetch coffee and biscuits.

The barely concealed surprise evident as he received this command confirmed Gideon's impression that guests were rarely welcomed to Lyddon Grange. He had a feeling that Renson had been expecting to escort him out rather than fetch refreshments for him. And he was quite sure which task the man would have preferred. Gideon favoured him with a particularly sweet smile as he left the room.

Milne was eager to continue their interrupted discussion on the relative merits of board and canvas, but recalling the reason for his visit, Gideon drifted over to one of the windows. Below him rough-cut lawns and rhododendrons covered the fifty metres or so to the tree-lined boundary, beyond which he could see the Sanctuary's field and the back of the stables.

'You've certainly got a nice position here,' he remarked into a slow spot in the rather one-sided debate. 'How far does your land extend?'

Milne was rather taken aback by this sudden change of subject. 'Oh, there's fifteen or so acres. I don't go out there much, it's always too damned cold and there's nothing to paint.'

'It's wonderfully quiet and secluded here. No bother from road noise or neighbours, I should imagine.'

'I must have it quiet. I can't concentrate with noise going on around me.' Milne frowned at the very thought.

'I expect Slade takes care of all that.'

'Slade takes care of everything. I don't know how I'd manage without him,' he said with a surprising degree of warmth.

'Still, you'd hardly know the wildlife sanctuary existed from here, would you?' Gideon probed gently. 'I shouldn't think you'd hear anything of them at all.'

Milne's bushy brows were beginning to lower again. 'Well, they're only rabbits and things, aren't they? Though why anyone would want to bother with vermin like that is beyond me entirely. Look, I didn't ask you here to admire the view. If you want to do that, I'll get Renson to give you a guided tour of the gardens!'

Gideon turned away from the window. He'd learned little or nothing but had obviously pushed as far as he could without arousing suspicion. 'I'm sorry,' he said. 'I'm not really into gardens, it just seems such a lovely haven for an artist.'

'That,' Milne explained, much as you would to a backward child, 'is precisely why I bought it.'

'How long have you been here?'

'Oh, forty – fifty years, I forget exactly. I bought it after my first London exhibition, soon after the war. It'd been used by the army as an intelligence HQ or somesuch.' He waved a hand at Gideon. 'And you, Mr Blake? Where do you live? One of these horrid, modern, two up-two down places, I suppose.'

'Three up-three down, actually. But sixteenth-century, not twentieth.'

Milne grunted. 'Yours?'

'No,' Gideon admitted wryly. 'I haven't had my first London exhibition yet.'

The older man favoured him with a long, hard look, eyes narrowed. 'Are you laughing at me?' he asked abruptly.

'At life.'

Once again the look, then, 'Where's that wretched man got to?' and an imperious prod at the bell push.

Coffee and a selection of chocolate biscuits duly arrived, were dispensed and enjoyed, and after another in-depth discussion on technical matters that were, quite frankly, beyond Gideon, Milne decided that the audience was over and Renson was summoned to show the visitor out.

As Gideon left he paused beside a handsome

seascape hung on the wall opposite the studio door.

'I like that. One of yours?'

'No, no, of course not! It's a William Templeman. There's another one downstairs. If you come again I'll show you,' Milne offered. 'I don't buy a lot; mostly only if there's a danger of something decent being sold abroad. I can't abide the thought of classic British art being hung in foreign galleries. The Americans especially have no real appreciation, they're just acquisitive. You're too young to have heard of Darius Sinclair, I suppose?'

Gideon shook his head. 'Actually, no. My mother's the proud owner of two small charcoal sketches by Sinclair.'

'Then you're probably aware that the Americans would have made off with the major part of his life's work if they'd had their way, the thieving magpies! And for what? For status, that's all. Philistines!'

'Some other thieving magpie got that collection, if I remember rightly,' Gideon observed. His mother had kept the newspaper cuttings in a scrapbook. A number of very highly rated oils and watercolours by Darius Sinclair, stolen while in transit to the auction rooms.

'Yes, well, that's as maybe.' Milne pursed his lips. 'Anyway, when I can afford to, I buy one or two pieces destined for export, and when I die they'll be gifted to the nation.'

Gideon smiled as he shook the man's gnarled

brown hand. Rude and intolerant Milne might be; even so, you couldn't help admiring his dedication.

At the foot of the stairs, closely followed by the sullen Renson, Gideon came face to face with a man he hadn't met before, but needed no introduction to tell him that this must be the infamous Slade.

Of no more than average height and build, he nevertheless filled the gloomy hallway with his presence. Maybe ten years or so older than Gideon, Slade had dark hair flecked with silver, and steel-grey eyes in a strong-featured, deeply tanned face, the whole giving an impression of latent power and determination.

'What the hell are *you* doing here?' were his opening words, and Gideon was slightly taken aback.

'I was invited,' he replied. 'What business is it of yours?'

Beside him, Renson drew an audible breath.

'Is that true?' Slade demanded of Gideon's escort, who shrugged unhappily but didn't answer. Slade obviously hadn't expected him to, for he continued with barely a pause, 'Well, don't just stand there like an idiot, show him out!'

Whereas Milne snapped and shouted, Slade's voice was low and controlled but with an underlying air of menace that spoke volumes. Gideon was reminded of his sister's description of the man: 'Smooth. Like a dangerous snake, beautiful but deadly.'

He felt she was probably right. He was certainly

handsome: white teeth, expensive haircut, and clothes that needed no labels to advertise their designer credentials. Also, maybe as a statement of personal toughness, a gold earring in one ear.

Meredith Milne must be a more generous employer than one would imagine, Gideon mused. But then to a man who wanted the world kept from his door, Slade would presumably be worth his weight in gold earrings and designer suits.

He allowed himself to be ushered to the front door where he paused on the threshold. 'Nice to meet you, Mr . . . er . . .?'

'Slade.'

'Mr Slade, of course. Well, I expect I shall see you again. Meredith said to drop in any time. 'Bye for now.'

Gideon turned his back on Slade with satisfaction. He and Milne had certainly not reached first-name terms but for some reason his presence in the house had put Slade out, and some spark of contrariness made him want to punish the man for his rudeness.

It wasn't until he was aboard the Norton and halfway down the drive that he remembered that Slade hadn't asked 'Who the hell are you?' as one might expect, but 'What the hell are you doing here?' And yet he'd never met the man before.

Had Slade seen him that day from the helicopter? Whatever the case, it seemed probable that Joey had warned him of Gideon's interest in the Sanctuary. It looked almost as though Slade was the driving force behind the campaign against Tim and Naomi, as Milne appeared to have little interest in his neighbours, either for or against. But what possible reason could Slade have for driving them off their land?

With a sigh, he went to report his lack of progress to Tim and Naomi.

Rachel's new clients had returned from their holiday and telephoned that evening to arrange for her to view the seafront apartment she was to work on. They wanted her to come the next day – Sunday – and Gideon saw her off in the morning with a sense of relief. She was expecting to be out for most of the day.

Since coming back from her ride with Pippa the day before, she'd been strung as tight as a bowstring with suppressed anxiety. Time and again he'd caught her peering out of the gothic arched windows of the Gatehouse from behind the curtains. And every time he'd opened an outside door, even if only to take rubbish out to the bin or let the cat in, she had immediately wanted to know where he was going. By bedtime he was in a state of suppressed tension himself.

Gideon had promised to ride with Pippa the next day, as he often did on a Sunday, and it was with a feeling of release that he set off to walk up to the Priory through a light, mizzling rain.

He rode Blackbird once more, at Pippa's invitation, and apart from trying to mash Gideon's knee on a gatepost at one point, still with an expression of perfect innocence on his handsome black face, the horse behaved immaculately.

Pippa was incensed.

'Last week, when I had somebody here to try him with a view to buying, he refused point-blank to leave the yard!' she complained in exasperation. 'And when I led him out for exercise beside Cassie yesterday, he suddenly put the brakes on after a couple of miles and nearly pulled me off over her tail. If I hadn't let go . . . The thing is, there's no rhyme or reason to him. One minute he's fine and the next a sod!'

'He gets bored,' Gideon said, surprising himself but knowing, even as he said it, that it was true.

'Oh?' Pippa said, raising an eyebrow. 'He told you so, did he?'

'You may scoff!' Gideon retorted, affecting lofty unconcern. 'You'd be surprised the things your horses tell me about you.'

Pippa laughed. 'That would be even funnier if I were a hundred percent sure it was nonsense,' she said. 'Oh, and while we're on the subject, I heard from Jenny Weatherfield yesterday. She said to tell you she's staying with friends in Somerset and that Willow hasn't growled once since your visit.'

'Oh, that's great news. I thought it might take a lot longer than that but she was very sensible about it. You'd be surprised how many people pay for advice and then ignore it.'

'Yes, she's a lovely person. She used to be a friend of Mummy's,' Pippa said, looking wistful for a moment. 'Anyway, you seem to have made quite an impression on her. She couldn't praise you enough. Which is odd,' she continued with a mischievous gleam in her eye, 'because I used to think she was quite a good judge of character.'

'Everyone makes mistakes now and then,' Gideon agreed solemnly. 'I mean, she's obviously stayed in touch with you, too!'

'You beast!' Pippa exclaimed. They were riding along the bottom of one of the Priory's fields, close to the stream, and with no warning she suddenly cried, 'See you at the top!' and urged Skylark into a gallop from a standing start, heading away towards the horizon.

Caught unawares, Gideon was nearly ignominiously piled as Blackbird responded to his companion's unheralded departure with a huge, lurching buck and acceleration that would have done justice to a drag racer.

Swearing under his breath, Gideon caught at his mount's flying mane like a novice to keep himself in the saddle and then, balance restored, leaned forward to help him take the hill.

He caught and passed Pippa and her mount a few yards from the top, as she pulled up, laughing.

'Oh, I hoped he would buck you off!' she declared as he reined in beside her.

'He almost did, thanks to you! But he's got quite a turn of speed on him, hasn't he?'

'He has, damn him! He's everything a horse should be, except reliable.'

'He's just a poor, misunderstood fellow, aren't you, lad?' Gideon said sympathetically, patting the warm, black neck.

Pippa snorted. 'Why don't *you* give him the understanding he craves then? Tell you what, I'll sell him to you. Fifty quid and he's yours.'

'Oh, no, you don't! What would I want with a horse?'

'Well, you could ride it out on Sundays with me,' Pippa said.

'I can do that anyway.'

'At *my* expense!'

'I thought I was doing you a favour . . .'

'Big of you, I'm sure.'

Gideon shrugged. 'I guess I'm just a naturally generous sort of guy,' he said modestly.

Pippa gave him a look that would have curdled milk. 'You're just a naturally annoying sort of guy, if you ask me. Are you ever short of a smart answer?'

Gideon frowned. 'Er . . .'

'Very funny.' Pippa glanced at her watch. 'I think we'd better turn for home now. I've got a vet coming to look at one of the horses at twelve o'clock.'

'On a Sunday?' Gideon was surprised. Veterinary fees were frightening at the best of times, and a Sunday call-out was certainly not the best of times. 'What's the problem?'

'There isn't one. And *I'm* not paying,' Pippa assured him. 'It's somebody who's interested in buying Sebastian. She wants him vetted and she insists on being there. Apparently Sunday is her only free day this week. I don't know how she thinks she'll get him fit enough for eventing if she's that busy, but that's not my problem.'

'Perhaps she has someone to do it for her.'

'Mm, maybe. Nothing would surprise me about her, she's a first-class snob and absolutely rolling in money.'

'Pretty?' Gideon enquired, affecting interest.

'Oh, for heavensakes!' Pippa exclaimed. 'Slim, blonde and hard as nails, if you must know. Daddy's something in the City and buys her whatsoever her little heart desires. A couple of years ago he bought her a stallion to play with, and now she wants an eventer. Six months time it'll probably be a dressage horse or a string of polo ponies.'

They headed back to the stables to prepare Sebastian for his examination.

The horse looked, to Gideon's fairly experienced eye, the picture of health but he knew, only too well, the horrors that could lurk beneath the surface of an apparent bargain. The possible pitfalls involved in buying a horse make the purchase of a second-hand car seem like childsplay in comparison, and no sane person would contemplate dipping in their pocket to the tune of several thousand pounds without a full vet's certificate.

Almost before the stableyard clock had finished striking twelve, a vaguely familiar, mud-splashed green car swept through the archway, pulled up in front of the tack room and disgorged Sean Rosetti on to the gravel.

'You didn't tell me it was Rosetti who was coming,' Gideon said quietly as they went forward to meet him.

'You didn't ask,' Pippa retorted. 'Anyway, how was I to know you knew him? He's Stephanie's vet, not mine.'

'Hi,' Rosetti called. 'Miss Barrington-Carr?'

'Oh, Pippa, please,' she said, holding out her hand.

'Pippa,' he amended obediently, smiling with easy charm as they shook hands. 'Sean Rosetti. And Gideon I've already met. Hi, again. You certainly get around!'

Gideon greeted the young vet with genuine pleasure, feeling the instant return of the comradeship they had begun to build on their previous meeting.

'Ms Wainman not here yet?' Rosetti asked, glancing round.

'No,' Pippa confirmed. She squinted up at the heavy grey sky from which persistent drizzle was falling. 'Come into the tack room and have a cuppa while you wait.'

Ms Wainman finally appeared nearly half an hour later, rolling up in a sleek dove-grey Jaguar that sat on the gravel beside Rosetti's car like a Siamese next to an alley-cat. She unfurled herself from behind the wheel and stood up in an impossibly immaculate cream-coloured riding mac, beige cord jodhpurs and short boots. She, too, squinted up at the rain and reached back into the Jag for a wide-brimmed hat to cover her jaw-length sleek blonde bob.

'Sorry to keep you,' she called, not looking in the least sorry. 'Daddy had people round for drinks and I just couldn't get away. I hope you'll forgive me . . .'

'Of course,' Rosetti assured her, with the smile she had expected. 'The meter's running and you're paying the bill. It's no skin off my nose.'

Gideon gave a silent cheer and sensed Pippa stifling a giggle beside him. For a fraction of a second, Stephanie was thrown off balance but she recovered almost immediately. 'Well, in that case, we'd better get on with it, hadn't we? Your bills are quite big enough as it is.' She smiled sweetly, but it was clear the gloves were off. 'Hello, Pippa darling. And who would this be?'

Gideon had joined the others in the yard and, as he was formally introduced, found himself subjected to a brief but thorough assessment by the lady's steel-grey eyes. They lingered a moment or two as she took in the length of his hair and the still-visible scars. Then she smiled a small, brittle smile that didn't touch her eyes, and dismissed him as of no account. Gideon was not troubled in the least.

He watched the ensuing examination with interest and a growing respect. Rosetti was quick, quiet and extremely thorough. He handled the restless thoroughbred with patience and firmness, and carried out tests on heart, lungs, teeth, joints and eyes with the confidence born of long experience. He checked the horse's feet at great length and asked what kind of work Stephanie was intending to do with him, all the while making notes. At the end of his examination he filled in a chart, noting all the white markings and hair whorls in Sebastian's coat, his breeding as certified by the papers Pippa produced, and other vital statistics, such as height, approximate weight, and size of bone, measured below the knee.

At the finish, he announced that he would prepare an official report but that as far as he had been able to determine, the bay gelding was sound in wind and limb, and fit for his projected career as a three-day-eventer.

'Good,' Stephanie said briskly. Then with a sideways look that showed that Rosetti's earlier remark still rankled, she added, 'So if he breaks down next month, I can blame you, can I?'

Rosetti shook his head, smiling thinly. 'I can only say as I see today. You can blame whoever you like next month, but honestly you'd do better to save your breath for sorting out some decent insurance.'

Gideon found himself liking Rosetti more and more, but Stephanie was determined to have the last word. Having arranged to contact Pippa to finalise details, she turned to get into the Jaguar and then paused, looking back.

'I used to know another Italian once,' she announced, smiling sweetly. 'He didn't have a sense of humour either.'

Without waiting for a comeback, she slid behind the wheel, said, 'Ciao, Pippa darling,' and drove smoothly away.

Pippa darling, Rosetti and Gideon looked at one another and dissolved into helpless laughter.

'Have you done her horses for long, Sean?' Pippa asked when they'd calmed down.

'About six months. I've only met her once before, though. Usually I deal with her groom.'

'Do you think you'll *still* be doing her horses?' Gideon enquired, pointedly.

'Oh, yes, I expect so,' Rosetti replied, packing the tools of his trade into a box in the back of his car. 'She's a spoiled little rich girl who's used to having her own way. I think she sees me as a challenge.'

He looked at his watch. 'Well, I'd better be getting along. My wife's cooking a roast and she'll murder me if I'm late. It's been nice seeing you again, Gideon, and Pippa, good to meet you.'

'I mean to take you up on that invitation to look round your surgery sometime,' Gideon warned him as they shook hands.

Rosetti looked pleased. 'Yes, please do,' he said. 'Look, why don't you come over this afternoon, if you're not doing anything? It's not strictly my weekend on, so I shouldn't be called out. Pippa, you're welcome too. Just give me an hour or so to get lunch out of the way.'

Both Pippa and Gideon accepted the invitation and after seeing Rosetti off, fed the horses before making their way to the Priory kitchens in search of Mrs Morecambe and a bite to eat.

Pippa drove Gideon to Dorchester that afternoon in her runabout, having declined the offer of a ride on the Norton in the worsening rain.

188

'Where's the Merc today?' Gideon asked as they set off down the drive, just after half-past two. He knew Giles wasn't out in it as he'd joined them for lunch, complaining that while they were 'having fun' he was having a nightmare day going over the estate accounts. 'Don't tell me you've finally made room for it in the garage!' It was a standing joke with them that the only things not to be found in their full-to-bursting coachhouse-cum-garage were the cars.

'No,' Pippa said, frowning slightly. 'As a matter of fact it's in Blandford having a re-spray. Some kind soul threw acid over it when it was parked in the village yesterday. Can you believe it? Why should anyone want to do such a thing?'

Gideon experienced an uncomfortable twinge of guilt. *He* had been driving the Mercedes quite a lot lately. Both Giles' cars had personalised number-plates and it didn't need a very great stretch of the imagination to picture either Curly or Duke Shelley venting their frustration on what they probably thought was Gideon's pride and joy. He knew from their conversation earlier that Rachel had given Pippa a potted version of her life history and the besieging of the Gatehouse by her husband, but it seemed that Pippa hadn't yet recognised the possible connection between that and the fate of the Mercedes.

He wrestled briefly with his conscience, and lost.

'Er, I suppose it could have been a case of mistaken identity. I mean, I have been driving the Merc a fair bit and, having the same initials, I suppose it's just possible that somebody might have thought it was mine.'

Pippa turned her head momentarily to glance at him.

'For heavensakes, Gideon! Surely this hasn't got anything to do with that stallion business, has it? What on earth have you got yourself mixed up in?'

'I wish I knew,' he said truthfully. 'But I should think this has more to do with Rachel's delightful ex-husband, who I had the pleasure of meeting the other night. We didn't exactly hit it off in a big way.' It was a good thing Duke hadn't had the acid handy when he'd called then, Gideon thought, but kept it to himself.

'Rachel told me,' Pippa said dryly. 'She seemed half out of her mind with worry. Kept saying she wished you hadn't hit him because he wouldn't forget. I said it sounded just what he needed!'

Gideon laughed. 'Trust you! Next time he turns up I'll let you know and you can come and sort him out! But, for the record, I didn't actually hit him. He was trying to hit me and I stopped him, that's all. I admit, he wasn't best pleased but it was his fault, not mine.'

Pippa clearly wasn't interested in the technicalities. She darted another, frowning look at him. 'You think he *will* come back, then?'

'If the police don't catch up with him first, then yes, I'd put money on it.'

'And it doesn't bother you?'

'Worrying won't stop it happening. We'll just have to be a bit careful, that's all.'

'I suppose so.' She didn't sound entirely convinced. 'I don't know what it is with those sort of people. I mean, just because things aren't going your way, you don't go round taking it out on other people, do you?'

'Well, speaking personally, no,' Gideon agreed.

'I didn't mean you personally, so don't be awkward. I was speaking generally. I mean, the average person doesn't. I just can't understand the mentality.'

'That's because you're a balanced, well-adjusted human being who knows her own worth and is sure of her place within the structure of society,' Gideon stated gravely.

There was an astonished silence for the space of a few seconds and then Pippa said, 'Bull!'

Gideon laughed. 'Actually, I thought it was rather impressive,' he said with assumed dignity. 'My psychology tutor would have been proud of me.'

'So he might have been, if you'd had one,' Pippa observed dampeningly. 'But I happen to know that you studied philosophy and history.'

'Maybe that was where I went wrong . . .'

'Why *did* you take those subjects?' Pippa asked with interest, changing down a gear as she negotiated roadworks.

'Well, I had to take something,' he said. 'And as the university wasn't offering anthropology, which Dad would have liked me to take, I decided on those two. I don't think at that age you really know what you want to do.'

'We were all dead jealous of you, having a father like that,' Pippa recalled. 'But I guess it wasn't all fun and games, was it?'

'Hardly any of it,' Gideon said dryly. His father, a world-renowned anthropologist, had on occasion taken his young son to some far-flung outpost of humanity in the pursuit of his passion and those trips had been very exciting for a teenage boy. Far more frequently though, he, his sister and his mother had stayed at home and not seen the celebrated Professor Blake for weeks, sometimes months, and on one occasion over a year. His studies and documentaries on the lives and customs of relatively obscure peoples of the world were said to be ground-breaking; be that as it may, Gideon had often thought he probably knew less about his own family, deep in darkest Sussex, than any man alive.

'Where is he now, do you know?'

'Nepal, the last I heard,' Gideon said. 'Mother had a postcard from him about a month ago.'

'That's unreal!' Pippa said. 'Getting a postcard from your own husband. Poor lady!'

'She's used to it. I sometimes wonder how Naomi and I ever came to be. We must be the eighth and ninth wonders of the modern world!'

Pippa giggled. 'What did your milkman look like?'

Gideon assumed a look of shocked indignation. Then he said; 'He was a remarkably handsome fellow, I believe.'

*

They reached Rosetti's surgery in good time, having followed his directions to the letter, and found themselves pulling up in front of a mellow stone farmhouse and sprawling range of farm buildings. The house itself stood in a well-tended garden sprinkled with snowdrops and crocuses, and where daffodil leaves stood in stiff clumps, promising colour to come. With red-berried evergreens against the walls and a well-stocked bird table, the effect was like something on the cover of a lifestyle magazine rather than the home of a busy vet but a white, shiny board on the wall of the nearest outbuilding proclaimed the existence of the equine surgery they had come to see.

The car had scarcely stopped rolling when the front door opened and a small child erupted through it in a flurry of curls, flounces and flying limbs.

As Gideon and Pippa got out of the car, this mini tornado whirled towards them and stopped barely three feet away, resolving itself into an enchanting two- or three-year-old girl, with a head of tousled curls and a pair of huge, dark-lashed brown eyes. She was dressed Victorian-style in petticoats and a long pinafore dress of green corduroy.

'Hello,' Pippa said, smiling at this vision. 'What's your name?'

Having precipitated the meeting, the child seemed suddenly shy and looked back for reassurance to where a slim, dark female followed at a more leisurely pace, wiping wet hands on a dishcloth.

'Please excuse my undisciplined daughter,' the woman begged with a smile as she came up to them. 'Try as I might, I can't make her see that all visitors have not necessarily come to see her.' She bent to take the little girl's hand. 'Daisy, you are an exasperating child. I told you to wait for me, didn't I?'

Emboldened by the proximity of her mother, Daisy peered up at the visitors. 'Are you Giddy an' Pips?'

With a carefully straight face, Gideon nodded at the child. 'We are,' he confirmed gravely. 'I'm Giddy and this is Pips.'

8

The grand tour of the surgery and accompanying buildings took nearly an hour, all told. Gideon and Pippa were deeply interested in all that they saw and Sean Rosetti, seeing their interest, needed no further encouragement to show off his pride and joy.

The conversion of the outbuildings to surgery, recovery room, drugstore and residential stabling was very recent, and the whole place was as modern and hi-tech on the inside as it appeared ancient on the outer. They learned that it had in fact only opened to patients within the last year. Sean told them that, at present, he shared the practice with one other vet, a trained anaesthetist he referred to as Eddie, with whom he eventually hoped to go into partnership.

At the stables, where they started the tour, Gideon and Pippa were introduced to one of the two veterinary nurse-cum-grooms who, between them, manned the yard twenty-four hours a day whenever there were horses in residence.

'They've got a bedsit where they can relax when everything is quiet,' Sean said. 'And we're having another one put in so owners can stay here if they arrive in the middle of the night or just want to be near their horses. I expect, once we really get busy, we'll have to have more stable staff, but at the moment we're managing.'

The stables were all equipped with state-of-the-art fittings, including an automatic watering system, and were linked to the nurses' station and Sean's office by closed-circuit television. 'It saves having to keep coming out to check on them, which is a pain for us and disturbing for them,' he explained.

At present the hospital held just one patient, who stood looking quietly contented in her luxury accommodation. They were told that she was recovering well from a deep, abdominal wound that had required cleaning and extensive stitching in a sterile environment. She was due to go home shortly.

In the main block of the buildings, which bore no resemblance to their former life as a milking parlour and dairy complex, Gideon and Pippa were shown the reception area where horses could be unloaded from horseboxes under cover. Various metal trolleys stood tidily around the walls with emergency equipment at the ready, Sean saying that some of his patients arrived in a state of virtual collapse.

From reception, he led them through a door that opened on to a flight of half a dozen or so steps leading upward to a corridor. From this corridor, windows looked down into both the surgery and a smaller room with padded floor and walls, which he explained was the area where horses were first anaesthetised, and to where they were returned to recover consciousness after surgery.

'We needed a corridor to bypass the surgery, for reasons of hygiene,' Sean said. 'And it actually makes quite a good observation area.'

'For whom?' Pippa asked.

'For owners – if they feel like it – and for visiting vets. Even for me if we have to call a specialist in. And maybe, one day, for students.' His eyes shone with thoughts of possibilities for the future.

The tour concluded with a brief look at the room that housed the X-ray equipment, the drugstore, the office and two rooms that were for general storage. The storerooms were locked, as was the office with its three large filing cabinets and its hot drinks dispenser, and all the connecting doors were fire-doors, made of metal and hung to swing either way. Everywhere was scrupulously clean and tidy. Gideon and Pippa were impressed, and said so.

'Come over to the house for a drink,' Sean suggested when they'd seen all there was to see. 'Cathy would love to meet you properly and I promised Daisy you wouldn't go without saying goodbye.'

'She's a sweet child,' Pippa said as they made their way across to the farmhouse.

'*You* don't have to live with her,' Sean declared with feeling. 'She can be a little monster!'

'Is she an only child?'

'At the moment,' he said, opening the front door and ushering them through. 'But not for much longer. We've just found out that Cathy's expecting again. No doubt that'll put Madam's nose out of joint for a bit, but I think it'll do her the world of good in the long run.'

Cathy appeared, accepted their congratulations and invited them through into the kitchen, which was a practical mixture of new appliances in an old farmhouse setting.

'I'm sorry, I don't normally entertain guests in the kitchen,' she said. 'But the sitting room's in a frightful mess. I'm decorating and all the furniture is piled in the centre of the room with dustsheets over it. I had intended to leave it until the summer but by then I might not be in the best shape for climbing up and down stepladders.' She put a hand on her stomach a little self-consciously.

'I'm sure Sean would have done it for you,' Gideon said provocatively, with a sideways glance at the vet. 'Do him good to have something to do in his spare time.'

Sean favoured him with a sour look. 'Ha, ha,' he said.

Cathy laughed. 'On the rare occasions that he does have a few minutes to spare, he disappears into his wine cellar,' she complained in a tone that conveyed tolerance.

'Oh?' Gideon said with interest. Wines were one

of Giles' passions and he was trying, with limited success, to educate Gideon in the subtle art of wine appreciation. 'Do you collect it, make it, or just enjoy drinking it?'

'All three,' Sean said.

'Pippa's brother has a very good cellar.'

'And guards it like the crown jewels,' she put in. 'I think he's afraid I'll use one of his precious Château-something-or-other's for cooking. Like most men, he doesn't believe a mere female could possibly have any knowledge of such things.'

Gideon and Sean both reacted with predictable indignation to that but Cathy swung round from her coffee-making. 'I agree completely! Sean won't even let me go down to the cellar on my own. I'm beginning to think he keeps another woman down there!'

'My secret is out,' he declared dramatically, but behind the smile Gideon thought he detected a trace of annoyance. 'Seriously though, a fella needs somewhere he can go to get away from the stresses and strains of everyday life.'

'And which am I, darling? A stress or a strain?' Cathy asked as she brought a coffeepot and cups to the scrubbed pine table where they were sitting.

'If I were you, I'd be careful how I answered that!' Gideon warned, laughing.

'You're so right!' Sean said, looking stricken, then seizing thankfully on the diversion. 'Ah, hello, Daisy. What have you been up to?'

'I bin good,' she declared defensively, coming into the room and up to her father's knee.

'I'm sure you have,' he assured her. 'Good God, what is it with you women? You always think you're being accused of something.'

'Well, we have to stand up for ourselves,' Cathy said, laughing as she put a plate of chocolate muffins next to the coffeepot. 'Otherwise you great rough bullies would make our lives a misery. Isn't that right, Daisy Doolittle?'

Daisy climbed on to a vacant chair, eyeing the muffins. 'Daisy's hungry!' she announced, re-adjusting her priorities. 'Daisy needs two muffins!'

'Daisy won't get any muffins at all if she doesn't mind her manners,' Cathy told her, severely.

In the hall a telephone trilled. Sean groaned and Cathy went to answer it.

'She's very good at sifting out the time-wasters,' he explained, but within a minute or so she was back.

'It's Rita Morgan. You'd better talk to her. It's something about the powders you gave her for her broodmare. She seems worried. I'll find her notes.' She flashed an apologetic smile at her guests as she followed her husband out of the room. 'Please excuse us for a minute. Oh, and help yourself to coffee and muffins.'

The minute lengthened to ten and still Sean and Cathy hadn't reappeared. In the meantime Pippa had poured coffee for herself and Gideon, and milk for Daisy, and they'd each had a muffin. Daisy ate her muffin with messy enjoyment, getting almost as much around her mouth as in it. Apparently abandoning the idea of a second helping, she slid off her chair, holding her sticky fingers high, and made her way towards the door into the hall.

'Hey, hang on!' Pippa exclaimed. 'Let's wipe those fingers, shall we? I'm sure Mummy won't want sticky muffin all over the house.' She led the child towards the sink, taking care to hold her wrist rather than her hand, and wiped the offending digits with a wad of damp kitchen paper.

'That's better.' Pippa released the child's hands and looked round for a bin.

'Try that corner cupboard,' Gideon advised, pointing.

A short search revealed the bin under the sink and as Pippa turned back to the table she stopped short. 'Oh, Lord! Now where has she gone?'

In the corner behind Gideon a door stood open eight black inches or so and there was no sign of Daisy.

'The wine cellar?' Pippa suggested.

'I'll get her.'

On the wall just inside the open door Gideon found a light switch and flicked it on. Daisy stood a little way down a flight of steep, stone steps, gazing up at him. 'Daddy's den,' she said. 'Daisy show you,' and pattered on downwards.

'Oh, no, you don't!' Gideon ran quickly down after her, catching up with her just as she reached the bottom. He grasped her hand firmly, glancing around with interest at the racks of bottles and benches of winemaking equipment as he did so, then led her back up the steps. 'I'm quite sure you're not allowed down here. Come on, up we go.'

He pushed Daisy ahead of him through the doorway and turned to pull the door shut.

'What are you doing?' Sean demanded sharply, coming through from the hall. 'That door should be locked. Where have you been?'

'Well, it wasn't locked,' Gideon replied, somewhat taken aback by the implied accusation. 'Daisy opened it when we weren't looking and I went down to bring her back. I'd no intention of prying.'

Cathy had come in behind her husband and now put her hand on his arm. 'Oh, come on, Sean. Aren't you taking this a bit far? We should be grateful to Gideon. Daisy could easily have fallen and hurt herself down there.'

'That's exactly why I keep it locked.' He paused and then said with a rueful smile, 'I'm sorry, Gideon. I didn't mean to be rude. It's just that those steps are treacherous. I must remember to take the key out of the lock in future.'

'It's all right, forget it,' Gideon said, and was rewarded by a grateful smile from Cathy.

Daisy had tired of the drama. 'Are Giddy an Pips staying to dinner?' she asked, her wide eyes looking from one to the other and back to her father.

'Er . . .?' Sean looked enquiringly.

'You're very welcome,' Cathy assured them.

'Thanks, but I'm afraid I have to get back to feed the horses,' Pippa said regretfully.

Cathy looked a lot more disappointed than her husband, Gideon thought. It appeared that he wasn't completely forgiven, in spite of the apology.

*

By the time Pippa dropped Gideon off at the Gatehouse, refusing his offer of help with the horses, it was getting on for six o'clock and completely dark. Rachel's Mini was parked by the gate, and as Gideon turned from waving to Pippa, Rachel herself emerged from it, almost as if she had been waiting for him.

'Hi,' he said cheerfully. 'Did you have a good day?'

'Busy. I've got to go back on Thursday. You?'

'Great, yeah. Thoroughly lazy, I'm afraid.'

They began to walk towards the house together and Gideon could sense Rachel's tension like electricity in the air.

'What's the matter? You haven't seen Duke again, have you?'

'No. I've been watching the house. I don't think there's anyone around.'

Gideon turned to look at her in the glow of the porch light, which he'd taken to leaving on as a precaution in these uncertain times.

'How long have you been watching the house?'

Rachel avoided his searching gaze. 'About half an hour, maybe longer.'

Gideon tilted her chin up with a finger. 'The truth,' he said quietly.

'All right, nearly an hour. I was scared. I knew you weren't there and I didn't want to be trapped again. At least in my car I'm mobile.' She was patently agitated, and Gideon felt a twinge of guilt. He should have been back earlier.

He let them both into the house and proceeded

to check all the rooms for intruders, ostensibly for Rachel's benefit but in truth, ever since the night of his abduction, he'd experienced some difficulty in relaxing until he was sure the house wasn't harbouring any undesirables.

The night was quiet. A steady drizzle fell outside, and inside Gideon worked on his portrait while Rachel curled up in front of the fire with a novel and a glass of wine.

Around eleven o'clock Gideon rubbed tired eyes, pushed his tray of chalk pastels away from him and switched the angle-poise off. Yawning, he wandered into the sitting room and discovered Rachel fast asleep in the corner of the sofa, her book spread-eagled on the floor and Elsa on her lap. Remembering what had happened the last time he'd awakened her in a similar situation, Gideon bent and blew softly on her face. Slowly, and with no fuss, Rachel's eyelids flickered and began to open.

Immediately Gideon stepped back.

'It's all right for some. Having time to fall asleep in front of the fire!'

'Mm. Well, it's been a long day,' she said, stretching with feline grace. 'And some of us had to work.'

Elsa jumped off her knee, cross at being disturbed, and Gideon tried not to look at Rachel's slim curves; they encouraged thoughts that for the time being were much better not explored.

*

Gideon had an appointment the next day with a farmer in a neighbouring village who trained point-to-pointers for a hobby. He'd recently taken on a young horse that showed a great deal of promise, 'If,' as his exasperated trainer had complained to Gideon the previous week, 'we can ever get him to the bloody racecourse!' The problem seemed to be a deep-rooted fear of travelling by horsebox, and the trainer, with whom Gideon had worked before, had appealed to him for help.

When he had agreed to see the horse the Duke Shelley situation hadn't existed, but it was obvious as he got ready to leave the house that morning that Rachel was not at all comfortable with the prospect of being left on her own. She had come down to breakfast pale and heavy-eyed, and had shadowed him ever since, as if afraid he would go without telling her.

Finally, as he shrugged his leather jacket on over a thick jumper, uncomfortably aware that she was watching him, dark-eyed, from the sitting-room doorway, he took pity on her and, warning her that she'd probably be bored stiff, offered to take her along.

They made the short journey in the warmth and relative comfort of the Mini, and were met at their destination by a ruddy-cheeked, middle-aged man wearing a flat cap, tweed jacket and trousers held up by baler twine.

Gideon introduced Rachel as a friend of Pippa's, come to watch him work.

Rachel smiled at the farmer; a wide, sweet smile

peculiarly her own, and said anxiously, 'I hope you don't mind my turning up like this? Gideon said it would be all right.'

'Mind?' Quentin repeated. 'You've made my day! Well, I suppose we'd better go and sort out this pesky animal. I've parked the box in the drive because I've been working on it all morning, but actually I think that's as good a place as any to try and load him. Come and see what you think.'

They left the Mini in front of the plain red-brick farmhouse and skirted the building and the towering bulk of the lorry, to reach the yard at the back, where alongside a tractor shed, henhouses and a barn, six looseboxes stood. Six long aristocratic heads appeared as if by magic over the half-doors and six pairs of nostrils fluttered in greeting.

'They're pleased to see you,' Rachel observed with pleasure as they stopped a few feet short of the stables.

'They think it's getting near their lunchtime is more like it,' Quentin said with a laugh. 'But it's nice to see, even so.'

'Which is the problem boy?' Gideon asked.

Quentin opened his mouth, half-raising his hand, then stopped. 'You tell me,' he invited.

Gideon raised an eyebrow. 'It'll cost you extra,' he warned.

'Well, I've got to call your bluff now and again. Make sure you're not having me on.'

Without further ado, Gideon went forward.

All the horses strained towards him except one, a coltish bay with wide-spaced, intelligent eyes, which regarded his approach with a slight flattening of its small ears. He ignored it, walking past without stopping and pretending not to notice the flash of temper that was directed at his back as he passed. He spoke to the other five: two amiable bays, a grey that was touchy about its ears, another grey, and one a chestnut who tried half-heartedly to nip him.

Gideon turned back to the first bay, who by now was banging its door, furious at having been passed by. The horse quieted as he approached, once again flattening its ears and, when he turned to face it, backing off a pace or two into its box, from where it continued to eye him.

Gideon deliberately went closer, leaning provocatively on the half-door.

After a moment or two of indecision, the bay took two quick steps forward and snaked its head towards him, teeth bared and ears flat against its skull. Instantly, and without conscious thought, Gideon slapped it hard across the nose.

The bay threw its head up and retreated hastily. Then, thoughtfully and from a safe distance, it proceeded to regard the human who had challenged it.

Gideon half-turned away as if losing interest. This was the crunch point. If he'd read the horse right it would take the opportunity he'd offered to approach without losing face. If not, he'd have to move fast to avoid being the victim of a powerful set of teeth.

A long moment passed, during which Gideon sensed rather than saw the horse capitulating, its ears flicking back and forth, its jaws working in a chewing motion. Then, with one slow step and a pause to gauge his reaction – carefully non-existent – the bay made up its mind to approach. Within moments it was standing with its head over the half-door, next to Gideon if not precisely close. He didn't attempt to touch it. It had made sacrifice enough for the time being. After they'd studiously ignored one another for a minute or so, he spoke quietly to the horse before walking back to the waiting pair.

'That was one of the strangest things I've ever seen,' Rachel said as he approached, then turning to Quentin, 'He got it right, didn't he?'

'We'll see,' the farmer said, watching Gideon through narrowed eyes. 'Well, young fella. What do you say? Which one is my problem horse?'

'The grey in the middle box,' he stated.

Rachel frowned. 'But, I don't understand . . .'

Quentin chuckled delightedly. 'That's why this guy is doing what he's doing and the likes of you and me's standing here watching, my girl. Yes, Molly is the one. I thought Rattler might try it on with you,' he added to Gideon.

'Yeah, he's an absolute classic Alpha. He'd need another session or two before I'd be sure of him.'

Quentin grunted. 'Took me two months.'

'Nice horse, though. They're nearly always the most intelligent. The most trouble and the greatest reward.'

'Not always the best for racing.'

'There is that.'

Rachel cleared her throat pointedly. 'If you're trying to make me feel left out, you can stop now. Mission accomplished.'

They apologised.

'So at the risk of sounding a complete ignoramus, what *is* an Alpha? And why is the grey horse the problem and not the bay?'

'An Alpha is what it sounds like – literally; the first one, a natural leader,' Gideon explained.

'A stallion.'

'A stallion *is* usually an Alpha, yes. But there are Alpha mares too. Usually the Alpha mare is second-in-command to the stallion. She's his favourite and often has more say in what the herd do and where they go than the stallion does. He's got other things on his mind, such as sex and fighting off challengers. You get Alphas in every species that naturally lives in herds or packs, but dogs and horses are the most noticeable because they're the ones we mostly try to train. Alphas are usually very intelligent and also very strong-willed, so they're not about to give up their dominant position to any Tom, Dick or Harry. You have to win their respect but, if you can do it, the relationship is very special.'

'I never realised it was so complicated, though I suppose I've never really thought about it.'

'Not many people do,' Gideon said with regret. 'And probably something like eighty percent of the problems people come to me with are the result of the wrong people owning the wrong animal. Alpha dogs and horses need Alpha people.'

'And Molly? Is she an Alpha too?'

'No. Molly is a nice everyday sort who suffers badly from claustrophobia.'

'Honestly?' Rachel said warily. 'No. You're having me on, surely?'

'I knew she wasn't happy,' Quentin put in. 'She doesn't do well when she's stabled. Picky about her food, that sort of thing. But what can I do? I can't get her hard fit on grass.'

'You're serious!' Rachel said, looking from one to the other in wonderment. 'I thought horses liked being stabled. Warm and dry and safe.'

'Most do,' Gideon agreed. 'They usually become accustomed to it very quickly but it goes against all their natural instincts nonetheless. I mean, what does a horse do if you startle it?'

'Runs away? Ah, I see what you mean. In a stable it can't.'

'That's right. But most horses soon learn to settle indoors. I suspect the grey mare has had a bad experience or has been shut in too small a space at some time.'

He glanced at Quentin who shrugged his shoulders. 'I wouldn't know, lad. She was bought at a sale. Are you saying she won't be any good?'

Gideon shook his head. 'I wouldn't go that far. If it's possible, and you think she's worth it, I'd try to get her into a covered pen with open sides. Even if you have to put a New Zealand rug on her. She'd feel a lot less shut in.'

'She's worth it. One of the most promising I've

ever trained. But what about the lorry? Will we ever get her into that?'

'Well, I don't s'pose she'll ever enjoy it but maybe we can get her to tolerate it at least. We'll give it a try.'

Quentin went in search of a headcollar but Rachel was still puzzled.

'So, how do you know what's going on in these horses' heads? You're surely not expecting me to believe that they talk to you?'

Gideon smiled faintly and shook his head. 'No.'

'Then how?'

He looked up and away to the horizon, trying to find the words to explain, but as always, they wouldn't come. He sighed. 'It's . . . well . . . instinct, I suppose,' he said lamely. 'You have to see the world from the animal's point of view. There are only a limited number of issues that figure in a horse's world, when all's said and done. It's purely a matter of hitting on the right one. Discounting the misplaced Alpha's, almost all problems have their root in fear.'

Quentin led the grey from the stable and took her rugs off. She was a tallish, good-looking animal that could have done with a bit more flesh on her bones. Even from where she stood, some thirty feet away from the lorry, she eyed the vehicle with apprehension.

Quietly, Gideon went to work.

After ten minutes or so of familiarisation, he was satisfied that he'd established his role as leader. The grey was following him around happily with no pressure at all on the lead rope, stopping and turning whenever he did. She'd walked past the lorry several times; the ramp was raised and lowered beside her; the engine switched on and off; and finally, when she'd accepted these things as harmless, Gideon attempted to lead her inside.

The lorry had been positioned on a slight slope so the angle of the ramp was not too steep, and although Molly approached it without any trouble she stopped short of actually stepping on to the slatted walkway. Tossing her head, she tried to pull back towards the other horses.

They had opened the groom's door at the front of the compartment and removed all the partitions but the grey still viewed the gloomy interior with trepidation. Gideon could feel the horse's conflict. She was conditioned to do as she was told and wanted to, but instinct held her back.

Careful not to look at her, Gideon stepped on to the ramp himself. The grey stiffened and threw her head up but didn't pull back. After a moment, Gideon walked slowly all the way up the ramp and into the box with the horse one step behind.

Once inside the lorry, the grey began to regret her co-operation. She shifted her weight restlessly, pushing Gideon with her nose and trying to turn round. Gideon spoke softly to her, gently rubbing circles on the dappled grey neck. The horse quietened but Gideon could feel her trembling and her coat was damp with sweat.

Somewhere at the front of the house a car door slammed and Molly started, eyes rolling anxiously.

'Whoa, silly girl. You know what that is. Nobody's going to hurt you. Just a moment more and we'll go back out, okay?'

The horse flicked her ears to and fro, not understanding the words but taking comfort from the tone. Feeling she'd done enough for one day, Gideon gave her one final scratch under her mane and prepared to turn her towards the ramp.

Beside the lorry someone shouted, 'You in there, Pops?' and thumped on the metal sheeting of the bodywork with enough force to wake the dead.

Molly's nerve broke. Instinct took over and flight became imperative. Too bad for Gideon that he was in the way.

With his size, Gideon was probably a good deal stronger than the average man, but compared to that of a panicking horse his strength was totally inconsequential. Molly whipped round, cannoning into him and slamming him into the inner bodywork of the box with an impact that drove every vestige of breath from his lungs. The lead rein that he'd been loosely holding whipped round his arm and dragged him sideways for an instant before it pulled free, as with a flurry of iron-shod hooves the thoroughbred launched herself down the ramp.

Lying full-length on the rubber matting that carpeted the floor of the lorry, Gideon could think of nothing for a moment except to be glad he'd learned at an early age never to wrap any kind of lead rein around his hand for better grip. If he'd done so in this instance, he could now have either been short of several fingers or being dragged across the gravel of the yard behind the wildly galloping horse. Neither prospect held much attraction.

The sense of having had a lucky escape filled him with gratitude for all of ten seconds. That was about how long it took for the multitude of ill-treated nerve endings to organise their protest to his brain. As the brief stunning effect of the impact passed, his left arm, shoulder and shoulder-blade all began to shout for his attention, but they had to compete with the agony of his forcibly deflated lungs.

He could hear Quentin and Rachel approaching, calling his name with touching concern, and wished them a million miles away. All he needed, for a moment, was time alone.

He wasn't going to get it.

'Gideon lad, are you all right? Did she tread on you?'

Gideon shook his head. No to both questions, he thought grimly. With an effort he looked up. Quentin stood at the top of the ramp, bending towards him, his face creased with anxiety. Behind him, Rachel looked white and shaken. He supposed he must look at least as bad as he felt. In an attempt to reassure them both he managed a smile.

It didn't seem to have the desired effect. Rachel burst into tears.

'I never meant to frighten her,' a new voice protested. 'I thought it was you in there, Dad, working on the lorry like you was this morning.'

Gideon was coping with shallow breaths now.

He gritted his teeth and sat up. The faces above him swam about in an annoying fashion until he blinked and they settled again.

Quentin was finding release for his fright in berating his unhappy offspring, who had begun to whine and deny all responsibility. Rachel was sniffing quietly.

'Look, it was a misunderstanding,' Gideon said soothingly. Back on his feet, he felt battered and bruised but didn't think there were any broken bones. It was much like falling off the bike, really, and he'd done that a few times, heaven knew.

'See? It was a misunderstanding,' Quentin's son declared sulkily. 'I told you!'

'Why don't you do something useful?' his father asked. 'Go and catch the horse.'

'Er . . . No offence meant but if you don't mind, I'd rather do that myself,' Gideon suggested. 'I want to make sure she doesn't associate me with the fright she's had.'

A quarter of an hour later, having politely refused all anxious offers of hospitality, Gideon eased himself gingerly into the passenger seat of the Mini, wincing a little as his back came into contact with the seat.

Rachel was watching him closely. 'Are you *sure* you're all right?' she asked for the umpteenth time.

'It's nothing that a good hot bath and a stiff drink won't put right,' he reassured her, wishing he could believe it himself. He'd a notion he was in for an exceedingly uncomfortable night and, judging by her expression, his optimism didn't fool Rachel either.

She was very quiet on the return journey, in spite of Gideon's assurances that incidents like the one she had witnessed were very much the exception rather than the rule. He could see she'd convinced herself that his line of work was second only to Mafia bodyguard in its potential for serious risk. He gave up, attempting instead to divert her thoughts to other matters.

They arrived back at the Gatehouse with Rachel having been coaxed into a marginally less anxious state of mind, which good work was abruptly overturned by the discovery of a note from Duke pinned to the front door.

Gideon cursed under his breath as he detached the slip of paper and read the angular, childish writing. It was written on a small sheet of lined paper that had obviously been torn from a spiral-bound notepad. Dated at the top of the sheet with yesterday's date, the next few lines consisted of precise times listed on the left-hand side, coupled with observations on the right.

08.45 – Rachel leaves in Mini.
09.15 – Gideon leaves the house on foot going to the Priory.
14.35 – Gideon and Pippa drive past in Volkswagen heading for main road.
17.05 – Rachel back. Sits in Mini. (Scared to go in?)
18.17 – Gideon back.

And so it went on, up to and including the hour and minute that they had left the house that morning.

Underneath this meticulous list he had written:

Just wanted you to know I was still around.
D.S.

Beside him, Gideon could feel Rachel beginning to tremble. He quickly unlocked the front door and, putting his arm round her shoulders, marched her firmly indoors.

'No, don't look back! It's what he wants, if he's still there. Don't give him the satisfaction.' He pushed the door shut with his foot and turned Rachel to face him. Her dark eyes looked helplessly up at him, and the terror in them moved Gideon to uncharacteristic anger.

'He won't hurt you, you know. I won't let him get to you.'

Rachel scanned his face, desperately seeking reassurance. Whatever she saw there obviously didn't do the trick, for her eyes became misty with tears.

'I know you'll do everything you can, but what if he's got a gun? If he's over there in the wood, we'd never even see him . . .' She gulped. 'I don't want you to get hurt on my account.'

Her words jolted Gideon. He hadn't considered the possibility of a gun.

'Has he had guns before?'

'Once.' Rachel nodded. 'He brought one back

217

from the pub one night and teased me with it but I don't know if it was loaded. It didn't matter, he knew I was terrified.'

Gideon put his undamaged arm round her and pulled her gently towards him, kissing the top of her head. 'Poor lamb,' he murmured softly. 'When they locked him up, they should've thrown away the key.'

Rachel leaned against him, clinging like a child and bringing Gideon's bruises sharply to his attention.

'I used to hope he'd die in prison,' she said in a voice that was perilously close to breaking. 'You hear of it, don't you? People being found dead; attacked by the other prisoners. Five years seemed such a long time. I thought anything might happen. I suppose I just didn't want to face the fact that one day he'd be free again.'

'Shhh,' Gideon said, sensing her rising panic. 'Let's get something to drink, shall we? I know I could do with it. Coffee would be good.'

She nodded, drawing away from him reluctantly and heading for the kitchen. The sudden ringing of the telephone stopped her in her tracks and she looked sharply at it, and then back at Gideon.

'I'll get it,' he said, walking forward. 'You get the coffee.'

He lifted the receiver, warily.

'Gideon. Hi!' the voice on the other end of the line greeted him cheerfully, and he breathed a small sigh of relief, in spite of himself. He was tired and aching and not over anxious for any more tussles that day, be they physical or verbal.

'Giles,' he said gratefully. 'What can I do for you?'

'Pippa and I are having a small dinner party this evening,' Giles announced. 'And we wondered if you and Rachel would like to come along?'

'How small?' Gideon asked doubtfully, feeling that Rachel probably wasn't in the best of moods for socialising, and that after the effects of several hours' stiffening on wrenched muscles and joints, he mightn't be either.

'Well, just us four, actually,' Giles admitted. 'But I thought "dinner party" sounded more impressive.'

Gideon laughed. 'Well, okay, thanks. As long as we're not expected to wear evening dress,' he added, reflecting that on balance it would be for the best if Rachel were out of the house that evening.

Giles was pleased. 'Great! I've got a new case of wine I want your opinion on. Just bought it at an auction.'

'You mean, you want to use me as an excuse to open a bottle of it.'

'Well, wine is meant to be shared and it's wasted on Pippa. She can't tell a five-hundred-pound bottle from supermarket plonk. "As long as it's fruity," she says. I ask you! What *did* they teach her at that catering school?'

'Goodness knows,' Gideon said, not at all sure he could do any better than Giles' sister in the matter of wine-tasting.

When Giles rang off, Gideon telephoned the local police, who were inclined to take the business of the note with its record of observations seriously, and promised to send someone round right away.

They were as good as their word. Barely had Gideon reported the gist of the two conversations to Rachel as she made coffee on the Aga than somebody knocked heavily on the front door.

Rachel jumped visibly, spilling hot milk on to the hotplate, where it smoked and burned.

'That'll be the police, I expect,' Gideon said, hoping it was.

The two officers at the door, Constables Hillcott and Roach, were the two who'd come when Gideon had reported his abduction, what now seemed like a lifetime ago.

He showed them into the sitting room, where they perched awkwardly on the edges of the soft leather armchairs, as if to relax would somehow undermine their authority. Gideon sank back on to the sofa with an inner smile. Body language spoke volumes, whatever the species.

Rachel, who made extra cups of coffee and handed them out, seemed a little ill-at-ease around them but Gideon noticed wryly that they unbent noticeably in the presence of a pretty girl and became far more eager to please.

They listened to Gideon's report of Duke Shelley's activities, read and took charge of the note, and told Rachel that everyone at the station had been made aware of her case and that they were confident Duke would soon be apprehended.

Rachel didn't appear much comforted.

As Gideon showed the officers out, one of them stopped on the doorstep.

'We heard from the lads at Chilminster that *they* had a visit from you too, on *another* matter. Busy sort of chap, aren't you? If you go on like this you'll have to have a task force assigned 'specially to you!' He leaned closer to Gideon. 'I think perhaps you like the attention, that's what *I* think.'

Gideon forced himself not to recoil from the waft of smoky breath that accompanied the remark. He leaned even closer. 'You know what? As long as you do your job, I don't give a damn what you think.'

Unable to come up with a suitable reply, the constable gave him a look heavy with dislike, turned on his heel and followed his colleague to the car.

9

The evening went well, all things considered.

The grey skies had cleared after dusk and it was a cold, frosty night. Gideon's first impulse was to walk up to the Priory but thoughts of Duke Shelley lurking menacingly in the undergrowth made him decide, reluctantly, that the car was a safer option. He hated to let the man dictate his actions – it was like acknowledging a defeat, however small – but there was another person in the equation and in his present, less than athletic, state he couldn't guarantee Rachel protection. Besides, he added to himself, there was the possibility of a gun to consider. Much better to concede the skirmish for the sake of the war.

They travelled the few hundred yards to the Priory with Gideon at the wheel of Rachel's Mini, in spite of her protesting that she ought to drive.

'Well, what would you do if Duke jumped out in front of us?' Gideon quizzed her.

'I think I'd run him down,' she said darkly.

Gideon gave her a hard look and wasn't at all sure she was joking. 'My point exactly,' he said, twitching the keys out of her hand. 'I'll drive.'

Pippa and Giles were in high spirits. Mrs Morecambe had been given the evening off and Pippa was revelling in having the kitchen to herself. Or at least, she would have been, she informed Gideon and Rachel on their arrival, if she could only get Giles out from under her feet.

'Now you've come,' she said thankfully to Gideon, 'you can go off together and admire cases of dusty old bottles down in the cellar with the spiders, while Rachel and I put the finishing touches to the meal. I'll apologise in advance for the red wine sauce. It's had to be white wine as that's all I could find in the larder and Giles wouldn't let me have anything from his precious store.'

'For cooking?' her brother exclaimed, scandalised. 'I should think not! You don't know what you're asking. Come on, Gideon. Let's leave these Philistines to their crude arts and occupy our minds with higher things!'

He headed for the door, leaving Gideon to shrug helplessly and follow, as Pippa spluttered with indignation behind him.

'I take it you won't be interested in the product of these crude arts,' she called after them.

Giles' voice floated back accompanied by laughter. 'Oh, I expect we'll force ourselves.'

Giles Barrington-Carr's wine cellar was deep in the bowels of the old Priory and quite as dusty and spidery as Pippa had suggested. Remembering the neat, almost surgical cleanliness of Rosetti's cellar, Gideon was struck by the contrast. Now he came to think of it though, there had been an armchair and a filing cabinet in the corner of Rosetti's cellar, and his wife said he spent a lot of time down there. Giles' cellar definitely didn't lend itself to thoughts of relaxing in armchairs.

He proudly displayed for Gideon's benefit several dozen bottles adorned with the name of some revered French château that he'd frankly never heard of, and promised they'd sample the contents of one of them with their meal.

'Even the Philistines?'

'Well, I suppose they could have a little glass,' Giles conceded.

'How do you know, when you pay thousands for a case of wine, that it's any good?' Gideon asked, his mind, as so often, running on unconventional lines. 'Or even,' he said, going a step further, 'that there's any wine in them at all? It might be Ribena or something.'

Giles looked askance. 'They *do* come with provenance.'

'Yes, but who's to say the wine is really as good as it's reputed to be? It's a bit like abstract art. It's given so much hype by the promoters that everyone's afraid to admit they don't know what the hell it is, and that it's hideous anyway.'

'But you'd know when you tried it, wouldn't

you?' Giles pointed out. 'The wine, I mean.'

'Yes, but who's to say that *your* taste is the same as Joe Bloggs' in the next château?' Gideon persisted. 'One man's vinegar might be another man's nectar.'

Giles looked at him suspiciously. 'You're arguing for the sake of it, aren't you, you bugger? Just trying to wind me up!'

'It's good sport,' Gideon agreed. 'But seriously, I've had home-made wine produced in a year or so on somebody's kitchen table that was as good as anything I've had with a fancy name on it, that's spent decades maturing in oak vats or whatever you call them.'

Giles looked disgusted. 'You're as much a Philistine as my sister. I'm obviously wasting my time trying to educate you.'

'Think of it as a challenge,' Gideon said helpfully, wishing at the same time that Giles' cellar actually did have an armchair. His sore muscles were aching. 'Actually, I saw another wine cellar yesterday, not as venerable as this one, perhaps, but it was a working one with all the gubbins for production of the noble juice.'

'Yes, Pippa told me. At the vet's place, wasn't it? Does he have his own vines, or does he use concentrate?'

'I don't honestly know. I shouldn't have thought he had time for vines but I suppose his wife might have, she seemed the efficient sort.'

'And pretty, according to my sister,' Giles remarked with a sidelong look.

'And taken,' Gideon said firmly.

'Yeah, shame. Anyway, I'm going to try making wine myself in the old pantry. I might even set up a vineyard.'

'Well, it's an improvement on ostriches, I suppose.'

Giles gave him a withering look. 'You've no sense of adventure, that's your problem. Come and have a look at the gear I've bought.'

'Okay. But only if I can look sitting down. I got mown down by a startled horse this morning and I'm in dire need of a soft chair to sink into.'

'Not having much luck with horses lately, are you?' Giles observed, selecting two bottles from his store. 'Ever occur to you, you might be losing your touch?'

'Frequently.'

Giles' new purchases occupied most of the shelves in what was known as the butler's pantry; a small, windowless room whose white-painted, stone walls were divided into cubicles about two feet square.

Gideon looked around him at the wealth of equipment accumulated. There seemed to be at least a dozen of everything. Ear-handled glass jars, wooden casks, plastic buckets, funnels, a pack of wooden spoons, rolls of white muslin, several large plastic dustbins, yards of tubing, multitudes of squiggly devices that Giles identified as fermentation locks, empty bottles by the boxful and corks by the hundred.

'Wow!' Gideon said, taken aback even though

he should have been accustomed by then to Giles'
whole-hearted immersion in anything that caught
his imagination. 'All you need now are some
grapes. What's that instrument of torture over
there?'

Giles followed his gaze. 'It's a fruit crusher.'

'Only one?' Gideon queried, an eyebrow raised.
'Besides, I thought you were supposed to trample
the grapes.'

'Grapes you can trample – if you want to –
apples and pears are not so comfortable.'

'Oh, I see. Branching out already. Well, I'm all
for expansion.'

'You may scoff now, but just you wait. I might
surprise you.'

'You might at that.' Gideon looked around
again. 'Rosetti had a couple of big metal canisters.
You don't seem to have got any of those. Don't tell
me you've missed something.'

Giles frowned. 'They could have been boilers, I
suppose. I can't think what else. You usually steer
clear of metal in winemaking, especially for
storage. It taints the wine. Ends up tasting metallic.
Foul!'

Gideon smiled to himself. Giles was already an
authority.

Dinner, when it was served, was predictably
excellent. The combined talents of Pippa, with her
training, and Rachel, with her natural flair, had
produced a meal that would have aroused justifiable pride in the breast of any top chef.

'I've always said you were wasted as an equestrienne,' Giles told his sister handsomely. 'Women should confine themselves to the kitchen where they so obviously belong. I've said it time and time again.'

Rachel gasped with indignation but Pippa merely smiled sweetly. 'I refuse to rise to that kind of male chauvinism. But just for that, you can do the washing-up!'

Giles groaned. 'Can't we leave it to mournful Millie?'

'Well, that's hardly fair, is it? Giving her the night off and then letting her come back to a loaded sink! And don't keep calling her that. You'll say it to her face one day!'

Gideon laughed at Giles' expression, enjoying the banter between brother and sister. Enjoying too the ambience of the centuries-old, candlelit dining room, the food, and the all-too-rare relaxed happiness evident in Rachel's face. She was laughing now as Giles related the latest chapter in the terriers' ongoing harassment of Mrs Morecambe, her clear skin honey-toned in the soft light and her huge dark eyes sparkling.

Gideon looked from her to Pippa's strong, boyish features, under her mop of wayward curls, and wondered how two people could be so completely different and yet equally attractive.

'Giddy's looking very serious,' Pippa said then. She'd been calling him by Daisy's childish name all evening. 'Too much wine? Or not enough, perhaps?'

'He's brooding over his lost powers,' Giles told her. 'He got flattened by a horse again this morning.'

'What do you mean, *again?* I haven't been flattened for months,' Gideon responded indignantly.

'And it wasn't *his* fault!' Rachel stepped in defensively. 'It was the farmer's stupid son, banging on the horsebox.'

'It's not the animals you have to worry about, it's the people,' Pippa agreed, adding solicitously, 'Were you very much flattened?'

'Completely,' Gideon said ruefully.

'The horse wasn't hurt, I hope?'

'The horse was fine.'

Rachel looked from one to the other incredulously. 'Why shouldn't the horse be all right? She wasn't the one who got flattened!'

Pippa laughed. 'It's a long-standing joke of ours, Rachel. You see a crashing fall point-to-pointing or eventing, and everyone's first concern seems to be for the horse; never mind that the rider's breathing his last a few feet away.'

'Oh, I see,' Rachel said doubtfully. 'Still, it *was* very frightening.'

'Oh, you don't want to worry about Gideon. He bounces.'

'No sense, no feeling,' Giles put in heartlessly.

'When you've quite finished . . .' Gideon protested. 'If you can't be sympathetic, then kindly keep your thoughts to yourselves. Now, I don't know about you, but I think I should move from

229

this chair before it becomes an integral part of my anatomy!'

The four of them cleared away the dinner things and transferred them to the kitchen where they discovered that somebody had left the door open, allowing Yip and Yap access to the remains of the first course; access of which the terriers had taken full and unashamed advantage.

The party broke up shortly after midnight, with Pippa complaining that *she* had to get up early the next morning, even if nobody else had to, and Gideon drove sleepily home, glad he wasn't on a public highway, with Rachel drowsily content at his side.

With deference to his bruises, Gideon spent most of the next couple of days at the Gatehouse working on the portrait. Rachel was also busy preparing plans, drawings and samples for her clients in Bournemouth.

They had heard nothing more from or about her ex-husband, and a shopping trip to Blandford on the third day passed without incident, but on their way back to the Gatehouse, Gideon began to wonder uneasily if it had been a wise idea to leave the place unprotected.

What if Duke had broken in, in their absence? He wouldn't put it past the man to trash the place out of spite. Elsa was too wary of strangers to come to any harm but the portrait was there on its easel; hours of work that could be completely undone with barely any effort at all. Starting from scratch

on a project that was all but finished was something that didn't bear thinking about.

Happily, there was no evidence of unwanted
visitors either outside or in. Wondering briefly if he
was allowing himself to be unduly affected by
Rachel's paranoia, Gideon nevertheless made a
call to his picture framer and arranged to drop the
portrait off after lunch.

Rachel had arranged to go riding with Pippa that
afternoon and Gideon accompanied her to the
Priory to beg the use of the runabout.

'Why don't you get yourself a sensible vehicle,
for heavensakes?' Pippa protested. 'I should have
thought you'd grown out of the motorbike phase at
your age.'

'Well, my free bus pass should be coming
through any day now,' Gideon told her through the
open window of the vehicle. 'But seriously, if I had
my own car, I wouldn't have any excuse for coming
up here to be scolded by you, would I? And you
know how gorgeous you are when you're cross!'

He made a prudent getaway at that point,
driving the thirty miles or so to Bridport with one
eye on his rear-view mirror – which remained
empty, as far as he could tell, of any suspicious
vehicles – and with his thoughts on the complex
turn his life had taken of late.

What with the unresolved affair of his abduction,
which seemed even to him oddly remote and
dreamlike now; his involvement with the troubles
at the Sanctuary; and now the business with
Rachel and Duke, he could well believe he'd

occasioned some comment amongst the local constabulary. How could someone as laid-back and instinctively solitary as himself become embroiled in so many other people's troubles in such a short time? he wondered.

It was a relief to offload Tom's portrait on the framer. Framing and mounting can make or ruin a picture and Gideon had never been tempted to do the job himself. The Bridport man had an unerring eye for style and colour, and the end result always justified the last nought on Gideon's prices.

Having accomplished his mission, he found himself back on the road with a couple of hours to spare. It occurred to him that he hadn't heard from Naomi and Tim for the best part of a week – not, in fact, since he'd rung them to report on his meeting with Milne the previous Saturday – and keyed in their number on his mobile phone.

There was no answer from the Sanctuary office, and as he headed back towards Dorchester, Gideon tried to raise Naomi on her own mobile with equally negative results. Maybe they'd got trouble with one of the animals.

He decided to investigate.

It was by this time getting on for four o'clock and although the sun wouldn't actually set for another hour and a half, the dull skies made it seem like twilight already.

It was more than that, Gideon realised after a few minutes as he turned off the A-road on to the back road that led ultimately to Lyddon Grange and the farm. The low sun was being obscured not only by clouds but also by a haze of smoke emanating from somewhere beyond the trees.

The road dipped between high hedges and for a moment the sky was lost to view but as he emerged from the trees Gideon saw that the volume of smoke had not diminished. It had if anything increased, rolling and eddying as the wind caught it, and the vague hope that it was the product of an oversized bonfire rather than something more serious was reluctantly abandoned.

An uneasy suspicion began to form in Gideon's mind and he stood on the accelerator, at the same time tapping nine, nine, nine into his mobile phone with his left thumb.

The operator listened and then thanked him. 'We are aware of that incident, sir, and already responding. An appliance should be with you shortly. Please keep well back and don't block the road.'

Gideon threw the phone on to the seat beside him and concentrated on his driving. The acrid smell of the smoke had begun to filter through the car's ventilation system now, and as he approached the Grange it became obvious that the seat of the fire was beyond it. It had to be the Sanctuary.

Flinging Pippa's hatchback round the last bend and into the farm track, Gideon nearly put it into the hedge as he came face to face with two careering donkeys. The poor creatures skidded to a halt, heads high and jostling one another in fright, but clearly the horror they had fled from was greater, for they made no attempt to retreat up the track.

Gideon got out of the car, cursing under his breath. Desperate as he was to get up to the farm and find out what the situation was there, the donkeys could clearly not be abandoned to their fate. Left to their own devices they would almost certainly run out on to the road where, even if they escaped being mown down by the approaching fire engine, it was highly likely that they would be involved in some kind of accident.

There was no time for calming techniques or subtle body language. The two creatures were patently terrified. They crowded into the hedge as Gideon approached, their minds muddled by panic and unable to separate real threat from imagined. About five yards beyond them he could see a gate that led into the adjacent field, and edging cautiously past he went to investigate, hoping they wouldn't, in the meantime, try to squeeze past the car which he'd left parked across the track.

The gate, which proved to be one of the few metal ones Gideon had seen at the Sanctuary, was securely locked with a very business-like new padlock; legacy, no doubt, of the trouble they had been having over the past few weeks. He swore and transferred his attention to the hinge end.

Bingo! How utterly like Tim to bar the front door and leave the back door open, as it were.

Lifting the long farm gate off its rusting post required a lot more effort than his damaged shoulder appreciated, but it couldn't be helped. Way off in the distance he could hear the siren of the approaching fire engine and, as he struggled with the gate, had an awful picture in his mind of it crashing into the stationary car, flattening the hapless donkeys and effectively blocking the lane completely to any further access.

With the gate as wide open as the protesting catch would allow, Gideon slipped back past the two mouse-coloured beasts and advanced upon them once more, waving his arms up and down and slapping his thighs. They regarded him warily but refused to budge, so he ran at them, pulling off his jacket and walloping the nearest animal with it to great effect. They both took to their heels, one giving voice in its terror, and rocketed straight past the gateway.

Gideon could have screamed his frustration. The next moment, however, the two fleeing donkeys were met by another coming equally fast in the opposite direction. They turned back again and the three of them, faced with Gideon once more, diverted into the field and relative safety. Hoping that there were no more donkeys heading his way, Gideon dragged the gate shut but didn't attempt to lift it back on to its hinges. He'd no idea how many donkeys might be running loose around the farm. He'd already seen three more than he'd expected to see.

He sprinted for the car, which he'd left with its door open and the engine running. A quick shunt to and fro straightened it up and with wheel-spinning acceleration he resumed his interrupted journey.

The yard was in chaos.

Gideon left Pippa's car well away from the buildings, where he hoped it would be both safe and out of the way of the emergency vehicles when they arrived.

There was so much smoke it was difficult to see which part of the buildings was actually ablaze. The wind blew it everywhere in choking black clouds, and every now and then a tongue of flame would shoot skywards with a roar and a shower of sparks. As a gust of wind lifted the dark veil momentarily, Gideon saw with a sinking heart that not only the newly renovated farmhouse but also the mobile home and both blocks of stables were well alight.

He could hear someone shouting, possibly Naomi, and pausing only to dunk his cotton neckerchief in the water trough and tie it over his nose and mouth, he headed for the long gravel walkway between the animal quarters.

Halfway across the yard, and with a feeling of unreality, he almost collided with yet another donkey. Where were they all coming from? In the next instant though, all thoughts of donkeys were abruptly driven from his mind as something tangled around his running feet and brought him crashing to his knees. The 'something' turned out to be a child's bicycle.

Jez's bicycle?

My God! Gideon begged silently. Please don't tell me *she's* here!

'Jez!' he yelled as he scrambled to his feet. 'Jez!'

Someone loomed out of the gloom, too tall to be the child.

'Naomi! Where's Jez?' Gideon shouted urgently, his relief at seeing his sister quickly overwhelmed by his fear for the child.

'Gideon!' Naomi's face was partly covered by what had once been a white tea towel and her eyes, above it, were red-rimmed, watering and wide with surprise at seeing him there. 'Thank God you're here! Tim's trying to catch the owl in the end cage and I don't know where the donkeys have gone, I just let them out. They could be anywhere!'

Filthy dirty and trying to subdue the frightened struggles of a rabbit she held to her chest, Naomi sounded desperate but Gideon had no time even to reassure her about the donkeys.

'Where's Jez?' he repeated, grasping her arm and speaking close to her ear.

'She's not here. She's gone home,' Naomi shouted back. 'Look, can you help Tim? He won't leave that bird and I'm afraid he'll be trapped. The fire's awful down there. Where the hell is the fire brigade?'

'They're coming, I could hear them. But are you sure Jez has gone home? Her bike's still here.'

Naomi stared uncomprehendingly. 'It can't be! I saw her go. She said Joey was picking her up down the lane.'

Somewhere along the row of buildings behind her a roof timber gave way with a crash and a shower of sparks. She jumped and turned instinctively to look.

237

Gideon shook her arm once more to regain her attention. 'Then she's come back. Where would she have gone?'

A look of utter horror crossed Naomi's face. 'Oh, my God! The fawn!' Then as Gideon started to move, 'But you can't get down there. Beyond the owl house the whole place is ablaze. It's just too hot!' The rabbit kicked again and she started to move away. 'I've got to put this somewhere. There's more to get.'

Gideon stood for a moment, undecided, then headed for the owl house and the old stables beyond.

Naomi was right. Beyond the owl house, which was thankfully empty, the heat was so intense and the smoke so chokingly thick that it was plainly impossible to go any further without breathing apparatus. Gideon withdrew a step or two, shielding his face with a forearm and desperately trying to remember whether the old stables had windows at the back. Surely they did. High, and possibly too small, but there – surely.

Sprinting back as fast as he dared in the reduced visibility, he rounded the last building and ran the few yards down the lane to the gate that led into the field behind the stables. He half-vaulted and half-fell over the dilapidated gate, landing on his knees in the tangled mass of brambles and scrap iron on the far side. The flashing, shrieking clamour of the approaching fire engine was appreciably closer now but not near enough to wait. He'd have to rely on Naomi telling them about Jez and the fawn.

Beside him as he scrambled hastily to his feet was a rusty iron bath, listing heavily but nevertheless half-full of greenish water. Gideon tugged his neckcloth loose once more then paused, recalling the shocking intensity of the heat from the burning buildings. Without giving himself time to think, he stepped into the trough, sat down in the icy water and then leaned back to immerse himself completely. The shock of it, as the water closed over his head, took his breath away and he swallowed a mouthful before he surfaced, gasping, into the icy wind.

Along the back of the row of Victorian brick buildings, Gideon could see that there were indeed windows, lit with a warm glow that was not, under the present circumstances, either welcoming or comforting. Gideon suppressed a groan. Surely the fire had claimed two or three more stables than it had when he'd approached from the other side. He loped along the row, frantically trying to remember how far down the fawn had been housed. Why, oh, why, hadn't he counted them from the top?

'Jez!' he yelled. 'Jez! Can you hear me? Where are you?'

If there had been a reply it was doubtful whether he would have heard it. Down this end the fire sounded like a hot-air balloon burner. The windows were high, too high to see through from the ground, but luckily, because they were so high, they weren't barred, there being no chance that their Victorian occupants could have accidentally broken the glass and injured themselves.

Gideon paused, trying to picture how far down the row he would be if he were the other side, and as he did so a timber inside the nearest stable collapsed, causing a shower of tiles to fall from the roof and shooting a jet of flame and sparks skyward. Gideon's instinct was to retreat to a safe distance but a thin, terrified scream halted him in his tracks.

Could it have been the child? When in acute pain or terror, animal screams could sound amazingly like human ones. *Was* it Jez?

Gideon stepped closer and yelled once more.

He was answered by a faint but unmistakable cry for help and experienced a rush of relief, instantly smothered by the knowledge that his troubles were far from over. The lower edge of the window was about level with the top of his head and although it appeared to be large enough to admit his rather bulky person, it would be a squeeze. Through the broken panes he could see the fierce orange blaze of the remaining burning beams.

There was no time to waste. Hunting around amongst the rubble and scrap iron that was scattered all along the back of the stables, Gideon found a piece of rusty angle iron with which he cleared the rest of the broken glass from the window. A couple of well-aimed swings took out the centre of the rotten wooden frame, and tossing the iron aside, he launched himself at the opening.

His initial leap left him with his head and shoulders in the aperture, resting his weight on his elbows and scrabbling at the brickwork with his boots. Luckily, the old bricks were crumbling in places and consequently very uneven, so it wasn't too difficult to gain purchase and push himself further through.

There was no easy way to climb over the sill. If he tried to sit on the ledge to get his feet through he was afraid he'd get stuck, but quite apart from that, the hot air rushing out through the opening felt like a blast furnace and what paint was left on the window frame was melting and burning his hands. As it was, he took advantage of a toehold in the bricks to continue his forward progress and sprawled almost head first into the stable.

A bale of smouldering straw broke his fall and he bounced off it to land on his knees on the floor. Glancing quickly about him, he discovered that although the beams overhead were blazing, at ground level the main fire was still one stable away. It could only be a matter of moments though, before falling debris ignited the thick golden straw underfoot.

'Jez!' he yelled, scrambling to his feet. That was a mistake. At head height the smoke was considerably thicker. It caught in his throat, stinging his eyes, and he dropped to his knees once more. To his right, in the other back corner of the stable, a wooden cross-member had fallen from the roof and lay smouldering, one end on the straw bales that lined the base of the walls. Beneath the beam he could see a flash of colour that could only have been blue denim.

He scuttled across on all fours. Behind him, in

the next stable, another part of the structure gave way and the fire roared in triumph. Gideon resisted the urge to look back. It wouldn't be good news and there wasn't a moment to spare.

The beam trapping Jez was, thankfully, not a main one but quite big enough. The child was lying, face down, in a strange, unnaturally hunched position under the lower end of it, trapped by her legs. Gideon could hear her coughing; a painful, racking sound that shook her whole body.

He put a hand on her shoulders.

'Jez! Can you hear me? It's Gideon.'

'Gideon?' she managed incredulously, between the coughs. 'I can't move my legs . . . It hurts. I've got Kizzy. Help me!'

She'd turned her head to try and see Gideon as he knelt beside her and through the swirling smoke he could see the helpless tears pouring down her face as she began to cough again.

'Steady, Jez,' he said, much as he would to a panicking horse. 'We'll have you out of here in no time.' The words caught in his throat and he too began to cough, taking in more of the thick grey smoke as he inhaled convulsively, and making it worse. 'I'll lift. You slide out.'

Eyes streaming, Gideon grasped the end of the beam and heaved. Where it had rested the straw was already alight and the wood was painfully hot to the touch. In these circumstances the pain was incidental. Speed was everything. The heat from the approaching blaze was unbelievably intense and the suffocating, energy-sapping pain in his chest left no room for any other considerations. He had to get the child and himself out while he still had the strength to do so.

The beam came up more easily than he had dared hope and he was able to move it sideways away from Jez before he let it drop, which was lucky because the girl showed no signs of being able to slide herself out from under it as he'd suggested. Without further ado, Gideon scooped her up and turned towards the window, forcing himself to ignore her whimper of pain. She was no heavier than a medium to large dog but almost immediately began to thrash about in his arms, making his task twice as difficult.

'No!' she cried in his ear. 'Kizzy!' Then she hit out at him with her fists before collapsing weakly in a bout of combined coughing and sobbing.

Suddenly Gideon realised what she'd been lying on and why she'd been hunched in that strange way. In the urgency of the situation he'd completely forgotten the reason the child had been in the stable in the first place. The muntjac fawn; Kizzy.

'You first,' he shouted, in a voice that hardly sounded like his own, his throat was so sore. 'I'll come back, I promise.'

The child was racked with coughing once more as he stumbled across to the window, seeing with heart-stopping horror that the straw bed was well alight now and their way almost blocked by the leaping flames. Beneath the window he paused, desperate to lift the child up and out into the life-giving air but doubled up and incapacitated with the torture of his own smoke-filled lungs.

Jez was much quieter now, ominously so. Repositioning her in his arms, Gideon stood on the crumbling straw bale and posted her through the window feet first. Still holding her, he hitched himself up by his elbows until his head and shoulders were outside the building, then let her slide through his grasp until she was hanging by her wrists with her feet perhaps eighteen inches above the ground.

The broken wood of the window frame was digging into his torso but he hesitated momentarily. He couldn't be sure whether one – or even both – of her legs weren't broken and his heart quailed at the thought of her landing on them.

He leaned even further out. Her head hung back and her eyes were almost closed, feet nearly touching the ground now. It was the best he could do. He opened his fingers and Jez slid down and fell sideways into the long grass at the base of the wall.

Gideon's legs, still hanging inside the stable, felt as though they were on fire and in a moment of panic he almost dived out of the window head first, but the certain knowledge that his falling body couldn't fail to land on the child, lying limply below, held him back. And then there was the fawn. He had promised. He wriggled back to stand on the straw once more.

The heat was fearsome. Somewhere within ten feet or so of him was a muntjac fawn, helpless and terrified. Ten feet or so, that was, of burning straw, thick smoke, and the possibility of being brained by a falling beam. Ten feet that stretched away like miles.

Hardly believing what he was doing, Gideon stepped off the fast-disintegrating straw bale and plunged back through the grey and orange chaos to where he had found Jez.

The fawn was still there, cowering in the corner against the bales that lined the walls. Coughing almost non-stop and struggling to see through the tears that threatened to blind him, Gideon could nevertheless tell that the animal was in a bad way. It pressed against the straw as if hoping that a gap would appear to allow its escape. It blinked terrified, watering eyes and gasped for air through an open mouth but Gideon could see that even were he to get it to safety it would be to no avail. The fawn was scrabbling at the ground with its front legs but its hindquarters dragged uselessly in the straw. In trying to save it, Jez had fallen with the fawn beneath her and broken its back.

The falling beam had brought with it a quantity of other woodwork and, groping in the debris around his feet, Gideon found a short piece that was not too badly burnt. Pausing only to aim as accurately as he could, he hit the stricken animal hard behind its left ear. To his relief it dropped immediately, kicked a time or two, and then lay still.

Above him, something gave way with a crack like a pistol shot and a shower of burning laths and tiles rained down upon his head and shoulders. The wind rushing over the hole in the roof drew the fire upward like a chimney and it roared with renewed vigour. The heat made the skin on Gideon's face feel unbearably tight and there was an acrid smell of singeing hair; whether his or the fawn's he wasn't sure.

He shook like a dog to rid himself of any clinging embers, worrying as he did so about Jez lying unprotected beneath the window. He should have taken the time to drag her away from the danger of falling debris.

What if the wall collapsed?

What if she stopped breathing?

At the same time, he knew that if he'd left the burning stable, he would never have had the courage to climb back in again, fawn or no fawn.

He stumbled through the smoke towards the window, glad of the protection of his heavy-duty motorcycle boots. The layer of straw bedding had burned away to just so much ash now but he could still feel the heat of it, even through the thick soles. With a flash of sick humour he pictured a fireman saying 'We couldn't find the rest of him, I'm afraid, but his feet are fine.'

The next moment, humour of any kind was extinct.

The window wasn't there.

Gideon groped his way sideways along the wall on a rising tide of panic. It had to be there. He couldn't see more than eighteen inches in any direction. It could be just an arm's-length away.

But *which* way? It was all taking too long.

His chest and throat were contracting from lack of air and as he paused, trying to think logically, his overwhelming urge was to sit down and rest for a moment.

Move, damn it! he scolded himself. You've got to move, for Jez's sake. She can't be left where she is.

Coughing hard now, he forced his leaden limbs into action, trying not to give room to the thought that pushed insistently at the edge of his mind, whipping up panic once more.

What if it's the wrong wall?

It *had* to be the right one. He'd always had a better than average sense of direction and this was definitely not the time to start overriding it. And, given that it *was* the right wall, he must be nearer to the right-hand end of it than the left. So, if he worked his way to the right and couldn't find it, then he'd just have to work his way back left-handed until he did. No point in admitting that the smoke was almost certain to beat him before he completed this methodical search.

No point at all.

Such was the woolly state of his mind that he'd moved two arm's-lengths sideways before he remembered that the window was just above head height, and if he carried on feeling his way along as he was, he would miss it anyway. Cursing his stupidity, he stretched his left hand upward and felt – nothing!

It took another long moment for this to penetrate his senses, and when it did, the surge of joy was stifled by a sudden frustrated despair. He may have found the window but with the straw bale stepping-stone just so much crumbling ash beneath his feet, and limbs that felt as though they were weighed down with lead, the aperture might as well be six feet above his head as six inches. Every time he coughed he inhaled another lungful of smoke and it was steadily killing him.

He just hadn't the strength.

Head bowed and eyes screwed tight against the smoke-induced agony, Gideon leaned weakly against the wall and thumped it helplessly with his fist. Shouting was beyond him, even if he could have made himself heard over the roaring blaze. And even had there been anyone to hear.

Then, suddenly, desperation gave way to resignation and a relief of sorts. He could stop struggling. It was all right; no one would blame him. He'd done all he could. And somebody would find Jez, surely. *Wouldn't they?*

There was nothing he could do but sit down and wait for it all to be over.

It was the water that stopped him.

A jet of it shot through the window above him just as he was about to release his hold on the sill. Shockingly cold, some of it hit the frame and cascaded down over his head and shoulders.

It was too much.

Gideon put both hands up to try and ward off the deluge and, incredibly, a strong, gloved fist closed around one of them and pulled.

10

It was a long time before he stopped coughing.

In the period of time between his lowering Jez from the window and being pulled from it himself, the field behind the stables had become host to two fire engines, an ambulance and a large, powerful-looking private car.

The firefighter who hauled him out had handed him over to a fluorescent-green-jacketed paramedic, who removed Gideon's own somewhat charred waxed jacket and immediately cocooned him in a shiny silver blanket. He was then led past the vast red and silver bulk of the busy fire engine, sat down on the back step of a waiting ambulance and had an oxygen mask held over his nose and mouth. Gideon drew in one or two shuddering gasps of the blessedly sweet gas, coughed and then pushed the mask aside to speak.

No words came, only an unintelligible croak.

The medic put the plastic firmly back in place.

'Don't try to talk, okay?' he advised. 'Don't worry about the kid. She's on her way to hospital already. She's going to be all right. She's a tough one. I guess she owes you, too. Big time!'

Gideon closed his eyes thankfully and tried to concentrate on his breathing. All around him he could hear the bustle and noise of the emergency crews in action and even through his closed eyelids the rhythmic blue light flashed, but he was content just to sit and let it all wash over him. His arms and legs felt boneless and shaky, his chest was tight and his eyes on fire. There was nothing he could usefully do except keep out of the way and the thought was bliss.

'Breathing any easier yet?' the paramedic enquired after a while.

Gideon opened his eyes and nodded. 'Better all the time,' he croaked.

'No other injuries that you're aware of?'

He shook his head. Scrapes and bruises he probably had aplenty but nothing of significance. As a matter of fact, aside from the smoke-induced discomfort, his shoulder was bothering him the most. Being hauled out of the stable window by his wrists had done little to further the healing process.

'Best have a look at those hands, then,' the medic suggested, removing the oxygen mask and producing dressings and bandages from a box.

Gideon looked down in surprise. His hands, when he turned them palm up, were indeed looking decidedly the worse for wear; blackened, bleeding in places from cuts and grazes, and blistering wetly. He held them out obediently.

Around him, the noise and bustle seemed to have abated a little. The shouts were a little less urgent, movement a little slower and the sky a shade or two darker as the flames died down. The pump was still powering on and the resultant jet poured salvation on to what was left of the buildings in a beautiful silvery stream. Sulky black smoke billowed up into the evening sky as the flames gradually gave up the battle. Already a wet, dank smell was beginning to pervade the air.

'I think those'll do for now,' the medic said, winding bandage over the second dressing. 'This gel should stay cold for about four hours. They'll re-do the dressings later, when we get you to hospital.'

'Er, I'd rather not, if you don't mind. I'll be needed here.'

'I don't think so, mate. Hospital's the best place for you right now.'

'But I'm okay. It'd be a waste of time,' Gideon asserted. 'These feel great. Really soothing.'

'It'll wear off though, and you've inhaled a lot of smoke; you'd be wise to get yourself checked over.'

'But I don't have to, right?'

'I'm not going to force you, if that's what you mean. I can only advise,' he confirmed, shaking his head. 'But smoke inhalation is dangerous. You could experience breathing difficulties later, and my advice is that you should get along to Casualty as soon as you can. The quickest way is obviously with us. But whatever you do, get those hands looked at by your GP in the morning.'

'Thanks. I will,' Gideon said gratefully, and succumbed to another bout of coughing.

A shadow fell across them as somebody approached. The ambulance man stood up, shaking his head once more, and melted into the background.

'Station Officer Hanley,' the bulky silhouette introduced itself. 'How are you doing?'

'Oh, not so bad, thanks to you guys,' Gideon told him, in a voice that at last sounded something like his own, if only barely. 'It was a close-run thing, though.'

'You were certainly lucky,' Hanley agreed. 'But, tell me, what on earth made you go back after you got the girl out?'

Gideon was surprised. 'How did you know I had?'

'Old gentleman from down the road was watching the fire and saw you lower the girl out of the window and then disappear again. He came across and pulled the girl away from the building, then came to find us. Luckily for you, we were on our way round, looking for the little girl. We couldn't get close enough at the front.'

'Me neither,' Gideon said. 'The thing is, the kid went in to try and save the fawn and she wouldn't leave without it. I had to promise I'd go back for it.'

'I take it you were too late.'

'Its back was broken. I put it out of its misery.'

'You know it was a bloody silly thing to do? Going back, I mean.'

'Tell me about it,' Gideon said wearily.

Hanley put a hand on his shoulder. 'If it's any consolation, I'd have done just the same, and I guess that goes for most of the lads too, but we'd have had BA – Breathing Apparatus,' he added, remembering he was talking to a layman.

'If I'd known you were so close on my heels, I'd have waited. I've no desire to play the hero, I can tell you!'

'Well, there's one little girl who's glad you did anyway,' the paramedic said, coming back unheard. 'I've just been in touch with my colleague and he says she's conscious and recovering well. But a few minutes later . . . Who knows?'

'Is she badly hurt?'

'I don't know, mate, but she's out of danger.'

'And the others? Is everyone else all right?'

'All accounted for, I understand.'

Gideon sighed, his most immediate worries laid to rest. If Naomi, Tim and Jez were safe, then the other inevitable problems could be dealt with in due course.

One of the firefighters came up to claim Hanley's attention and he drifted away, warning Gideon that he might want to ask him one or two questions later.

'Is there something suspicious, then?'

Hanley pursed his lips. 'Just routine, sir, that's all. Unless you know something?' His gaze intensified.

Gideon shook his head, coughing again. He knew nothing.

'You should get along to hospital.'

'Yeah, so I'm told.'

It was another half an hour or so before the fire was pronounced under control, and the damping down operation carried on for a long time after that.

Having thanked the paramedics and assured them at least twice more that he really didn't need a trip to the hospital for a check-up, Gideon made his way round to the yard to see what the position was there. The ambulance crew, their job done, departed for base and, no doubt, many other urgent calls before their shift was through.

It was by now almost completely dark, and in the yard, someone, presumably the firemen, had rigged up a powerful spotlight to illuminate the scene. By its light Gideon could see a little of the havoc wrought by the blaze.

The mood of the fire crew had changed now from one of brisk determination to workaday cheerfulness. The fire was as good as out; human casualties were nil and animal casualties apparently low. It was a job well done. The destruction of property was something they saw day in and day out, regrettable but not their problem.

They methodically doused any and all combustible materials within reach of their hoses that could possibly be suspected of harbouring a spark. Water was everywhere. It poured on to the still-smoking roofs of the stables and animal cages, and through the roof and windows of the blackened mobile home and farmhouse beyond. It deluged the hay shed and its contents, which had survived mainly intact, and lay all around in huge, muddy pools, reflecting the blue flashing lights.

As Gideon stood on the edge of the lighted section, trying to assimilate the scale of the destruction and also scanning the area for Tim and Naomi, somebody touched his elbow. He turned to see a diminutive lady with a shawl over her head and a basket on her arm.

He blinked. She looked like a refugee from a children's fairy tale.

'I didn't know if you'd have electric so I brought a thermos,' the apparition said, looking anxiously up at Gideon who was wondering if he should know who she was. 'Tea,' she added helpfully. 'If you'd like it.'

He gathered his wits. 'More than anything,' he assured her with a smile. Anything, that was, except a good stiff measure of spirits. *Ah, well.*

'Gideon!' Naomi materialised out of the darkness beside him. 'Are you okay? One of the firemen said you nearly got buried alive in the old stables!'

'It wasn't quite as dramatic as all that,' he protested. 'Jez went in looking for the fawn and I got a bit singed getting her out. She had a far narrower escape than I did.'

Naomi took hold of his arms and pulled his bandaged hands forward. 'Oh, yes? And the rest! Still, I'm just so glad you're all right.' She wrapped him in a huge hug and added, into his jumper, 'I can't afford to lose my big brother. He's the only one I've got!'

Gideon returned the hug, more moved than he would have cared to admit but unable to think of any reply that wouldn't make him cringe in retrospect. 'And what about you? Are you all right, Sis? Really?'

'Yes, I'll be okay. Just bone weary,' she said, standing back and summoning a brave smile.

'And Tim? Where's he?'

'He's over by the surgery with the birds and smaller animals. He's okay.'

'Well, this kind lady – I'm sorry, I don't know your name – has brought us a thermos of tea,' Gideon said.

'Rose,' the lady put in. 'My name's Rose Callow. I live just down the lane there. My husband, George, was the one who helped the little girl.'

'Oh, is he here?' Gideon glanced round. 'I'd like to thank him.'

Rose shook her head. 'No, he's gone home to sit down. His heart's not too good and he needed to rest after all the excitement.'

Gideon began to express his sympathy but was cut short by a commotion at the entrance to the yard, where at least three policemen were struggling to deny access to a rather large individual who appeared desperate to gain entry. He watched for a moment and then recognition dawned.

'It's all right,' he called out, making his way over. 'He's the girl's brother.'

He was obliged to repeat himself before the officers took in the information and reluctantly released their hold on the blond giant. This they did cautiously, as if afraid that, once free, their captive would turn on them.

Joey had other matters on his mind. 'What's going on? Where's Jez? She was supposed to meet me down the lane.'

'But you were late, weren't you?' Gideon stated coldly. After all, if Joey had picked the child up at the appointed time she would have been gone long before the fire even started. 'And while she was waiting she saw the smoke and came back.'

'Your sister, is it, sir?' one of the policemen enquired, keen to regain his position of authority. 'Yes, well, I'm afraid she was taken to hospital about half an hour ago. Smoke inhalation, of course. Apart from that, I can't say.'

'But she's all right, isn't she?' Joey towered over the policeman, grabbing the man's waterproof jacket in his agitation. 'Isn't she? Tell me, damn you!'

The officer looked a little startled, as well he might. Joey was a formidable figure even at the best of times, which these clearly weren't.

'Take your hands off me, sir!' he spluttered. 'Thank you. Yes, I'm told she's out of danger but she's a lucky little girl, it could have been very different.'

But Joey was no longer listening. He swung savagely towards Gideon. 'It's your bloody fault!'

he hissed. 'If you hadn't brought her here, this would never have happened! You've been nothing but bloody trouble!'

Gideon didn't rise to the bait. Whatever his quarrel with the man, the outburst was provoked by Joey's own feelings of shock and guilt, and this was neither the time nor the place to rake up what was past. Nor was it the moment to point out the injustice of his accusation.

'Now, look here!' someone said firmly and to no noticeable effect.

Out of the corner of his eye Gideon saw one of the policemen start forward and then hesitate, the headlights of Joey's idling vehicle picking out the fluorescent strips on his jacket with startling intensity. Joey's face was no more than six inches from Gideon's and his expression was not encouraging. He held his ground and waited for reason to reassert itself.

'You smug bastard!' Joey spat the words and accompanied them with a forcible shove against Gideon's shoulder, which sent him staggering back a pace or two. Sod's law it had to be his sore one. His sharp intake of breath set off another bout of coughing.

'Here!' one of the policemen protested, reaching for Joey's arm.

He shook him off as one would a troublesome insect and advanced upon Gideon once more.

At this point the other two officers took a hand, fastening themselves with grim determination, one to each arm, and at the same time Naomi reached the group and stepped in front of her brother in an unconsciously protective gesture.

Joey sneered. 'That's it, pal. Hide behind a woman.'

'Come on, sir. You're upset.' Another policeman had appeared. 'Don't make things worse for your sister by getting into trouble yourself. It won't help anyone, least of all her.'

Gideon thought his voice sounded familiar but couldn't place him. He wondered how many more there were around. It must be a quiet night in Dorset.

'The best thing you can do is get along to the hospital,' the newcomer continued. 'She'll want her family around her.'

The calm good sense had its effect. Joey ceased to glare belligerently at Gideon and turned to glare instead at the policeman, a slim five foot ten or so of easy, quiet authority.

'Well, I'd have been there by now, if someone would just tell me where she's been taken.'

'Just let me take your details: name, address and phone number. Then you can be on your way.' He nodded to the two PCs who were still clinging to Joey's arms as if their jobs depended on it, and they obediently stepped back.

With no more than a darkling glance at Gideon, Joey turned to follow the slight figure back towards the gate, but Gideon was under no illusion that the matter would be forgotten.

'*That* was Jez's brother?' Naomi asked incredulously. 'Poor little mite!'

'Half-brother, yes, I'm afraid so. Though, to do him justice, I think he's very fond of her,' Gideon said. 'You should see the other one!'

'Thanks, but no thanks!'

'Are you all right, sir?' one of the remaining two policemen asked. The third was nowhere to be seen; presumably he'd returned to the fire scene.

Gideon assured him he was fine and the two fluorescent jackets headed back towards the gate where, despite the farm's isolation, a number of sightseers were pushing eagerly against the police tape.

'Come on, Sis. Let's have that cup of tea,' Gideon suggested, putting his arm round her shoulders and steering her back to the spot where they'd left Rose Callow. 'Have you lost weight, Naomi?'

As a dancer she was of necessity slim, but just now she seemed, even through the waxed jacket that she wore, positively bony.

'I have, a little,' she admitted. 'We've been working *so* hard, Gideon. Tim's really determined to make a success of this place and there's been so much to do. And then . . .' Her voice caught on a sob as exhaustion and the horror of the situation threatened to overwhelm her. 'And then there's been all the trouble, it's been so . . .' She sobbed again and sniffed. 'So frightening. And now this. What are we going to do with all the animals?'

'Shh.' Gideon gave her shoulders a gentle shake. 'We'll get it all sorted out. Don't worry about it now.'

'But how can we? It'll take ages to rebuild, and what do we do with the animals in the meantime? We've got all those donkeys . . . what'll we do with them? They need shelter. Oh, it's all such a mess!'

'First things first. We all need a cup of tea,' Gideon said firmly as Tim appeared from the direction of the surgery. 'Let's find dear old Rose. Ah, Tim, is there somewhere – anywhere – warm and dry, where we can sit down for five minutes?'

'As a matter of fact, I was coming to suggest just that. One of the firemen – chap named Smiley as far as I can make out – has rigged up a lamp in reception for us, and Rose is making more tea on the primus.'

'The woman's a marvel!' Gideon declared. 'Well, what are we waiting for?'

The small block comprising surgery, reception and Tim's office had come off best of all, the wind having blown the flames in the other direction, and it was bliss to collapse on to the upholstered reception area chairs and sip the hot tea Rose had brewed.

The old lady dug down in her basket and produced a packet of chocolate digestives which she passed round, and for several long moments Gideon was content to let all thoughts of the outside world pass him by.

It couldn't last though. Beside him sat Naomi, her blonde head drooping with fatigue and telltale clean streaks in her sooty complexion. In the opposite corner Tim was sitting hunched on his chair, hands clasped around a mug and red-rimmed eyes staring into the steaming liquid with a blank unfocused gaze. Under the grime his face was burned red, as Gideon could feel his own was. The skin felt as if it would split if he smiled too widely. Not much chance of that, but he did have one idea that might help raise morale.

'Back in a minute,' he said, climbing to his feet with an effort and leaving the haven of the lighted building. Tim barely glanced up.

Outside, surprised by the wobbly weakness of his legs, Gideon headed for where he'd left Pippa's car, answering a firefighter's call of, 'All right, mate?' with a wave of his hand. He supposed 'all right' was a relative term; his throat and chest burned deeply and he was constantly fighting the need to cough.

The small crowd of onlookers by the gate had dispersed, uninterested now the drama was over. The two fire engines from the field were packed up and lumbering away down the lane, blue lights off. Only the one in the yard remained, and one police car. Close by, he could see Hanley deep in conversation with one of the police officers but made no move to approach them.

Pippa's runabout seemed mercifully undamaged, although one window was partially open and when Gideon reached through it, the seat on which his mobile phone lay felt suspiciously damp.

He got through to the Priory almost immediately and Pippa answered.

'Gideon! Where are you? I thought you'd be back ages ago. Rachel was convinced you must have run into that psychopathic ex-husband of hers, and she's been picturing you lying in a ditch on some deserted country road.'

'No. Nothing like that,' he assured her. 'I haven't seen hide nor hair of him. I'm at the Sanctuary – you know, where my sister's been helping out. They've had a bit of a calamity and I shall probably be here most of the night, so do you think Rachel could possibly bunk down with you? She won't want to be on her own in the Gatehouse.'

'No problem,' Pippa said instantly, as he'd expected she would. 'But what's happened? Is everyone all right?'

Gideon explained briefly and finished by asking to speak to Giles.

Ten minutes or so later, when Gideon made his way back to the others, he found Tim sitting almost exactly as he'd left him, except that he'd put his empty mug on to the floor beside him and was resting his chin on his hands. The blank gaze was unchanged and he looked worn out and desperately depressed. Naomi, in the other chair, was curled up asleep, and he'd passed Rose in the yard, dispensing tea to the thirsty firefighters.

'Tim?' he said softly.

He blinked and looked up.

'How many donkeys are there altogether?'

He could see the effort as Tim tried to concentrate. 'Er, thirteen, I think. Yes, thirteen. They won't have gone far, though I suppose we ought to go and look for them. Naomi got some of them into the barn field, so the others will be around, they're practically inseparable.'

'No, it's okay. There were seven in the barn field and three hanging around outside, which I let in. And there are three in the field down by the gate. I nearly ran those over on the way in.'

Tim sighed. 'God knows what we're going to do with them now, though. Some of them are pretty ancient. They belonged to an old lady who had to go into hospital. The thing is, they need shelter and we haven't got any now, except the old barn, and that's full of hay.' He ran his filthy fingers through his hair. 'Oh, God, what a mess!'

'Well, I think I've found them temporary accommodation, if they can travel, that is,' Gideon said. 'And any other of the animals.'

Tim's reaction was subdued. 'Thanks, but I'm afraid we'll have to try and manage here. There's no way I can afford to pay rent for them all. God knows how long it'll be before we're back on our feet again.'

Gideon shook his head. 'There's no question of rent. My friend Giles has offered to have them at Home Farm, about half a mile from the Priory. You'll have to supply whatever feed they need and the stables might need a bit of a spring clean, but there's grass and water for free, if you want it.'

'If I want it?' Tim echoed. 'Where's the catch? There has to be one.'

'Not that I know of. Unless I phone to cancel, a

horsebox will be here in the morning. So it's up to you.'

'Thanks. That's brilliant,' Tim said, his eyes at last registering a spark of renewed optimism. 'I owe you one.'

Gideon shook his head and smiled, then wished he hadn't, as his cracked lips protested.

Having completed her mercy mission, Rose returned to her cottage and George, with heartfelt thanks ringing in her ears.

Tim and Gideon spread a blanket over Naomi and left her sleeping in the chair for want of a more comfortable place to offer her, and because, as Tim rightly said, if they did wake her up to move her, she would no doubt insist on helping them with the animals.

The firefighters attached to the remaining engine turned their attention to what was left of the straw bedding, raking it out into the walkway between the sad remnants of the two stableblocks, and thoroughly sousing it.

Tim had put most of the animals and birds in the fenced-off area of grass behind the surgery, some in transport carriers, some in boxes, and one or two rabbits loose. With the temperature rapidly falling, he decided it would be best to move them all into the surgery for the night, where they could at least be kept warm. One or two were exhibiting signs of severe stress, and he told Gideon he was quite prepared to find that they'd lost some by the morning.

They had just finished settling the last of the birds into their makeshift homes when they were joined by Naomi, followed closely by the police officer who had handled Joey so skilfully.

'The constable would like a word,' Naomi said, looking much better for her hour or two of sleep. She'd washed her face and tied her hair back and seemed ready for whatever was to come.

'PC Logan,' the officer supplied, edging into the surgery, which was by this time decidedly cramped.

In the light of the emergency gas lamp Gideon recognised him as the first officer he had seen at Chilminster, when he'd reported the low-flying helicopter. About the same age as Gideon, he wore his light brown hair cropped short under his peaked cap, and pale blue eyes regarded the world with a patient cynicism from a lean, uncompromising face. Although he was no taller than Naomi, there would never be any question of dismissing him as of no account; his easy self-confidence was completely unassumed. A good man to have on your side, Gideon thought, and a relentless adversary.

'How're they doing?' Logan asked, gesturing at the multitude of cages. 'Will it affect them badly?'

'Most will be okay, I think,' Tim replied. 'It's a bit early to say, for sure.'

'Did you lose many?'

'One or two. It spread so fast. Do they know how it started yet?'

'As a matter of fact, that's what I wanted to see

266

you about. Station Officer Hanley has notified the FIU and until they arrive I must ask you to stay away from the area of the fire, especially the house and the mobile home. At the moment it looks as if that's where it started.'

'FIU?' Naomi repeated.

'The Fire Investigation Unit.'

'They think it's arson, then?' Tim asked. It was a possibility he had been talking over with Gideon while they worked.

Logan shook his head. 'I'm afraid I can't discuss it with you at the moment. Let's just say that the cause of the fire is not immediately obvious and it's Fire Brigade policy to investigate when that's the case. There may be a completely innocent explanation.' He paused, pursing his lips slightly. 'I understand you've had a bit of trouble here . . .'

'Yes, we have, but I never thought . . . I mean, if it *is* arson will you be able to find out who did it?'

'We'll do our best,' Logan promised. 'But for now, if you feel up to answering a few questions . . .?'

White-faced and strained, with bloodshot eyes and a nagging cough, Tim hardly looked eager to undergo a cross-examination, but he assented wearily and followed Logan back into the reception area.

'Poor old Tim looks rough,' Gideon remarked to his sister, as the door shut behind the pair.

'He's not the only one,' Naomi responded. 'I've seen you looking better.'

*

The sun rose cheerfully in a dazzling blue sky the next morning oblivious to the havoc below. During the night, the wind had dropped and along with it the temperature. When Gideon and Tim ventured out into the scene of devastation that the farmyard had become, there was ice on the puddles in the lane and a white frost on the fields and hedges.

The final fire engine and its attendant crew were ready to leave, having kept an eye on the blackened ruins throughout the night. The dour-faced leading firefighter officially took his leave of the two men, informing them that the long awaited FIU had recently arrived, having been detained at another incident the previous night.

With the fire engine gone, the extent of the damage seemed suddenly to hit home. Somebody, presumably Logan or one of his colleagues, had cordoned off the main area of the blaze with fluorescent orange tape, and beyond it the blackened skeletal remains of the old brick stables were all that remained upright. The new wooden stables and the range of small animal and birdcages that had stood at the end of the rows were just so much debris lying amidst the icy pools.

On the far side of the row of charred stumps that had been the hedge, the twisted shell of the mobile home promised no hope of salvage, and behind it the farmhouse stood with glassless windows staring blankly, like a familiar friend without their spectacles. The roof had been completely destroyed and soot coated all that could be seen of the inside and rose in fan-shapes from the window openings.

The air was heavy with the acrid smell of smoke.

As for himself, Gideon had come through his ordeal surprisingly well. His hands were worst affected, throbbing uncomfortably under the dressings. His eyes still smarted, and every now and then his breath caught in his sore throat, causing him to cough, but he knew he'd been incredibly lucky.

He glanced across at Tim, whose lean, wiry frame drooped with a mixture of weariness and despair. As he watched, the vet's face became suddenly tight and bitter, and following the direction of his gaze he saw a helmeted figure come round the corner of the house, apparently intent upon inspecting the ground beneath his feet. He wore a fireman's protective jacket with FIU across the back in large, fluorescent lettering.

'Do you know, last night Logan actually asked me if *I* had started the fire?' Tim said then, scowling with remembered anger. 'What the hell does he think I've been working my guts out here for, these last months? I couldn't believe it!'

'It's his job,' Gideon pointed out reasonably. 'He doesn't know you and he spends his life around criminals. I expect he was just testing your reaction. This place is your dream; I know that, but he doesn't. You can't blame him for his suspicion, it's what he's paid to do, the same as those guys.' He nodded towards the farmhouse.

'Yeah, I know.' Tim sighed. 'It's just . . . Well, it's hard, when you've come close to losing everything you've worked for and dreamed about, to be more or less accused of starting the fire yourself!'

'Mm. Well, if it's any comfort, I got the distinct impression that Logan had more or less crossed you off his list of suspects after he'd questioned you last night. He's pretty shrewd.'

'Well, he'd have to, surely? I mean, I'd be a bit bloody stupid to set fire to the place and then almost get myself toasted rescuing the animals, wouldn't I?'

'Yes, but I suppose he could argue that you hadn't realised how quickly it would spread. That you only meant to burn the farmhouse and underestimated the strength of the wind.'

'Why would I want to do that?' Tim protested. 'It's in the middle of being renovated!'

'Perhaps it was taking longer than you expected. Perhaps you couldn't afford to pay the builders,' Gideon suggested. 'It happens.'

'Yeah, I guess so. But not this time. I presume he's gone off to question the builders now. He asked me when they left yesterday, and to tell the truth, I couldn't remember. They've been here so long now they're like part of the fixtures and fittings. I couldn't even tell him how many were here yesterday. They come and go as they need to. It's not always the same ones.'

'You're very trusting,' Gideon observed.

'Well, there's nothing of value to go missing; the building inspectors visit to oversee the structural work; and I've got a quote for the work, in writing, so it's up to them how long they take – within reason. Besides, Tom Morgan, the contractor, is a good sort. I trust him. So as far as this goes,' he gestured at the dismal scene before them, 'if it wasn't an accident, then I guess we all know where to look.'

'There's just the little matter of evidence,' Gideon said. 'We'll have to hope our friends over there turn something up.'

The door of the reception area opened and Naomi appeared. She had spent the remainder of the night on the narrow camp bed that Tim kept in the surgery for emergencies. He and Gideon had taken turns on a mattress compiled of chair cushions for the four or five remaining hours; one sleeping, one keeping an eye on the animals.

Naomi looked heavy-eyed and depressed. She shivered and hugged herself as the icy air found its way through her denim jacket and jumper.

'Brrr! I hate the cold.' Winding an arm through one of Tim's, she reached up to kiss him fondly on the cheek. 'I think you'll have to shave off what's left of your beard and start again,' she told him. 'It looks rather the worse for wear.'

'I know.' He rubbed the singed remains, ruefully. 'And I can't even claim it on the insurance!'

'How are the animals?' Naomi asked. 'I gather poor old Ferdy didn't make it.'

Tim shook his head. They'd found the pheasant dead in the early hours. 'He was very sick even before last night, so I wasn't surprised. We seem to be short of two rabbits, as well. I can only think they got through the hedge somehow, if you put them all in the garden.'

'But I didn't,' Naomi said, remembering. 'I put the first two in Gideon's car. Oh, my God! They must still be there! I meant to move them after we had our cup of tea but I fell asleep and then just clean forgot. The poor little sods!'

'This might seem a silly question,' Gideon ventured cautiously, 'but is it standard emergency procedure to house rabbits in cars?'

Naomi had started towards Pippa's runabout, which stood with frosted windows near the gateway to the lane.

'I was panicking,' she explained. 'The fire was spreading so fast. I had to put them somewhere safe for the time being and there it was.'

She reached the car and paused to try and rub the side window free from ice. 'I hope they're okay. I can't see them.'

The rabbits were eventually run to ground snuggled under a dog blanket on the floor behind the front seats. They were huddled together for warmth and seemed unconcerned by their odd surroundings but were, nonetheless, quite pleased to be transferred to more appropriate accommodation.

The animals accounted for, the three of them made their way in Pippa's car to the nearest pub, and breakfast in front of a roaring fire. Though, as Gideon remarked, it was only a scant few hours since he would have sworn that he never wanted to see another fire as long as he lived.

272

It was a busy day, one way and another, and quite late in the evening when Gideon finally turned Pippa's car towards the hospital to visit Jez.

Pippa herself had turned up at the Sanctuary shortly after ten o'clock driving her horsebox in which to transport the donkeys to their temporary home on the Graylings estate. The donkeys, however, had other ideas, and it took the four of them almost two hours to load the stubborn beasts into the lorry.

Pippa complained that Gideon's supposed powers of communication and persuasion were not being a great deal of help, whereupon he replied, quite straight-faced, that he had never learned to speak donkey. The truth was, in fact, that with one or two exceptions, the donkeys weren't particularly apprehensive, merely obstinate, and no amount of communication would have made any difference at all. They had made up their minds.

The breakthrough came when they identified the ringleader, who went by the highly imaginative name of Murphy, and having almost bodily picked him up and carried him into the horsebox, found the others much more readily coaxed up the ramp. In fact, the last two, terrified that they'd be left behind, charged in by themselves, almost pulling Tim over in the process.

Deciding that at least one of them should stay at the Sanctuary, Tim sent Naomi off in the wake of the horsebox to see the donkeys safely installed in their new quarters. Gideon followed shortly after in Pippa's car, stopping briefly at the Callows' tiny cottage to thank them both for what they had done.

Rose was anxious to ply him with coffee and a full fried breakfast despite the lateness of the hour but he declined, stressing the importance of his being present when the donkeys were unloaded. He thanked them both warmly, well aware that he owed his well-being, if not his life, to George.

He, a gaunt eighty-something with pale rheumy eyes and a pronounced tremor in his hands, positively glowed under the praise, and Gideon guessed that it had probably been a long time since he'd felt of much use to anyone.

Rose told Gideon how pleased they had both been to see Mr Reynolds doing something with the farm. George had apparently been gardener at the Grange before the war, when the farm had been part of the estate. Then, at the outbreak of war, the military had taken both properties over and the whole area was declared out of bounds.

'They was coming and going at all hours. All very hush-hush. There was rumours of spies, code-cracking, a secret bunker and all, so I heard,' George told him. 'Some folk even said they was interrogating POW's there. Said you could hear the screams on a quiet night. I don't know about that. I never heard anything. Anyway, they put wire up and I wasn't allowed anywhere near the place. Fair broke my heart it did, seeing that beautiful garden go wild, but then I was called up and I had other things to worry about, didn't I?'

Gideon agreed that he probably had, and

eventually took his leave, promising to visit the pair again when things were a bit less hectic. They seemed pathetically pleased and he realised they were probably very lonely, living as they did, miles from the nearest town.

The installation of the donkeys at the Priory's Home Farm had gone smoothly enough. Pippa backed the lorry up to the doorway of the barn that had been made ready for them, and they more or less installed themselves, bustling down the ramp to explore the interior with obvious and rather comical delight.

Rachel, who with Giles had helped prepare the barn, was enchanted by the new arrivals, exclaiming over each of them in turn. Giles responded with helpful comments like, 'Oh, you mean the one with the long ears?' but knowing him as he did, Gideon could see that he was quite taken with the creatures.

After seeing the donkeys settled, Gideon had dropped in at the Gatehouse to feed Elsa, who'd missed her supper the night before and was understandably put out. A quick look round reassured him that nobody had taken advantage of his absence to make any mischief, and leaving Rachel in Pippa and Giles' capable care, and Naomi keeping an eye on the long-eared guests, he had returned to the Sanctuary to see what help he could offer Tim.

When he got there, Tim was in the surgery, drinking tea and gloomily awaiting the advent of the insurance assessor. He told Gideon the FIU had just left, and that if they had turned up anything interesting, they weren't telling.

They ate fish and chips that Gideon had had the foresight to pick up on the way and then set about making habitable those stables that had suffered the least damage. Having all the animals in the confined space of the surgery was far from ideal, and stressful for all concerned.

Parking in the hospital multi-storey was comparatively easy, due to the lateness of the hour, and Gideon took his hands off the wheel with some relief. Urged by Naomi and Pippa, he had made time to call in at his local surgery to let the nurse redress his hands but even so his blistered palms were proving something of a trial and he'd done a fair amount of driving around that day, one way and another.

He gave himself a mental shake. Leaning back on the headrest, he'd been within a whisker of falling asleep right there in the car park. With a groan he climbed out of the car, purchased a ticket and headed for the hospital building.

Inside the building it took Gideon a good ten minutes to discover exactly where Jez was, and as he hurried down the corridor, the general tide of people was in the opposite direction. It seemed that visiting time was probably over.

Passing an open-plan coffee shop area, he caught sight of Big Ellie at one of the tables and, opposite her, the back of what was almost certainly Joey's blond head. He ducked his own and hurried by, hoping he hadn't been seen. It had been a long day and a confrontation with Jez's brother he could well do without.

Jez lay in the end bed of a smallish ward that appeared to be peopled with geriatrics. She wore a pretty flowered nightdress and someone had combed out her tousled locks. The effect was astounding, notwithstanding her dark-shadowed eyes and unnatural paleness. For the first time since he'd known her, she actually looked like a girl.

'Hey there, Shorty, I almost didn't recognise you,' Gideon remarked, making room on the already overcrowded cupboard beside her bed for a puzzle magazine and a bag of toffees he'd picked up in the hospital shop. 'How's it going?'

'Gideon!' she exclaimed in a voice that, like his own, was a little huskier than usual. 'What happened last night? Did you get Kizzy out? Is she all right?'

Gideon hesitated. It was a question he'd rather unrealistically hoped to avoid for the time being. There was no easy way to say it.

'I'm afraid there wasn't anything I could do, Jez. Her back was broken.'

Jez was silent. The dreaded tears didn't come but her stillness was almost worse. Then she fixed Gideon with an intense gaze from her startling blue eyes.

'You did go back though, didn't you?'

'I said I would.'

'I know, but . . .'

277

'But adults often say things just to keep kids quiet, is that it?'

She nodded, unsmiling.

'Not this one,' he promised.

'So . . .' She paused and her lip trembled slightly. 'So, if I killed her – when I fell on her, I mean – you'd say so?'

Her eyes were huge now and the desperate plea in them unmistakable. Gideon was pretty sure she'd known all along that the fawn wouldn't survive. She wasn't stupid. What had been tearing her up inside was wondering if she had caused the injury herself.

'If it was your fault,' he agreed steadily, 'I would tell you. But it wasn't. It was the beam that killed her and there was nothing anyone could have done. She didn't suffer,' he said then, anticipating her next question.

She scanned his face intensely, wanting to believe him.

Behind him a voice said softly that visiting time was over and they were sorry but he would have to go.

'Did you kill her?' Jez asked bluntly, totally ignoring the nurse.

'I had to.'

Behind him, the nurse cleared her throat. 'Five minutes,' she said. 'I can see this is important. But if Ward Sister catches you, I shall deny everything.'

Gideon thanked her, sat himself on the chair beside Jez's bed and took one of her small, bandaged hands in one of his own. 'I'm sorry, but it's the way things go sometimes.'

'Joey was mad at me for going in there.'

'Joey's had a fright,' Gideon said. 'He knows that if he'd picked you up on time, this wouldn't have happened. People often get mad with other people when they're really mad at themselves.'

'That's silly.'

'That's life.'

To cheer her up Gideon told her of their antics with the donkeys that morning and, as he talked, her eyelids began to droop. By the time the nurse returned to see him on his way, Jez was fast asleep. The nurse told him that the child's injuries were confined to minor burns, bruising and the effects of smoke inhalation. She would be out in a day or two.

The frosty night air was a shock after the stuffy warmth of the ward, and Gideon pulled his leather jacket closer about him as he headed back to the car. The multi-storey was dimly lit and unwelcoming, and his footsteps echoed hollowly as he passed between the few remaining vehicles to where he'd left Pippa's runabout. He was desperately, achingly weary and his mind was on hot soup, crusty bread, and collapsing on the sofa at the Gatehouse in front of the woodburner.

Suddenly, as swift and silent as a cat, someone stepped out from behind a van as he passed. Instinctively, Gideon whirled, crouching slightly.

Joey held up his hands in mock surrender.

'Kinda nervous, ain't we, pal?' His eyes scanning the shadows, Gideon slowly straightened. Joey appeared to be alone. Ellie would have been a comfort, Curly a decided minus.

'You bastard!' he said, low-voiced. The adrenaline rush in his over-tired system had produced an unpleasant shaky light-headedness. 'What do you want? I'm not in the mood for any more of your threats. Save them for another day.'

Surprisingly, Joey's cocky self-assurance seemed to ebb a little and his gaze shifted to a point somewhere above Gideon.

Managing to resist the temptation to look up, Gideon nevertheless felt a shiver, as though someone had walked over his grave.

'I didn't know, yesterday, what you'd done. For Sis, I mean,' Joey said awkwardly. 'We saw the fireman today, the one from last night. He came to visit Jez. He said if it hadn't been for you . . .' He broke off, his eyes meeting Gideon's once more. 'I said some stuff yesterday . . .'

'Oh, forget it,' he said wearily. 'I don't give a damn what you think of me. I like your sister, she's a good kid. Too bad she has to have you for a brother!' He turned away from Joey, back towards the car, but in two swift steps Joey had caught up with him and detained him with a hand on his arm.

'I know you don't give a shit what I think, but I owe you.'

'I didn't do it for you,' Gideon cut in roughly,

shrugging the hand off. He'd had enough.

'I owe you,' Joey said stubbornly. 'And I don't like feeling obliged to you, so you can soddin' listen! That night with the horse . . . I can't tell you who we were working for. He'd know who bloody told you and then I'd be dead. But there was another bloke there, a foreigner. I don't know his name but he was dark – Spanish maybe.'

Gideon's eyes narrowed. This was unexpected indeed. 'And the horse?'

'I don't know where that came from. We were only called in, Curly an' me, when they wanted you fetched.'

'Well, what did it look like? That'd be a help.'

Joey thought hard, his brow furrowing. 'It was a kind of copper colour, I guess you'd call it, with white legs and white on its face. It was a big sonafabitch, I'll tell you that for nothing.'

Gideon's head was a whirl of unwelcome thoughts.

'Did anyone use a name?' he asked, almost afraid to hear the answer.

'Not that I heard, pal. I can't tell you anything else, and I didn't tell you this, you understand? The debt's clear now. If I get any grief over this, I'll come looking for you and my conscience won't trouble me. D'you understand?'

'What? Oh, sure.' Gideon's response was probably not what Joey had hoped for, but he had other things on his mind.

A copper-coloured stallion and a Spaniard. *A chestnut and an Italian?*

Was it possible? Popsox, the Collinses' ex-showjumping stallion, and Sean Rosetti, the vet?

But *why*, for Christ's sake? Where was the sense in it?

11

Early on Sunday morning, two days after the fire, somebody rapped on Gideon's front door just as he was making his way downstairs. He looked at his watch, frowning.

Five-past eight.

Elsa met him in the hall, winding herself affectionately around his legs in her ritual greeting. He picked her up and draped her over his shoulder as he slid the bolts back and turned the key. Situated as it was in a porch, and being of solid oak, there was no way of seeing who was waiting at the door, and having learned from previous experience, Gideon stood well to one side as he opened it.

A slim frame in jeans and a jacket, short hair and shrewd blue eyes; Logan, out of uniform.

Gideon's heart missed a beat. 'What is it? Has something happened?' he asked, with nightmare visions of Naomi and Tim in dire peril.

'Er, no – nothing,' the policeman said. 'I was just passing.'

Gideon raised an eyebrow. 'Don't you guys ever sleep?' he asked, with a touch of asperity. 'Eight o'clock on a Sunday is barely civilised.'

Logan had the grace to look a little discomfited. 'I forgot it was Sunday. You tend to lose track of the days in this job. I wondered if I might have a word?'

'An official word?'

'Well, about official matters,' Logan hedged.

'Yeah, well, you'd better come in, I suppose.' There was a sharp frost outside and Gideon's feet, as yet bootless, were beginning to freeze on the flagstones of the hall. He stood back to let Logan pass, gesturing in the direction of the kitchen. Elsa, still on his shoulder, bristled at the intrusion and he soothed her as he followed.

'Coffee?' Without waiting for a reply he filled the kettle and stood it on the Aga. Elsa dropped lightly on to the top of the cooker and glared at the policeman from behind the hotplate cover.

'Thanks.' Logan propped himself against the table. 'How're the hands?'

Gideon had removed the original, rather bulky dressings the day before and replaced them with light bandages. The blisters were drying out well. In fact, the nagging cough he'd been left with was far more troublesome. 'Soon be as good as new,' he said. 'How do you like your coffee?'

'Strong, black and sweet. I need the caffeine.

I've just finished a double shift. Haven't slept for twenty-six hours.'

He didn't appear to be seeking sympathy and Gideon didn't offer any. 'So what was so urgent that it couldn't wait?' he asked, feeding the Aga to encourage it to greater effort with the kettle.

Logan shrugged. 'You get a lot of time to think, on surveillance, and I found myself thinking about your friend Tim Reynolds at the Sanctuary. He seems pretty sure the trouble he's been having has its roots next door.' He paused. 'What do you know about Slade?'

Gideon had his back to Logan, so was able to hide his surprise at this unexpected question.

'A lot less than you do, I expect,' he replied over his shoulder.

'You went to visit,' Logan stated.

'I went to see Milne, not Slade.'

'He invited you?'

'Sort of. Casually. I don't think he expected me to take him up on it.'

'So why did you?'

Gideon thought for a moment. 'Call it curiosity.' He spooned instant coffee into mugs and poured on the water.

'I wouldn't have thought he was your type . . .'

'We're both artists,' Gideon pointed out. 'We had coffee and biscuits, we talked about art, and he showed me some of his pictures.'

'And you didn't even try to find out if or why he's been making trouble for Reynolds?' Logan stuck to the scent like a bloodhound.

'Yes, I tried, but to be honest, he just didn't seem interested in the Sanctuary. He only wanted to talk about things artistic. He's got tunnel vision. I'd say he's a man obsessed.'

'And do you share his views on that subject?'

'His views?' Gideon stirred three spoonfuls of sugar into Logan's mug and handed it to him.

'Thanks.' Logan pulled out a chair and slid into it. 'He used to be a troublemaker, apparently. Protested about English masterpieces being sold overseas. Picketed the galleries. Lobbied the Heritage people and the government. Made himself a real pain in the arse, from what I can gather. I thought you'd have known about it, being an artist yourself.' He glanced up at Gideon under his brows.

'I paint animals,' Gideon observed mildly. 'That doesn't make me an authority on the history of art and artists. But anyway, that must have been years ago. He's practically a recluse now. Beyond the odd letter to *The Times*, I shouldn't think he's bothered anybody for a long time.'

Logan shrugged again. Once a troublemaker – always a troublemaker, his body language intimated. 'So, did you see Slade while you were there?'

'On the way out. He wasn't exactly overjoyed to find me there. I'd kind of side-stepped the security man.'

Logan blew on his coffee and sipped it. 'Was that the first time you'd met him?'

'It was.'

286

'And?' He gave the appearance of being far more interested in the business of cooling his coffee than the conversation he'd initiated.

'And . . .' Two could play at that game. Unhurriedly, Gideon pulled a chair out, sat sideways on it and stretched his feet towards the warmth. 'And, I wondered what a man like him was doing buried in the depths of the country, working for a man like Meredith Milne.'

'Ah,' Logan said. 'So it wouldn't surprise you if I said he was known to us?'

'It would surprise me a lot more if you said he wasn't,' Gideon replied frankly. 'What's he done?'

Logan rubbed a hand wearily over his forehead and eyes. 'Well, he's had a couple of speeding tickets,' he said after a moment.

'And?' Gideon said, mimicking Logan, who flashed him a brief, amused smile of acknowledgement.

'And – nothing,' he admitted, regretfully. 'We've nothing else on him but a handful of suspicions. He's been suspected of illegal gambling activities, of fraud, even of extortion, but he always seems to wriggle out of the net. The boys down at Bournemouth nick had him in for questioning after they raided an unlicensed poker club four years ago but they couldn't make anything stick and they had to let him go. He's very good at finding other people to do his dirty work and it seems those people would rather go down than risk pointing the finger. He must have some very unpleasant friends. Of course it's all conjecture. As far as his official record goes, he's a fine upstanding citizen who probably helps old ladies across the road and is kind to small children and animals.'

'Yeah, well, I don't think I'd trust him with *my* granny,' Gideon said. 'So what do *you* think he's doing at Lyddon Grange? Is he behind the troublemaking?'

Logan pursed his lips. 'Almost certainly, but he didn't start it. Milne tried to buy the farm as soon as Mr Reynolds arrived, three months ago; Slade has only been working for him for two months. Before that, he was running a club in Dorchester for a couple of years. When we realised who he was we made a point of keeping a close eye on his activities but somehow he got wind of it and before we could act, he'd upped and left.'

'You think Milne got Slade in specifically to shift Tim from next door? But why? And how would Milne get hold of someone like him? I can't see the old guy visiting Slade's club, can you? Or did he look in the *Thompson's Local* under T for Troublemaker?'

'I should imagine Renson may have had something to do with it,' Logan said.

'Renson the low-flying helicopter pilot? It *was* him, wasn't it? What's been done about that?'

'He's been given a caution,' Logan said. 'Any more stunts like that and he'll lose his licence. My sergeant seemed to think that was all that was needed.'

'Your sergeant didn't seem very interested at all, to be honest,' Gideon observed. 'One might almost have thought he was trying to protect someone he knew . . .'

Logan's eyes narrowed. 'One might think it, but it would be very difficult to prove.'

'All right, so why are you telling me all this?' Gideon asked, after a moment. 'It's not *me* who's being driven off my land.'

'Joey Dylan is a known associate of citizen Slade. You seem to know Joey. I want to know how.'

'My sister helps at the Sanctuary, as you know. Jez spends a fair bit of time there. Joey is Jez's brother and he picks her up sometimes. I've met him once or twice, that's all. No mystery.'

Logan wasn't going to be so easily put off. 'I'd say there was a lot more to it than that. And according to Mr Reynolds, it was you who first introduced them to Jez,' he remarked.

'I met her just outside,' Gideon explained patiently. 'Her dog was injured and Tim's a vet. It made sense to take her there.'

'So you're saying that you first met Joey at Hermitage Farm. Saying, in fact, that Joey Dylan has no connection with the six foot five, fair-haired Joey who was involved in your reported abduction?'

Gideon cursed silently. He should have known that Logan would do his homework and make the connection. He conjured up what he hoped was a suitably embarrassed expression. 'Oh, that! That was just a bit of a practical joke that got out of hand.'

'Yeah, and I'm Eskimo Nell! You've still got the

scars, Mister, so don't give me that crap!' He regarded Gideon thoughtfully for a moment. 'But something's happened to make you change your story. I don't suppose you're going to tell me what it was, are you?'

Gideon got to his feet. 'I've withdrawn the allegation. More coffee?'

'I don't mind if I do,' Logan said, swallowing the last dregs and holding out his mug. 'I know you've withdrawn it. Your statement's still on record, though, and if we feel it needs to be followed up, it will be. Are you saying now that you knew Joey Dylan all along?'

Gideon hesitated. Once again Logan was driving him into a corner. Knowledge brought with it responsibilities. A few days before, he would have welcomed Logan's interest, but what Joey had told him about that night had sent his thoughts along unwelcome avenues, and he wanted to know more before he took the matter any further with the authorities.

He shrugged. 'What do you want me to say? It's over, as far as I'm concerned. I've spoken to Joey and we've sorted it out.'

Logan regarded him through narrowed eyes. 'I think you're lying, but I can't figure out why. Is someone threatening you?'

Gideon handed him his second mug of coffee. 'No,' he said, returning Logan's look steadily. Above their heads the floorboards creaked as Rachel went across to the bathroom.

Logan held his gaze for several long seconds and

then sighed. 'Well, it's up to you, I guess. I just hope you know what you're doing.'

Elsa mewed plaintively and Gideon opened a tin for her. He was beginning to feel hungry himself, so he fished a loaf of bread out of the cupboard, cut several slices and put them in the toaster. 'Do we know how the fire started yet?'

Logan nodded. 'In the farmhouse. It seems one of the workmen was careless. Some unfinished wiring, some old wallpaper and woodshavings, the power left on . . . These things happen.'

'So, it was an accident?'

'Looks that way.'

'But accidents can be arranged, right?'

'You'd have a job proving it. There were no suspicious circumstances, no use of accelerants, nothing obviously out of place. You'd be surprised how many fires are started by workmen. I mean, look at Windsor Castle . . .'

'I suppose so.' Gideon wasn't convinced and he didn't think Logan was either, though his expression gave nothing away.

Rachel came downstairs with her characteristic quick, light tread and through to the kitchen.

Gideon saw Logan's look of mild enquiry sharpen into appreciation as he took in elfin features surrounded by a mane of dark curls, and the slim curves that weren't completely disguised by the huge mohair jumper she wore over her jeans.

She paused, then advanced hesitantly.

'Rachel, this is Constable Logan. Logan, Rachel Shelley, my temporary lodger.'

'Mark,' he said, standing up to shake her hand with a brief smile.

Rachel took the proffered hand shyly, her dark-fringed eyes glancing anxiously from Gideon to the policeman and back again. 'What's happened? Have they caught Duncan? Is he back in prison?'

'He's here about the fire, Rachel.'

'Duncan?' Logan looked at Gideon. 'Ah, Duncan Shelley. The man who broke parole and has been making a nuisance of himself.'

'Yes. Rachel's ex-husband,' Gideon said. The toast popped up, and as Logan showed no signs of leaving, he put three plates on the table and more bread in the machine. Rachel fetched butter, marmalade and knives.

Logan helped himself.

'Well, well,' he said. 'And are you involved in any other criminal matters I should know about?'

Surprisingly, it was Rachel who became fired up in Gideon's defence.

'That's not fair! It's not Gideon's fault he got mixed up in this, it's mine, and all because he was kind enough to help me! He didn't have to.' She glared at Logan who appeared a little bemused by this unexpected attack.

'In fact, I'm thinking of putting in for canonisation,' Gideon told him.

Logan's mouth twitched but Rachel coloured up unhappily.

'I know you're teasing me. But it's not fair to criticise you for something that's not your fault! That other policeman was just as bad!'

'*What* other policeman?' Logan asked through a mouthful of toast and marmalade.

'Hillcott, I think his name was,' Gideon said. 'He and his pal were here the other day about Duke Shelley and more or less accused me of attention-seeking. As if I hadn't anything better to do!'

'Ah,' Logan said, as if things had become clear. 'You get prats in every walk of life. Unfortunately, the police force is no exception. I know Hillcott. He was stationed with us at Chilminster for a while and he's not a particular friend of mine.'

Small talk occupied the remainder of the meal. Rachel's hostility was apparently dissipated by Logan's opinion of Hillcott and she joined in the conversation as if she had known the policeman all her life. Gideon couldn't be sure whether this was due to Logan's undoubted skill in managing people or to Rachel's growing confidence. She seemed to have come on a lot, even in the short time he had known her.

'So, what did you come about, really?' Gideon asked as he eventually showed Logan out. 'Or were you just hungry?'

Logan flashed his boyish grin, then said frankly, 'I was checking up on you, actually. I found myself going over the connection between you and Joey, and Slade and the Sanctuary, and none of it made a lot of sense.'

'Join the club,' Gideon said.

'I needed to know more about you.'

'And now you do?' he asked, trying to remember what might have been said to this end.

'Enough,' Logan said. 'For now, anyway.'

'Well, let me know if you're coming again,' Gideon suggested. 'And I'll get extra bread in.'

For a couple of days it seemed as though things had settled down a little in Gideon's orbit. The donkeys appeared to have adjusted quite happily to life at Home Farm and, unexpectedly, Giles had taken to them in a big way. Although so far he'd drawn the line at actually mucking out, he seemed fascinated by them and was often on hand to help Naomi when she came over to see them.

At the Sanctuary itself, Tim reported no further disturbances. The insurance company was dragging its feet, which left him treading water, unable to do more than maintain the remaining animals as best he could while waiting for the okay to begin rebuilding. When Gideon visited him, on a cold and frosty day the week after the fire, he was busy hand-feeding an injured kestrel that somebody had brought in.

'How often do you have to do that?' Gideon asked, watching with interest as Tim patiently coaxed the bird to accept food from a dropper.

'Every couple of hours to start with,' he said. 'She's very weak and won't take much at a time.'

'She? How do you sex a kestrel? Or is the plumage different?'

'Yeah. The male has a grey head and tail.' Tim refilled the dropper but the bird appeared to have lost interest. 'The hell of it is, you wear yourself out doing this all day and night and think you're doing well, and then they up and die on you with no warning. Delayed shock, heart attack, stress – I'm never sure, but it happens again and again. You can't not try though, can you?'

Gideon agreed that you couldn't.

'Seen or heard anything of the neighbours?' he enquired.

'Well, strangely enough,' Tim said, laying down the pipette and carefully returning the kestrel to its cage, 'Milne was here yesterday.'

'*Milne* was?'

Tim nodded. 'The man himself. I was busy in the yard, clearing some of the rubble from that old wall that came down, and when I looked up he was there. Just standing looking at the mobile home – or what's left of it. He hadn't said a word. When I spoke to him, he looked at me for a moment as if *I* was the one who was trespassing.'

'Then what happened?'

'Well, not a lot, really. He said he hadn't realised that there'd been so much damage and asked how long it would take to clear up. No explanation of what he was doing here or anything. Oh, and he asked if we'd be rebuilding it all as it was.'

Gideon frowned. 'That's odd. No, not that he didn't explain, he's a bad-mannered bugger at the best of times. I mean, asking about the rebuilding. What did you say?'

'Well, to be honest, I didn't see that it was any of his business, so I said we hadn't decided for sure but we'd probably take the opportunity to expand on quite a grand scale.' He looked a little sheepish.

295

'It probably wasn't the wisest thing to say but I was feeling a bit peeved.'

'No! Good for you!' Gideon declared. 'What did he have to say to that?'

'Not a lot. He muttered something about how distressing it must've been for us, and then left. It was all very strange.'

Gideon pondered the riddle of Meredith Milne as he headed on from the Sanctuary to visit some clients and then pick up Mary Collins' picture from the framer.

It would have been easy to pass off this interest in Tim's plans for the future of the Sanctuary as mere curiosity, if it hadn't been for the fact that Milne was self-interested almost to the exclusion of all else. If he *had* instigated the burning of the buildings, it had surely been with the intention of driving the occupants out, not because the present layout offended him. After all, he could hardly see the Sanctuary buildings from the Grange.

Gideon abandoned the puzzle.

The clients he'd journeyed to see were John and Yvonne Radcliffe, a young husband and wife whose hobby was three-day-eventing. They were friends of Pippa's and it was she who'd passed on Gideon's name.

He was taken to see the problem horse, a big, rangy gelding called Bouncer who, he was told, was as quiet as a lamb to handle with practically everyone except John.

Gideon asked to see the horse alone first and

went into the stable talking softly and with palms held uppermost for the horse to sniff. The gelding snuffed both hands and then his face in a perfectly relaxed fashion, then stood calmly while Gideon ran his hands over the bay coat with its hard, fit muscles beneath.

Leaving the stable, he asked John to approach the horse and watched carefully. John was a fairly burly individual but his body language was good. Immediately, though, the black-edged ears went back and the horse retreated a step or two, showing the whites of its eyes and blowing distrustfully through distended nostrils.

'That's enough,' Gideon called. Then turning to Yvonne, 'Does he react like that to anyone else at all?'

'No, only to John. Oh, and yes, now you mention it, one of my friends. A girlfriend. But she isn't horsy, so we thought nothing of it. Before that, we were thinking maybe he just didn't like men, but then he's been all right with Ted, an ex-jockey who helps me out sometimes when John's working.'

'And how far will the horse go? I mean, is it all show or does he get physical?'

'He bit me once. Hard, too.' John fished a packet of cigarettes out of the pocket of his waxed jacket and lit one. 'And he's threatened to kick. I leave him to Yvonne these days but it's not an ideal situation. I mean, it's one thing at home, but come the spring, when we want to travel to events, I'm going to have to be able to handle him

297

too. To be honest, if we can't sort it out he'll have to go.'

'D'you think you'll be able to do anything?' Yvonne asked anxiously. 'We really don't want to have to sell him, he jumps like a dream.'

They were talking less than ten feet from the gelding's stable door and Gideon had been watching the horse closely all the while. Now he transferred his attention to the waiting couple again.

'No, I'm afraid I don't think there's much I can do,' he said, and saw their faces drop with disappointment. 'But I think maybe John can.'

'Me? What can I do? I can't get near him.'

'Tell me,' Gideon said to Yvonne. 'Does your girlfriend have any bad habits?'

'Bad habits?' she echoed, looking utterly bewildered. 'What d'you . . .?' Then the coin dropped. 'Oh! You mean smoking! Of course! John smokes and so does Clare but neither Ted nor I do. You've got it, I'm sure you have. Ha!' she exclaimed triumphantly, turning to her husband. 'Now you'll *have* to give up.'

He withdrew the offending object from his mouth and looked at it ruefully. 'Damn!' he said. 'Why couldn't it have been my after-shave he didn't like?'

Gideon laughed. 'I expect he associates the smell with someone who's abused him in the past. Horses have exceedingly long memories when it comes to that sort of thing. And they have a very acute sense of smell.'

'I suppose you're sure?'

'Reasonably. I'll tell you what. You give up smoking for, say, three months, and if there's no improvement, I'll come and see him again, free of charge. But I warn you, there probably won't be an overnight change. For one thing, the smell of tobacco will linger for quite a while, and after that you've got to give the horse time to adjust to the new you.'

'Bugger!' John said succinctly. 'I can't believe I've just paid a small fortune for somebody to come and tell me to quit smoking!'

Yvonne was highly amused. 'Personally, I think it's well worth it,' she said. 'I've been on at him for ages to stop. Come on, Gideon. Come and tell me what you think of my baby while you're here.'

The 'baby' turned out to be not a bawling pink bundle wrapped in a blanket, as Gideon had feared, but a leggy, dark chestnut yearling colt with two long white stockings and two white socks. As they leaned on the stable door, Gideon was able to say with perfect honesty, 'He's gorgeous, isn't he?'

Yvonne glowed.

'No need to ask who the sire is,' he added. 'He couldn't be by any other horse, with those trademarks.'

'Let's hope he jumps like his dad,' John remarked. 'The stud fees were phenomenal.'

'I suppose you can't blame them for trying to make as much as they can while Popsox is still a household name,' Yvonne said reasonably. 'I think he'll jump. He's got the pedigree and he's going to have the right build, and the mare was a jumper, but of course there are no certainties in breeding.'

'Only that you're going to lose money,' John put in.

'Never mind, dear,' Yvonne said sweetly. 'You'll just have to go out and make some more.'

The portrait, when Gideon collected it from the framer's, was a triumph. Framed in a dark oak, with a dusky, mushroom-coloured mount, the horse and man depicted were thrown into relief so they appeared almost three-dimensional.

Gideon was absolutely delighted with it. This was the moment that made all the hours of hard work seem worthwhile – until the next time. He drove home with it wrapped in soft cloth and a wealth of bubble plastic, and with Duke in mind, decided to leave it stowed safely at the Priory when he took Pippa's car back.

There was nobody about in the yard when Gideon arrived, but as he let himself through the back door into the kitchen he found not only Pippa but also Giles and Rachel, apparently in hot debate over the parentage of Fanny's puppies.

'Ah, Gideon. Just the man,' Giles said, seeing him come in. 'Come and give us the benefit of your learned opinion. I say these pups are no more purebred Labrador than I am, but Pippa refuses to see it.'

'That sounds remarkably like, "Gideon, come and take sides with me against my sister,"' he commented warily. 'I'm no expert on puppies.'

'Well, come and look anyway,' Pippa urged. 'They must be Lab. I paid a fortune in stud fees.'

It was the second time that day he'd heard that particular protest, Gideon reflected, as he obligingly approached the huge, and much-chewed, wicker basket that housed Fanny and her six pups.

The puppies, five weeks old now, squeaked and wriggled across one another in mock aggression, two of them tumbling out on to the rag-rug as they wrestled. Gideon regarded them judiciously for a long moment, aware that three pairs of eyes watched his face for a clue as to his thoughts.

'Well,' he said cautiously, 'as I said, I'm no expert but they *have* got rather long noses, haven't they? And one of them looks suspiciously brindle.'

Two howls greeted this observation. One unmistakably of triumph and one of something approaching anguish.

Gideon felt sorry for her. 'I'm sorry, Pips, but it's true. I'd say dear Fanny pre-empted your expensive stud dog with a choice of her own. Maybe that lurcher from the farm.'

'Oh, God! And I thought I'd been so careful! How am I going to find homes for six bloody mongrels? That's what *I* want to know,' she wailed. 'I've got orders for five blue-blooded Labradors. I can't see those people saying, "Oh, that's all right. I don't mind if he's got a long nose and a curly tail." Most of them want gundogs, for heaven-sakes.'

'Well, they are half-Lab,' Giles pointed out. 'Tell them it's a new, dual-purpose breed – the

Tarrant Labra-lurch. Ideal for gunwork or a spot of poaching.'

'Well, I think you're being really rotten!' Rachel said from her position on the floor, close to the basket. 'All of you! They're beautiful puppies and I don't think it should matter whether they're purebred or not.'

'Absolutely,' Gideon approved. 'A dog is a dog, as far as I'm concerned.'

'Oh, good!' Pippa said sweetly. 'I'll put you down for one, shall I?'

'Oh, go on, Gideon!' Rachel urged. 'It would be such fun!'

'For whom? You're not the one who'd have to mop up after it. No, I don't think it's a good idea. Elsa would be horrified, for a start. Look,' he said, judiciously changing the subject, 'I only came in to ask if you've somewhere safe I could leave this for a few days.'

'Is it very important?'

'Well, yes,' Gideon said, surprised.

Pippa looked meaningfully from the package he held to the writhing black mass at her feet and back again. 'I expect we could come to some arrangement.'

'That,' Gideon said, with narrowed eyes, 'is blackmail, and I won't submit to it.'

Three days later, after a preparatory telephone call, a bitterly cold but bright morning found Gideon on his way to the Collinses' stud to deliver the portrait. Once again he had had to beg for the use of Pippa's car, and it occurred to him, not for the first time, that he really should look round for one of his own.

Mary had assured him that Tom would be safely away at a cattle market until midday, and as Gideon turned into the yard he could see that although Tom's car stood on the gravel, the livestock lorry was indeed missing.

Mary met him at the door, hugging herself against the chill of the wind and patently excited at the prospect of seeing the picture. He greeted her with a kiss and followed her gratefully into the warmth of the kitchen, feeling the slight twinge of apprehension that unveiling a portrait invariably produced in him. No matter that he'd done dozens and had never yet met with anything but delight from his clients; a portrait is such a personal thing, and although he always tried to reproduce every detail faithfully, he still lived in dread of seeing the excited anticipation in someone's face fade into disappointment.

This was not that day. After the usual, heart-stopping moment of blank assimilation, Mary's face lit up with something approaching wonder and she turned to Gideon with tears shining in her eyes.

'It's beautiful!' she breathed. 'Thank you! Oh, thank you so much!'

Gideon let out the breath he had been unconsciously holding and smiled in return. 'I'm glad you like it,' he said. 'Let's hope Tom does.'

'Oh, he will,' Mary stated with certainty, still

303

gazing at the portrait. 'He'll love it. I just don't know how you do it.'

'Monkey see, monkey copy.'

'Oh, no. There's much more to it than that or we'd all be doing it. Oh, it's just perfect!'

Gideon watched her fondly.

'How are things now? Any better?' he asked gently.

Mary's rapt expression became wistful. 'Oh, I don't know. Some days are better than others. Sometimes I think maybe I'm imagining a problem that doesn't really exist. Perhaps we're just getting old and growing apart. I don't know what to think any more.'

'Perhaps it's a kind of mid-life crisis. The male menopause or something.'

Mary laughed and said she'd better put the picture away out of sight, as their anniversary wasn't until the following week. 'If you'd like to wander up to the yard, Anthony's up there somewhere,' she added. 'I'll put the kettle on.'

Gideon readily fell in with this suggestion. He had in fact been hoping for a chance to see Sox again. Ever since Joey's disclosure about the copper-coloured horse with white legs, he'd struggled to equate the animal he'd worked with for all those weeks with the frightened and aggressive stallion of that memorable night.

Anthony made it easy for him. When Gideon reached the yard he found the boy in Sox's stable, working hard to make his glossy coat even glossier.

'You've had him clipped,' Gideon noticed, after the usual greetings had been exchanged.

'Yes, well, we've started riding him again – or at least, I have,' Anthony said. 'He seems fairly sound now and he was getting so bored in the autumn with no mares to keep him busy.'

'He looks well. How is he in himself? Have you been having any trouble with him? You know – mood swings or aggression?'

'No.' Anthony looked surprised. 'Why do you ask? He gets a bit high-spirited at times, but don't they all? Come in and see him. He'd like that, he's fond of you.'

Gideon did so and the stallion did indeed seem pleased to see him. Moreover, he seemed very relaxed and content, not even displaying any characteristic stallion one-upmanship. Gideon was pleased to find him so settled, but also perplexed. What could have happened to him that night to make him so distressed? What had they done to him?

'He seems very happy. What a difference from when I first saw him after the accident. His new line of work must be suiting him.'

'He's back to his old self,' Anthony said, replacing the stallion's rugs before untying him. He slapped the shining neck and turned away as Sox began to pull at the hay in his net.

Gideon passed on the message from Mary about the kettle.

'Right-oh. I'll just put this stuff in the tack room and I'll be with you.'

Gideon watched the lad move about the yard and was struck by his quiet efficiency. 'I expect your dad'll be glad when you finish college and can help him full-time,' he commented as they began to walk back towards the house.

Abruptly, Anthony's face set into harder lines. 'You'd think so, wouldn't you?' he said. 'It's all I've ever wanted to do, and he knows that, but now he turns round and says it'd be better if I went away to another stud to gain experience for a couple of years.'

Gideon pursed his lips. 'I suppose there might be some advantages but I should've thought he'd want you here. Especially since he hasn't got anyone else on site, so to speak. Is this a new idea?'

'Well, he did mention it in passing a few months ago but I made it clear that I wasn't keen and he never followed it up. I thought he'd forgotten it.' The boy made a sound of pure frustration. 'In the old days he was always reminding me that the stud and the farm are my future. That I should learn all I could about it. Now, he says my education is the most important thing. He even wanted me to go away to boarding school but Mum put her foot down.'

'Well, you must admit, farming's in a bit of a mess at the moment. It seems to be one crisis after another. I mean, it can't necessarily be regarded as the secure future it once was, can it? I expect your dad just wants you to get a good basic education that you can fall back on, if needs be.'

'Oh, I'm taking my education seriously, don't

you worry,' Anthony said. 'I've just started my second term of a business studies course at night school, and when I've finished that I'm doing one in book-keeping. By the summer, if everything goes to plan, I should have A-levels in maths, computer-aided design and biology. I think I'm doing my bit. Taking responsibility for my own future. I feel I'm mature enough to decide where I want to go from here.'

Gideon was impressed. 'Have you tried talking to him?'

The boy snorted. 'That's just the trouble – he won't talk! Or won't listen, more like. If I corner him about it, he just resorts to telling me to do as I'm told, as if I'm still a kid. Sean says I'll be eighteen soon and will be able to do what I want, but that's no help if what I want is to stay here. If I wanted to *leave*, it would be easy!'

Gideon shook his head. 'I must admit, it's an unusual situation. With most kids it's the other way round.'

'Yeah, I suppose . . .' Anthony paused, leaning on a field gate and gazing across the grassy acres through eyes narrowed against the cold wind. In the near distance a herd of red and white cattle grazed, all facing the same way, as cattle often will.

'This is all I want. To stay here and learn the business, and then someday take over from Dad when he retires. You'd think he'd be pleased! It's like he's changed lately. Mum's noticed it, too, even though she tries to pretend everything's okay. I know she gets upset sometimes.'

Gideon couldn't think of anything comforting to say. If he'd thought it would do any good he would have offered to speak to Tom himself, but knew him well enough to realise he wouldn't welcome any interference, and that once he'd made up his mind there was little hope of changing it.

He leaned on the gate beside Anthony, watching the cattle.

'Beef cattle?'

'Mm. Herefords.'

'You haven't got a bull, have you?'

Anthony laughed, the bitter lines disappearing in an instant. 'Where've you been for the last fifty years? Haven't you heard of AI?'

'Oh, yes, of course. Who does that, Rosetti?'

'No, a chap called Petersen. Have you heard of him? Comes from your way.'

Gideon hadn't. 'I thought you said Sean Rosetti did AI?'

'Not any more. He used to work for one of those centres, pioneering new techniques, but he gave it up to set up his own practice. But anyway, he's just our horse vet. We have a different vet for the cattle.' He turned his head as the sound of a heavy vehicle reached them. 'Dad,' he said flatly. 'Talk of the devil!'

They swung away from the gate and went down to meet him.

'How did the sale go?' Anthony asked. 'Are prices picking up yet?'

Tom grunted. 'Well, they made their reserve, but only just. Twenty percent less than I'd hoped for.' His eyes narrowed as he took in Gideon's presence. 'What are you doing here? Every time I go out for a few hours you turn up! Are you having an affair with my wife?'

'I would if she'd have me, but she won't,' Gideon said, hoping his credit would stretch that far.

Apparently it would. 'Cheeky bugger!' Tom said, punching him lightly on the arm. 'Well, as you're here you'd better come in for a cup of tea.'

Gideon was just breathing a sigh of relief for the safe negotiation of what could have been a sticky moment, when Anthony said, 'Gideon was asking if we'd had any trouble with Sox. I told him he's been absolutely fine. He has, hasn't he?'

Tom stopped and turned. 'What do you mean, trouble? What kind of trouble?' he asked, abruptly.

Gideon could cheerfully have throttled the boy at that moment, though it was said in all innocence.

'Nothing in particular. I was just thinking aloud what an incredible recovery he'd made,' Gideon lied. 'How's his stud work going?'

Tom frowned. 'Very well. Why do you ask?'

'Just interested. I'm fond of the lad.'

'Aye, well, you've seen his get. How do *you* think his stud career is going?'

'Very well, I'd say,' Gideon assured him.

'Well, the mares have no complaints and he's happy in his work,' Tom confirmed, opening the farmhouse door and standing back to let the others precede him. 'If you can call it work!'

309

Gideon hoped fervently that Anthony would let the subject rest at that, and whether by luck or intuition, he did.

Rachel was out working again that day, and when Gideon thankfully removed himself from the emotionally charged atmosphere of the stud, he took Pippa's car home and spent the rest of the day helping her with the horses.

With a jumble of half-formed possibilities churning round in his mind, it was almost inevitable that Gideon should offload some of them on to Pippa. By the time they stopped to thaw out with a mug of coffee in the kitchen at five o'clock, she was in possession of most of the facts and as determined to get to the bottom of the riddle as he was.

'But what makes you think it *was* Sox that night?' she asked, curling her fingers gratefully round the hot mug. 'You told us it wasn't a horse you'd worked with before.'

Gideon shrugged. 'I didn't think it was . . .'

'I mean, there must be other chestnut stallions with white legs, for heavensakes! Stephanie Wainman's got one, for a start. It's not that unusual a colour combination, is it?'

'Yeah, I know. I was thinking about that on the way home. But Joey's actual words were "copper-coloured" and that's not so common. I guess, too, it was because Joey mentioned an Italian in the same breath. I instantly thought of Rosetti and went from there.'

'You told me Joey said there was a *Spaniard*,'

Pippa protested. 'One way and another, it seems to me that you're stretching the facts to fit an idea you've had. And it's not much of an idea, come to that. You can't even say *why* they might have "borrowed" him – if that's what they did.'

Gideon sighed. 'Okay, I admit I got a bit carried away but there just seemed to be a lot of coincidences, and I reckon several coincidences add up to a probability.'

Pippa snorted. 'And that's accepted mathematical reasoning, is it?'

'Well, if it isn't, it should be,' he asserted, enjoying the exchange.

'If I were you, I'd speak to Tom about it,' she told him. 'After all, if Rosetti *is* up to something that involves his horse, he's got a right to know about it, hasn't he? One way or another, it would be better to get it out into the open.'

'Unless Tom already knows about it,' Gideon pointed out, thinking of the stud owner's sharp reaction that afternoon. 'What if he's involved?'

'Well, that wouldn't make sense,' Pippa protested. 'If it was *his horse* he wouldn't need to sneak around at the dead of night, would he?'

'I suppose not. But on the other hand, how could he not know? None of it makes sense. But maybe you're right. I'll talk to him.'

To that end, he fished his mobile out of his pocket and found the Collinses' number in its memory.

Mary answered. 'Tom's not here at the moment, I'm afraid, Gideon. Can I take a message?'

'I really wanted to speak to him. Would he be in later, if I were to come over?'

'No, I'm afraid not. He'll come in for his meal but he said he was going to do some work on the cottage this evening. You know, Roly French's old place. You could always pop in to see him there, if you wanted. I'm sure he wouldn't mind.'

'Okay, perhaps I will,' Gideon said. 'Sevenish be okay?'

Mary thought it would. 'I'll let him know you're coming. There's nothing wrong, is there?'

'No. Just something I wanted to clear up with him. Don't worry.'

Gideon disconnected, wishing it was indeed likely to be that simple. He didn't know how the hell he was going to broach the subject.

'I need to be there about seven this evening, so could Rachel possibly come over here for an hour or two?' he asked Pippa.

'She's welcome to, if she doesn't mind putting up with Giles. I shall be out myself for a bit. So if your next question is can you borrow the car, the answer is no!'

'The thought never crossed my mind.' Gideon was all innocence. 'So where are *you* off to? Got a hot date?'

'That's for me to know and you to wonder.'

'It's all the same to me, Pips,' he said, shrugging. 'Well, if you're sure Giles won't mind . . .'

'I'm positive,' she assured him. 'He's never yet complained about having to entertain a pretty female and I'm sure he won't start now.'

As Gideon rode the Norton towards Winterbourne Shires later that evening, he found himself going over their conversation again in his mind.

He recognised Pippa's argument, that there were probably dozens of chestnut stallions around, as a sound one, but he still couldn't shake his conviction that there were too many coincidences. The problem still remained as to just what anyone had to gain from kidnapping a well-known stallion that they couldn't name as a sire. He'd flirted with the idea that if Rosetti was involved, then maybe AI could have been used, but the same objections applied. There was only value in it if Sox's name could be revealed, and even had that been the case, it was a hell of a risk for what could only be a small return.

Turning off the main road in due course, he was wondering variously if Giles fostered any serious feelings for Rachel, and who, if anyone, Pippa was going out with, when he became suddenly and somewhat forcibly aware of a vehicle looming large in his mirror, its lights blindingly bright. Now it had been brought to his attention, he recalled that it had been on his tail for a while, certainly since the outskirts of Dorchester, and possibly longer.

He wasn't normally a nervous bike rider but something about the way the van was holding the centre of what was not a terribly wide road made it seem more than a little menacing. It couldn't have been much more than ten feet off the rear wheel of the Norton, and at the best part of fifty miles an hour in the dark, that was a great deal too close for comfort.

Gideon was certainly not out to prove anything. Playing games with other road users when you're on a motorbike seemed to him to be little short of suicidal, even if they are getting up your nose. He slowed down slightly and pulled in to his side of the highway. Although the road wasn't wide, there was room aplenty to overtake, and that's what the van did.

Unfortunately, what it also did was cut sharply across the front wheel of the Norton in a screeching, sliding swerve.

Gideon hadn't a prayer.

One moment the road ahead was clear, the next his vision was filled with a wall of white metal. His instinctive attempt at avoidance was a physical impossibility and he and the bike hit the side of the van together with a deafening bang.

Hardly losing any speed, the van swerved back on to the tarmac, and after weaving from side to side a time or two, straightened up and powered away.

This much, Gideon sensed rather than saw, for as he and the Norton rebounded off the van they parted company and Gideon was flung headlong into the hedge, ending up in the ditch below it.

When his world stopped doing somersaults, he found himself more or less face down in the muddy stream that flowed in the bottom of the ditch, with icy water soaking freely into all parts not immediately protected by his leather jacket.

His first thought, as he lifted his head and spat gritty water, was: That's it. No more bikes. I'll get a car.

His second, and very unwelcome, thought was that whoever had been at the wheel of the van hadn't run him off the road by accident, and given his recent history, he couldn't even rely on its having been a case of road rage. If the van had indeed been following him with this intent, then it was entirely possible that whoever it was would return to see the results of his handiwork.

With this in mind, Gideon lost no further time in pushing himself to his knees and climbing over the lip of the ditch. As he stood painfully upright, his sodden jeans stiffened almost immediately in the biting wind and the excess water made its way unerringly into his boots.

Gideon swore. It was a clear night but the moon was waning and gave little light. He could just make out the shape of the Norton, wrapped around a roadside oak in a very final manner, and didn't need any more than the available light to convince him that he wouldn't be going any further on that.

Removing his helmet, and the thick leather gauntlets that had very probably saved his hands from being badly cut, he reached to his belt for his mobile phone. He turned it on with little optimism, for the road he'd been following was in something of a river valley and the reception would never have been great, even had the crash not reduced the antenna to no more than a jagged stump. It beeped comfortingly but could locate no signal whatsoever.

The mini camera in its zipped leather case seemed to have fared better, and Gideon took a couple of shots of the wrecked motorbike for the record before deciding on his best course of action.

He could hear the roar of the traffic on the busy main road, half a mile or so away, but Gutter Lane, in which Roly French's old cottage was situated, was only two or three hundred yards ahead, and the most sensible option appeared to be to head for that as planned. With any luck, Tom would have a phone he could use to call for a salvage truck, a taxi, and the police. Shivering with cold, he set off.

The walk to the cottage took no more than five minutes but, chilled to the bone and in constant dread of the van returning, it felt much longer. Consequently it was with some relief that Gideon rounded the last corner and saw Tom Collins' Range Rover parked on the cinder track outside.

The ground floor was in darkness but there was a light at one of the upstairs windows, and as he approached over the twenty feet or so of frosty grass in front, Gideon heard the sound of the front door opening and by the faint light of the moon, could just make out a bulky figure in the porch.

'Tom,' he called, and the figure turned in the open doorway, one hand raised to the light switch.

There was a blinding orange flash, an instantaneous, ear-shattering boom, and a massive whoosh of air lifted Gideon off his feet and threw him back against the Range Rover, which in turn rocked on its wheels. For the second time that evening he rebounded off metal and hit the ground. The noise of the blast seemed to roll on and on, and after a moment a shower of fragments rained down on him, accompanied by thick choking dust.

Desperately winded, Gideon lay where he had fallen, face down, his ears ringing and the taste of blood in his mouth. Behind his closed eyelids was imprinted the last image he had seen, the black silhouette of a man against a billowing wall of flame.

Gradually the sound of falling debris died away, and the searing heat retreated. Gideon opened his eyes almost reluctantly, rolled on to his side and propped himself up on one elbow, still finding breathing difficult.

What was left of Roly French's cottage stood starkly against the starlit sky, lit here and there by small flickering flames in its depths, but Gideon hardly gave it a glance.

On the path in front of the devastated building, some six or eight feet away, lay a body. Gideon struggled on to his hands and knees and moved closer.

Within moments he could see that it was Tom Collins, and he didn't need a doctor to tell him that the stud owner was very dead.

12

The day of Tom Collins' funeral was wet and cold. Sleety rain blew lazily but relentlessly down from a slate-grey sky, obscuring the horizons behind a misty curtain. A few early daffodils bobbed and curtsied in the churchyard, determinedly cheerful but almost out of place, as if someone had had the bad taste to turn up in a party dress.

Gideon stood respectfully among the mourners, rain dripping off his hair and the end of his nose, and best shoes sodden in the rough, hastily cut grass.

The service had been fairly long; the church was packed and several people had wished to say their piece. Tom Collins had been generally liked and respected, it seemed. A rough diamond but a reliable friend in need. As an epitaph it was all one could ask really, Gideon reflected, and he wouldn't have hesitated to agree with it a few short days before. But now he had the uneasy feeling that there might have been a little more to Tom Collins than met the eye.

The body was committed to the earth and the necessary words spoken in what just stopped short of being unseemly haste, but none of the mourners, red-nosed and shivering in the misery of the drizzle, looked as though they were about to complain. Indeed, Mary, leaning on the arm of her son, looked as though she wished it was all over. Her eyes dark-ringed and swollen in her pale face, she kept her head bowed and held a handkerchief almost constantly to her nose and mouth. Beside her, Anthony held himself rigid and expressionless as he had throughout the proceedings.

Gideon felt for them both.

On the other side of Mary, and holding a large black umbrella over the three of them, was a plumply pretty blonde girl whom Gideon remembered as being Annabel, the daughter currently studying at university. She wore Doc Marten's and an assortment of black garments that none but a student would even contemplate wearing together, topped off by a multitude of earrings and a nose stud.

Gideon followed the assorted friends and family as they filed thankfully through the lych-gate and away to their cars, each stopping briefly under the tiled roof to offer their sympathy to Mary and the children. In his turn, Gideon shook hands with Anthony and Annabel and hugged their mother warmly, intending nevertheless to make his excuses and slip away without going back to the wake at the farm.

'You *will* come back with us, won't you?' Mary said, keeping hold of his hands.

'Well . . .' Gideon hesitated, his heart sinking.

'Please.' She drew him closer, adding in a low voice, 'I need to talk to you. It's important.'

'Of course I will,' Gideon heard himself say, resigned to the prospect of at least an hour, if not two, of polite small talk with people he'd never seen before and would probably never see again.

'Thank you.' Mary squeezed his hands tightly before letting go and Gideon felt slightly ashamed. After all, what was an hour or two in the grand scheme of things?

It was in fact over three hours before the company at the farm had thinned out enough to allow Mary to devote much time to Gideon. Grief had not dimmed her hospitality and she'd prepared a huge spread. Few of the assembled mourners allowed their distress to stand noticeably in the way of their appetite.

Gideon watched Mary bustling about carrying plates of nibbles, replenishing wine glasses and mopping up the occasional spillage with seemingly indomitable energy. His first thought was that it was wrong that she should have to work so hard on such an occasion but he quickly realised the non-stop activity was her way of coping. It left her less time to talk; less time to have to endure the well-meant but emotionally torturing sympathy of others.

Gideon had counted Tom amongst his friends but he'd always been closer to Mary, and in that sense the tragedy was in a way at second-hand to him. After the initial shock of Tom's violent death, his first thoughts had been for her. For as long as he'd known her, her family had been her world. How would she cope?

Most of the rest of that tragic evening had faded into a blur. He recalled his relief at finding the stud owner's mobile phone in the Range Rover; the irritation of having to keep at bay the half-dozen or so voyeurs drawn by the noise and glow of the explosion; and the eventual arrival of the emergency services, including the blessedly capable Logan.

Nothing, though, would ever erase from his mind's eye the heart-wrenching sight of Mary's face as she opened the door that night, expecting it to be Tom, surprised but pleased to see Gideon, and finally taking in the significance of Logan behind him, showing his warrant card as identification. Her eyes had searched Gideon's, urgently beseeching him to deny what she instinctively knew. The moment when the light went out of them had haunted his waking moments ever since.

The police surgeon had given Mary a sedative and Gideon had offered to stay with her at least until Anthony returned from his evening class.

In the end he'd stayed all night. Although Anthony had received the shocking news of his father's death with characteristic courage, it seemed hard to leave a seventeen year old to look after his widowed mother in such circumstances.

Suddenly, Mary was there beside Gideon, taking his arm and apologising profusely.

'I'm *so* sorry, Gideon. I'd no idea everyone would stay so long. If I had known I'd never have asked you to hang on.'

'It's not a problem,' he assured her. 'But are you sure it can't wait? You look worn out. Has anyone been looking after *you*?'

'Anthony's just making me a cup of tea,' Mary said, waving the matter away with a dismissive hand. 'No, I have to tell someone and you were the only person I could think of. You see, it's been worrying me ever since I found it – I didn't sleep a wink last night. I just need someone to tell me what I should do.'

Gideon frowned. 'I'm happy to help you, Mary, if you think I can, but what about your family? Isn't there someone . . .?'

She shook her head, hanging on to his arm as if to physically stop him from leaving. 'Nobody really. We're not that close, and this is so . . .'

Her voice shook and Gideon put his hand over hers, squeezing gently. 'It's all right.'

Mary took a deep breath and smiled bravely as Anthony appeared with the promised cup of tea. 'He's been so good,' she told Gideon, as her son walked away to help his sister gather discarded plates and glasses. 'He's so steady, such a comfort. His father would have been so proud of him.'

Tears stood in her eyes and the teacup rattled in its saucer.

322

'Come on. Sit down and tell me what's worrying you.'

'No, I think I'd better show you. Come upstairs and see what you make of it.'

Gideon followed her up the narrow staircase with some reluctance. He hoped he wasn't going to be required to untangle some kind of legal muddle because, if that were the case, Mary would very likely find her faith in his abilities misplaced. In his limited experience, papers drawn up by a solicitor were usually only comprehensible to another solicitor. It was as if they wanted to keep it in the family, so to speak. And they probably did.

As it turned out, the papers Mary produced had not been issued by a solicitor, but were no less legally binding for all that.

She led Gideon into a small room at the back of the house that had obviously been her husband's office-cum-study. Untidy bookcases covered one wall, stuffed partly with books on animal husbandry and farm management, and partly with folders and files. A filing cabinet stood in one corner, its top drawer so full that it wouldn't shut, and in front of the black square of the window a desk overflowed with letters, invoices, advertising literature, endless official-looking forms and other assorted paperwork. Amongst this muddle of ongoing business, a computer and monitor sat almost self-consciously, offering the possibility of order amongst the chaos.

Mary beckoned Gideon in and shut the door behind them, removing a telephone from the seat of a shabby leather wing-chair and inviting him to sit down.

'I was going through his papers looking for something the bank wanted. Tom would never let me touch this sort of thing; he said he'd take care of it and that I wasn't to worry. I wish he *had* let me. It's all such a muddle! *He* may have known where to find things but it's a nightmare for me.' She drew the curtains as she spoke, shutting out the lonely, rain-filled darkness, then picked up a brown envelope she'd put to one side. 'Anyway, I found this. It isn't marked, so I opened it to see and – well, you read it.'

With a sense of deep foreboding, Gideon took the envelope from her and removed its contents. It was a typewritten document, couched in simple but unequivocal terms, and signed and dated by the three parties involved. It was an agreement to divide in equal shares the ownership and stud proceeds of the stallion Popsox, presently standing at Winterbourne Shires. It was signed by Tom Collins, Sean Rosetti and Royston Slade, and was dated nearly three years previously.

Gideon re-read the document slowly, trying to take it in. *Slade*? How on earth had Tom got himself mixed up with Slade of all people? He looked at Mary, not knowing quite what to say. The document was clearly above board and legal. If she'd been hoping he'd tell her it wasn't, she was going to be disappointed.

'I didn't know,' she said, shaking her head helplessly. 'I don't even know who this Slade is.

Why would Tom do such a thing and not tell me?'

She was evidently totally bewildered and Gideon felt a wealth of pity for her. Hard enough to lose her husband in such a way, without coming so quickly upon evidence that he'd withheld part of his life from her. He hesitated to tell her what he knew of Slade, little though it was. Besides, it was just possible it was another, completely different, Slade.

Possible, but realistically Gideon recognised it as a forlorn hope.

'He must have run into financial difficulties, I suppose, and didn't want to worry you with it,' Gideon said, knowing this would be no great comfort.

Mary rubbed a hand across her eyes. 'But we often had hard times, that's the nature of farming. Tom never tried to conceal it from me before. He always used to moan and go round like a bear with a sore head for a few days and then we'd start to work round it. He knew I understood. I was a farmer's daughter before I became a farmer's wife, after all.'

'Can you remember what was happening about then?' Gideon prompted. 'That would have been the year Sox had his accident, wouldn't it?'

'He had the accident in the autumn – the *previous* autumn that would have been. What's the date on that thing? July? He was over the worst of it by then, as you know, because you were here just after Christmas, weren't you? Sox even served a few mares that summer and we'd just started advertising him for stud the following year. I remember I thought we'd pitched the fee far too high but Tom said people would pay almost anything to have a foal by a celebrity like Sox. And he was right, too. We were oversubscribed and had to turn people away.'

'I suppose the insurance paid for the vet's bills?'

'Yes, most of them. I don't understand it. That horse is the apple of his eye! *Was*,' she amended, swallowing hard. She smiled shakily at Gideon. 'I'm sorry. I still forget sometimes. It makes it worse, because then you have to remember all over again.'

'Don't apologise,' he said softly. 'You're doing incredibly well.'

'It's just . . . I can't believe that he'd sell any part of Sox, let alone *two-thirds* of him. Sean – I can maybe understand, we see so much of him he's like a family friend now, but this Royston Slade – whoever he is . . . It doesn't make sense. And why didn't he *tell* me?'

'I don't know, Mary. Have you mentioned this to Rosetti?'

She shook her head. 'I only found it last night. I had hoped Sean would come today but he rang this morning to say he had an emergency operation – colic, I think. Anyway, he couldn't make it.'

Gideon tried to think. Presumably Rosetti had met Slade, as co-owners of the horse, but then again, maybe not. It was hard to imagine Slade and the vet dealing together. It was hard to imagine Slade and Tom dealing together either. Slade and *anyone*, come to that. But how well was it ever possible to know anybody? Maybe Rosetti had brought Slade to the deal, rather than Tom. But the question remained: why should Tom be in a position to have to sell? As Mary said, it didn't make sense. The horse was about to become a mini-gold mine for them. Why make someone else rich?

If Slade was a friend of Rosetti's . . .

Mary was watching him anxiously.

'Would you like me to ask Sean about it?' he asked.

'Oh, would you?'

'Sure. And – um – have you said anything about it to Anthony?'

'Oh, no. I don't want to worry him. He's got enough to cope with.'

'You're probably right. He might be able to help you with some of this, though,' Gideon suggested, gesturing at the jumble of papers on the desk. 'Just to sort through it a bit. He told me he's doing business studies and he's got a good head on his shoulders. Put it to him.'

'I will. Thank you, Gideon. And thank you for everything you did last week. I don't know how we would have coped without you.'

'You'd have managed. You're a stronger person than you give yourself credit for,' he told her. 'But you're welcome anyway.'

'I'm just so glad you weren't both caught in the blast,' Mary said. 'One tragedy's bad enough, but if it had been both of you . . .' Her voice caught in her throat and she paused, fighting to keep control. 'They say he wouldn't have felt anything. Wouldn't even have known.'

'No, he wouldn't have. Something like that is instantaneous.'

'What makes it so hard is that I feel almost responsible. But then if it hadn't been Tom it would have been you and that would have been just as awful.'

Gideon was bewildered. '*Why* should you feel responsible? Wasn't it his idea to go to the cottage that evening.'

'Yes, it was, originally, but he was dragging his feet and I got cross with him. It was ten to seven and I said, "Gideon will think you're not coming," and he said, "Maybe I'm not." I'm afraid I lost my temper then,' she admitted. 'I said, "You may treat me like dirt, Tom Collins, but I'll not have you treating Gideon that way. He's been a good friend to us. Look at all the time he spent here with Sox." Perhaps I should have flared up at him before. He said, "I know, damn it! Don't you think I know that?" And that's when he left.'

'He didn't say anything else?'

'No. Only—' Her voice wobbled under the strain. 'Just as he got to the door he said, "I do love you, Mary Lou." It used to be his pet name for me. He hadn't used it for years.' The emotion proved too much and she buried her face in her handkerchief.

Gideon put his arm round her shoulders and waited, frowning slightly. It sounded as though

Tom had hoped to avoid meeting him that evening, which pointed to his having something to hide. But what?

'Mary? When you told Tom I was coming to see him at the cottage, did he say anything then?'

She sniffed and mopped her eyes. 'Um . . . he asked what you wanted to see him for, and I said I didn't know, you hadn't said.'

'How did he seem?'

'He was cross. Kind of agitated. He said I should have asked him before making arrangements. He left his meal unfinished and came up here. I didn't take much notice, to be honest. I've not been able to do anything right for a long time. Although I *was* a bit surprised because he's always liked you.' She turned to look at Gideon, her eyes red and swollen. 'What *did* you want to see him about? You hadn't quarrelled, had you? He seemed all right with you earlier.'

'Yes, he was fine,' Gideon said, not answering the question. How could he answer? 'I'm sorry, Mary. I shouldn't have reminded you. Forgive me.' He gave her shoulders a squeeze. 'Look, I shall have to go soon but is there anything I can do for you first – anything at all?'

She blew her nose determinedly and smiled shakily at him. 'No, I don't think so, Gideon. But thank you.'

'Well, if there is anything, you will call me, won't you?'

Mary assured him that she would.

'What will happen here now? About the farm

and the stud, I mean? It'll be too much for you on your own.'

'It's not up to me,' she said. 'It's held in trust for Anthony, until he's twenty-one. I can't do anything without the permission of the trustees, and then only on Anthony's say-so. The farm will be okay, we've got a farm manager, and the stud almost runs itself until the season starts. Then, well, I don't know . . .'

Gideon hesitated. 'I suppose it's not possible that you could get Roly French to come back?'

'I was thinking about that this morning,' Mary admitted. 'Though I felt awful about it. It feels almost like going behind Tom's back – silly, I know – but I *would* feel much happier if Roly were here. He knew all there was to know about running this place. Whether he'd come, though . . .'

Gideon shrugged. 'Whatever Tom's quarrel with him was, it was none of your doing. Try him and see. And don't feel guilty. Hard though it is, Tom's gone now and it's you who have to make this place work. You must do what's best for you and for Anthony.'

Mary pursed her lips. 'Yes, you're right. I'll ask around and see if I can track him down. After all, Anthony's schooling's the most important thing now. He must finish that.' She put her hand over Gideon's. 'Thank you, Gideon. Thank you for everything.'

After leaving Winterbourne Shires, Gideon drove a short way in the hectic, rush-hour traffic, then pulled into a side road, stopped, and keyed in a number on his replacement mobile phone. Logan answered fairly promptly but when Gideon asked if anything more had come to light regarding the explosion, said he was busy and would ring back shortly.

Gideon sat in the car – Pippa's – with his hands resting on top of the steering wheel and his eyes staring straight ahead into the blackness beyond the windscreen. It was raining still but the drumming on the roof was just background noise and hardly registered in his busy brain.

From what Mary had told him, it was obvious that for some reason his suggesting a meeting had upset Tom, though for the life of him he couldn't see why. As far as he could remember, most of their conversation that day had been fairly mundane. Admittedly, Tom had seemed a bit put out to find that Gideon had been asking about Sox's behaviour. But why should that have bothered him so greatly? If Sox had been giving cause for concern it was more likely that he would have *wanted* to discuss it with Gideon.

Tom had been agitated, Mary had said, and seemed reluctant to go to the cottage. But what would staying away have achieved in the long run? Avoidance could only have delayed the confrontation. After all, it was quite conceivable that Gideon, not finding him there, would have come to the farmhouse to look for him, unless . . .

Unless something happened to prevent him from doing so. With a fizz of actual, physical shock,

Gideon realised the unwelcome course his thoughts were taking.

Was it possible that the explosion at Roly French's cottage had not been an accident at all?

Contacting Logan earlier in the week, Gideon had learned that it had borne all the hallmarks of a gas explosion but as far as he could see, that didn't preclude its having been rigged. And, unpalatable as it might be, he had to accept the fact that if it hadn't been an accident, then the fatal blast had quite conceivably been meant, not for Tom but for himself.

Murder. Even thinking the word seemed ridiculous. It was something that happened in books and films, and on the news, not in rural Dorset to ordinary people.

Gideon dragged his thoughts back on track. This was cold hard reality. There was no getting round the fact that if the explosion had indeed been set, then murder had been intended. But Tom hadn't left the farmhouse between receiving Gideon's message and his final journey to the cottage, so somebody else must have been involved.

According to Mary, he'd left his meal unfinished and gone up to his study. Whom had he called?

It was clear that even if he had set up the trap, Tom hadn't known what form it was to take or he wouldn't have walked into it himself. But why go there at all? Had his conscience stepped in at the last minute? When he left, he'd told Mary he loved her, something he hadn't done for a while. Were they the words of a man who knew he was heading for trouble? Perhaps Tom had gone to the cottage intending to warn Gideon who, unbeknownst to him, had been delayed by his run-in with the maniac in the white van.

Considering what Gideon had discovered that afternoon, he had to consider the possibility that the third party – the one who had rigged the explosion – was none other than Milne's minder, Slade. Somehow he never seriously entertained the idea of Rosetti being responsible. Slade was the odd link in the chain; the one with the criminal background and necessary ruthlessness. But Gideon kept coming back to the same question. Where was the motive? There was no crime after all in selling shares in a horse and keeping it secret.

Another thought forced its way in. If Slade or one of his associates *had* blown the cottage up then it stood to reason that it hadn't been them who ran him off the road earlier. It would have been pointless to set such an elaborate trap and then waylay the intended victim before he reached it.

Who then had driven the van? Duke Shelley? Ironically, it if *had* been him, Gideon probably owed the man his life. That would make him spit if he knew!

He laid his head on his arms and groaned in sheer frustration. It seemed the more he knew, the less he understood. Maybe he was reading far too much into the whole affair. Maybe the explosion *had* been no more than a tragic accident.

One thing was for certain, though; his half-formed idea that Sean Rosetti was in some way defrauding Tom by using Popsox behind his back was obviously just as ridiculous as Pippa had thought it. If Sean part-owned the stallion and shared in the profits of his stud work, then any such motive was clearly redundant. Whatever was going on, Tom Collins had been in the very thick of it.

His fruitless mental wranglings were interrupted by the urgent trilling of his phone. It was Logan returning his call.

'Gideon. Hi, I can talk now. The official line is that the explosion at Gutter Lane was caused by a gas leak and triggered by Tom Collins turning a light switch on. The cottage had been unoccupied for some time but the gas was never disconnected.'

'So where was the gas leaking from, do they know?'

'As far as we've been able to determine, it came from a ruptured pipe in the sitting room. It appears that someone had broken in and tried to make off with a gas fire.'

'What, by wrenching it away from the wall?' Gideon didn't attempt to hide his scepticism.

'It would appear so.'

'And when do they think this happened? How long would it take for that much gas to build up?'

'It would depend on the size of the rupture. An hour or so . . . or a few days. It's difficult to tell with the kind of damage this explosion caused.'

'I wonder why there was a light on upstairs if Tom had only just got there?'

'Whoever broke in probably left it on. It's not that unusual. Some thieves turn everything on:

lights, bath taps, television. You count yourself lucky if they don't trash the place and spread filth on the walls,' Logan told him. 'I don't think the light is significant.'

Gideon had his own ideas about that. By leaving the upstairs light on, Slade, if it had been him, had ensured that Gideon would not just turn and walk away. Which was what he almost certainly would have done if he'd found the cottage in darkness and with no vehicle parked outside. Slade appeared to have prepared for everything, except the strength of Tom's conscience.

'Well, you certainly seem to lead a charmed life, Gideon Blake,' Logan went on. 'I suppose I don't need to tell you that if you'd been just a few moments earlier it would have been you face down in the front garden! Looks like the guy who smashed your bike up did you a favour after all.'

'Yeah, but not Tom. It's like tossing a coin,' he said. 'Somebody wins, somebody loses. Life or death. It's a sobering thought.'

'Mm. I see it again and again.'

'So that's the official line. What's the unofficial one?' Gideon asked after a moment. 'What do you, personally, think?'

'Ah, but I *am* an official,' Logan countered irritatingly.

'When it suits you.'

'My prerogative.'

'But what do you *really* think? Do you believe it was an accident?' Gideon persisted. 'Come on. I know you don't just follow blindly.'

'Can you give me a compelling reason why I *shouldn't* believe it?' Logan said slowly. 'What have you found out?'

Gideon hesitated. After all, what *had* he found out? All he could do at the moment was muddy the waters, and he felt it only fair to Mary not to cast any suspicion on Tom until he knew more. She had enough to deal with.

'Nothing definite,' he said at last.

'Yeah, well, trust works both ways, mate. You might remember that.' A faint click and Logan had disconnected, leaving Gideon feeling slightly unsettled. He liked Logan and wished he could discuss his thoughts and suspicions with him, but he couldn't let his instincts blind him to the fact that Logan was first and foremost a police officer and would be bound most strongly by the demands of duty.

Clearly, the best thing for everybody would be to get to the bottom of the riddle as soon as possible, and with that in mind, Gideon started the car and headed for Redbarn Farm Hospital and Sean Rosetti.

13

Redbarn farmhouse was aglow with light as Gideon drove up. He hurried through the rain to the porch and the bell was promptly answered by Sean's wife Cathy, two springer spaniels and a hairy terrier of unimaginable parentage.

'Gideon!' she exclaimed. 'My goodness, you're soaking! Come on in. Isn't it a foul night? If you want Sean I'm afraid you've missed him. He's at rugby practice – lovely, I should think, in this weather.'

'Oh, well, never mind. It's not urgent.'

'Is there any message? Look, come through to the kitchen. I've got dinner on the go and it'll be boiling over in a minute.' She turned to lead the way as she spoke, adding, 'Don't trip over the dogs!'

'Sean won't be back for a while, I'm afraid,' Cathy continued, as they emerged into the warmth and brightness of the kitchen. 'He usually goes on for a beer or two with the lads afterwards. Eddie's here though, if it's a veterinary problem. He's down at the stables at the moment, checking on a patient, but he'll be in later. These are his dogs.'

'No, no problem really,' Gideon assured her. 'There was just something I wanted to check with Sean but it was more in the way of a social call, really.'

'Well, I've just this minute made a pot of tea, so sit down and make yourself comfortable. Here, let me take that wet coat,' she said as he took off the navy blue stockman's coat, revealing shirt and jacket beneath. 'You look very smart. Where've you been?'

'It was Tom Collins' funeral today.'

'Oh, of course! Sorry. Sean was upset that he couldn't make it but he had an emergency op to do. Thoroughbred mare with a twisted gut. It was touch and go for a while but she seems to have come through it quite well.' Cathy took his coat back out to the hall, her voice echoing as she disappeared.

'Do sit down,' she said again, coming back in and taking two mugs from a rack. 'How did it go? The funeral, I mean. They're obviously never pleasant but if it runs smoothly, that's something.'

Gideon sat down. 'It went well, I think. Mary was very brave and so were the kids. There was a good turnout and she laid on such a spread that it took ages to get rid of everybody.'

'It was a dreadful business, wasn't it?' Cathy put

a mug of tea in front of him then resumed her interrupted task of chopping carrots and adding them to the contents of a large saucepan that bubbled on the hob. 'I've never met Mary but I know Sean's very fond of her. And Anthony's been over a couple of times. Sean plays rugby with him. He's a nice lad. Very grown-up and sensible. It's such a shame.'

Gideon was just agreeing with her when the door opened and Daisy skipped in. She stopped short when she saw him at the table.

Cathy swung round with a carrot in one hand and a knife in the other.

'Hello, Daisy Doolittle, where have you been? Look who's come to visit.'

'I'm having a baby sister, Giddy,' Daisy announced proudly, forgetting her shyness and stepping up to Gideon's knee. She looked into his face, her huge eyes earnest. 'She's going to be called Starlight.'

Gideon choked, trying not to laugh. 'Well, that's . . . er . . . unusual.'

'That's the name of the pony in the book I've been reading her,' Cathy said, smiling. 'I think she'd rather I had a foal than a baby, at the moment.'

'*Is* it a girl?'

'They think so. It was a bit difficult to see. To be honest, I don't mind which. I think Sean'd like a boy, though. He says he'd like a rugby team. I told him he'd better look elsewhere, then, because I've no intention of turning into a broodmare.'

'The way it's going, it looks as though he'd better start reading up on netball,' Gideon remarked.

Sean still hadn't returned when Gideon left Redbarn Farm, some three-quarters of an hour later, and if anything he felt even less enthusiasm for his self-imposed task than he had when he arrived. The warmth and happiness of the family atmosphere at the farm was a rare and beautiful thing in this day and age, and the thought of doing anything to upset it was abhorrent to him.

Useless to tell himself that any trouble was of Sean's making and not his. Drinking coffee and enjoying the company of the vet's family while doubts about Rosetti's honesty loomed large in his mind, he'd felt like a traitor. He could only hope that the business of the part-share of Sox, the connection with Slade, and Joey's information about a 'Spaniard' were just a coincidence, and that the vet would have some simple, innocent explanation.

By the time he stopped Pippa's car in the Priory stableyard it was gone eight o'clock and Gideon hoped, belatedly, that Pippa had had no need of it herself.

The yard was deserted. Giles' four-by-four was out and the horses had all been fed and were contentedly munching hay in their boxes. He let himself into the house by way of the back door and the old washhouse, and made his way to the kitchen.

At first he thought that this too was deserted, although the light was on, but then he spotted Pippa, kneeling in the corner by Fanny's basket.

'Hi,' he said, going over. Then, when she didn't reply, 'Is something the matter?'

Pippa turned and he could see she was cradling one of Fanny's puppies in her arms. It lay unmoving, and a glance at its limp form was enough to tell Gideon it would never move. It was dead.

What caught and held his attention, though, were Pippa's tear-filled eyes. The shock was like a physical blow. He'd never seen her cry before. It was a bit like seeing a parent cry for the first time. Pippa was always such a fiercely practical person, with apparently no time for sentimentality. Adversity made her determined; injustice made her angry; and grief she had in the past greeted philosophically. She was tougher than her brother by far and, although younger, had taken all the day-to-day decisions of life on herself, in the absence of their parents. Gideon had thought he knew her pretty well and this was out of character.

'Oh, Gideon,' she said in a voice that shook. 'Poor little puppy!'

Fanny licked her hand and nuzzled the small lifeless body, puzzled.

'What happened?' Gideon asked, crouching down beside her and putting out a finger to rub the dead pup's soft head. 'Was this the small one?'

Pippa nodded. 'He seemed all right this morning. A little quiet perhaps, but then he was always fairly quiet. I remember thinking I ought to get them all checked over by the vet but I didn't have time today.' She sniffed, her eyes filling with tears again. 'I should have made time.'

Gideon put an arm round her shoulders.

'You know it wouldn't have made any difference, love,' he said gently. 'There was obviously something not quite right with this little fellow. He was never going to make old bones, whatever you'd done. You mustn't blame yourself.'

Pippa looked up at him. 'Did you know then? Could you tell?'

Gideon shook his head, half-amused. 'No. Of course I didn't know. Who do you think I am? Doris Stokes? I just meant that he wasn't doing as well as the others. There was no spark about him. *You* saw that.' He gave her shoulders a shake. 'Now, would you like me to take him out in the garden and bury him?'

'It's raining.'

'No reason you can't have a burial in the rain. Went to one this morning, come to that.' Incredible that it had only been that morning. It seemed days ago, already.

'Oh, Gideon, I'm sorry, I forgot! You must be feeling dreary enough as it is, without me being such an idiot!'

'Don't be daft. I don't mind. Anyway, it's nice to see there's a soft and sentimental centre to that tough, practical shell.'

*

Fifteen minutes later and considerably wetter, Gideon and Pippa shrugged off coats and wellies in the washhouse.

'You don't really think I'm tough, do you?' she asked, almost anxiously.

'As old boots,' Gideon joked. 'No. Perhaps I should have said business-like.'

'I know I made a fuss about the pups not being pedigree, but I love them just the same.'

'I know you do. I was teasing,' he assured her.

They went back into the kitchen where Mrs Morecambe had appeared and was rattling pots and pans in a busy manner.

'Are you staying for a meal, Gideon? This silly child hasn't eaten yet, so busy she was, mooning over what couldn't be altered.'

'I'm sure Gideon would love to stay. I've never yet known him turn down the offer of a meal,' Pippa said with a sidelong glance.

Gideon acknowledged the truth of this and within minutes Mrs Morecambe had magically produced hot soup, warm bread, sausage rolls, ham, pickles and flapjacks.

As they ate, Pippa told him that Rachel and Giles had gone to see a film together, which caused him to raise an eyebrow, speculatively.

'You don't mind, though, do you?'

'Mind?' Gideon queried. 'No. I should think they'd be safe enough there.'

'No, I mean they seem to be seeing quite a bit of each other and, well, she *is* pretty.'

Gideon stared at her, tragically. 'You don't

mean . . .? Oh, no! You don't think Giles is being unfaithful to me?'

Pippa treated his play-acting with the contempt it deserved. She rolled her eyes heavenwards and then helped herself to a flapjack.

'So what are you saying? You think Giles is serious?' Gideon asked after a moment.

'I'm not sure. Would you mind very much?'

He bit into another sausage roll. 'I think she'd be good for him,' he said. 'But I'd miss having her around. What's that song called? "I've Grown Accustomed to Her Face". Perhaps I should put up a fight. What d'you think? I'd hate to have to cook for myself again!'

'I don't think you're in any imminent danger. At the moment, I think she regards Giles in the light of a big brother. You're her all-conquering hero.'

'What a weird feeling! I've never been a hero before,' Gideon said thoughtfully.

'Oh, I don't know. You've always been mine.'

Gideon laughed. 'Yeah, right! So how did your date go last night?'

'My date? Actually it was better than a date. I had a meeting with a course designer. Giles has offered to build me a cross-country course here on the estate. Isn't that brilliant?'

The telephone rang, saving Gideon the necessity of responding, and Pippa jumped up to answer it.

'Oh, heavens! I expect that's Stephanie. Stephanie Wainman – you remember her. I told her to ring tonight because I knew I'd be seeing you. She wants to know if you'll come and sort out her horse. What shall I say?'

'What horse? The one you sold her?'

'No. That stallion I told you about, Whitewings. He's getting out of hand, apparently. What shall I say?'

'Oh, God,' Gideon groaned. 'Okay. For the horse's sake, say I'll come.'

'When? Do you want to speak to her?' Pippa paused with her hand on the phone. 'Quick!'

Gideon made a face. 'Not really. Tomorrow, if she wants.'

From what Gideon could hear as he polished off two more sausage rolls and a flapjack, Stephanie did want, and Pippa confirmed it when she came back to the table.

'She says she'll be in all morning,' she reported. 'Actually, she sounds really desperate. I always thought that stallion would be too much for her but she would have it. I think it's a kind of status symbol, you know, like owning a Rottweiler. He's always been a handful but apparently he's got worse and worse. According to her, they can hardly get near him now.'

Gideon groaned once more. 'Why do people leave it until things are totally out of hand before they ask for help?' he wanted to know.

'Pride?' Pippa suggested. 'Or ignorance? But to be fair, Stephanie did get a behaviourist in a few months ago. Obviously it didn't work.'

The meal was completed in companionable silence and was followed by Irish coffee, served sacrilegiously in mugs instead of glasses. Gideon sat back to enjoy it in drowsy contentment, and if the Tom Collins affair nagged at the back of his mind, he lazily pushed it away. It had been a long day. Time enough for problem-solving tomorrow.

'I suppose you'll be wanting my car again,' Pippa remarked presently.

'Well . . .'

'Would you mind if I came too? It's a while since I've seen The Master at work.' She gave him a coy, sideways look.

'You can come if you promise not to mention the words "Horse Whisperer",' Gideon said severely.

Pippa laughed. 'Okay. I promise. Guide's honour.'

They arrived at Stephanie Wainman's Chilminster home shortly after ten o'clock the following morning. The house was not as large as Graylings Priory but a great deal more self-important. Whereas the Priory had the look of having evolved comfortably over the centuries into its present sprawling, haphazard form, the Wainmans' residence had all the pomp of some Georgian architect's ego, and stood foursquare with Doric columns flanking the front door and twin flights of steps leading down on to an immaculate, pea-gravelled drive.

Gideon thought it exactly fitted the first impression he'd formed of Stephanie herself: expensive-looking but lacking depth.

The stables were situated at a short distance from the house, round a brick-paved courtyard with a central flowerbed. Pippa parked her car outside and they walked in under an arch with a clocktower, to be faced with a scene straight from a manufacturer's brochure. Even in the rain the place looked spotless. Paintwork gleamed, the bricks underfoot were swept clean, each stable bore the name of its occupant over the door, and there was not a rug or tool in sight. Even in the flowerbed, winter pansies obediently bloomed in regimented rings.

As they entered the yard, a long grey head appeared interestedly over one of the shiny painted doors, trailing a mouthful of hay.

'He'll be out on his ear if he drops that!' Gideon murmured to Pippa whose mouth twitched.

They were met by a tiny, middle-aged man who identified himself as Mick Winters, the groom, and told them that 'Miss Stephanie' would be down shortly.

'Miss Stephanie' appeared on cue, less than a minute later, accompanied by two cocker spaniels and driving what looked like a covered golf-buggy, even though the walk from the house could have been no more than fifty yards. She disembarked at Gideon's feet.

'I'm so pleased you could come. You're a real life-saver!' she declared with her best smile and an outstretched hand, apparently forgetting that she'd barely acknowledged his long-haired presence on their last meeting. 'And, Pippa *darling*! How lovely to see you. You must come and say hello to Sebastian in a minute.' She kissed Pippa on both cheeks and hugged her, before turning back to Gideon.

'I *do* hope you can sort Wings out. Daddy says if you can't then he'll have to go, and that would be *such* a nuisance when I've got him this far. He cost a small fortune, you know. He's full brother to Popsox, the Olympic showjumper. I expect you've heard of him? Everybody has. Winters, have you got his bridle?'

'Yes, miss,' Winters said gloomily as they began to walk across the yard. 'I haven't tried to put it on him though, and neither will I.'

'Winters got bitten last week,' Stephanie explained. 'And last month Wings knocked him out and got loose. We were away at the time but luckily he didn't go far. Winters found him down by the lake in the morning. But it's gone on long enough, this business. He's got completely out of hand.'

She stopped by the closed doors of a large loosebox that stood on its own next to what looked like a storage barn. 'Well, here he is. Winters has the bridle.'

'Is the top door always kept closed?' Gideon wanted to know.

'This side is, but he can see out of the back, into the field. If we leave this one open the mares call to him and he gets randy. It makes him even more difficult to handle.'

'You don't use him as a stallion, then?'

'No. We were hoping to but at the moment we can't trust him.'

Winters held a stallion bridle towards Gideon but he waved it away. 'No, thanks, Mick. Just a rope or lead rein will do.'

'You be careful then, Mr Blake,' the groom said, looking doubtfully at Gideon. 'He's a real devil, he is! Evil!'

'Oh, I doubt it,' Gideon said lightly. 'I expect he's just got his problems, the same as the rest of us.'

'Oh, stop fussing, Winters! He'll be all right!' Stephanie stated impatiently. 'It's what he's paid for.'

You're all heart, lady, Gideon thought as he moved towards the stable door. Stephanie made to follow him.

'I'd like a little time with him, if you don't mind,' he said. 'Alone.'

'Okay. Whatever,' she declared airily. 'Be all mysterious.'

Gideon decided to ignore the taunt but Pippa was cross on his behalf.

'Oh, for heavensakes! It's not that at all. Sometimes it's the owner themself that's part of the problem, so it helps to see the horse on its own first.'

'Oh, it's all right, darling. I was only teasing. Gideon knows that, don't you, Gideon?'

'Oh, sure,' he responded blandly.

'So, Pippa and I will go and see Sebastian. And I'm sure Winters has plenty to do,' Stephanie said briskly. 'We'll leave Gideon to his whispering.'

As they moved away, Gideon opened the stable doors just wide enough to slip inside and did so, closing and bolting the lower half behind him. The stable was lit from the opposite corner by an open half-door that looked out over fields, which was exactly what its occupant had been doing before he turned to look at Gideon.

Neither of them moved a muscle.

In the yard outside, Stephanie's carrying tones could clearly be heard. 'I wish I'd sold him two years ago. I had an offer, you know. But he was all right then, and I'd got big plans for him. He was going to take me to the Olympics. If I'd known what trouble he was going to be . . .'

Her voice faded as she moved further away, but Gideon was no longer listening anyway, his mind already completely taken up with a far more compelling matter: the instantaneous and unshakeable certainty that he'd at last found the mystery stallion he'd been searching for.

He looked quite monstrous as he stood across the stable from Gideon. Over seventeen hands tall at a guess, and in the light from the open door his coat shone a deep copper chestnut, but it was neither of these things that triggered the recognition. The horse emanated a buzz of energy, or personality, that identified him to Gideon as surely as if he had been labelled.

There was no aggression in his body language as he turned to look at the man who was invading his space, merely curiosity and a thread of anxiety that made his ears flick to and fro a time or two. He was

350

a stunning-looking horse, and with his colouring and the long white stockings that gave him his name, it would have been impossible to have mistaken the identity of his famous brother, even had Stephanie not named him.

With an effort Gideon strove to push away the muddle of questions and thoughts that were crowding into his mind. He needed a clear head to focus on the stallion's own problems. He knew how dangerous this horse could be; he still had the fading bruise on his shoulder from their first encounter to remind him. The horse was quieter this time, of course, not stressed-out as he'd been before, but even so he began to show signs of agitation as Gideon watched, shifting his weight and raising his head slightly, nostrils flaring.

Keeping his own body language submissive and non-threatening, Gideon moved closer.

It was the best part of twenty minutes before he opened the top door on to the yard and nodded to the others, who were waiting a little way off.

'It was so quiet, we thought you were either doing well or else he'd murdered you!' Stephanie remarked as they approached. She didn't look as though she'd been unduly worried, to Gideon's eye.

'No, we're both okay.'

'So, what's the problem? Have you sorted him out?'

Gideon gave her a withering look. 'You've been having trouble for how long? Six months? A year?

351

You can't seriously expect me to sort it out in twenty minutes! I'm a behaviourist, not a bloody magician!'

'There's no need to be rude!' she said, her eyes flashing dangerously. 'Christ! You may have a way with horses but you certainly haven't got much of a way with people!'

Gideon looked up into the drizzle and took a deep, steadying breath. 'You're right. I'm sorry, okay? Now, about Wings. Do you always bridle him when you do anything with him?'

'We used to,' Stephanie said, a slight pout suggesting she still hadn't entirely forgiven him. 'He won't let us catch him now.'

'How on earth do you manage? Mucking out, grooming and such?'

'Winters puts hay out in the field in the morning and opens the door to let Wings out. Then he cleans the box out and Wings comes back in for a feed in the evening.'

'So you don't handle him at all?'

'Up until a month ago we did,' she said defensively. 'But he's got so much worse lately, and Winters won't touch him since he got knocked out.'

'I'm no coward!' the groom put in hastily. 'But he's a big horse and he goes mad. I'm not gettin' myself killed for nobody!' he finished, with a defiant look at his employer, who ignored him.

Gideon was standing just inside the loosebox with a rope held loosely around the stallion's neck. He rubbed his hand gently in a circular motion along the horse's powerful crest, and although Wings kept a wary eye on him, he seemed fairly relaxed. In spite of this, Gideon wasn't fooled. He knew that the closer his hand strayed towards the stallion's head, the tenser he would become.

'He's certainly not evil or mad,' he told them. 'What he is, is very uncomfortable. He's in pain from his mouth – teeth, I should think, or *a* tooth. Anyway, he's terrified of being bridled. I should imagine it's become agony to have a bit in there. He's obviously come to associate human contact with having a bridle on, and he knows that hurts. Before long the bridle doesn't even come into it. In his mind, humans mean pain. Has he lost weight lately, or is he normally lean like this?'

'A bit, the last few weeks, but he's never been fat.' Stephanie dismissed that with a wave of her hand. 'But what's wrong with his teeth? He's only six. What *could* be wrong? It's ridiculous!'

'Gideon's not a vet, Stephanie,' Pippa interposed quickly, anticipating the pithy retort that was forming on his tongue. 'I suppose it could be an abscess or too many teeth coming through, like kids get.'

'The thing is to get him somewhere where there are X-ray facilities and find out,' Gideon said, making an effort to hold on to his patience. 'Rosetti's place, for instance.'

'Well, how on earth am I going to get him there?' she asked peevishly. 'Can't you make him quieter? I thought that's what you were here for.'

'I can't do anything until we sort out the pain in

his mouth.' Gideon was exasperated, as usual, by the wilful stupidity of those who should know better.

'And then he'll be all right?' she persisted.

'No. Then we can start to rebuild his trust in us. But it won't happen overnight. There are months of learned behaviour to overcome. We'll have to see how he is. He may possibly benefit from being turned out to grass for a few weeks and then starting fresh. We could try join-up, perhaps. That might give him a good start.'

'Like I've seen on TV?' Stephanie lost her petulant look.

'Yeah, just like that,' Gideon said, wearying of her.

The natural method of bonding using discipline and reassurance through body language had been given a lot of publicity recently, and this obviously recommended it to Stephanie. It was probably something she could drop into conversation on social occasions, Gideon thought uncharitably: 'We used join-up, you know,' rather like having one's own therapist or fitness coach.

'How do you know he's in pain?' Pippa asked interestedly, as Gideon slid the rope off Wings' neck and let himself out of the stable. The stallion backed away instantly, ears close to his head. 'Couldn't he just be head-shy? I mean, it's not like lameness, is it? There's nothing to see – no obvious swelling or anything.'

Gideon hesitated. It was almost impossible to put into words. He didn't fully understand it himself and wished Pippa had kept her question for the journey home.

'Instinct, I suppose. It's difficult to say. It's in his body language.'

How to explain the sense of harmony he experienced from a healthy animal and the discord where pain or illness was present? It sounded wildly improbable even to himself, and he certainly wasn't going to try it on Miss 'Tough as Nails' Wainman!

'If you want to arrange it with Rosetti, I'll come and help load him into the box for you,' Gideon offered, more for the horse's sake than anyone else's. 'In fact,' he said, thinking quickly, 'I've got to see Sean later. I'll arrange it with him and let you know, if you like.'

Out of the corner of his eye he saw Pippa raise an eyebrow in surprise but Stephanie seemed to find nothing unusual in people exerting themselves on her behalf.

'Okay, let me know what he says,' she agreed, apparently not feeling that gratitude was called for. 'Pippa darling, you'll have a cup of coffee before you go, won't you? It's all in the tack room, so it won't take a mo.'

'You came over uncommonly helpful back there,' Pippa said quizzically, as they began their homeward journey some twenty minutes later. 'What happened? Did you fall for her warmth and charm?'

'She's a real sweetie,' Gideon said sourly. 'Prime spinster material.'

Pippa laughed. 'Actually, underneath that rich-bitch exterior, I think there's probably a shy, insecure person trying to get out.'

'It should try a little harder!'

'She's the classic spoilt only child. I should imagine she's never sure whether people are interested in her for herself or Daddy's money. It can't be easy.'

'My heart bleeds . . .'

'Okay. So she's a bitchy snob. In that case, why did you offer to arrange everything for her?'

'For the horse's sake, and . . . er, you remember the night I was abducted?'

'Of course. It's not the sort of thing you forget easily, is it?'

'Well, think about the half-wild stallion I had to catch. Joey said it was copper-coloured with white legs . . .'

'Not Whitewings!' Pippa exclaimed, and the car swerved towards the kerb as she turned her head to look at him. 'Are you sure?'

'Absolutely,' Gideon stated, calmly putting out a hand to steer them on to a safer course.

'But why?'

'That's the rub,' he said. 'The more I think about it, the less sense it makes. I mean, when I thought the stallion must be Sox – from Joey's description – it made sense in as much as he's valuable and his youngstock would be. But this Whitewings is a complete unknown.'

'Except that he's a full brother to Popsox. Surely they weren't trying to kid someone that the foal was his? After all, they do *look* alike. But why go to so much trouble for just one foal? I mean, how much could the stud fee be, for heavensakes?'

'You wouldn't. Not for one,' Gideon said slowly. Then he slapped his leg in triumph. 'That's it! You've got it! Well done!' He leaned across and gave Pippa a resounding kiss on the cheek, which made the car wobble dangerously again.

'Well, I'd be feeling pretty pleased with myself if I knew just what it was that I'd come up with,' she said, glancing at him in some amusement.

'Yeah, sorry. I just need to check something with somebody and then I'll explain,' Gideon promised, reaching for his mobile phone.

14

It was still raining when Gideon pulled up outside Redbarn Farm that evening, which suited his mood.

When he'd rung to arrange the meeting with the vet, he'd merely said that Mary had wanted him to come to sort out something about Tom's affairs. Rosetti must have known his part-ownership of Sox would eventually come to light, so he would have seen nothing strange in that. Nevertheless, Gideon had delayed ringing him until he was on his way to the farm, just in case the idea of contacting Slade crossed Sean's mind. He didn't really think it would but recent experience had made him cautious.

As Gideon slid out of Giles' Mercedes – generously loaned, as Pippa needed her car – he was hailed from the direction of the hospital yard. Rosetti was waiting under the stable overhang.

Gideon ducked his head into his collar and splashed across at a run.

'What a miserable night!' was Rosetti's greeting. 'Is it ever going to stop raining?'

He led Gideon into the hospital block and from there to his office, where an electric fire kept the winter chill at bay. He waved his guest into an upholstered chair and offered him soup, coffee or chocolate from a vending machine.

'Tea's run out, I'm afraid,' he said apologetically. 'Clare – our head nurse – is supposed to keep it stocked up but she doesn't drink tea, so it only ever gets re-ordered when the coffee runs out. Anyway, help yourself.' He sat down in one of the chairs and looked across at Gideon. 'Now, what can I do for you?'

Gideon hesitated. It was daft that he felt awkward, after all, *he'd* done nothing wrong. 'I went to see Mary the other day,' he said finally. 'She wanted me to look at some papers she'd found.'

'Ah,' Rosetti said. 'So she knows about Sox. Tom should have told her at the start. I always said so.'

'So why didn't he?'

'I think because he was ashamed to admit he was in trouble again. He'd promised Mary a new bathroom and he'd lost the money that he'd put by for it. He just couldn't face disappointing her.'

'But why sell to Slade?' That was the thing that had been puzzling Gideon most of all. 'Selling a share to you I can understand. But why get involved with someone like that?'

'You know Slade?' Rosetti sounded surprised.

'We've met.'

'Well, unfortunately he was already involved. It was Slade Tom owed the money to and he was getting impatient. What I could afford to pay for my share wouldn't cover it, so he let Slade in on the deal, promising him that it was an investment and that the stud fees would soon more than cover his debt. What he should have done was sell Sox outright to someone else, pay Slade off once and for all and be shut of him. But he couldn't bring himself to do it. He's very fond – *was* very fond – of that horse.'

'So when did it start to go wrong?' Gideon asked.

'Wrong?' All of a sudden, Rosetti looked wary. 'What do you mean?'

'I was called out to see a horse called Whitewings today,' he prodded gently.

The vet held his gaze for what seemed an age and Gideon could sense the flurry of frantic mental activity behind the black eyes, then Rosetti bowed his head and rubbed his brow with the palm of his hand as if he had a headache. All at once he looked desperately weary.

'So you know,' he said after a moment. 'Or you've guessed. How much? All of it?'

'Most of it. I think I know the how but I'm not so sure of the why, and I'd like to hear it from you.'

Rosetti got to his feet and absent-mindedly

helped himself to soup from the vending machine. 'Are you sure you won't?' he asked, gesturing at the machine.

'Okay,' Gideon nodded. 'Coffee, please.' Somehow it helped restore a measure of normality to a wretched situation.

Rosetti walked round behind Gideon to deliver the coffee but his body language signalled no threat. Then he sat heavily in his chair and sighed once more.

'I don't expect you to believe this, but I'm glad you know. I'm glad it's finally all out in the open.'

Gideon saw no reason to tell him that it was not yet common knowledge; that he'd told only one other person, and then not the whole story. The assumption that the facts were generally known was a kind of insurance, if he should need it. He didn't think he would.

'So how did Tom get mixed up with a rat like Slade in the beginning?' he asked. 'They're hardly in the same line of business.'

'No,' Rosetti shook his head sadly. 'But they *are* in the same line of recreation. Gambling. I gather Slade runs illegal poker games for big money. Tom met him over a friendly game of cards with some mates and got drawn in. He's always had a gambling problem, and although he had it under control for a while, it's like alcoholism, you're never really cured, only in remission. He told me he was feeling a bit low at the time, what with Sox's accident and Annabel going off to university. She was his little girl.'

'I never knew he had a problem.'

'Well, no, *I* didn't to start with. He hadn't gambled since he married but apparently, as a youngster, he got into big trouble. Cards, horses, the dogs, you name it. He told me his father was the same. Said it was in his blood, but that's a cop-out, if you ask me! Anyway, his mother knew all about it, as you might imagine. She never really trusted him, and when she died she left the farm to Anthony instead of Tom. She was a shrewd woman.'

'So Tom lost money to Slade, kept going back to try and recover his losses, and ended up in over his head?' Gideon suggested.

Rosetti nodded. 'That's about it. Slade let him win at first, of course. It's the old story. But what it comes down to is that the stallion was the only thing of value that Tom really owned for himself. He couldn't mortgage the farm because it wasn't his. He couldn't even sell off stock because there was hardly any market for British beef. So he decided to sell a third share of the horse to me. I'd already said I'd be interested as an investment, as I was still building the hospital at that time. So Tom offered the money I gave him to Slade as a down payment, with the promise that as the stud fees started to come in he'd pay back the rest plus the interest. Unfortunately he put his case rather too well. Slade said he'd waive the debt in return for a third share in Sox.'

'But over the years that would amount to a small fortune,' Gideon protested.

'Yes, but as you probably know, Slade isn't a man to be troubled by his conscience and Tom was in no position to argue. He'd already been turned down by his bank manager, who felt there were just too many potential pitfalls involved in using a projected stud career as security for a loan. As it happened,' he went on, shaking his head ruefully, 'he was only too right.'

'Sox was infertile,' Gideon stated.

Rosetti nodded once more. 'You *do* know, then. Who told you?'

'Nobody, actually. When I'd worked out the rest it was the only answer. But presumably you didn't find out yourself until it was too late?'

'No, more's the pity. You see, he'd sired one or two foals before, while he was competing, and the accident didn't directly affect his reproductive equipment. It simply never occurred to either of us that he wasn't as virile as ever. It wasn't until he covered half a dozen mares in the late-summer after his recovery and only one of them scanned in foal that we began to suspect all was not right. We can only think that somewhere along the way he must have picked up an infection that left him all but infertile. It's the only answer.'

'So what happened then? How on earth did you come up with such a crazy idea?'

'It was my fault,' Rosetti admitted. 'And you're right – it *was* crazy. That's just it. It was meant as a joke, nothing more. Tom was in a dreadful state about having to tell Slade the bad news, so I said I'd go along with him to add my professional weight, as it were. I'd not met Slade at that point, and although I could see that Tom was pretty rattled by him, I didn't know what a bastard he could be.' He almost spat the last few words and Gideon could sympathise with him.

'I wish I'd never gone,' the vet went on bitterly. 'Oh, he was charming enough on the surface but it was obvious he didn't believe us at first when we told him that his investment wasn't going to bring any rewards. I think he thought we were trying to trick him. I had to show him the actual lab report before he'd accept it. Then he turned nasty. Not loud or violent but sort of icy-cold. He said Tom would have to find some way to pay what he owed because he was through waiting.

'I suppose I was trying to lighten the atmosphere, I don't know, because then I said something really stupid. I said, "It's a shame we're not using AI, artificial insemination that is, because then we could use old Sovereign to service the mares."'

'As a joke,' Gideon put in.

'*Of course* as a joke,' Rosetti asserted with a touch of irritation. 'Tom knew that – though he wasn't in much of a mood for laughing – but Slade, God damn him, he took me seriously. "Why can't we?" he asked. I tried to tell him I'd been joking, and that it would be completely unethical to do any such thing, but he waved it all aside. He wanted to know if it was technically possible. I could only say yes, technically, but that it was totally unfeasible. I told him Sovereign was a heavy horse and completely different in every way from Sox. The first crop of foals would find the deception out. Slade just said, "Another stallion then?"

'Tom was keeping very quiet, so I tried to get him to back me up but then he came out with the information that Sox had a full brother! I couldn't believe it! It was like a nightmare. And of course, that was it. Slade had the whole thing planned within the hour. He's a bastard but he's a very clever bastard, I'll give him that.'

'They couldn't have done it without you, though,' Gideon pointed out. 'You were the one with the know-how and the equipment. You could have said no.'

'Yes, I could have,' Rosetti said, gazing at his hands that were systematically squeezing and releasing his plastic cup so that what was left of the contents rose to the brink and fell again, over and over. Suddenly he looked up at Gideon.

'Have you ever had a dream?' he asked, his black gaze intense. 'Have you ever wanted something so much that it becomes all you live for; so you feel it's what you were put on this earth to do?' His eyes held Gideon's for a moment and then the fire in them ebbed and died. 'No, I don't suppose you have. It's probably the fault of my ancestry. We're an emotional race, don't have the fabled English reserve.'

'My father's a visionary,' Gideon said mildly. 'He's followed his passion all over the world. I seem to have inherited my mother's phlegmatic and entirely unambitious nature.'

Rosetti smiled briefly. 'Sorry, I didn't mean to

be rude. It's just that this hospital was half-built, half-converted perhaps I should say, and I was running out of money. I got a last-ditch loan from the bank to pay for my share of the stallion because I knew I was helping Tom out of a jam and because the returns for me should have been enough to finish this off. Oh, I know I should have done a sperm-count on Sox before I paid out but, as I said, he'd sired foals before. The silly thing was, if it had been anyone else, I would have insisted on it. As it was,' he finished sadly, 'I was left facing ruin and the end of my dream.'

'So you decided to go along with Slade's plan.'

'No. Not at first. I thought it was crazy and said so, but Slade had got the bit between his teeth and before long he'd convinced Tom it was possible. Between them they badgered me until I said I'd think about it. I swear, I still didn't think anything would come of it. I thought when the others cooled down they'd realise how impossible, and in Tom's case how *wrong*, it was.'

'But they didn't.'

Rosetti shook his head. 'To be honest, I think Slade saw it as a challenge. I don't think the money Tom owed him was the issue at all. Looking back, I think the more I tried to say it couldn't, and shouldn't, be done, the more determined Slade became to do it. And Tom was so desperate I think he'd have tried anything to get out of the fix he was in. Also . . .'

'Also?' Gideon waited.

Rosetti hesitated, looking down at his hands.

366

'I'm not sure if Slade ever actually threatened Tom or his family. He's certainly done so to me. Though never in so many words.'

'To get you to go along with his scheme?'

'Yes, and to stop me pulling out of it, many times since. You see, it was only ever supposed to be for one year. Just long enough to cover our debts – well, the most pressing of mine anyway – and then we agreed we'd declare Sox infertile as the result of some mystery virus and retire him.'

'And what about Cathy and Daisy?' Gideon demanded. 'Slade may have implied harm if you crossed him but didn't you think about what would happen to them if you were caught, as, God knows, you were likely to be?'

Rosetti looked Gideon straight in the eye. 'I thought about it every minute of every day,' he said. 'Daisy wasn't even born then, of course. Cathy had just about a month to go. If I'd known how that child would make me feel, I'd never have risked what I did. Bad enough to let Cathy down, but my little girl? Never!' He checked himself, perhaps remembering with a spasm of mental anguish what Gideon's presence meant. 'Not until now anyway.'

'So how exactly did you pull it off?' Gideon asked, repressing instinctive sympathy. 'How on earth did you manage to "borrow" Whitewings for a night? Several nights, I imagine. This year wasn't the first time, was it? I saw a copper-coloured yearling the other day, supposedly sired by the great Popsox. Was Winters, the groom, in on it?'

'No. He knows nothing about it. We couldn't keep Wings for more than a few hours without him being missed, so we've had to collect from him every year; that's three times now. Honest to God, it was only ever supposed to be once, believe me!'

Gideon ignored this impassioned plea. 'Tell me about it? How many mares can you serve from one collection? I gather you can freeze the semen. How long will it keep?'

'It'll keep indefinitely. That's what made it possible. The usual method, using chilled semen, wouldn't have worked for us, as it can only be kept for two or three days, and obviously we couldn't have forty-odd mares at the stud at one time, even supposing they were all conveniently in season at once – which is ridiculous. We had to make it look as though Sox was serving mares naturally throughout a normal breeding season, so we needed to be able to store the semen until it was needed.'

'And you can collect all the necessary in one go?'

'One collection will normally cover between five and thirty mares, depending on the fertility of the stallion. We managed to collect twice from Wings each time we had him. He was exceptional,' he added. 'When did you guess that we were using AI?'

'Not until this afternoon. Something Pippa said made me wonder but I had to ring Anthony to be sure. I didn't know much about it myself.'

'Does Anthony know about all this?' Rosetti looked haunted, and Gideon could almost feel sorry for him.

'Not yet,' he said. 'He told me that freezing is a method that's used all the time with cattle but he said not all stallions are suitable.'

The vet nodded. 'That's quite true. It was my last hope – that Whitewings' sperm-count would be too low or his semen prove too fragile for freezing. You're bound to lose a percentage of fertility during the process and with many stallions it just isn't viable.'

'But Wings was just fine.'

'He was excellent,' Rosetti stated bitterly. 'One of the best, if not *the* best, that I've ever dealt with.'

'What's the advantage?' Gideon asked. 'Normally, I mean. Why not stick with the natural method? It must be cheaper.'

'Yes, it is much cheaper but AI, especially using frozen semen, makes it possible to breed from horses in circumstances that preclude conventional methods. Competition horses that can't afford the time off to stand at stud, for instance, or show horses and ponies whose bloodlines are sought after abroad. And, even more exciting, it can be used to extend the careers of famous sires of all sorts who are approaching retirement. Some mares are even now in foal to stallions that have been dead for several years.' Rosetti's eyes shone with the fervour of the trailblazer.

'Pippa says you can't use it for thoroughbreds. Something to do with Weatherbys.'

'That's right. Not racehorses registered with Weatherbys. It *is* used on thoroughbreds, of course. Eventers and other competition horses.'

'So, what if someone had wanted their foal paternity-tested? What would have happened then? Or is a full brother a close enough match?'

'No.' Rosetti shook his head. 'Full brother or not, it would show on a paternity test.'

'So you took a bloody big risk, then.'

'Not really. People brought their mares to Sox, most of them wanted to meet him, some even saw him at work, and in due time the mares produced foals that bore all the hallmarks of their famous sire. Why should anyone suspect?'

Gideon regarded the vet for a long moment then shook his head. 'It's a dirty trick.'

'I'm not proud of myself,' Rosetti replied quietly.

'So where did you take it to be frozen? Presumably it's quite a tricky procedure. You couldn't use the normal channels, surely? Questions would be asked.'

'They would,' Rosetti agreed. 'No, I have the equipment here. It's not as complicated as you might think.'

'In the hospital?'

'No.' He looked a little sheepish. 'The hospital wasn't finished when we started this, remember? As a matter of fact, it's in my wine cellar.'

'Ah.' Gideon remembered Giles' bewilderment when he'd described some of the vet's wine-making equipment to him. 'Of course. No wonder you were upset when I went down to fetch Daisy back.'

'It gave me quite a shock,' Rosetti admitted.

'Until I reminded myself that you couldn't possibly know what was going on.'

'If Winters wasn't in on it, how on earth did you spirit Wings away without being heard? His flat's over the tack room, and that stallion wouldn't be the easiest to sneak out quietly.'

'We tried to buy the horse at first, under an assumed name, of course. We planned to keep him at stud separately from Sox and collect from him as necessary, but Ms Wainman wasn't interested in selling. I hoped that would be an end to it but no, not a chance! Slade found out, don't ask me how, that Winters has a serious weakness for the demon drink. He also discovered that the entire Wainman family were in the habit of taking a skiing holiday for two weeks every February. Having discounted the idea of bribery – it seemed to be generally held that Mick Winters is as honest as the day is long – the next step, to Slade, was obvious.'

'Join him in his favourite watering hole,' Gideon said slowly. 'Encourage him to overindulge and then . . .'

'And then do the decent thing by escorting him back to his flat and laying him on his bed to sleep it off. Slade made sure of it by getting his man to slip a little something extra into his drink. Winters would have woken up in the morning with a heavy head and absolutely no idea that his prize charge had been missing for half the night. Slade arranged it all and it went like clockwork.'

'But not this time.'

'No. This time it all went pear-shaped. The

horse, who's never been easy to handle, was almost unmanageable. Stephanie Wainman has neither the know-how nor the instinct to deal with a stallion, and he's never been taught manners, but this time there was something else. He wasn't just awkward, he was really fighting us.'

'He's got a problem with his mouth,' Gideon put in. 'I think he's in a lot of pain.'

'I was beginning to think it must be something like that but Stephanie hasn't called me in, so what could I do?'

'Well, consider yourself called now. I said I'd speak to you about it. Is it likely to be teeth, at his age?'

'I'd need to X-ray him but it could be what we call a bone sequestrum,' the vet said, thoughtfully. 'That is, a small piece or splinter of bone that's separated from the main – in this case jaw – as the result of a knock or injury. It can be extremely sore, and if it happened to be just where the bit lies in his mouth you could hardly blame him for kicking up a fuss, poor sod!'

'So, this time he went ape?' Gideon prompted.

'Yeah, and to top it off, Slade was getting cocky. I think he was becoming bored with the whole thing. Anyway, he didn't wait to hear from his man that Winters was safely taken care of and, as luck would have it, the groom didn't go to the pub that night. He picked up a four-pack from the off-licence and came home to watch a football match. He walked right in on us.'

'So, what happened?'

'Well, the stallion had got himself pretty worked up and when Winters came over to see what was upsetting him, Slade coshed him with a shovel before he saw anything.' Rosetti grimaced at the memory. 'We weren't at all happy about that, Tom and I. I mean, he could have killed him! It was never part of the deal for anyone to get hurt, but Slade just brushed it aside. It was like it was an everyday thing for him. I think that's when we finally realised just what kind of man we were dealing with. It was frightening.'

'He's a real bastard,' Gideon agreed. 'I don't think he'd stop at much. So then you took Wings to the farm with the barn?'

'Yeah. We backed the horsebox up to the barn door but before we could get a proper hold on him, Slade let the ramp down and the horse was away. He broke through the safety gates on the lorry and hit the ground running.' Rosetti shook his head in wonder at the memory of it. 'I've seen a good few stallions in my time but never anything like that! He was fighting mad! There was no way any of us was going to get near him, even Slade could see that. We toyed with the idea of bringing the mare in to entice him over but we couldn't risk him mounting her before we were ready. As you can imagine, timing is everything. Then Tom suggested you.'

'That was nice of him!' Gideon observed dryly. 'Most of my work comes by word of mouth but there are times . . .'

'I think he said it without thinking,' Rosetti said

in his defence. 'He mentioned to me that you'd performed miracles with Sox after his accident and Slade, who was losing his temper by this time, said, "Well, where is he? Let's get him." Just like that! I think then Tom realised what he might be getting you into, because he said, "You can't. What would you tell him?" and Slade just said, "We won't tell him anything." Tom pleaded with him not to hurt you. He said you were a friend, but he told them where you lived, nevertheless; he didn't have much choice. Slade sent his two thugs and, well, you know the rest.'

'Yes, I remember it well. And I have the scars to prove it.'

'Tom was horrified,' Rosetti told him. 'I think he'd begun to regard the whole business as almost acceptable until that night. Then it was all brought home to him. I could see how his mind was working. After all, we were doing no one *actual* harm. It was just a little deception. Whitewings' get may well have been every bit as good as his brother's, for all we knew, and it's possible that some of the foals were actually Sox's; he was still carrying out his stud duties, as normal.'

'It's fraud,' Gideon stated, uncompromisingly.

Rosetti nodded sadly. 'This season I was going to be able to start work on a covered hydrotherapy pool,' he said. 'I'm ashamed to say that even in the circumstances, I couldn't help looking forward to that.'

Gideon said nothing. There didn't seem to be anything appropriate. In spite of his principles, he understood the dilemma Rosetti had found himself in and couldn't condemn him completely. It would be arrogant to assume that he wouldn't have been tempted to do the same, faced with losing everything and driven into a corner.

'Something I wondered,' Rosetti said then. 'When Slade told you what you had to do, when he said the horse had already kicked someone, weren't you afraid?'

'For a moment, a little,' Gideon admitted. 'But, as you yourself know, you can't let it show. With animals, confidence is everything, especially when they're frightened themselves. Once you make contact, you're too busy for fear.'

'I was watching you. There wasn't a flicker.'

'My phlegmatic English temperament again. Comes in useful sometimes.'

'I didn't think you could do it,' Rosetti said frankly. 'I didn't think anyone could. I know a bit about join-up techniques, but this was something different. When Slade suggested the blindfold, I told him he was mad. I thought the horse would kill you.'

'*I* didn't think I could do it, at first,' Gideon said. 'But I didn't have a lot of choice, did I? Tell me, how did you get the horse back unseen?'

'We set him loose in the grounds of the Wainman estate. It's quite likely that he made his way back to the yard and the other horses. When I saw Mick Winters a few days later, he told me the stallion had knocked him out when it barged out of its stable.'

'You've been bloody lucky!'

'I know we have,' Rosetti said. 'And in a way it's made me feel guiltier than ever, as daft as that may sound. I've been almost willing something to go wrong, and yet, at the same time, terrified in case it did. It's been . . .' He cut the sentence short, as though remembering he had no business to ask for sympathy.

There was silence for a moment. A silence that hung heavily in the air, punctuated only by a ticking noise from the vending machine and the monotonous buzz of the striplight overhead.

Gideon was aware that it was, metaphorically, his move; that Rosetti was waiting for him to say what he intended to do with the information he had. The devil of it was that Gideon didn't know. He had thought that confronting the vet with what he'd discovered would force the issue one way or another, but he found himself still unsure.

'Tell me how you do it – this freezing process?' he asked, playing for time but nevertheless genuinely interested. 'Is it legal for you to carry it out here, freelance, so to speak? Or is that against the law, too?'

Rosetti flinched at the roughness of Gideon's tone, much as one might when a dentist drilled too deeply.

'No, it's not against the law. You couldn't do it on a large scale though. There are too many regulations attached. For instance, any semen for export can only be collected from horses certified disease-free, and for countries outside the EC they

376

need to be kept in quarantine conditions for anything up to a month. Also they must not have
covered a mare for at least thirty days leading up to
collection. You really have to have the right set-up
to do it properly. There are four or five licensed
collection centres in this country. I used to work at
one myself. This, being a hospital, is in no way an
ideal place to do it.'

'So, you're telling me you can collect enough
semen in one night to cover mares for a whole
season? Forty mares, did you say?'

'Normally that would be pushing it,' Rosetti
admitted. 'But, as I said, Wings is extremely suitable for the process. Both the quantity and the
quality of his output are exceptional. Ideally you
would want to leave forty-eight hours between
collections for maximum yield but obviously that
wasn't an option for us.'

'So, you divide it up into smaller amounts . . .'

'Doses.'

'Doses. And then you freeze it. How? Surely not
in a normal deep-freeze? There must be more to it.'

Rosetti smiled faintly. 'There is.' He paused.
'Are you really interested?'

'Very,' Gideon assured him.

'Well, you need the services of a teaser mare and
at the point of mating you intercept, so to speak,
collecting the semen in an AV. Artificial vagina,' he
added, seeing the question forming on Gideon's
lips. 'It's a tube, about eighteen inches long filled
with warm water and with an inner tube for the
semen. It's important not to let the semen cool too

377

quickly. The contents are checked under a microscope for any signs of poor health, mixed with a milky fluid – an extender, we call it – and then spun. The centrifugal force makes it easier to divide the sperm into individual doses,' he explained, looking at Gideon to see if he still understood. 'Then the semen is re-extended using a mixture of egg yolk and glycerine, and packed in half-mil acetate straws for freezing. The straws are, in turn, packed in tubes and frozen in liquid nitrogen. Taken down to minus one hundred and ninety-six degrees centigrade over about forty-five minutes.'

'And that's all there is to it?' Gideon said wryly.

'Well, no, actually,' Rosetti said. 'Even when a stallion's semen appears to freeze well – that is, it survives the thawing process – it can sometimes still give a poor conception rate, for reasons we don't yet fully understand. Research is ongoing. Also, the health and fertility of the mare is of paramount importance. Only about twenty-five to thirty percent of stallion semen freezes well, and even when it does, the conception rate for a first covering is lowered significantly against that of fresh or chilled semen. Interestingly though, over subsequent seasons it evens itself out pretty much. A lot can ride on the skill of the vet handling the insemination process. The mare has to be scanned several times during her cycle to ensure that insemination takes place as close as possible to the point of ovulation. Between us, Tom and I got it down to a fine art. Oh, we had failures, of course, but that's to be expected with any form of covering. A lot of it is down to the mare. Sox's success rate seemed to the outside world to be average, if not above.'

'No wonder Roly French had to go,' Gideon said thoughtfully. 'You must have been constantly at the stud. There would be no way you could use AI without his knowing and he's not the kind of man who would lend himself to any sort of dishonesty. The same goes for Anthony, I suppose, poor kid. No wonder Tom was trying to keep him away.'

'It wasn't so bad at first, when he was younger and mostly at school, but lately he's wanted to be more and more involved in the stud work and he was starting to question what he saw as our obsession with the scientific side of it. Gerald, Roly's replacement, lives in the village so we could work round him but Anthony was becoming a problem. Tom was being more or less forced to drive him away and it was breaking him up.'

'I can imagine. He always used to be so full of pride that Anthony wanted to follow in his footsteps. The boy was totally bewildered by his turnabout.'

'I know. It was tearing the whole family apart. About three months ago Tom told me that he wished he'd owned up to Mary about the money from the start. I can't believe we were both so bloody naive as to think Slade would let it go after one season. Of course, by the time we realised, it was too late. I don't know what'll happen now,' he said wearily. 'I haven't heard from Slade since I left him a message about Tom's accident.'

Gideon gave a short laugh. 'Oh, I don't think Slade needed to be told about that!' he said bitterly. 'I think you'll find our mutual friend knows more about it than any of us.'

That clearly shocked Rosetti to the core. The colour drained from his face as he stared at Gideon. 'I thought – I was told – it was a gas explosion. Wasn't it?'

'Gas explosions can be arranged.'

Rosetti put a shaking hand to his face. 'Oh, my God! Slade? But why? Without Tom the whole thing falls apart.'

'I don't think he was the intended victim,' Gideon said quietly. 'I'd arranged to meet him at the cottage that night, but I was late. I haven't any proof but I think Slade set it up. Tom told him I'd been asking questions about Sox and he wanted shot of me. Tom was never even supposed to be there.'

'But Tom liked you!' Rosetti protested. 'I can't believe he'd do something like that. In spite of everything he was a good man. He would never have hurt anyone.'

Gideon shook his head. 'I don't think Tom stopped to think what he was doing when he contacted Slade. Mary had asked me to do a portrait for their anniversary so I visited the stud two or three times when he was out. All Tom knew was that suddenly, soon after the abduction, I turned up out of the blue a couple of times and then started asking questions about Sox. Looking back on it now I can see that, unknowingly, I asked the one thing that was guaranteed to set the alarm bells ringing. I asked how his stud work was going.'

'Ah,' Rosetti said.

'Yes,' Gideon said wryly. 'The worst thing I could have asked. And Tom panicked. To be fair to him, I think it was because he began to have misgivings about Slade's intentions that he got caught in the trap that had been set for me. It was all a horrible mix up.'

'My God!' the vet said again. 'What have we done? Oh, dear, dear God!'

15

Gideon's visit to Rosetti left him with no clearer
idea of what he should do about the Sox affair than
he'd had before.

Before they'd spoken he was a fair way towards
convincing himself that he'd been mistaken in his
first instinctive liking and respect for the vet. If
Rosetti had been belligerent or had tried to excuse
his actions when faced with the knowledge that
he'd been found out, it would only have served to
reinforce that conviction, but he hadn't. Not once
in his interview with Gideon did the vet try to shift
the blame or plead his case in any way. Gideon
could not help but like him for it and was surprised
at the degree of sympathy he felt.

None of it helped when trying to decide what
should be done with the knowledge he possessed.
Useless to wish he'd never discovered the con-
spiracy. Life wasn't like that. The real sticking

point was that he hated to let Slade get away Scot-free, but in bringing him down – even if it could be done – he would drag Sean Rosetti's and Tom Collins' good names down with him. The people who would suffer the most would be Mary and Anthony, Daisy, Cathy and her unborn child. Rightly or wrongly, he couldn't believe there was justice in ruining so many innocent lives.

He said as much to Rosetti before he left, admitting that he'd not yet told anyone the whole story and warning him to say nothing for a day or two. Also, he arranged with the vet for Wings to be booked into the hospital for an X-ray the following week.

As Gideon was on the point of leaving, Rosetti had said quite quietly, 'That horse has a huge jump on him, you know. I saw him being loose-schooled over fences one day when I called to see one of Stephanie's other horses. He was only three then, but he jumped like a stag.'

The fact had obviously been a small sop to his troubled conscience, and Gideon felt it was as this that Rosetti offered it rather than as any kind of justification for his actions.

After the internal moral wrangling that followed his meeting with the vet, Gideon wouldn't have been surprised to have found sleep elusive but mental exhaustion cut in and he slept long and soundly, to wake to the sound of drumming rain and the telephone ringing.

'Hi, Bro. How are you?' It was Naomi, sounding

more bright and breezy than anyone had a right to on a dark, wet, late-winter's morning.

'Hi, Sis. What can I do for you?'

'Um, well, I was wondering if you were by any chance thinking of visiting us today?'

'And if I was . . .?'

'Well, Giles was kind enough to offer us a couple of tarpaulins the other day, and what with this foul weather, we could really do with them now. Someone has brought in an injured badger and there's nowhere dry to put him.'

'And you thought, if Bro wasn't doing anything . . .'

'We'd love to see you anyway, of course,' Naomi put in earnestly. 'But I just thought, if you *were* coming over, it would be a shame for you to come all this way without them.'

'It would be, wouldn't it?' Gideon agreed. 'Okay. I'll be an hour or more, though.'

'You're not still in bed?' Naomi exclaimed with sisterly scorn. 'It's nearly half-past nine!'

'It *is* Sunday,' Gideon protested. 'What happened to the good old traditional lie-in? Everybody seems to leap out of bed at the crack of dawn these days, if they even bother to go there in the first place,' he added, remembering Logan's visit. 'I'm sure it's not good for you.'

'Early to bed, early to rise,' she suggested primly.

'Yeah, well, I wasn't early to bed. Look, do you *want* me to bring these bloody tarpaulins over?'

In spite of what he'd said to Naomi, Gideon

384

couldn't truthfully have said that his lie-in had done him much good. Prolonged sleep had left him heavy-eyed and with a muzzy headache that paracetamol made no impression on at all. Nevertheless, barely half an hour later he was at the Priory, rooting three grubby green tarpaulins out of the tractor shed. Pippa had loaned him her car, yet again, though not without protest. She and Rachel had planned to spend the morning exploring a new shopping centre together and only Rachel's offer to take Pippa in her Mini saved the day.

'If I find any more rabbit droppings in it, though, I shall have it professionally valeted and send you the bill,' she warned.

Gideon could not be completely happy about the two of them setting out in a car which Duke Shelley would so easily recognise, but, on the other hand, the man was so thorough, he probably knew all the Priory vehicles anyway. He didn't believe Duke wished Rachel any actual harm, it was more a case of extreme possessiveness. Surely not even *he* would consider abduction from such a public place as a busy shopping centre? Gideon took Pippa aside to remind her of the danger, and beyond that had to trust to her resourcefulness.

'Brother dear, you look awful,' was Naomi's greeting. 'What was it? A night on the town? You're getting too old for that, by the look of it!'

'And you're getting too old for me to give you a brotherly kick-up-the-pants, but I won't let it stop me!' Gideon told her. 'The tarpaulins are in the back of the car. Where do you want them?'

Naomi took an armful of green canvas and led the way to what was left of the old stables. Two bays of the old brick buildings had been roughly shored up, their roofs patched with sheets of corrugated plastic that appeared, in the main, to be tied on with baling twine. The next two bays were completely roofless. Only the main central joists remained, blackened but surprisingly stout. It was to these two that Naomi led Gideon, skirting the muddy puddles and piles of roof tiles that littered the way.

Following her, looking at her mud-caked boots and mud-spattered jeans, and listening to her cheerfully cataloguing what they had so far done and what remained to be done before rebuilding could start, Gideon found it hard to see in her the neat, well-groomed, ultra-feminine dancer of days past. Of course, dancing was not a soft option as a career. It was hard, often painful, slog, but it was just *so* different.

As though she was reading his mind, Naomi paused in her detailing of the plans for the Sanctuary to say, 'Jack's found me some work in Bournemouth, isn't that great? It's a three-month run in a musical. Three months at least – maybe more.'

'And that's what you want?'

She glanced over her shoulder at him. 'Sure, why wouldn't I? I'd always want to dance. It'll be nice to wear pretty clothes again, something that's not caked in dirt and, well – you know what! Besides, the money will come in really useful here.'

She turned into the doorway beside her and dumped her armful of tarpaulin on to a sodden straw bale. The rain had almost stopped for the moment, only a light, misty drizzle disturbing the pool of water on the concrete floor.

'The Victorians knew how to build stables, didn't they?' she observed. 'The water has all collected at the front, here. If the drain wasn't blocked with ash, it would have run away completely.'

Gideon dropped his tarpaulin on top of hers.

'Sis? What aren't you telling me?'

Naomi avoided his eyes. 'What d'you mean?'

'I mean you're all buoyed up with something – positively bursting with it! You can't tell me something hasn't happened.'

'Oh, I never could keep a secret from you, could I?' she exclaimed, giving up all pretence at normality. 'Tim has asked me to marry him! He asked me last night, and I said yes. You don't mind, do you?' She scanned his face with comic intensity.

'All the same if I did!' Gideon laughed. 'No, of course I don't, you idiot! If it's what you want, that's all that matters. I'm thrilled for you! Come here!' He held out his arms and she hugged him joyfully.

'I hope he did it properly – this proposal. Down on one knee in a candlelit restaurant somewhere, with a serenade of violins.'

Naomi chuckled, and from the doorway a voice

spoke apologetically. 'Well, I *was* on my knees, but we were trying to force some water and glucose down a badger's throat at the time.'

'Oh, nice timing!' Gideon approved. 'Very romantic!' He leaned away from Naomi to get a better look at her. 'Well, I don't have to ask if you're happy, you're absolutely glowing! Well, well. My little Sis, getting married!'

'I am nearly thirty!' the bride-to-be protested. 'It's high time *you* started thinking about settling down.'

'Mm. Well, congratulations, both of you!'

'Thanks.' Tim coughed, slightly embarrassed by the whole situation. 'What I came to say is that I've put the kettle on, if anyone's thirsty.' He turned and headed towards their new caravan that stood not where the mobile home had but in the lee of the old barn.

Gideon put his arm round Naomi's shoulders and followed him.

'So what's the story with you and this girl Rachel?' she asked, slanting a look up at him.

'There's no story. She's staying for a few days, that's all.'

'No romance, then?'

Gideon groaned. 'Why is it that as soon as someone makes a commitment, they can't wait to sort out the lives of everyone around them?'

'I'm not! But she seems a nice girl.'

'Oh, she is. She's a lovely girl. But she's not my type. She's too,' he paused, searching for the right word, 'too delicate.'

388

'I thought that's what men liked,' Naomi commented. 'Someone pretty and fragile to take care of.'

'Not all men,' he stated firmly. 'And not this one. You can't tell me Tim does either. He wants someone to work beside him as an equal. Someone he can rely on in a crisis. You give each other strength, I've seen it.'

Coffee and biscuits were consumed in high good humour. The talk was all of plans for the future. No reference was made to past troubles, which disturbed Gideon a little. Surely whatever grudge the occupants of Lyddon Grange had had against Tim and the Sanctuary had not gone up in smoke with the buildings. Or, if for some reason it had, surely it would return when they were rebuilt.

'You've not had any more trouble, then?' he asked eventually, reluctant to spoil the mood but having to know.

'All's been quiet since I found Milne here that time,' Tim said, shrugging. 'He asked all those questions about my plans – our plans – for the place,' he amended with a smile for Naomi. 'I told him that when we'd had new plans drawn up they'd be available for all to see, and he just took himself off. I've not heard a peep out of any of them since. Suits me,' he added, getting to his feet and collecting the empty mugs. 'Actually, I've got an architect coming to have a preliminary look this afternoon.'

'On a Sunday?'

'Yeah, well, I think he's moonlighting but his

rates are very good, so who am I to ask questions?'

'Quite. Well, if you want a hand putting those tarpaulins up, we'd better get on and do it now,' Gideon remarked. 'I thought I might drop in on George and Rose on the way home. Mrs Morecambe sent some tomato chutney for Rose, and I promised I'd call in again.' He paused. Naomi was looking stricken. 'What?'

'Oh, Gideon, I should have phoned to tell you, but what with this business about your friend Tom, I didn't want to add to everything. Poor old George had a heart attack and died two nights ago. I'm sorry. The funeral's next week. I *was* going to let you know before then.'

'Oh, God! Poor old chap!' Gideon said. 'Poor Rose, too. She must be lost without him.'

'I went to see her yesterday. She seems to be coping well. It wasn't completely unexpected, of course, but it's always a shock. Apparently he got up in the night for some reason and she found him dead in the sitting room in the morning. There was some theory that he might have disturbed an intruder and the shock set it off, because they found a window open. But nothing was taken, so they think he must have opened the window himself when he felt unwell. The dog was upstairs with Rose, but then he never barks anyway.'

'Poor Rose,' Gideon said again. 'What a shame.'

'Pop in and see her anyway,' Naomi suggested. 'She'd like to see you. I don't think she's got many left to care about her.'

*

Hauling the heavy tarpaulins into place was hard and wet work, and it was almost an hour later when Gideon knocked on Rose Callow's tiny front door. After a moment or two it opened the six inches or so that its chain allowed and Rose peered anxiously round it. From ground level, the wizened face of an elderly terrier peered silently up at him.

'It's all right, Mrs Callow. It's Gideon. You remember me, don't you?'

'Of course!' she declared warmly. 'Hold on a minute. Mind your nose, Benny!'

The door closed and reopened, minus the chain. 'Gideon! Come in, come in.'

He hesitated. 'Well, look, I don't want to trouble you. Naomi's just told me about George and I had to come and say how sorry I am.' He seemed to be saying that a lot lately. 'After all, if it wasn't for him that night . . .'

'Bless you, my love. He was just so proud that he'd helped. Come on in, you're letting all the warm air out!'

Ducking his head, Gideon stepped past her into the narrow, dark hallway and on into the sitting room. Rose carefully closed the door and followed.

'You'll have a cup of tea, Gideon? The kettle's on.'

Having consumed two mugs of coffee at the Sanctuary, a cup of tea was not precisely at the top of his wish-list but Gideon knew Rose would be much happier if allowed to provide for her guest, and so accepted with a show of gratitude.

While she busied herself in the kitchen, he

glanced round the tiny, chintzy room. Everything was neat but worn. It all looked as though stuck in a time warp since the nineteen-forties or -fifties, and Rose apparently lived by the wartime adage of make-do and mend. Two worn armchairs and a small settee all bore lace-bordered antimacassars and covers on their arms to hide the signs of age. The rugs on the stone-tiled floor, and the curtains at the tiny windows, were also thin and faded but the room was spotless and the furniture polished to a mirror finish. In the narrow grate, coal glowed red behind a burnished bronze rail, and partly worked embroidery had been hurriedly shoved into a basket containing silks beside one of the chairs. The whole effect had a certain poignant charm.

Preceded by the terrier, Rose returned with a tray that held, not only teapot and cups but jam, cream and scones too. The dog stepped neatly into a basket near the fire and settled down with a deep sigh, looking depressed.

'I know it's not teatime,' Rose apologised, 'but I haven't got anything much for lunch, and everybody likes scones, don't they?'

'Well, *I* certainly do,' Gideon said as he hurried to move a vase of daffodils that stood on the coffee table.

'Thank you, Gideon. Just pop them on the desk in the corner, will you? Aren't they pretty? Naomi brought them for me.'

'They're lovely,' he agreed, thinking that it was typically thoughtful of his sister. As he set the vase down carefully on its lace mat, he noticed an old document lying partly unfolded on the desktop, underneath a tatty-jacketed book entitled *Gardens to Treasure*.

'Oh, is this an old map of the area?' he asked, seeing the name on the bottom of the sheet.

'Yes. It shows Lyddon Grange and the farm, with the old boundaries,' Rose told him. 'There's a picture of the gardens in their heyday in the book, too. Before the military took it over in the war. George was always looking at that book. He was looking at it the day before he died. Mr Slade from the Grange called in and George was telling him all about how it used to be. Happy as a sandboy he was that afternoon, that's what I try to remember.' The hand wielding the teapot shook a little. 'Here you are. Come and help yourself to scones.'

'Did Slade often come to see you?' Gideon asked, considerably surprised. He accepted a cup of tea and sat in one of the chairs by the fire.

'No. He'd never been before,' Rose echoed his puzzlement. 'He knocked on the door with our hanging basket in his hand. You know, the one from by our front door with the winter pansies in. He said he'd found it in the middle of the road, which is odd, unless it was kids playing about, but it was kind of him, wasn't it?'

'It was,' Gideon agreed. And completely out of character. But it was a convenient way of introducing himself if he had wanted to. But why should he have wanted to? 'Did you know him?'

'Well, George came to see who it was, and Mr Slade said he was from the Grange and asked him if it was true that he used to work there. Apparently somebody along at the pub had mentioned it. Well, that was all it needed. Within the minute George had him in here and was telling him all about the history of the Grange and the farm. I gave them tea and cake, and he was here nearly an hour. I thought he'd be bored silly, because George did go on a bit when he got talking about the old days, but Mr Slade said he was very interested in the history of the Grange.'

She leaned forward to offer the plate of scones to Gideon. 'George was very taken with him. He even said he'd come again and George was looking forward to it.'

Her voice faltered and Gideon tactfully changed the subject. While he made small talk he was, however, pondering the possible reason for Slade's sudden and unlikely fascination with things historical. The only answer that made any sense was that it had something to do with Milne's enduring desire to get his hands on the Sanctuary land. Could it be that he was hoping to learn something that would help his employer dispute the boundaries? But surely Milne would have explored all those possibilities long ago? Gideon resolved to have a good look at the plans for himself, before he left.

Half an hour, and several jam-and-cream scones later, he prepared to take his leave.

'Has Tim seen this?' he asked, wandering over to the desk as he donned his jacket. 'He'd be fascinated. Do you mind?' As he spoke, Gideon

394

moved *Gardens to Treasure* and smoothed out the document beneath.

'No, you carry on. Can you make out what's what all right? Here, let me put the light on.' Rose switched on a wall light over the desk and Gideon could at last see the map clearly.

It was a little disappointing. Not nearly as detailed as he'd hoped, it covered an area of several square miles, and Lyddon Grange and its adjoining farm were shown as not much more than named plots.

Rose stood beside him, the top of her white-haired head barely reaching his elbow. She bent over the map for a moment, then shook her head.

'No, that's not the one. You want the other one. Where is it?'

Gideon lifted the sheet. There was nothing underneath except the inkstained wood of the desk.

'It must have slipped down.' Rose rifled through the other papers on the desk, and peered hopefully down between it and the wall. 'Well, that's very odd,' she said then. 'George got it out to show Mr Slade. He was telling him about the wartime bunker that he always swore was there.'

'Perhaps he lent it to him?' Gideon suggested.

'No. I don't think he would have done that,' Rose said slowly. 'No, he didn't, because I remember seeing it there when I collected the tea things. I can't think where it can be.'

Gideon had his own suspicions forming about that, but he wasn't going to worry Rose with them.

'Well, never mind. I expect it'll turn up. What made George think there was a bunker there?'

'Well, the Lyddon Estate *was* taken over by the military during the war, and on the map it does look like steps in one place, and George would have it that the steps went down into the ground. He said it was one of those places they built during the war for the top brass to hide away and make their plans and such. I suppose it's possible but I never really took it seriously. I put it down to his imagination. A very fertile imagination my George had.'

'But something must have given him the idea.'

'I think it was something old Mrs Harvey said. Her that used to own the farm. But then she was as nutty as a fruitcake, if you ask me.'

'And what did Slade think of the idea of a bunker?' Gideon probed casually.

'He didn't seem to think it was very likely, as far as I could gather. I only had one ear on them really,' she said apologetically. 'I was doing my knitting. I'd heard it all before, you see. George got quite excited in the end, trying to convince him. I had to tell him to calm down because of his heart. Silly old fool!' she added fondly, with tears shining in her faded, blue eyes. 'But I did love him, you know, Gideon.'

On an impulse he put an arm round her thin shoulders and squeezed gently. 'Are you going to be all right, Rose?' he asked. 'Isn't there anyone who can come and stay with you for a while?'

'No. I'll be all right. I've got Benny. And

everyone's been so kind. After all, I've known I would lose him for a while now. In a way, I was ready for it, even if it was a bit sudden. Much better for him though,' she said with determined brightness. 'But, you know, he never minded the thought of going – only of leaving me. He used to say he'd had more than most and been very happy. So I really shouldn't grieve, should I? He *was* eighty-seven, you know.'

'Was he really?' Gideon gave her another squeeze. 'You're a remarkable woman, Rose Callow,' he said warmly. 'And George was indeed a lucky man.'

Gideon left the cottage in a thoughtful frame of mind. As far as he could see, the possibility of there being an underground bunker at the Sanctuary did nothing to explain Milne's obsession with the place, but nevertheless Tim really ought to know about it. Gideon made a mental note to ring him that evening.

The Gatehouse looked deserted when he got back. Rachel's Mini was nowhere to be seen, no lights showed at the windows, and the kitchen chimney was the only one to send a thin plume of smoke into the leaden grey sky.

Gideon concluded that if Rachel and Pippa were home from their shopping trip they had gone straight back to the Priory and, as he had anyway to return Pippa's car, he followed them.

Sure enough, the Mini was parked in the stable-yard but when Gideon let himself into the kitchen he found only Fanny and her five remaining pups, and Mrs Morecambe, who was up to her elbows in floury dough.

'You've missed the girls,' she told him, when greetings had been exchanged. 'They've gone out riding. I told them they'd catch their deaths in this rain, but Pippa would have it that the horses needed their exercise. Personally I should've thought they'd be just as happy not going out in this, but who am I to have an opinion?'

'Actually, it's almost stopped now,' he informed her. 'So, where's Giles?'

'He's down at the farm with the donkeys,' she said, pummelling her dough. 'Funny how he's taken to them. Can't see no good coming of it.'

Gideon was amused. 'Whyever not?'

'Talking about starting a sanctuary now,' she said, wrinkling her nose disapprovingly. 'That won't make him a living, will it?'

'He's not exactly short,' Gideon pointed out. 'Still, I expect he's got some scheme in mind. I might go down there, actually, as the girls aren't back.'

'I think that's where they were going, too. But, you'll have to go the long way if you're taking the car,' Mrs Morecambe informed him. 'The ford will be full to bursting after all this rain.'

'Thanks, yes, I will.'

The local radio news that morning had been followed by a list of rivers on flood alert due to the recent rain. These included the nearby River Tarrant that flowed through the village, and the

Tarr, one of its minor tributaries that crossed the Priory estate, was certain to be equally high. A gravel lane ran from just outside the stableyard down beside the park to join the one that led from the village to Home Farm. However, it forded the stream on the way, so Gideon would be safer going back past the Gatehouse, to the village and down the farm's own drive.

He picked up Pippa's keys from the table where he'd just dropped them and turned towards the door.

'Oh, there was some policeman here too, a while ago, looking for Rachel,' Mrs Morecambe said as an afterthought. 'I'd have told him about the ford too, if he'd not been in such a hurry. He didn't even have the grace to apologise for calling me away from my baking, so high and mighty he was. I thought it might do him good to get his feet wet. Bring him down a peg or two.'

'What policeman?' Gideon asked sharply, pausing with his hand on the door handle. 'Was it Logan? What did he want?'

'That might have been his name. I'm sure I don't remember.' Mrs Morecambe sniffed with remembered indignation. 'He came hammering on the door fit to break it down and asking for Rachel. I said she'd ridden down to the farm with Pippa and he wanted to know how to get there, so I told him. Didn't seem any call to mention the ford.'

'When was this?'

'Oh, I don't know, ten – maybe fifteen – minutes ago.'

Gideon was uneasy. Brisk and to the point he might be but Logan's manners had always been exemplary.

'What did he look like, this policeman?'

'Oh, I can't remember. Nothing out of the ordinary, I don't think. I was too busy to notice.'

'It might be important,' Gideon persisted. 'Please.'

Mrs Morecambe stopped kneading and looked at the ceiling as if to see his face there. 'Plain clothes. In his thirties, I suppose. About Giles' height but quite stocky, and he had very short brown hair.'

You wouldn't describe Logan as *stocky*, Gideon thought, his suspicions mounting. 'What shade of brown, light or dark?' he asked, trying to keep his voice calm. On the other hand, Duke Shelley was fairly heavily built.

Mrs Morecambe frowned for a moment, then her face cleared. 'Dark,' she stated decisively. 'Oh, and he had a tattoo on his neck. In my day you would never have seen a policeman with a tattoo, but anything goes these days, it seems.'

Gideon didn't wait to hear any more, and her indignant tones were cut off as the door swung to behind him.

Outside in the yard he paused. The route back through the village to the farm was a good three miles, as opposed to maybe half a mile the other way. Even if Duke's car *had* got stuck at the ford, he would almost have had time to reach the farm on foot by now. The quickest option for Gideon was clearly on four legs rather than four wheels, and Blackbird's long black face was watching him with interest over one of the doors.

He swung towards the tack room and retrieved the key from its ledge above the door. Blackbird, originally having come to the yard for schooling, had his own tack, which hung on the wall under a nameplate bearing his name. Gideon scooped up both bridle and saddle. Although he'd ridden bareback many a time in his youth, he hadn't done so for quite a while, and he had a strong suspicion that false heroics at this point would leave him sitting very unheroically in the mud somewhere between the Priory and the farm.

He managed to tack Blackbird up in reasonably good time, ignoring the evil looks and snapping teeth that expressed the horse's feelings at being commandeered in such hasty fashion. Before he had time to organise a more efficient protest, Gideon had him out of the stable, mounted, and cantering across the yard and down the lane.

Resentment quickly gave way to excitement, and as Blackbird's hooves touched the grass verge of the lane he lowered his head and arched his back ominously.

'Oh, no, you don't, you tricky bastard!' Gideon muttered through gritted teeth as he wrenched the black head up and booted him ruthlessly forward. 'Go on. If you've got so much energy, you can bloody well run!'

Blackbird bloody well ran.

For Gideon, the exhilaration of the cold wind

blowing through his hair and whipping tears to his eyes lasted about as long as it took for the ford to come into view round a bend in the track. Cursing, he sat back, wrapping his long legs round Blackbird's body and hauling at his mouth with all the strength he could muster. He might just as well not have bothered for all the effect it had.

The stream was in spate; twenty feet or so wide where it met the road and coming well up the side of the white van caught halfway across the ford. The muddy torrent swirled and eddied around the black-and-white marker posts, which showed nearly three feet of water.

To the right of the ford a narrow footbridge spanned the stream but it might as well have been a tightrope for all the hope Gideon had of slowing Blackbird enough to use it.

It wasn't that three feet of water would have presented a problem to the horse under normal circumstances. It was just that running at full speed into a deep, fast-flowing current is enough to unbalance anybody, and horses are no exception, as shown by the number of competitors that come unstuck at water obstacles on cross-country courses.

With ten feet or so to go, it didn't look possible.

It wasn't.

Blackbird floundered helplessly as the water dragged at his galloping legs and although he leaped and plunged to try and maintain his balance, his momentum carried him on and down, finally collapsing some two-thirds of the way across. Gideon felt the murky water close over his head and the churning cauldron of noise as the horse scrabbled for footing alongside him was almost unbelievable. Grimly, he held on to the reins, finally feeling the pull as Blackbird regained his feet and splashed clear of the stream. Twisting to get his own feet underneath him, Gideon waded out of the flood and pulled the horse to a halt.

Looking back, he found it hard to see how they'd avoided hitting the abandoned van on their way through. He supposed he should think himself lucky, but soaked to the skin in ice-cold dirty water, with a litre or so of the same in each boot, somehow the feeling eluded him.

Blackbird stood, steaming and trembling, with rivulets of stream water pouring off him and one stirrup caught over the top of his saddle.

'What a good thing I put a saddle on,' Gideon remarked, as he patted the horse and prepared to climb aboard once more. 'I might have fallen off!'

He settled back into the saddle with an audible squelch and gathered up reins that had become horribly slippery, but thankfully the shock of his ducking seemed to have calmed Blackbird down. With another look back at the empty van, Gideon sent him on into a canter. Impossible to be sure it was the one driven by Duke Shelley – one white van looks much like another – but he didn't like the way the evidence was piling up.

They reached the farm drive proper, swung into it and in a matter of moments were through the gateway and trotting alongside the massive wooden granary that stood on staddle stones, end-on to the yard.

Gideon almost missed Giles. There was a tractor parked at the far corner of the barn and as he rode past, Blackbird shied violently away from it, causing his rider instinctively to look down. There, behind the tractor and partially under the raised wooden floor, lay Giles, face down in the grass.

'Shit!' Gideon leapt off the horse and ran over, dropping to his knees beside his friend. 'Giles?'

There was no response, so he rolled him over with gentle hands, guiltily aware that it probably wasn't good first-aid practice to do so without first discovering the extent of his injuries. Wet hair was plastered on to a pale forehead that sported a large, rapidly purpling bruise. It looked as though he might have hit his head on the staddle stone.

'Giles? Can you hear me? Giles!'

His eyes were closed but, as Gideon watched, they screwed tighter shut and then partially opened.

'Bugger!' Giles said distinctly.

Gideon grinned briefly but there was something he urgently needed to know.

'Can you remember what happened? Did you fall or were you pushed?'

Giles struggled to focus on Gideon's face. 'I don't know,' he said dazedly. 'There was a bloke . . . I'm not sure what happened.'

Gideon had heard enough. He got to his feet and collected Blackbird who was happily cropping grass.

'Look, when you feel able, get to the farmhouse and call the police,' he said, remounting. 'Tell them Duke Shelley is here looking for Rachel. Tell them to get over here fast!'

Giles tried to sit up. 'Duke? Oh, shit! I'm sorry, Gideon!'

'Yeah, well. You didn't know. I'll try and find the girls. I suppose Henry isn't about?' Henry Williams, the tenant manager of Home Farm, was five foot ten of pure muscle and would have been a good man to have backing him up.

Giles shook his head and winced. 'No. Out in Five Acre with Bob. The girls were going to see the donkeys. Watch yourself! I'll be with you as soon as I can.'

To reach the donkeys' barn and paddock, Gideon had to go through the farmyard itself, round the old pigsties and then down a narrow corridor formed by the back of the milking parlour on one side and the barn itself on the other. The mass of outbuildings belonging to the farm formed a veritable labyrinth and there was still just a hope Shelley had not yet located the girls if he hadn't been very far ahead of Gideon.

As they passed the pigsties, Blackbird gave a soft whicker and Griffin's chestnut head appeared over one of the low doors. After a moment, Cassie came into view next door.

The girls were still about then. Gideon toyed with the idea of sticking Blackbird in one of the sties but thought better of it. He was more than capable of clambering out over a door that low, and would almost certainly create havoc with the other horses, once free.

He was halfway down the muddy corridor when Pippa and Rachel came into sight, laughing and chattering, at the other end. He jumped to the ground and hurried forward to meet them. Pippa was quick to notice his bedraggled state.

'Gideon! What *have* you been up to, for heavensakes?' she exclaimed, laughing. 'Did you fall in the stream?'

'Listen, Duke's here somewhere!' Gideon cut across her laughter. 'Get the horses and get out of here! Ride over to Henry in Five Acre and stay there until I call you.'

'Oh, my God!' Shock drained the colour from Rachel's face and she clasped Pippa's arm convulsively. 'Pippa!'

'It's okay. Come on.' Pippa was briskly efficient as always. She made to move past Gideon and then stopped short, her eyes widening.

Blackbird shifted nervously, head up and eyes rolling, and the hair on Gideon's neck stood up.

'Very good advice,' a voice commented in approving tones from behind him. 'But about five minutes too late. Ain't that a shame?'

Gideon turned and looked back some three feet past Blackbird's flank to where Rachel's ex-husband stood grinning in a thoroughly unpleasant fashion. He was wearing jeans and an army jacket but had removed the eyebrow stud, presumably to lend credence to the tale he'd told Mrs Morecambe. In his right hand he held a throwing knife with a four-inch blade, and from his left dangled a length of heavy, rusty chain. No gun then.

'Anyone moves and this knife ends up in the redhead!' Duke promised. 'Pippa, isn't it?'

'He can do it!' Rachel said on a rising note of panic. 'Do what he says!'

'Oh, yes, I can do it,' Duke agreed. 'And don't think I won't.'

'Why don't you leave Rachel alone?' Gideon asked, trying to divert Duke's attention. 'Go and bother someone else.'

'Why don't you fuck off?'

'You told me not to move,' Gideon pointed out. 'Make up your mind.'

'Oh, funny guy, huh?' Duke said, moving closer. 'Laugh a fuckin' minute! I hoped I'd settled you when I trashed your bike the other night!'

'I bounced.'

'You'll do more than bloody bounce when *I've* finished with you!'

'Ah, you're just sore because I've laid your woman,' Gideon taunted.

'Gideon, don't!' Rachel pleaded. 'It's not true, Duncan.'

'Shut up, you little whore! You slept with all my friends when I was away, didn't you? But you were too busy with your precious career to give me the son I wanted!'

'That's not true!' she protested, perilously close to losing control. Pippa put a steadying hand on her arm.

On the other side of the wall beside them, one of the donkeys, disturbed by their voices, noisily began to gather its breath in preparation for braying, and Blackbird's ears snapped forward in astonishment.

Out of the corner of his eye Gideon could see Pippa trying to edge Rachel backwards. Duke saw it too. His knife hand lifted.

'I said, stand still!' he hissed.

The donkey completed its build-up and began to trumpet in a wonderfully raucous voice. The glory of it passed Blackbird by completely. He was horrified. It was quite possible he'd never come across a donkey before and certainly nobody had ever explained that it was a close relation. He went into a high-speed reversing manoeuvre, almost pinning Duke against the wall of the milking parlour.

'Hey! Keep that fuckin' animal still!' Duke jumped sideways, ending up alongside the panicking horse.

'I'm doing my best!' Gideon lied through gritted teeth. With his back momentarily to Duke he looked straight at Rachel, mouthed, 'Run!' and then, hating to do it, turned and slapped Blackbird hard across the nose with his free hand.

The startled horse whirled away from him, cannoning into Duke with his shoulder, and would have run if Gideon hadn't held determinedly on to the end of his reins. Blackbird was an advantage he was loath to relinquish.

A hurried glance over his shoulder served to

408

reassure him that the girls hadn't wasted the opportunity he'd given them and he returned his attention to Duke.

Blackbird had reverted to his reversing strategy, his head high and open mouth spattering gobs of grassy foam as he tried to get away from the human being who had suddenly and inexplicably turned on him.

Behind him, scrabbling on all fours, Duke was desperately trying to get out of range of his trampling, steel-shod hooves and, as he finally made it to his feet, Gideon could see that somewhere along the line he'd lost his grip on the deadly little knife. He sent a prayer of thanks winging upward.

Having evened the odds a little it seemed that the gods were prepared to sit back and watch the fun because Duke took one stride forward and, with a satisfied smirk, retrieved the length of rusty chain from the mud at his feet.

At this point, Blackbird proved to be something of a double-edged sword. With one full swing of his arm, Duke brought the chain round to strike the black horse hard across the rump. He exploded forward with a grunt of fear and pain, catching Gideon with his shoulder and spinning him into the wall of the barn as he made his escape. The reins were ripped from Gideon's grasp and clods of muddy earth rained down on him and Duke. Fleetingly he hoped that the girls had had time to get well out of Blackbird's way.

He peeled himself painfully off the brickwork to

find Duke Shelley regarding him from about half the chain's length away. The expression on his face was not encouraging. Gideon's plan to divert the man's anger from Rachel to himself had succeeded beyond his wildest expectations.

It seemed to be no part of Duke's plan to let Gideon get his breath back. He had barely straightened up when the chain wrapped itself around his shoulders with brutal force, the end flicking up to catch him on the jaw. Instinct made him bring his arms up to try and shield his face, and by the time his brain sent an override it was too late. Although he grabbed at it, the chain was already back out of reach.

'Too slow!' Duke jeered, beginning to swing the chain in a circular motion at his right side. 'You big bastards are all the same! Slow and clumsy!' He caught his lower lip in his teeth and swung the chain faster until it hummed through the air.

Gideon eyed it warily.

This time when it came he was ready for it, flinging his left arm upwards to grab it close to Duke's grasp. He wasn't, however, ready for the numbing shock of it catching the bone of his elbow, with the result that, once again, the end lashed round his shoulders with wicked force and then pulled tantalisingly through his nerveless fingers and out of reach.

Duke apparently found the whole thing highly amusing but Gideon found his own sense of humour had taken a sabbatical. His shoulders, even covered as they were with a thick jumper and his stockman's coat, felt extremely sore, and his left arm hung uselessly from the elbow, filled with pins and needles.

Duke began to swing the chain again, an almost demonic grin on his face, and it occurred to Gideon that he was almost certainly high on something. There was a light in his eyes that had little to do with sanity, and his movements were jerky and tense. The realisation was no comfort at all.

'Not so fuckin' cocky now, are you?' Duke observed. 'What's the matter? Cat gotcha tongue?'

Somewhere to Gideon's right, probably upset by the fracas, another of the donkeys began to trumpet, joined after a moment by a second and a third, and behind him, over the humming of the chain and his own heavy breathing, Gideon became aware of hoofbeats once more. Presumably Blackbird had found no way out and was returning. The sound gave him renewed hope but Duke seemed not to have noticed, so intent was he on his own sadistic satisfaction.

'I did karate at university,' Gideon informed his opponent, in an attempt to keep his attention.

'Ooh, tough guy! Bruce fuckin' Lee!' he sneered. 'I'm shakin'.'

The chain whirled faster, lifting to cut through the air above Duke like a lasso. A swift vision of the havoc it would wreak if, as obviously intended, it wrapped itself about his head, prompted Gideon to make his move.

'I preferred rugby,' he added conversationally, and had the satisfaction of seeing Duke's right arm

411

falter as the apparent irrelevance of the comment threw him for just a fraction of a second.

Gideon launched himself under the whirling length of rusty metal in a desperate, diving tackle. He caught Duke round the waist and bore him backward and down into the wet grass against the parlour wall. The chain landed with diminished force across Gideon's legs as the breath left his opponent's lungs with a rush.

With thundering hooves and flattened ears, Blackbird swept past them, leaping high into the air to avoid their legs and showering them with mud once again as he galloped on.

Duke shrank back involuntarily and Gideon took advantage of the moment to locate the end of the chain and wrench it from his grasp. He flung it away and reached for a handful of Duke's combat jacket, bracing himself for violent resistance, but Shelley's attention was fixed on something over Gideon's shoulder.

He would have resisted the urge to follow his gaze, had not a sound like a distant roll of thunder intruded on his consciousness. He had to look.

An incredible sight met his eyes. What could best be described as a tidal wave of donkeys was approaching at breakneck speed, jostling one another for space in the narrow passageway.

Duke used Gideon's momentary distraction to pull out of his grasp and scramble out from under him, scampering on all fours for a moment like a chimpanzee before he gained his footing. With a horrified look over his shoulder, he took to his heels.

Gideon decided it was too late to run. He swiftly turned his back upon the approaching stampede and curled himself tightly into a foetal position close to the wall, instinctively protecting his face and stomach like a fallen jockey. There was no time for fear. The donkeys were upon him in an instant, flowing round and over him in a tide of long ears, wide eyes and tiny, stiletto hooves.

The noise was deafening but, incredibly, all but a couple of the little hooves missed him entirely, and those that did hit him caught him only glancing blows. Gideon uncurled in time to see a crowd of furry rumps squeezing round the corner by the pigsties, and then they were gone. He wondered how far Shelley had managed to get.

'Gideon! Are you all right?' Pippa was running towards him in the wake of the donkeys, with Rachel close on her heels, eyes huge in a white face.

'Fine.' He climbed stiffly to his feet. 'You'd better wait here, though. I don't know where Duke is.' He began to jog back towards the yard, fervently hoping that Rachel's ex didn't spring out at him. He'd had about enough of fisticuffs for one afternoon.

Rounding the pigsties cautiously, he heard a slithering noise on the tiles above him and saw Duke drop to the ground some ten feet away.

He landed on his feet and swung his head to look at Gideon but was apparently unwilling to take him on without the advantage of a weapon, for he immediately turned and sprinted away across the yard.

413

Without much expectation of catching him, Gideon ran on, wondering whether the police were on their way, and also where Blackbird and the donkeys would end up if they found their way down the drive to the village.

Ahead of him, Duke had reached the corner of the granary and glanced back over his shoulder to see where Gideon was. As he did so, Giles appeared running from the direction of the farmhouse and launched himself at Duke's legs in a tackle that would have instantly won him a place with the British Lions. He followed it up, however, with a move that would just as quickly have lost him that place.

Gideon jogged up with a wide grin on his face. 'Foul!' he declared.

Giles was by now sitting firmly upon his captive, breathing heavily and leaning on one hand which was, in turn, pushing Duke's face uncompromisingly into the mud of the farm track.

Gideon tilted his head on one side, looking down at his erstwhile opponent.

'You know, I'm not sure he can breathe,' he announced after a moment or two.

'How sad,' Giles said lightly, but he relaxed the pressure a little.

Duke spat mud and curses, and wriggled violently.

'There's gratitude,' Giles observed, leaning hard once more.

'Would this be useful?' Pippa came up behind Gideon, holding out the lead rope from a headcollar. Rachel stood some distance away, apparently not yet convinced that Duke was sufficiently contained.

Gideon took the rope, and with Giles' assistance, bound Duke's wrists to his ankles with ruthless efficiency and great enjoyment. They stood back and surveyed their handiwork with satisfaction.

Duke was not nearly so content. He spat some more mud and then let loose an incredible string of verbal abuse, his extensive vocabulary presumably acquired during his army days.

'Oh, for heavensakes!' Pippa exclaimed. She pulled a cotton scarf from around her neck, and kneeling behind him, wrapped it around his face, pulling it into his protesting mouth and knotting it at the back of his head.

Gideon was impressed. 'Where did you learn to do that? At catering college?'

'No. At the cinema,' she countered. 'You see what you're missing?'

'Obviously.' Gideon turned to give Rachel a reassuring grin. 'Come on, we've got him now. Or rather, Giles did.'

'He can't get free again?'

'No.' Giles went towards her and put his arm round her shoulders. 'He's trussed up like the proverbial chicken and the police are on their way. They'll have him locked away in no time, I should think.'

'Did he hurt you?' she asked, frowning as she noticed the bruise on his forehead.

'No, I'm fine,' he assured her.

Gideon raised his eyebrows significantly at Pippa. 'Who's the hero now?' he murmured. 'By the way, how did the donkeys escape? Did Blackbird crash the gate?'

'No, I let them go. They were milling around in a semi-panic, and I thought if I let them out they might stampede and cause a diversion.'

'They did,' Gideon said heavily. 'Unfortunately it was me that was diverted! I'd just got hold of our friend at that point.'

Pippa bit back a giggle. 'Oh, I'm sorry! Only I saw Blackbird had deserted you and I thought you might need some help.'

'O, ye of little faith. Was that another of your tricks learned from the films?'

'Well, it always worked for John Wayne,' she told him.

16

It was a good hour and a half after the police arrived to relieve them of Duke Shelley that Gideon, Giles, Pippa and Rachel finally arrived back at the Priory in Giles' four-wheel-drive Mercedes.

The police, two officers Gideon had not met before, dealt with the situation with brisk efficiency, releasing Shelley from his makeshift rope bonds and securing him with handcuffs before taking statements from his four weary captors. They were very gentle with Rachel, who looked, and probably was, on the verge of mental exhaustion.

Duncan Shelley was also wanted, one of the policemen told them, on suspicion of involvement in a drugs-related stabbing the night before. Gideon mentioned the knife and a short search turned it up at the scene of the confrontation.

'You were very lucky, sir,' one of the policemen told him. 'He's a nasty piece of work.'

Gideon flexed his bruised shoulder muscles gingerly. Once again, he didn't feel very lucky.

The bulk of the time after the police had hauled their unwilling captive off was taken up with retrieving the donkeys from the various parts of the farm to which they had fled. Rachel took no part in this operation, staying instead in the farmhouse under the motherly eye of Henry's wife, where they found her in due course, kneeling on the rug by the fire, playing with a litter of boisterous kittens. She looked up eagerly as they came in, and Gideon immediately said, 'No! Elsa would murder it!'

The skies had opened again and it was decided to leave the horses at the farm to be collected the next day. Blackbird had been found pulling hay from a stack of bales in the barn but allowed himself to be caught with no trouble and appeared to bear Gideon no lasting grudge for the treatment he had received.

The Priory kitchen, with its assortment of old armchairs, ancient range pumping out heat, basketful of puppies and deliciously fragrant cooling loaves of bread, seemed like heaven as they came in from the cold, wet dusk outside.

Mrs Morecambe fussed round them all, exclaiming at the state of Giles and of Gideon, who now also sported an impressive purpling bruise where the end of the chain had caught him in the face. She made them all sit down, ignoring Pippa's protests that she had horses to feed and settle for the night.

'They can wait five minutes while you have a cup of tea. They're not that fragile, and you can't make me believe they are. You look fit to drop!'

Pippa gave in, admitting that she could do with a cup of tea, though, as she pointed out, she had come through the whole thing the fittest of all of them.

Gideon was the wettest, his clothes never having completely dried out since his ducking in the river, but Mrs Morecambe's suggestion that Giles lend him a change of clothes was greeted with a chorus of mirth.

'I'm quite a bit bigger round and a good four inches longer in the leg,' Gideon explained, seeing that Mrs Morecambe was looking a little put out.

'Well, I know *that*,' she said. 'But you're not going in for a fashion show.'

'Actually, I'm drying out quite nicely now I'm next to the range,' he told her. 'Sort of steaming gently.'

She pursed her lips in a way that showed she wasn't completely mollified but he knew her well enough to be sure she would soon come round.

Quite apart from being decidedly damp, he was feeling the ongoing effects of Duke Shelley's efforts with the chain, and they were not very pleasant. Even the soft upholstery of the armchair generated more pressure on his bruised shoulders than was comfortable, and now he was resting, the injured muscles had begun to stiffen and set up a protest every time he shifted his position.

He was glad no one had been witness to the worst of the confrontation. If Pippa had known, she'd probably have had him stripped to the waist and rubbed liniment into his bruises, and that kind of attention he felt he could well do without, just at the moment.

Having consumed cups of tea and slices of newly baked bread, they were sitting round feeling warm and somewhat sleepily discussing the events of the afternoon when Gideon's mobile phone trilled.

'Hi, Bro, it's me,' Naomi's voice announced. 'Look, I just wondered if you'd seen or heard from Tim this afternoon? I had to go to Bournemouth to see about this job I've been offered, which took forever, and when I got back he wasn't here. I wouldn't worry but some of the animals obviously haven't been fed and I wondered if there was a problem with the donkeys or something, and he'd come over to you? His car's gone.'

'No, he's not here,' Gideon told her. 'You've obviously tried his mobile . . .'

'Yes. That's the silly thing. It's here on the table. Wherever he is, he forgot to take it. Oh, well. Never mind. I expect he'll turn up. Speak to you later.'

'Yeah.' Gideon was frowning. 'Give me a ring when you find him, won't you?'

'Okay,' she said lightly. ''Bye for now.'

Gideon ended the call, still frowning. 'None of you have heard from Tim today, have you?' he asked thoughtfully.

Nobody had. They discussed possibilities for a moment and then the talk turned to a discussion of the character traits of Fanny's remaining five pups, but Gideon felt unsettled. She had sounded casual enough, but he was sure there'd been an undercurrent of real anxiety in his sister's voice.

'Well, I still think the black pup is more intelligent than Gideon's brindle one,' Pippa said, standing up and stretching. 'But I'm not going to sit here arguing about it any more. I've got horses to feed. Volunteers gratefully accepted,' she added hopefully. 'Gideon?'

'I'm sorry,' he said. 'What?'

'Stables?'

'Yeah, sure. Look, I'll be with you in a minute. I just want to ring Naomi back.'

'Okay. But you're not really worried about Tim, are you? After all, what can have happened? He's probably just nipped out for something, met a friend and stopped for a drink.'

'Yeah, maybe. But I would have thought he'd have let Naomi know.'

'Well, he hasn't got his mobile, has he? She told you that.' Pippa collected a coat from the washroom on her way out, calling, 'See you in a minute, then,' and the door banged behind her.

Gideon keyed in the Sanctuary's number, noting as he did so that Rachel had fallen asleep with her head against Giles who was sitting perched on the arm of her chair. He smiled to himself.

He wasn't smiling a minute later as he cancelled the call and keyed in Naomi's mobile number, and when he cancelled that call too, his heart was beginning to beat a little faster.

Giles was watching his face. 'She's probably outside looking for Tim,' he offered.

'She'd surely have taken her mobile,' Gideon said. 'In case he called.'

'You're really worried, aren't you?' Giles said, surprised. 'What on earth do you think has happened? The Invasion of the Bodysnatchers, Part Two?'

Gideon didn't smile. 'I'm probably getting paranoid in my old age,' he said, climbing stiffly to his feet. 'But they've got some pretty nasty neighbours. I've just got a feeling something's not right. D'you think I could . . .?'

'Yes,' Giles said resignedly. 'Take the Merc. It's faster. Just don't crash it.'

The country roads of Dorset don't lend themselves to great speed, but the Mercedes' speedometer touched ninety-five a time or two on the straighter stretches and Gideon tested its cornering ability to the limit. It wasn't until the last few miles of narrow lanes forced his speed down that he noticed a vehicle following him, lights flashing urgently. It was almost completely dark by now but the absence of blue lights suggested it wasn't the police, and on the remotest chance that it might be Tim or Naomi, Gideon slowed to a halt, keeping to the crown of the road so he couldn't be boxed in.

The vehicle behind stopped about six feet from his rear bumper and a figure got out. Even in silhouette, Gideon could tell it was Logan; he had a certain way of moving. He waited for the policeman to come up to the window and then lowered it four inches or so, blinking in the light of Logan's torch.

Logan dispensed with the expected remarks about Gideon's driving, saying simply, 'I followed you from the Priory. What's up?'

'Maybe nothing,' he said. 'Naomi phoned looking for Tim, and now I can't reach her either. Too much has gone wrong lately. I need to know they're safe.'

'Okay. I'll be right behind you.'

Gideon thanked him but he'd already disappeared, and when the Mercedes moved off, the other car was once more on its tail.

The yard appeared deserted when Gideon and Logan drew up in front of the office. The security light came on illuminating their vehicles, Naomi's yellow MG, the open area of rain-puddled gravel, and the buildings beyond. Several piles of sand and shingle stood around. Of Tim's Volvo there was no sign.

Logan was out of his car and shining his torch into the MG as Gideon came round the back of it.

'My sister's.'

'She's still here somewhere, then.'

'It looks like it. I'll take a look in the caravan and the farmhouse. You look in reception,' Gideon suggested, though with little optimism; there were no lights to be seen anywhere.

The caravan was indeed empty; the heater not

even warm. Nobody had been in there for quite a while. The burnt-out shell of the farmhouse stood dejectedly in its overgrown garden with chipboard across the windows and a tarpaulin on the roof. All was quiet, and as far as he could tell, nothing had been disturbed. Gideon padded round to the front of the offices again. He was wearing desert boots, his soggy footwear being the one item of clothing he *had* stopped to change. The rest was more or less dry now anyway.

Logan was waiting.

'Nobody in the office or surgery,' he confirmed. 'But there's a white pick-up parked round the corner. Any idea whose that might be?'

Gideon shook his head. 'Sorry.'

'I'll call it in,' Logan said. 'Then we'd better take a look round the rest of the place. What there is of it.'

He produced his mobile and sweet-talked someone at the station into checking the numberplate for him, waiting only a few moments before saying, 'Right, thanks. I owe you one.'

Pocketing the phone he looked at Gideon. 'Well, well. It belongs to your friend Joey Dylan.'

Gideon frowned. 'Joey? Why would he be here?'

'You tell me,' Logan invited. 'He's been here before, though, hasn't he?'

'Only when Jez – his sister – was here. I don't know whether she's been back since the fire, or even if she's out of hospital yet. Naomi didn't mention her. I have seen Joey next door, though. At the Grange. I think he works for Slade

424

sometimes, when he needs some muscle.'

Logan glanced sideways at him. 'Such as abducting people in the middle of the night?'

'Yeah, things like that.' It wasn't the time to hold back on Logan.

'Someday, when we've got a little more time, we'll have a beer and you can tell me all about that,' he said. 'But for now let's take a gander, then decide what's best to do. It might be worth taking a little look next door to see who's at home.'

They set off past the foodstore and down the row of old stables, which grew less serviceable the further they went. On their right lay the open areas of concrete foundations where the new, wooden stables had stood before they had burned to the ground, and beyond that the hard-standing for the mobile home, the remains of which had finally been carted off to the scrapyard a couple of days before. Several piles of bricks and timber promised rebirth in the near future.

They searched all the remaining buildings, shining Logan's torch into the corners and disturbing the badger in one stable, who blinked and tried to push himself deeper into his straw bed. Then they tramped round the fence that separated the yard from the fields beyond, calling out every few strides for Naomi and Tim, but they saw and heard no one. Gideon battled with a rising sense of unreality. They couldn't just have disappeared.

'It's like the *Marie* bloody *Celeste*,' Logan commented, as they came to a halt in front of reception once again. 'Any ideas?'

'I wish I had,' Gideon said. 'One person going missing is bad enough, but two, and separately . . . ?'

'Right. Well, I think I'll shoot along to the Grange,' Logan suggested. 'I don't think Slade's into wholesale kidnap but it won't hurt to account for his whereabouts. You take the torch and stop here in case either of them turns up. But watch your back, okay? There's still a chance Joey's around here somewhere. I don't want you disappearing too!'

'Me either,' Gideon agreed.

As the sound of the car's engine receded, he stood debating whether he should take another look round or whether it was worth trying to find Tim's diary to see if that held any clues. Surely Naomi would have thought of that, though. A faint smell of petrol hung in the air, causing him to wrinkle his nose. Logan's car could do with a service, he thought inconsequentially. The security light went out, leaving him in darkness, and after a moment he waved a hand to bring it on again.

Right in front of him, about twelve feet away on the edge of the pool of light, stood Joey.

Gideon caught his breath. 'Christ! Where did you come from?'

Joey's attitude was wary but non-threatening. 'I was waiting 'til the cop buggered off,' he said.

'How did you know he was a cop?' There was nothing about Logan's clothing or vehicle to suggest it.

'It pays to know, pal. He comes from Chilminster nick, that one.'

'Well, he'll be back in a minute, he's only gone next door,' Gideon warned him. 'So, what are you doing here? Do you know where Tim and Naomi are?'

As he spoke, Gideon took a step or two sideways, out of the direct glare of the light. He didn't want to be a sitting duck if Joey wasn't alone.

'No, I don't. But I think they're in trouble. I bin trying to reach you for the last hour or more.'

'I haven't been home,' Gideon said, his heart beginning to thud. 'Why do you think they're in trouble?'

'Because when I saw him this afternoon, Slade was talking about getting out. He said he'd got wind of a nice little haul that was just there for the taking, and he was gonna cut his losses and go. Then he started muttering about you. Said you were unfinished business and how he had a score to settle.' Joey shook his head, almost despairingly. 'I don't know what you did, pal, but you really pissed him off and he's not one to let that sort of thing go. That was when he remembered your sister. He said if he could get hold of her, then you'd be sorry you crossed him.'

Gideon's fists were clenched by his sides. 'What? Did he say what he was going to do?'

'I'm sorry, pal. I should've kept my mouth shut. I told him I don't hold with hurting women, and he clammed up. Said he didn't need me anyway. I should've waited 'til I knew more. I tried to ring you but I haven't got your mobile number, so I

427

came to warn your sister but she wasn't here. Don't know if she'd have listened to me anyway, after the other night.'

Gideon was wary. 'Why should I believe you? What's in it for you?'

'Sod all but trouble,' Joey admitted. 'It's just . . . Well, I know how it feels. You know, sisters.' He dried up, palpably embarrassed. 'Oh, shit! I don't know what I'm saying.'

'But you work for him. How do I know you're not doing his dirty work right now?'

'Not since I found out he was behind that fire,' Joey stated.

'So where's Slade now?' Gideon wasn't convinced.

'I don't know. His car's at the Grange but he wasn't in his flat. I even asked Milne if *he* knew – he's a miserable old bugger, that one! – but he didn't know either. Renson was there but if he knew he wasn't telling, and he's gone out now to refuel the chopper.'

'So, where else might Slade go? Does he have any other hideouts?'

'Well, I'd've looked there if he had, wouldn't I?' Joey pointed out reasonably. 'Anyway, his car's there. It's like a friggin' alien abduction or a black hole or something.'

Gideon frowned. 'And Naomi's car is here . . .' Then sharply, '*What* did you say?'

'What did I say when?' Joey was bewildered.

'A black hole. That's it! George Callow's bunker!'

428

Joey shook his head. 'You've lost me now, pal.'

'There's supposed to be an underground wartime bunker somewhere on the farm, or rather under it,' Gideon explained, starting to walk back towards the stables. 'Slade must have got wind of it – don't ask me how – and he visited George Callow to find out where it was. George had a map, you see. At least, he did have. I've a strong suspicion that your friend Slade has it now. You see, George had a heart attack the other night. A window was open when they found him and they thought he might have surprised an intruder, although nothing appeared to be missing.'

'Except the map,' Joey supplied.

'Well, his wife was going to show it to me but she couldn't find it.'

'So you don't know where the entrance to this bunker is?'

'Somewhere round the farm buildings,' Gideon said helplessly. 'Rose couldn't say for sure and I didn't know it was going to be important.'

'What the hell would Slade want with a bunker?'

'How the bloody hell would I know?' Gideon demanded. 'He's not *my* mate.'

He stopped in front of the old stableblock. 'It would be a lot easier if we knew what we were looking for precisely. I suppose the trapdoor, or whatever you call it, would be made of concrete or iron.'

'Somebody's been digging over there.' Joey pointed in the direction of the farmhouse.

'That's where the new stables were. The ones they lost in the fire.'

'No. Further over,' he said, impatiently. 'There's a spade or something.' He started to move. 'And a crowbar. This could be it, pal.'

Gideon moved with him. 'That's where the mobile home stood.' He shone Logan's torch ahead of them. 'Hey, I think you're right. Some of the paving's been moved.'

They reached the spot and stood looking down. Four paving slabs had been lifted, to expose a square of concrete underneath, and within that, a rectangle measuring about three feet by two, outlined by a thin line of metal. Also, a matter of two feet away to one side, another slab had been removed, under which was a cavity containing a heavy iron handle, shaped like a ship's wheel. In the light of the torch it appeared to be remarkably rust-free.

It was easy to see how Gideon and Logan had missed it earlier. In the muddle of devastation and imminent rebuilding, the significance of loose slabs lying around was easy to miss, especially when there was no thought of hidden trapdoors.

'Now what?' Joey asked quietly.

Gideon wished he knew. If Slade *was* down there, just what was he up to? Was access to the bunker the reason Milne had been so desperate to drive Tim and Naomi off the farm? What could possibly be so important about a derelict military bunker? Gideon would have been tempted to think that Milne had had nothing to do with it, if it

430

weren't obvious that Slade had only recently discovered its existence.

'Have you really no idea what he's up to?' Gideon asked.

'Sweet FA, pal. I wish I did.'

'Well, I suppose I'd better go down and have a look,' Gideon said, with a marked lack of enthusiasm. 'I'll just have to hope this hatchway doesn't open straight into the business department of whatever's down there, or I could be in big trouble!'

Joey put a hand on Gideon's arm, his head up and listening. 'Hold on a moment. There's a chopper coming. It could be a coincidence but I wouldn't bet on it. Renson pretty much answers to Slade these days, even though it's Milne who pays him.'

They waited a moment. The helicopter drew ever closer and then began to circle the field behind the farmhouse.

'Best if I go and see who's on board,' Joey suggested. 'If it's Slade, it'll be easier for me to talk my way round it than it would be for you. If it's just Renson, I'll give him some story about a change of plans and tell him to come back later. The fewer we have to deal with, the better.'

'Er . . . Okay, thanks.' Gideon was finding it hard to adjust to the idea of he and Joey batting for the same team, and the doubt must have sounded in his voice because Joey paused, looking back.

'Yeah, I probably wouldn't trust me either, pal,'

he said helpfully, and with a gleam of white teeth in the darkness, was gone.

Oddly enough, Gideon felt in some way reassured. His head was telling him he was mad to believe anything Joey Dylan said but the instinctive liking he'd felt on their first meeting was still there, and his instincts rarely let him down, with animals or people.

In the field, the helicopter sank ever lower, the draught from its rotors reaching Gideon even where he stood. He shivered. Now the rain of the last few days had stopped, the sky was clearing and the temperature dropping fast. If *he* was cold, what would it be like underground? Were Tim and Naomi really below his feet somewhere? It seemed unreal.

The word 'underground', with all its funereal connotations, gave rise to a sudden feeling of panic in Gideon. It was intensely frustrating to be standing there doing nothing while his sister almost certainly needed help.

'Come on, Logan. *Where are you?*' he muttered, gazing impotently into the surrounding darkness, although to be fair, it could only have been five minutes or so since he'd driven off and the Grange was the best part of a mile away by road. Gideon wondered how Joey was getting on. The helicopter had landed now, its engine idling and rotors turning slowly. What was he saying to whoever was in the machine?

Was he mad to trust the man?

After a minute or two more, the helicopter

engine died completely, leaving an almost deafening silence. Gideon crouched to listen at the bunker entrance but could hear nothing and stood up, stepping back and stretching his tense limbs. Stiffening muscles pulled across his shoulders, reminding him painfully of the earlier conflict. He groaned wearily. What he wanted most in the world was to see Naomi safe and then sink into a steaming bath.

A noise behind made him turn. Was that Logan back? Over the racket of the approaching helicopter, he'd never have heard him.

'Logan?'

No answer.

His skin prickled. Had Joey ever gone to meet the helicopter? Had he, instead, circled round to come up behind Gideon? Or was someone else waiting in the darkness?

Another slight sound, like a pebble being dislodged, made him swing the torch to his right, and in that instant he heard a step behind him and knew he'd fallen for the oldest trick in the book.

In a flash, a length of wire was brought down over his head and pulled viciously tight round his neck. Gideon managed to get the fingers of one hand inside the loop before it tightened and, dropping the torch, clawed at the other side desperately as it began to bite.

He wasn't sure if the intention was to strangle him or slit his throat, and either way he didn't fancy it. He knew that if his windpipe collapsed he'd be beyond help.

Even in the heat of the moment, struggling for breath as he was, Gideon's self-defence training didn't desert him. Still gripping the wire, he dropped his bodyweight downward and back, landing at the feet of his assailant and crashing into his lower legs.

For a brief, agonising moment the wire felt as if it would cut his fingers off but then his weight unbalanced the man behind him, pulling the top half of his body forward. Gideon continued to roll backwards, bringing his feet over to drive into his attacker's chest.

Instantly the pressure was released and Gideon completed the roll, coming up on to one knee, gasping for air. He was very aware that, a few feet away and barely discernible in the darkness, his assailant was also recovering and would doubtless renew his assault, but for a second or two all Gideon could do was massage his throat and gulp in life-giving oxygen. The fallen torch lay at his feet, still miraculously unbroken and wasting its light on the muddy ground. Gideon scooped it up, turning as he clambered upright, and it lit Curly's unlovely countenance just as he gathered himself to charge.

The beam from Logan's powerful torch caught Joey's half-brother full in the eyes, causing him to pause, blinking and turning his head away slightly.

'Where's my sister?' Gideon hissed.

'That blonde bitch?' Curly sneered. 'She's dead meat, mate. Her and the vet. You'll never see her again.'

'You'd better hope I do,' Gideon advised in a low, furious voice; goaded in spite of himself. 'If I find out you've laid a finger on her . . .'

Curly laughed. 'Oh, we've all had a piece of her,' he said roughly, enjoying himself. 'She screamed a bit at first, but there was no one to hear. Best lay I've had in a while—'

The words were cut off abruptly as Gideon's self-control, rendered precarious by tiredness and anxiety, finally snapped. The torchlight bobbed and swung as he charged across the half-dozen feet between them and aimed a haymaker at Curly's smirking face.

This furious, unwary approach was obviously what Curly had anticipated. He took a quick step back, and before Gideon's swinging fist had a chance to make contact, the end of a short length of timber caught him squarely in the solar plexus, stopping him in his tracks and bringing him retching to his knees.

'Not such a clever bastard now, are you?' Curly observed, and accompanied the words with a chopping blow across Gideon's head and shoulders that dropped him on the spot.

Even through the pain and dizziness, Gideon was conscious of a stab of desperate disappointment that he'd let Naomi down. He could expect no mercy from Curly – the very concept was entirely alien to him – and he was powerless to prevent him finishing what he'd started. He had a feeling that a mere roughing-up wouldn't satisfy the man. He'd seen before that only Joey kept the brakes on his violence, and Joey, unfortunately, wasn't here. How could he have been so *stupid* as to let his temper flare like that?

Curly pushed Gideon with a booted foot, rocking his body and rubbing his cheek against the cold paving on to which he'd partially fallen. Feebly, Gideon attempted to grab the boot, but a sharp kick loosened his grasp easily. He bit back a groan. That satisfaction, at least, he would deny his tormentor.

'Got any last wishes?' Curly enquired, bending over Gideon who lay on his side feeling lousier than he would have believed possible. Above them, the moon suddenly broke free of the clouds and Curly's face became dimly visible, full of savage enjoyment. 'Oh, yes, your sister. Oh, well. We can't have everything we want, can we?' He hefted the length of wood again, tapping it on the ground in front of Gideon's face so the threat didn't escape him. 'If you believe in God, this might be a good time to pray,' he suggested.

Gideon almost wished he would get on with it, then remembered Logan. Surely he must be on his way back by now. How to stall for time? He could think of only one thing that might influence Joey's thuggish half-brother.

'What about the money?' he asked, his voice coming in such a pathetic grating whisper that for a long moment he thought Curly hadn't heard.

The word 'money' obviously found its way through the gloating though, for he leaned forward. 'What did you say?'

'The money,' Gideon reiterated, slightly more strongly.

There was a pause. 'What money?'

Gideon devoutly wished he knew.

'If you kill me, you'll never find it,' he said, forcing his brain back into gear.

He was finding breathing difficult. Anything more than the shallowest of inhalations set off a knifing pain in his side. Dully, he supposed he had one or more broken ribs. It didn't seem important.

'Why d'you think Slade . . . wanted to lure me here?' he went on, groping for inspiration. 'He won't be too pleased . . . if he finds you've interfered.'

'Slade didn't say anything about money.' Curly still sounded bullish but a tinge of doubt had crept in.

'Well, he wouldn't, would he?' Gideon pointed out, relentlessly pressing home his slim advantage. He pushed himself up on to one elbow, grunting with the effort. 'He didn't tell you to kill me either, did he?'

'Stay still!' His movement had unnerved Curly a little, which amused Gideon. His faith in Gideon's powers of recovery obviously bordered on the miraculous. Gideon himself severely doubted if he could even stand up, let alone pose a threat to a sixteen-stone thug with a length of timber in his hands.

'What money are you talking about?' Curly demanded. 'I'll give you five seconds to tell me, and it'd better be good!'

437

Gideon stared up at the vague outline of his head and shoulders against the sky and could think of absolutely nothing convincing to say.

'Fuck you!' Curly spat the words. 'There's no money! You're just fuckin' me about!'

Gideon watched with a strange, detached fascination as, in what seemed like slow motion, Curly raised the timber, holding it vertically and preparing to drive it downward like a stake. He braced himself for the impact, knowing he should try to roll at the last minute but seriously doubting that he would be quick enough.

'I've been waiting for this a long time,' Curly told him, determined to milk the last ounce of sadistic pleasure from the situation, but before he could bring the timber down, another silhouette silently joined his against the moonlit clouds. There was a quick movement, a thud, and Curly fell senseless, wood and all, across Gideon's legs.

'You'll have to wait a while longer, pal,' a familiar voice remarked.

Gideon wouldn't have believed he could ever be so glad to see Joey. He closed his eyes and let out a groan that was a mixture of pain and relief.

'I don't really know why you did that,' he said. 'But thank you.'

Joey bent and pulled his half-brother off Gideon's legs, pausing briefly to check that he still breathed. 'It beggars belief that this man-rhino is any relation of mine, but Ma says he is so I have to accept it. I don't, however, have to like him.'

He switched on the torch he held – presumably

what he'd used to club Curly – and shone it at Gideon. 'Jeez, you look a mess!'

'I *feel* a mess,' Gideon assured him, gritting his teeth as he began the daunting climb to his feet. 'What happened with the helicopter?'

'Oh, Renson was getting awkward,' Joey said, casually. 'So I took the keys off him and locked him in.'

'Just like that?'

'Well, something like that,' he amended, his teeth flashing white in the torchlight. 'I 'cuffed him to the seat support, too.'

Gideon paused, crouched on one knee, while a dizzy spell came and went. *More* handcuffs? Joey was unbelievable!

'What are you going to do with sleeping beauty, there? He'll be fighting mad when he comes round.'

'Won't he just?' Joey agreed. 'Perhaps I'd better put him in one of those stables.' He bent and grasped a handful of clothing and then dragged Curly's unconscious figure unceremoniously across the open ground and disappeared into the shadow of the old stable-block.

'Naomi and Tim are somewhere down there,' Gideon said, when Joey came back. He'd made it to his feet and was cautiously straightening up. He gasped as a rib moved where it shouldn't. 'I don't know where the hell Logan's got to, but I don't think I can wait for him much longer.'

'That might be my fault, pal,' Joey admitted with a hint of an apology. 'I made a little hole and drained off most of his petrol while you were looking round. I reckon he might've got a mile or so up the road but no further.'

Gideon groaned. 'You bloody idiot! Why?'

'Yeah, well, he may be *your* buddy but he's no friend of mine!' Joey stated defensively. 'I knew when he didn't find Slade he'd come straight back and I wanted to slow him down a bit. I figured it'd give me time to fill you in on what I knew. Look, if we're going down there, we'd better do it before someone starts wondering why Curly hasn't reported in. Slade's very hot on regular personnel checks and I think we could do with surprise on our side.'

'We could do with a squad of commandos on our side!' Gideon observed. 'Okay. Let's see if we can get that hatch open.'

Opening it was fairly straightforward. To one side of the wheel-shaped device, a large, well-oiled padlock lay, disengaged and with the key still in it. If it hadn't been for the hostages below, it would have been the work of moments to re-apply it and seal in Slade and whoever else was down there until Logan came back. As it was, and with that thought in mind, Joey removed the key and hid the padlock under a tarpaulin near the stables before operating the mechanism that opened the hatch.

With a slight grating noise, the heavy, reinforced concrete cover slid down and sideways to reveal a steep flight of steps, dimly lit by a recessed bulb behind thick, yellowed glass. Gideon peered unenthusiastically into the opening.

'I hope there's more than one room down there,' he said softly, revoicing his earlier comment. 'Otherwise we're going to get a warm welcome when we start down those steps.'

'Only one way to find out.'

'That's what's worrying me!' Gideon said with feeling.

'I'll go first, if you like,' Joey offered. 'Slade won't react so badly to me as he would to you.'

Gideon had an uneasy feeling that, as it was *his* sister, it ought to be *his* risk, but he decided it would be silly to let his principles get in the way of common sense.

'Okay,' he agreed. 'You've talked me into it.'

'And by the way, if you've got a phone on you, switch it off. I doubt you'd get a signal down there but you don't want to find out the hard way!' Joey warned.

His broad shoulders almost filled the opening as he stepped carefully downwards and Gideon was extremely grateful that the Liverpudlian's conscience had caused him to change sides, at least for the time being. He followed, trying not to let the recurrent suspicion that this might be an elaborate trap get in the way of forward thinking. Surely, he told himself, if Joey were still working for Slade, then he wouldn't have rescued Gideon from Curly. It wouldn't make sense.

At the bottom of the steps they found themselves in a corridor some thirty feet long, with three pairs of heavy metal doors leading off it at regular intervals. All the doors were closed and fitted the frames so tightly that no light could have escaped to hint at occupancy. Feeling like someone out of a TV detective series, Gideon joined Joey in flattening himself against the cold corridor wall as they cautiously opened each door in turn.

The first two rooms they revealed were obviously derelict. Each about fifteen feet square, a quick flash of the torch showed a dusty old desk and filing cabinet in one, and a number of metal-framed chairs with khaki canvas seats in the second. The rooms smelled musty and were cold and deeply depressing. Gideon found himself hoping, as they approached the next, that there wasn't a mouldering skeleton seated at a desk, pen still in hand.

The third was a kind of radio room, presumably once wired to an outside mast, and the fourth a bunkroom with eight bunkbeds, still draped with blankets. These rooms also appeared dry and dusty, and had at some time supported a colony of busy spiders, which had almost certainly met a hungry end.

They walked ever more softly towards the last pair of doors and paused.

Joey looked sideways at Gideon.

'Fifty-fifty,' he whispered. 'Which one d'you fancy?'

'Neither,' Gideon replied frankly. 'You choose, pal.'

Another gleam of teeth rewarded this mimicry, and Joey leaned towards the door on their right and stood listening.

442

After a moment he pursed his lips and shook his head. He swung the door open and flashed the torch inside before moving across to the other. Gideon held his breath. They had to be there. Curly had said as much, and this was the last door.

Joey looked back over his shoulder and gave the thumbs up, with a nod. He returned on silent feet to where Gideon waited.

'They're in there all right,' he whispered. 'What now?'

Gideon wished he knew. 'Do you know how many there's likely to be?'

'Couldn't say, pal. Slade can lay his hands on just about whoever he wants. If I knew what he was up to, I might have more idea.' He looked at Gideon with an air of expectancy.

'What?' Gideon demanded in quiet exasperation. 'You think I know, is that it? Well, I don't. I'm only interested in getting my sister back.'

'So, that stuff you told Curly – about the money – that *was* a load of crap, was it? I thought so.'

'I was trying to stall him, that was all,' Gideon said. 'Just how long were you there before you stepped in?'

'I only caught that last bit,' Joey told him. 'So what now?'

'Well, we can't just go charging in, so we'll have to get them – or some of them – to come out. Divide and conquer.'

'Okay,' Joey said briskly. 'I'll give it a try. Here, you might need this.' He held the torch out.

Gideon took it, startled. 'What are you . . .?'

443

The question died on his lips as Joey stepped up to the door, rapped jauntily on the metal skin and opened it, as bold as brass.

Gideon hurriedly flattened himself against the wall, biting off a gasp as his ribs protested again. From this position he heard Slade's sharp exclamation, 'What the bloody hell are *you* doing here?'

'If that ape up there was supposed to be guarding this place, you're out of luck, pal.' Joey sounded completely relaxed. 'Someone's laid him out cold. I thought you'd like to know.'

'Shit! You, Smithy! Go and see what's going on. And find out where the chopper's got to while you're at it.'

Gideon heard footsteps as Smithy presumably made to do as he was told, and saw Joey angle his body to let him pass. He was barely through the doorway, however, when he appeared to trip and measured his length on the concrete floor at Gideon's feet with a muffled curse.

'Whoops!' Joey said. 'Sorry, pal. Are you okay?'

He was, that is until Gideon made use of Logan's invaluable torch. A brief check assured him that the man still breathed – he had no desire to have a death on his conscience, however deserved – and then, gritting his teeth against the effort, he swiftly bent and rolled the inert body against the wall out of sight. Straightening up with the aid of the wall, he completed the charade by padding up and down on the spot for a moment with decreasingly audible footfalls. Joey gave the slightest of winks before turning back towards the light of the room.

'What the hell's going on?' Slade was clearly unhappy.

'He's okay,' Joey said blithely. 'Just tripped over his own feet, clumsy bastard! He's gone now.'

'How did you find this place?'

'Jeez, that's easy.' Joey advanced into the room, out of Gideon's view. 'You didn't think Curly would keep his mouth shut, did you? And besides, I followed your friend Blake.'

Slade swore sharply. 'Blake's here? Where?'

Gideon held his breath, his heart pounding, and with a sickening jolt of shock, heard Joey say lightly, 'Sure he is. He's just outside the door.'

There was a pause during which Gideon's mind was racing. Damn Joey Dylan for a twisty, treacherous bastard! He waited, almost frozen with fear, for Slade to order him taken.

There came instead a short bark of laughter.

'You're full of shit, Joey!' Slade grunted. 'And you're wasting my time. Come and make yourself useful. If there *is* someone up there, Smithy will deal with them but we need to get out now!'

The relief was almost as shattering as the shock had been. Gideon leaned against the wall, bathed in sweat and trying to steady his breathing and his nerves. What game was Joey playing now?

'What's with the pictures?' Joey asked.

'Milne's had them stashed here for donkeys' years, apparently,' Slade told him. 'They're by some artist called Darius Sinclair. I only found out about them the other day. I happened to be having a little look through Milne's filing cabinet—'

'Like you do,' Joey put in.

'Like you do,' he agreed. 'And I came across a load of press clippings about these paintings going walkies from one of the London galleries way back in the sixties. It seems my good friend Meredith has a shady past. I faced him with it and he gave me some shit about keeping them for the nation. In other words, he nicked them. So if they're not his, they might just as well be mine.'

'Well, well. All this time and I didn't know you were an art lover,' Joey said in wondering tones. 'I suppose they might be worth a bob or two?'

'They're priceless,' Slade said shortly. 'And because they're priceless, they need to be wrapped carefully. The thing is, I had no idea how big the sodding things were and these bags aren't big enough. If they get wet, they'll be ruined, so they'll have to be covered. I suppose it's still raining?' he queried with little optimism.

'Pissing down, pal,' Joey lied. 'Cats and friggin' dogs!' There came the crackle of plastic and the sound of tape being pulled from a roll.

Gideon grinned to himself. They were still a team.

'So what's in it for me?' Joey wanted to know. 'I don't work for nothing.'

'I'll see you right. Just get on with it, okay?'

'So Milne was all right with you going through his filing cabinet, was he? Should have thought he'd hit the roof!'

'Ah, but he's sweet on me, you see,' Slade explained. 'And he's a very lonely old man. He'd forgive me almost anything.'

'But, you're not . . .'

'No, but it would have been cruel not to give him some hope.'

'You're unbelievable, you know that, pal?' Joey remarked. 'Still, it was trusting of the old boy to tell you where he'd stashed 'em. Not to say stupid.'

'He didn't. But it didn't take much working out. Daft bastard took me on as extra security, then offered me a bonus if I could shift the vet and his fancy woman. Said if the Sanctuary grew into a tourist attraction he'd get no peace and quiet. *Yeah, whatever*. A bonus is a bonus. But then the other night, some morons down at the Bell and Broom were arguing about old George Callow's bunker, and knowing what I knew, I started to wonder. When I called on the silly old codger he couldn't wait to tell me all about this place. Even had a map, would you believe? *Did have*, that is.'

Slade chuckled, and Gideon clenched his jaw bitterly. He looked down at Smithy who showed no sign of stirring, and wondered if he should strip his belt off and secure the man's wrists. Joey's next words put the thought out of his mind.

'Thought you'd be gone by now,' he remarked casually.

'Yeah, well, Reynolds had some bloke round here half the afternoon taking measurements. When he'd gone we nabbed the vet, got rid of his car and came down here. But then the girl came back and started prowling around looking for lover boy. My lucky day! A chance to get my own back on Gideon "pain in the arse" Blake.'

Gideon went cold. There was no sound from Naomi and Tim. Were they gagged? Or unconscious? He felt sure his sister would have said something by now had she been able to.

'What are you going to do with them?'

'Nothing.'

'Nothing? Then why . . .?'

'I'm going to do nothing,' Slade repeated. 'I'm just going to turn off the light, wave goodbye, lock the outer door and throw away the key. I expect somebody'll figure out where they are sooner or later. Maybe even while they're still alive. Anyway, I'll be long gone.'

'You're a cold bastard, Slade,' Joey said, almost conversationally. 'And what if I don't go along with that?'

'Oh, I think you will,' he said, unperturbed. 'I think there are a number of things you've done for me that you'd rather the police didn't know about.'

'Not murder,' Joey pointed out.

'Oh, I wouldn't call it murder. More – neglect.' Slade chuckled at his own wit.

With an effort, Gideon forced himself to remain still. Joey would presumably let him know when it was time to move. It was as hard a thing as he had ever had to do, though. Slade couldn't have provoked him more thoroughly had he known he was listening outside the door.

Or did he know? Had Joey confirmed his words

by way of some silent signal? Was it, after all, just part of some elaborate plot? Gideon made himself think logically. What could either of them possibly gain by keeping up the deception? All they would have to do was step outside the door and grab him. The way he felt, if he moved too fast he'd probably fall over and Joey knew that, even if Slade didn't.

'So, who's the other bozo?' Joey asked. 'Why isn't he doing this?'

'What *is* this? Twenty soddin' questions? Because he's a ham-fisted idiot, if you must know. He's already dropped one of them and broken the frame. I can't afford that at maybe half a million a time. Now shut up and hold that corner tight.'

There were two of them left, then. Gideon wished he knew whereabouts in the room Tim and Naomi were. Presumably they were tied and gagged. He felt sure Naomi wouldn't have stayed quiet otherwise. Did the 'other bozo' have a weapon?

'Smithy, Curly, Whatsisface over there – why so many?' Joey persisted.

'Because there are eight pictures and they're bloody heavy! What did you think I was going to do? Tuck four under each arm? Where the shit has Smithy got to? He should have been back by now. Am I surrounded by imbeciles?'

There was a significant pause and then Slade said with heavy emphasis, 'Who *did* slug Curly? If there's someone else about, then why haven't they found this place yet? You did.'

'Actually, I hit him,' Joey admitted. 'But he started it. Tried to stop me coming down.'

'*You* did? What the hell are you playing at?' Slade sounded understandably testy. 'Well, where's Smithy, then? And what about Renson? He should've been here by now.'

If Slade didn't know where Joey was coming from, he wasn't the only one. Gideon was struggling to keep up with his constant changes of direction. He could only hope that confusion was part of his plan, if indeed he had one.

'Choppers go wrong,' Joey suggested helpfully.

'You're fucking me around!' Slade cut in abruptly. There was a sharp click followed by deep silence, then he spoke again. 'If you're out there, Blake, you should know there's a gun pointed at your sister's head. Your little game is over. You may as well come in.'

Shit! Gideon thought. *Now what?*

The silence lengthened as he desperately tried to weigh his options. If he did as Slade said he was surely throwing away any chance for Naomi or himself. But if he didn't and Slade carried out his implied threat, the consequence was unthinkable. On the other hand, did Slade even know for sure that Gideon was out there? He could be bluffing.

Whilst he wavered Joey spoke again. Soft, joshing; no sign that he was on a knife-edge. 'Oh, come on, pal. You're not serious? What d'you think he's doing? Standing outside the door listening? You're getting paranoid!'

'He could have come looking for his sister,' Slade pointed out with unsettling accuracy. 'He wouldn't have any trouble dealing with Curly, he's a powerful bastard, you told me that yourself.'

Oh, no, no trouble at all, Gideon thought ironically. He could feel the sticky warmth of blood on his neck and scalp even as he stood there.

'Well, whatever,' Joey said dismissively. 'Blake's no friend of mine, so do me a favour and point that thing somewhere else. I don't know why the hell you think *I'd* team up with him.'

Slade grunted. 'Because you've got principles, and that makes you unpredictable,' he said.

Gideon was unwillingly impressed by his perception, but whatever Slade's reservations, after a moment he heard the crackle of plastic once more.

Behind him, without warning, Smithy stirred and groaned.

Gideon whipped round but Smithy already had his eyes open and was drawing breath to shout. Hating to do it, Gideon bounced the unfortunate man's head off the concrete wall with his foot.

He wasn't quite quick enough. Just before contact was made, Smithy managed to utter the beginnings of a warning shout, and even as he subsided again, Gideon heard Slade swear and there was a flurry of violent activity inside the room, followed by a stifled but unmistakably feminine cry.

Fear for his sister overrode any thoughts of personal safety. Gideon pushed the heavy door wide and plunged straight in, eyes instinctively seeking out Naomi's figure before all else but compelled to stop instead on Slade.

He was standing in the far corner of the room,

surrounded by pictures and packaging, with Joey a pace or two in front and to one side of him. As Gideon entered the room Slade was looking straight at him, a roll of parcel tape in his right hand and a small but deadly pistol in the other.

The pistol was pointing unwaveringly at Gideon's chest.

17

The round, black muzzle of the gun was a very effective brake. Gideon stopped so suddenly he almost overbalanced. From his right he heard another muffled sound of alarm from Naomi but he didn't look across. Even had he done so, he didn't feel that a reassuring smile would be very credible in the circumstances.

'So, Gideon Blake. Come to join our little party,' Slade purred. 'My cup runneth over.'

Gideon dragged his eyes away from Slade's left hand. The pistol looked plastic, like a toy. Hard to think that such a tiny black hole could deliver such a deadly payload. Too much to hope that Slade was really right-handed.

He transferred his gaze, with an effort, to Slade's smoothly handsome face. There were triumph and vicious intent there, in equal measures. The small gold ring in his ear gleamed in the light of the overhead bulb.

The bulb. Gideon wondered for a fleeting second if he could smash it with the torch but dismissed the idea. Even if he managed it, and with the pain in his side he wasn't at all certain that his aim would be true, the best he could hope for was chaos, and with the gun in his hand, Slade was best placed to take advantage of that.

'I wouldn't,' Slade remarked.

'I wasn't going to,' Gideon said. There was a pause during which he felt that everyone must be able to hear the heavy pounding of his heart, and he risked a quick glance round the room.

It was bigger than the others they had looked into, with contemporary if minimalist furnishings comprising one leather swivel-based chair, a small round table, and what looked like a drinks cabinet. The walls were covered with some sort of hessian and each one supported two chrome picture lights. One picture remained hanging, one was half-packed in bubble-wrap, and the others leaned against the far wall behind Slade, swathed in plastic and brown tape.

Milne's private gallery.

All this Gideon absorbed in an instant before shifting his gaze over his right shoulder towards Naomi. She and Tim were sitting propped against the wall, bound at the wrist and ankle with quantities of brown parcel tape and gagged with what looked like dusters. Their faces reflected the severe strain they were under and Naomi's eyes met Gideon's imploringly. More than averagely resilient, she nevertheless appeared near the end of her tether. Tim also looked dazed and disbelieving.

Gideon returned his gaze to Slade and said in a surprisingly steady voice, 'So what now?'

'Now we put you with your precious sister and her boyfriend, and you can all keep each other company when I leave and turn out the lights.'

'All because I spoilt your little game with the horses?' Gideon asked incredulously.

'Oh, that! No, that was a nuisance but I was getting tired of it anyway. It was too bloody slow. And I'd had enough of working with gutless, whingeing amateurs.'

'So you blew up Tom Collins' cottage and him with it.'

'The stupid bastard wasn't even supposed to be there!' Slade said contemptuously. 'He rang me in a panic, saying you were on to us and almost blubbering with fear, so I told him to stay at home and I'd take care of you. He thought I was just going to slap your wrist and ask you politely to mind your own business but I had something a bit more permanent in mind. I'd had about enough of you poking your nose where it wasn't wanted.'

'He just can't stand to be crossed, can you, pal?' Joey commented. He was standing a few feet to the right of Slade and nearer the wall. 'Whether there's fifty grand at stake or just a parking space, he can't bear to be beaten.'

If Joey had been trying to distract Slade's attention, it didn't work. The dark eyes didn't waver as he said quietly, 'Shut up, Joey! I'll deal with you in a minute.'

'Well, you've won in the end,' Gideon pointed out reasonably. He had no real expectation that reason would weigh with Slade but he didn't know what else to try. He would rather, by far, have been dealing with a dangerous animal, however unpredictable. 'What have you got to gain by killing us? You've got the pictures and you've got the helicopter waiting.' He tried not to linger on the thought of Renson locked inside it and the key – heaven knows where. 'Naomi and Tim have got nothing to do with any of this. At least let *them* go.'

Slade smiled nastily. 'Why should I? Why should you get to be the hero? This way you'll have time to remember that if you hadn't been such a persistent pain in the backside, they wouldn't be dying in this shit-hole with you.'

'Somebody will find us. Logan knows I'm here somewhere.'

'Yeah, but how soon? What if something were accidentally to block the ventilation shaft? How long do you think the air would last? Each of these rooms is individually sealed, you know.'

A low chuckle came from the other side of the room and Gideon glanced across to where Joey's bozo stood, enjoying the show. He was of medium height and thickset, possibly an ex-boxer by his facial scars, but something less than a heavyweight in the brains department if first impressions were anything to go by. Gideon dismissed him as of little account.

'Hey, you! Catch!' Slade tossed the roll of tape towards the grinning man. 'Bind him up tight. But,

456

whatever you do, don't get in my line of fire.'

Gideon made a snap decision. Once bound, his chances would be virtually non-existent. So, as the man began to move towards him, Gideon began to walk towards Slade, feeling that it would be better to try and force his hand in the hope he could be pushed into making a mistake, than submit meekly to a certain fate.

'Stand still!' Slade said immediately.

Gideon ignored him, but he wasn't dealing with another Curly or even a Duke Shelley; Slade's brain was ten times quicker and he wouldn't be rattled so easily. As Gideon continued to walk he saw, too late, where his gamble was leading. With no further warning, Slade set his jaw and calmly swung his gun-hand away from Gideon and towards Naomi.

With a mouth that was suddenly dry with fear, Gideon stopped in his tracks.

'No!' he begged, putting out a hand as if to stay Slade's arm, but he was still feet away and had no hope of reaching him. As if in slow motion he saw Slade's knuckle whiten as his finger tightened on the trigger and, vaguely aware that across the room, Joey was starting to move, Gideon launched himself forward in a futile attempt to throw Slade off balance.

He didn't make it.

'No!' Gideon's anguished cry was lost in the sharp crack of the gun as, simultaneously, Slade's henchman took him in a crashing, rugby-style tackle from the side. As he hit the ground, Gideon heard a terrified squeal from Naomi and wide-eyed, with a horror verging on panic, twisted desperately under the weight of his assailant to try and see his sister.

With his face pressed uncomfortably firmly to the heavy-duty carpet, Gideon's field of vision was somewhat limited but mercifully he could just see Naomi. She was staring at Slade with a mixture of terror and disbelief in her eyes but as far as Gideon could make out, somehow, miraculously, Slade's shot had missed her.

Before he had time to make sense of the situation, the fifteen stone or so of thug that had wrestled him to the ground twisted his fingers in Gideon's hair and jerked his head up and backwards. He gasped as his spine took the pressure and pain knifed through his side.

'Should get yer hair cut, girlie!' a coarse, garlicky voice breathed in his ear. 'On yer feet. And I don't want no trouble.'

Gideon wasn't at all sure he could make it to his feet but his captor thoughtfully assisted him, with his hand still firmly twisted in Gideon's hair. It was either get his feet under him somehow or risk having a painfully large handful pulled out by the roots. It was wonderful what you could do if you tried.

Just as he reached something approaching vertical, another shot rang out, and a sound like a bee in flight passed his ear, surprising an oath from the man behind him. Through watering eyes, Gideon became aware that across the room Joey

458

and Slade were locked in a deadly wrestling match, the bigger man evidently badly hampered by the need to keep Slade's gun-hand from pointing at himself or any of the other hapless occupants of the room.

The bozo started to fidget, as if he felt it incumbent upon himself to go to the aid of his boss, so before his resolution hardened, Gideon provided a distraction by sagging at the knees and reeling back against him as if in a faint.

Sagging and reeling was not, as far as he knew, listed as a karate technique but for the moment it was all Gideon could manage, and it worked. The man behind him staggered slightly and swore as he took Gideon's weight but it seemed to have put all thoughts of rushing to Slade's aid out of his head.

As he was hauled upright once more – though thankfully not by his hair – Gideon could see that despite being a good six inches shorter and goodness knows how many pounds lighter, Slade was, incredibly, gaining the upper hand over Joey. With his face set in a mask of vicious determination he was slowly but surely drawing the taller man's arm in towards his body, with the obvious intention of turning the gun on him. Joey's expression was a grimace of pain and effort. Sweat beaded and ran from his forehead, and it was clear to Gideon that he was in desperate trouble.

Drawing on reserves of strength he'd thought long exhausted, he got his feet under him a second time, and before his captor had time to step away, drove his head back to smash him brutally in the face, much as he had done to Curly in the front hall of the Gatehouse, what seemed a lifetime ago.

The result was much the same, too. The man staggered back, cursing, and received a vicious elbow to the ribs to add to his woes. Gideon left him doubled up and stumbled to Joey's aid, hesitating involuntarily as Slade's gun went off again, the bullet burying itself harmlessly in the ceiling.

With a Herculean effort, Joey had managed to force Slade's gun arm away from his body once more and Gideon instinctively latched on to it, jerking the wrist towards him with his right hand, while forcing his own left forearm into the back of Slade's elbow joint. Slade screamed with pain and the gun dropped with a clatter from nerveless fingers as he staggered back under Joey's continued pressure.

Gideon had little enough time to enjoy the moment. Slade's heavy had recovered swiftly from his treatment, and powered by an understandable, if regrettable, desire for revenge, a meaty fist slammed into Gideon's ribs from behind.

Pain exploded through him, arching his back and leaving him powerless to resist as he was swung round and measured for a follow-up blow to the head. What he could see of his attacker's face behind the bloody mess of his nose promised little hope of mercy.

Gideon's body had had enough. The damage Duke Shelley, and then Curly, had done to it before this guy had even got started, was too much.

His eyes closed and he swayed on his feet, almost welcoming the blow that would put an end to the misery.

It never came.

There was a rushing noise in his ears and a familiar voice said, 'Whoa, steady there, mate!' almost as if he were a nervous horse. Eyes still closed, he was conscious of being lowered gently to the floor, his nose pressed into what, from the smell of it, was a newish leather jacket. Under the prompting of firm hands he leaned back against a wall that felt surprisingly soft and tried to force his eyes open long enough to make sense of what had happened.

Legs clad in blue denim jeans stepped back from him and crouched, bringing Logan's clean-cut features into view. Gideon looked past him to where his erstwhile assailant lay, stretched motionless, on the floor.

'Are you *allowed* to do that?' he asked quizzically, in little more than a whisper.

Logan's quick, boyish grin showed itself. 'It comes under the heading of reasonable force,' he assured Gideon.

The grin disappeared in a haze of dark blotches as Gideon's head began to spin again.

'Get your head down,' Logan advised, but leaning forward would squeeze up the ribs and Gideon elected to stay where he was.

'Slade?' he murmured, closing his eyes.

'We've got him. Everything's under control. Just sit still for a minute.'

461

Gideon was aware of Logan moving away but didn't try to open his eyes again, content to trust the man. There was still a fair bit of frantic activity and a certain amount of swearing going on, but there were new and commanding voices. Obviously Logan had brought the cavalry.

'Gideon?' Naomi's voice, anxiously enquiring.

He opened his eyes reluctantly to find that the world was a lot clearer this time.

'Hi, Sis.'

A radiant, if watery, smile greeted this effort.

'Are you all right?'

'Better all the time,' he responded truthfully.

'You don't look it,' she told him, scanning his face with worried eyes. 'You look awful.'

'Thanks. It's been one of those days. But what about you?'

She shook her head. 'He didn't hurt us. We were just in his way at first. I don't think he really cared about us at all until he realised he had a means of getting back at you. He was utterly cold and ruthless. Terrifying! What on earth did you do to him?'

'It's a bit complicated. I'll tell you one day. But I'm *so* sorry, Sis. Really.' He broke off with a groan, seeing, over her shoulder, the fluorescent green jackets of two paramedic officers. 'Oh, my God! What are *they* doing here?'

'Well, let me see,' Naomi said, pretending to think. 'We've got one with a broken arm; one with a broken nose and concussion; one who's been shot; and one who looks as though he's been knocked down by a freight train! No, I can't imagine what they might want!'

'Shot?' Gideon exclaimed, grabbing her arm. 'Who's been shot? Not Tim? Where *is* Tim?'

'No, not Tim. He's gone on up. A call of nature.' Naomi said. 'It's your friend, Joey. At least, I wasn't sure whether he was on your side or Slade's until he went for Slade's gun. He saved my life, Gideon. That bastard would have killed me!'

Her voice cracked as a sob shook her, and Gideon pulled her down beside him, putting his arm round her silently shaking shoulders. Now the danger was past, her valiantly preserved brave front was abandoned, and she buried her face in his rough wool jumper and wept out all the terror of her ordeal.

Over her tousled blonde head, Gideon watched as police and ambulancemen went about their business, admiring their efficiency and immeasurably glad that the responsibility for decision-making had been removed from him.

After a minute or two, Naomi sniffed and sat up, fishing in her pocket for a handkerchief. 'I'm sorry,' she said.

Gideon squeezed her shoulders. 'You know, for an intelligent girl, that's a remarkably idiotic thing to say,' he observed, and was rewarded with the ghost of a smile.

Across the room, Joey was sitting on the swivel chair, arguing with two paramedics who apparently thought he should occupy the stretcher they'd laid on the floor beside him. He'd already been stripped bare to the waist, exposing a powerful pair of shoulders, the sight of which had Gideon thanking God, for the umpteenth time that day, that Joey had chosen to side with him instead of against.

Judging by the area now padded and heavily bandaged, he'd been shot just below the ribs on the left-hand side, but his mobility suggested that the bullet hadn't touched anything vital.

In another corner, under close police guard, Slade was having his right arm splinted. Watching the pain flicker across his white face, Gideon experienced no remorse whatsoever. In fact, he felt it was a shame it was just his arm that was broken, and not his neck. What prompted this reprehensible train of thought was the realisation that, driven by the implacable hatred he obviously felt for Gideon, Slade was quite capable of dragging both Sean Rosetti and Tom Collins' reputations down with him.

As if to reinforce this belief, Slade caught Gideon's gaze on him, and returned it with one of pure venom. Beside him, Naomi gasped, and he shook her gently. 'He can't hurt you now. Come on, help me up.'

Naomi frowned. 'Do you think you should?'

'Got to sometime,' he said with undeniable logic.

Shrugging, she climbed to her feet and obediently held out a hand to him.

He made it to his feet with the additional help of the wall, which seemed to be insulated with polystyrene and yielded a little under the pressure of his hand. The effort set off a wave of dizziness and he paused, leaning heavily on his sister who was watching his face anxiously.

'I'm not sure this was a good idea,' she told him.

Gideon wasn't sure it was, either, but he had as little wish as Joey to be consigned to a stretcher just at the moment. Even as he stood, swaying slightly, a green-jacketed officer hurried over.

'I really think you should be sitting down, sir,' he advised.

'Tried that. I'm fine now,' Gideon lied.

'I don't think . . .'

'I need to see Joey,' he said firmly. 'If I feel faint, I promise I'll sit down. Or fall down.'

The officer didn't appreciate his humour. 'Now come on, sir.'

'You may as well give up.' Logan approached from behind him. 'He's an obstinate bastard.'

'Thanks.' Gideon flashed a dry smile at the policeman. 'I promise I'll come quietly in a minute.'

He made his way, on horribly weak legs, over to where Joey had finally given in to his escort and been strapped on to the stretcher. As he reached them, the stretcher-bearers lifted their reluctant cargo, for which Gideon was grateful; he wasn't at all sure he could handle either crouching or bending at present. He put a hand out to detain the leading bearer.

'Just a minute.'

He turned towards Joey but stared at the ground

465

for a moment, struggling to find the right words. 'I can't believe you did that,' he said, finally meeting his eyes.

'Ah, shit,' Joey said uncomfortably. 'You couldn't reach him, I could. I didn't plan on this.' He waved a hand to indicate his wound.

'He was going to kill her,' Gideon stated, fixing Joey's clear, ice blue gaze with his own.

'Yeah, well, I hate seeing women hurt. Guess we're even now, pal.'

Gideon nodded, not trusting himself to speak. The physical and emotional battering of the day had left him in a mess. The ambulance men were fidgeting now but there was something else he had to know. 'About the other . . .?'

'*I've* got nothing to say,' Joey assured him. 'Even if I knew anything. And Curly knows when to keep his mouth shut. But Slade? I'm sorry, pal. I don't know.'

It was no more than Gideon had expected. 'Thanks anyway,' he said resignedly, a cloak of depression settling on him as the paramedics bore the big man away.

It was such a waste.

Tom Collins and Rosetti had been by no means blameless but without Slade's muscle and intimidating tactics it was inconceivable that they would ever have acted on what was, after all, never meant as a serious proposal. There had been more than enough distress already; it seemed so unfair that the future happiness of two families could hang on the whim of a vicious chancer like Slade.

466

As if conjured by his thoughts, Gideon turned to find Slade approaching, flanked by medics and the police. His splinted right arm was in a sling of sorts, his left handcuffed to the officer at his side, but as he passed Gideon he leaned closer to him, hatred twisting his handsome features. Under his Mediterranean tan Slade's face was pale and beaded with sweat, and he was so close that Gideon could clearly see the individual hairs of his eyebrows. He resisted the instinctive urge to flinch away.

'Your friends are finished!' he hissed in Gideon's face. 'I'll ruin them. And I'll get you yet! I've got mates who owe me.'

'Get him out of here!' Logan had appeared at Gideon's side, accompanied by Naomi and the hopeful paramedic. Slade's escort jerked on the handcuff and dragged him away.

'Now, are you going to tell me what happened here and why?' Logan queried.

'The pictures are by Darius Sinclair,' Gideon told him. 'The ones stolen in the sixties, I presume. No need to ask by whom.'

'Yeah. I've sent someone to pick up Milne. But that wasn't all that was going on here, was it? What's the history with you and Slade? He meant what he said, you know. He'll have contacts on the outside.'

'Constable, I really think this man needs medical attention,' the hovering paramedic interposed hesitantly.

Gideon blessed the man's overriding sense of

duty. He *did* need medical attention, but most of all he needed time to consider what he was going to tell the police.

'I do feel a bit faint,' he agreed. 'I think I need some fresh air.'

Having received his mandate, the green-jacketed one immediately took over, brushing Logan aside as he moved to take Gideon's arm and steer him towards the door.

'I'll see you later, you crafty bugger!' Logan murmured as he passed.

Whatever the motivation for the move, it was a relief to get out of the bunker and into the cold night air. The steep flight of steps was more of an effort than Gideon cared to admit and the more deeply he breathed, the more his ribs hurt him but all in all, he knew his injuries – however painful – were largely superficial, and he was incredibly thankful to be alive.

Escorted by his sister and the medic, Gideon made his way across the concrete towards the brightly lit interior of one of two waiting ambulances. Once again the whole yard seemed to be a mass of blue flashing lights. Fire engines and police cars a fortnight ago, now ambulances and the police; the old farm had probably not seen this much activity since the end of the war.

In the back of one ambulance, Gideon could see Curly sitting, watched over by a uniformed policeman. His head was swathed in bandages and Gideon wondered if he'd realised yet that it was his own brother who had dealt him the knockout blow.

Preparing to embark was Slade, now wrapped in a blanket and obviously in a great deal of pain.

There was a sudden stir in the ranks of navy blue beyond the ambulances and a figure strode past Gideon's party with a purposeful step. Lit briefly by the light from the vehicle, he caught sight of white hair and a sailor's cap. Milne, with his face set in a mask of grim determination and a fanatical gleam in his eye.

Gideon twisted away from the paramedic and saw the artist homing in on Slade's unsuspecting group like an Exocet missile.

'No!' he cried, without pausing to think whom he was trying to protect.

But he was too late anyway.

Calmly, Milne took his right hand out of the front pocket of his painter's smock, revealing a large, old-fashioned handgun that had probably been out of date before the Second World War. Any doubts as to its serviceability, however, were dispelled in the shockingly loud report of its discharge.

Even as the ears of those closest rang with the sound, Slade was already dead. Shot through the heart at almost point-blank range with surprising efficiency for a man of the arts, he was knocked backwards and down, dragging his accompanying officer with him.

For a moment there was shocked silence. Slade lay on the frosty ground, his eyes flickering weirdly with reflected blue light, and whatever vengeful intentions he may have had, extinguished forever.

18

'I still can't believe it!' Pippa declared, tucking a wayward, newly bleached curl behind her ear as she poured coffee into mugs on the Priory's huge kitchen table. 'And Sean Rosetti, of all people!'

Gideon shifted to try and ease his various aches and pains. Nearly a week had passed since the horror of the events at the Sanctuary, but it would be a long time before his body would begin to let him forget it. 'Yeah, well, like I said . . .'

'Oh, I know. Keep it under my hat. But within these walls it can't hurt, can it? And I'm still trying to get my head round it. I mean, how could Sean have just stood by and let them treat you like they did that night? I thought he'd have had more backbone!'

Gideon had had much longer to think about it than Pippa. 'He couldn't do a lot about it at that point, could he?' he pointed out. 'Slade was more or less holding his family to ransom by then, to say nothing of his career. To be fair, I don't think he would have carried on for any other reason. Slade was a past master at manipulating people, and he guessed Rosetti wouldn't do it for the money alone, however much he needed it.'

Pippa topped the mugs up with milk, pushed one towards Gideon and shouted 'Coffee, Giles!' towards the open door, before settling down on the other side of the table. 'They were taking a hell of a risk, though, weren't they? I mean, what if someone had wanted a paternity test?'

Gideon nodded. 'That's what I thought but then, as Sean said, why should they? A lot of the foals were apparently perfect little carbon copies of their illustrious uncle. Most of the mares' owners would have visited Sox at the stud when they booked his services. He looks happy and healthy. What earthly reason would they have to suppose that anything was amiss?'

Pippa frowned. 'You almost sound as though you admire them for what they did. It *was* criminal. And whatever you say, I'm still not convinced that they should have got away with it.'

'Me neither,' Gideon agreed, 'in principle. But what's done, is done. And who's to say some of them won't turn out to be just as good jumpers as Sox might have sired? After all, there's no certainty that *he* would have produced talent either.'

'No-o,' Pippa said slowly. 'But the fact remains that those people paid a lot of money for something they didn't get. However you look at it, it's fraud. There should be compensation.'

'And who's going to foot the bill?' Gideon asked. 'Anthony?'

Giles came in and flopped down in a chair beside Gideon, rubbing his hands together. It was a cold, bleak day and the kitchen was by far the warmest place in the house. 'Not still chewing over the Great Stallion Scandal, are you?' he asked, reaching for his coffee. 'A horse is a horse, as far as I can see.'

'Well, thank you for that intelligent input,' his sister said, dryly. 'So I suppose it would also be true to say a wine is a wine?'

'Ah. Now that would be the remark of a truly uneducated person,' Giles said, comfortably sure of his ground. 'The two bear no relation.' He looked at his sister questioningly and said, apparently out of context, 'Has he?'

She frowned heavily at him and answered quietly, 'I don't think so.'

'The thing is,' Gideon said, ignoring them and still trying to justify his silence on the Sox affair, 'with Tom and Slade dead, the person – or people – who'd be most damaged by revealing the truth are Mary and Anthony Collins. Now all that boy ever wanted was to help his father run the stud and take over when he retired. He's got a good head on his shoulders and he's a far stronger person than Tom ever was. If the truth ever came out about his father, he would be devastated. The press would crucify the family and the stud's credibility would be shot to pieces. He's done nothing to deserve that. Neither of them has.'

'I suppose . . .' Pippa relented, still doubtful. 'But Sox can't go on standing at stud, can he? How are they going to get round that?'

'Sean's going to break it to Anthony in a day or two that Sox's sperm-count is dramatically down. He'll say Tom asked him to do some tests just before he died because he was worried that the horse was a bit under the weather. It'll be a shock to him, but he won't be able to argue with the figures.'

'But surely he's booked up for the season?'

'That can't be helped,' Gideon said sadly. 'It could never be painless, but this is the best way out for all concerned. There'll have to be an announcement in *Horse and Hound*. You know, "Olympic Gold Medallist Retires from Stud" or something similar. Anthony will cope.'

'It doesn't seem right, though, Sean getting off Scot-free.'

'Oh, I think he's suffered more than you could imagine. And think of Cathy and Daisy,' Gideon added, persuasively. 'It would ruin their lives too.'

'He's right, you know,' Giles put in, helpfully for once. '"Let sleeping dogs lie" and all that. Leave well enough alone.'

'What the eye doesn't see . . .' Gideon contributed.

'Yeah, all right, all right!' Pippa exclaimed. 'I think I get the idea. I'm not saying I agree with it, mind. I mean, innocent people often get caught in

473

the crossfire; surely the responsibility lies with the criminal not with the people who come along to pick up the pieces. But,' she held up her hands, 'it's not up to me, is it? So, how are Tim and Naomi getting on? Have you spoken to them today?'

'No. I called them earlier,' Gideon told her, 'but they weren't in. I'll try again, later. They seem to have come through it remarkably well though, considering. Naomi is incredibly tough.'

'Like her brother, I'd say,' Pippa remarked casually. 'First a confrontation with a chain-wielding maniac, and then taking on the Dorset Mafia! Getting beaten up once in a day is enough for most people, but not masochistic Mr Blake! Honestly, what on earth possessed you to take on Slade on your own?'

'I *wasn't* on my own,' Gideon protested. 'Joey was there. I told you how it happened. We had no way of knowing how long Logan would be and we didn't know what Slade might be doing to Naomi and Tim. What was I supposed to do?'

'You could have been killed,' Pippa persisted stubbornly. 'And I don't know how you could trust that Joey bloke after all he'd done to you, for heavensakes! Not to mention emptying Logan's petrol tank.'

'Yeah. Logan was pretty pissed off about that, too. It ran out before he even got to the Grange.'

'So it was Joey's fault that Logan wasn't there, yet you *still* trusted him! That's plain daft!'

Gideon didn't have an answer. He took a long

sip of his coffee and stared broodingly at the tabletop.

'Well?' she demanded.

'Er . . . it's a guy thing,' he suggested with an apologetic grin. 'Male bonding.'

Beside him, Giles spluttered into his mug and Pippa favoured them both with a withering look. *'Oh, please!'* she said with heavy emphasis.

The old range spat and popped as a log shifted inside it, and looking round the old kitchen in warm contentment, Gideon became aware that Fanny the Labrador was busy washing just one remaining pup. Pippa had successfully homed three of the puppies in the last week but there had still been two there the night before. With a mixture of relief and wistfulness, he saw it was the brindle pup that had gone.

'When did the brindle go?' he asked.

'Oh, this morning,' Pippa said. 'It's going to a smashing home. Local too, so I'll be able to see it.'

'So, have you got someone lined up for the last one?'

'Why? Do *you* want it?' she asked, regarding him quizzically, head on one side. Then she laughed. 'No, actually I'm thinking of keeping it myself. I've been thinking about it ever since we lost the smallest one. I don't know why.'

'It's that soft centre again,' Gideon teased. 'You want to watch it, you're becoming quite sentimental in your old age.'

'Perhaps I am,' Pippa said thoughtfully. Then,

changing the subject again, 'So, Milne *was* behind all the trouble at the Sanctuary, after all.'

Gideon nodded. 'Apparently. He and another idealist – who's since died – stole the Darius Sinclair collection back in the sixties to save it from being sold to America. Milne then installed it in that specially adapted room in the bunker where, I gather, he regularly used to sit and admire it. The farm was derelict for nearly fifty years, you see, until the old lady that owned it inconveniently died and left it to her great-nephew, Tim. According to Logan, Milne assumed that there'd be ample notice of any change in the status quo; you know, For Sale boards or builders dropping off supplies. Plenty of time to remove the paintings before anyone moved in. If the farm had come on to the market he would have bid for it. Nothing had changed for such a long time that I suppose he'd become complacent. But, as it happened, he was away for a few days and when he returned Tim was already there.'

'And he plonked his mobile home bang on top of the entrance,' Giles said. 'That was a bit of a bummer for Milne, wasn't it? So he hired Slade to shift him.'

'Well, he could hardly have come and gone without being seen, wherever the mobile home was,' Gideon pointed out. 'I suppose the idea was that if he could get rid of Tim, even for a short time, he'd be able to rehouse the pictures somewhere else. But it didn't work out that way.'

'And then Slade found out what a fortune Milne

was sitting on, and decided to relieve him of it,' Pippa put in.

'Yeah. The scam with Sox and Whitewings had gone belly up, though I think he was probably already getting bored. And once he discovered Milne's secret, he must have thought it was easy money.'

'Which it would have been, if you hadn't turned up,' Giles added. 'He could have got Tim and Naomi out of the way and whisked the paintings away without anyone being any the wiser.'

'Except Milne, of course, but *he* couldn't say anything without incriminating himself,' Pippa said. 'Slade would have been home and dry. Do you think he really would have blocked the ventilation shaft and left you to suffocate?'

Gideon shrugged. 'Who knows? I wouldn't have put it past him. After all, dead men tell no tales. But who's to say that room was even airtight after all these years? The rubber seals on the doors were probably perished, and anyway Logan would pretty soon have worked out where we were.'

'I'd have been petrified,' Pippa said soberly. 'It's a good thing Logan was there. So how did he come to be following you in the first place? You never did tell us.'

'Well, I'd spoken to him Friday – after Tom's funeral – when I was still trying to figure out what was going on, and I pushed him for his opinion on the explosion at the cottage. He was convinced I knew more than I was telling and he's like a terrier when he gets hold of something, so after his shift on Sunday he came on over to see if he could get me to open up. He was almost here when he met me haring in the other direction and decided to tag along and see where I was off to in such a hurry.'

'Well, it looks like his terrier instincts may just have saved your life,' Pippa observed. 'It sounds as though Slade had it in for you in a big way!'

'Yes, in the end, I think getting back at me was almost more important to him than the money,' Gideon said, remembering the look of vicious loathing that Slade had directed at him as he was led away. 'Joey said he could never bear to be beaten.'

'What would you have done if the old guy hadn't shot Slade?' Giles asked curiously. 'I mean, he was hardly going to keep his mouth shut, was he? If he couldn't get at you, I should think he'd have jumped at the chance to take it out on your friends.'

'Yeah, he said as much. And he said he hadn't finished with me, either. I just hope he hasn't got half a dozen brothers who're going to come looking for me!'

It was said lightly, but Pippa looked aghast.

'You don't really think . . .?'

Gideon shook his head with a grin. 'No, I don't,' he said firmly.

'So this Milne character saved the day,' Giles said.

'Mm. In a rather drastic way. It seems that after Logan had been there asking where Slade was and what he was doing, Milne began putting two and two together. When Logan found out about the paintings he sent someone to arrest him, but by that time Milne had already set off across the field to the Sanctuary with the gun in his pocket.'

'Pretty extreme,' Giles commented.

'Yeah, well, he was a man obsessed. He lives and breathes art and he'd jealously guarded the Sinclair pictures for the best part of forty years. And that wasn't all. I gather he was one for the guys, if you know what I mean, and I think Slade had led him on a bit. I guess that made the betrayal twice as hard to stomach. I think he just flipped.'

'Wow! Lust, betrayal and murder in darkest Dorset,' Giles exclaimed. 'You never know what's going on behind closed doors, do you?'

'Too true. By the way, where's Rachel?' Gideon asked.

Pippa had been deep in thought but now she gave herself a mental shake. 'Oh, she's down at the farm with the donkeys. Confronting her demons, she said. She hasn't been down there since the business with her charming ex.'

'She's a brave girl,' Gideon said approvingly, glancing at Giles. 'And from what I hear, you're a lucky guy!'

Giles blushed a little. 'I don't know what I've done to deserve it. After all, you had a far more heroic role in the drama than I did.'

'That's just it,' Pippa stated wisely. 'I think Gideon is altogether too much for her to cope with. You're more homely,' she added with sisterly sweetness. 'Any more coffee?'

The companionable sibling bickering faded to the edge of Gideon's consciousness as he closed his eyes against the onset of another throbbing headache. They were troubling him less frequently now than they had a few days ago. He groped in his pocket for the bottle of double-strength painkillers his doctor had prescribed, and took two with the dregs of his coffee. They usually made him feel a little woolly but the compromise was well worth it.

The events following Slade's death were not much more than a blur now. Milne had surrendered his weapon without a struggle, his face blank and his whole body shaking with the shock of what he'd done.

Shock had had its effect on Gideon too, seeming to drain his body of its last reserves of strength. His head swimming once more, his legs had threatened to let him down, and a sharp call from Logan had brought a second paramedic to his aid. Once in the ambulance, with Naomi at his side, the relief of relinquishing all responsibility was immense and he'd closed his eyes and gratefully let consciousness slip away.

They had kept him in hospital for several days, until the doctors were as certain as they could be that his head injuries were not going to develop into anything life-threatening. He was then discharged with the proviso that he should immediately report any sharp or worsening pains, double vision or impaired co-ordination. He was fortunate that he hadn't suffered a fractured skull, they told him shaking their heads solemnly, and he was left with the feeling that they held him in some way to blame for his injuries, as if he'd been involved in a pub brawl.

Gideon had looked forward to the peace and quiet of the Gatehouse after the ceaseless, if well-meant, attentions of the staff at the hospital. His dream of solitude was soon to be shattered, however. Pippa met him at the door of the hospital with the information that, with Rachel out working most days, there was absolutely no way she and Giles were going to let him go back to the Gatehouse on his own. He was to stay at the Priory until he was fully recovered.

His lengthy protests fell on deaf ears but in the event he had to admit that he was grateful. Still uncomfortably weak and feeling emotionally below par, Pippa's unfussy good sense and Giles' undemanding company were the best possible aid to his recovery. His usual sense of humour was soon restored too, by Mrs Morecambe's dire predictions of his likely demise if he failed to follow the doctor's instructions to the letter. His strength had quite quickly returned with good food and complete rest, and all in all, he felt better after just six days than he could have dared hope.

Logan and a senior officer had visited him twice and from them he'd learned that Milne had been arrested and charged with the murder of Slade and the theft of the paintings but appeared to regret neither. In turn, he'd given them a truthful, if incomplete, account of recent events, and if Logan was aware that they were being fed a budget version – and Gideon was almost certain that he was – he didn't say anything in front of his superior. At the end of their second visit, however, he lagged behind as they got up to leave.

'If I let it go at that,' he said quietly, 'then I'll expect the full story one day, off the record. I think you owe me that.'

Gideon had to agree. It was just a fraction of what he owed the man.

A growing babble of voices brought him back to the present and he glanced at Pippa who was trying to hide a smile. The door from the main hall burst open and suddenly the room was full of people. Gideon looked up, wonderingly, scanning each face as they came in.

Naomi led the charge, followed closely by Tim and Rachel, Sean, Cathy and Daisy Rosetti, Mary and Anthony Collins, and a woman Gideon felt he should know but couldn't place.

Gideon got hastily to his feet. 'What the . . . ?'

Naomi looked at Pippa with mock despair. 'He still hasn't, has he?'

Pippa shook her head. 'It's his age, poor old chap! And that knock on the head didn't help.'

'Oh, my God! It's my birthday, isn't it?' Gideon exclaimed, and then through the general laughter, 'Why didn't someone tell me?'

'We couldn't believe you'd really forgotten!' Pippa said. 'All except Naomi. She said you quite probably had. I must say, it's a completely new twist on a surprise party to me!'

'There's someone else outside,' Tim announced

over the hum of amused comment. 'Someone special!'

He opened the door with a flourish to reveal Joey's half-sister, Jez, looking uncharacteristically pretty in a flowered dress, and a little overawed by the occasion. She came in glancing shyly up at Gideon, who rewarded her with a huge grin.

'Wow! Don't you look nice!' he said. 'How are you doing? Feeling better now?'

'This is for you from Ma,' Jez said, holding up a large, expensively labelled, bottle of whisky. 'She said to say thanks for everything.'

'Well, thank you.' Gideon accepted it, greatly surprised. 'That might have an interesting effect, mixed with my painkillers! It's lovely,' he assured the child, who was looking a little uncertain.

'Joey says he's going to buy me a pony, and Tim says we can keep it at the Sanctuary,' she announced, moving on to matters of greater importance.

'Hey, that's brilliant!' he said. 'And how is Joey?'

'He's home again now but he said he wouldn't come here,' Jez confided. 'But Curly isn't coming home for a long time, Ma says. Joey says it's a bloody good thing too!'

Gideon coughed to hide a smile. 'Joey's probably right,' he agreed amidst the general amusement.

'Gideon, you remember Jenny, don't you?' Pippa prompted, touching his arm and drawing his attention to the older lady at her side.

'Of course I do,' he responded gallantly. 'How are you doing? And how's Willow?'

'She's fine. We both are, thanks to you.' The intense gratitude in her expression made Gideon fidget, and she said quickly, 'Oh, I'm sorry. Pippa said you'd be embarrassed if I thanked you.'

'Oh, she did, did she?' he asked, raising an eyebrow. 'Who's the behaviourist around here?'

Sherry and fruit punch were offered and the gathering settled into easy companionship, everyone blending well. Gideon was inclined to think that Joey had been right to decline the invitation. His presence might have been a little unsettling for some.

After a while Mrs Morecambe appeared and a buffet lunch was served on the kitchen table, after which everyone sat chatting in the various chairs, comfortably full and basking in the warmth of the range.

As coffee and tea were passed round, Naomi and Tim produced their birthday gift of a new waxed jacket, to replace the one that was ruined on the night of the fire. Mary and Anthony gave Gideon a top-notch pocketknife and the Rosetti family produced a beautiful, silver half-hunter watch.

Rachel gave Gideon a lavishly wrapped package and a huge, uninhibited hug, her face radiant with the release from worry and the joy of her burgeoning relationship with Giles.

'I can't get used to the new look,' she said.

'Me either!' he admitted. A visit from Pippa's hairdresser, the day before, and painful memories of his tussle with Slade's heavy, had resulted in not only Pippa changing her gingery mop to blonde, but also in Gideon sporting a short head of hair for the first time since his mother had last cut it when he was fourteen.

Rachel's parcel contained an antique carriage clock which prompted him to exclaim, 'Hey, are you lot trying to tell me something? Either there's something wrong with my timekeeping or you're hinting I should retire!'

Jenny Weatherfield and Jez had both brought small gifts and, after all had been admired, Pippa announced with a gleam in her eye that if he wanted to see what she and Giles had got him, Gideon would have to go outside. Giles, it seemed, had already slipped out.

Muttering audibly about the proper consideration due to an invalid, Gideon hauled himself out of his chair, aided laughingly by his sister, and joined the general exodus towards the front door.

'Like the hair, Bro,' Naomi commented, taking his arm. 'I see Pippa's had hers done too.'

'Yeah, well, I'm fed up with being called "Girlie" and Pips wasn't happy when Rachel's charming ex-husband called her a redhead.'

'Well, I think you make a charming couple,' she said with a playful look.

'Now don't start that again! Just let me organise my own love life, will you?'

'Ah, so I'm on the right track, then?'

'Mind your own business,' Gideon said severely, and Naomi laughed.

Outside, parked on the gravel, was a dark green, short-wheel-based Land Rover. Not new, it was nevertheless in very good condition, and Gideon was speechless for a moment.

'You're not serious?' he asked finally.

'Quite serious,' Pippa told him. 'We decided the only way to be sure of having our own cars when we needed them was to provide you with some sensible transport of your own. Now you've finally wrapped that prehistoric motorbike round its last tree!' she added with what Gideon felt was rather an unkind degree of satisfaction.

He ignored it.

'I don't know what to say,' he said, shaking his head. 'It's incredible!'

'Well, before you work yourself up to a thank-you speech, I should warn you, it comes with a condition.'

'Er, yes?' Gideon said warily. 'Go on.'

'Look inside. Try it for size.'

He walked across to the driver's door and was about to open it when a small, brindle face and two paws appeared behind the glass. Gideon stopped, his hand on the door handle, and started to smile in spite of himself. As the puppy began to wriggle with glee at the prospect of company, the female portion of the party uttered a synchronised 'Aahh!' and he knew protest would be useless.

An hour or so later, with just the dogs for company, Gideon sat in the Priory kitchen with the brindle pup on his lap. The guests had departed, Pippa was out in the yard seeing to the horses, and Giles and Rachel had offered to feed Elsa for him.

486

'I suppose I'll have to find a name for you now,' he told the drowsy pup. 'See, I knew you were going to make work for me!'

He was wondering if he could really live with a dog called either Logan or Joey, and also whether either of them would receive the tribute in the spirit that it was meant, when he made a discovery. Inspecting his birthday gifts once again, he turned the Rosettis' watch over and opened the back to look at the works, and there, inscribed inside the silver cover in tiny but clearly legible script, were the words, *With Thanks for Second Chances.*

The new fast-paced and absorbing thriller from the author of CUT THROAT will be published by Hutchinson in August 2004

DEADFALL

Lyndon Stacey

Lincoln Tremayne, heir to a viscountcy and manager of his father's Dorset estate, has one burning ambition – to be selected to ride on the British Olympic three-day eventing team. But his dream is about to be put on hold. Arriving at the stables late one night, Lincoln walks into a crisis. Thieves have targeted the tackroom and viciously attacked the stable owners' daughter, leaving her unconscious.

As she lies in a coma, what appears to be freak chance sets Lincoln on the trail of the attackers. Disregarding the advice of the police and increasingly unpleasant warnings from those involved, he juggles sleuthing with his demanding job and a competitive riding career. But, as the violence escalates, it becomes chillingly clear that someone is trying to kill him for reasons of their own, and the race is on to find out who, before they succeed . . .